THE
COOPERMAN
VARIATIONS

A BENNY COOPERMAN MYSTERY

HOWARD ENGEL

THE OVERLOOK PRESS
WOODSTOCK & NEW YORK

First published in the United States in 2002 by
The Overlook Press, Peter Mayer Publishers, Inc.
Woodstock & New York

WOODSTOCK:
One Overlook Drive
Woodstock, NY 12498
www.overlookpress.com
[for individual orders, bulk and special sales, contact our Woodstock office]

NEW YORK:
141 Wooster Street
New York, NY 10012

Flow chart on page 70 compiled by Jacob Engel.

∞ The paper used in this book meets the requirements for paper
permanence as described in the ANSI Z39.48-1992 standard.

Library of Congress Cataloging-in-Publication Data

Engel, Howard.
The Cooperman variations : a Benny Cooperman mystery / Howard Engel
p. cm.
1. Cooperman, Benny (Fictitious character)—Fiction. 2. Private investigators—
Ontario—Fiction. 3. Television broadcasting—Fiction. 4. Ontario—Fiction. I. Title.
PR9199.3E49 C66 2002   813'.54—dc21   2002070410

Manufactured in the United States of America
ISBN 1-58567-233-5
1 3 5 7 9 8 6 4 2

for

Harry J. Boyle

THE
COOPERMAN
VARIATIONS

A BENNY COOPERMAN MYSTERY

ONE

◖ Tuesday in April

I should have seen the writing on the wall. It was writ large, as my friend Dr Frank Bushmill says. "You have to pay attention to the signs and portents, Benny," he says, and he should know. Frank has remade his life a couple of times based on his reading of the signs. How he rejected his well-to-do family, abandoned a promising career at Trinity College, cleared out of Dublin and came to live here is a history of a man who won't take "yes" for an answer.

The first sign, which I ignored, was the closing of the United Cigar Store, which cut me off from my usual lunch counter. Then the other places along St Andrew and James streets, the Columbia and the Crystal, where I used to go for coffee and meals, went out of business or changed beyond recognition. Then the thunderbolt: a few weeks ago the Diana Sweets went broke. Not only did the Di close for business, but one night some enterprising wiseguy with a truck took all the tables, booths and mirrored cherrywood walls off to some location across the Niagara River. Here, the Di will be recreated for trendy diners in the great Empire State of New York as an evocation of the 1930s. A couple of irate citizens asked me to try to trace the Di, but even with all my experience as a private investigator I never had much luck in tracing people, let alone restaurant interiors.

Out on the street, where a nippy April wind cut up the sidewalk, lifting shreds of green garbage bags and pasting them against the bricks of Helliwell Lane, I ran into Wally Skeat from the radio station.

"Benny Cooperman! As I live and breathe."

"Hi, Wally." Wally's street voice sounded almost human. But once he got his hand cupped behind his ear in front of a microphone in the studio, he treated you to his bell-cracking lower register.

"You hunting for your morning coffee, Wally?" Wally kept getting hired by bigger and bigger TV stations. He disappeared for a year or two, and then turned up in Grantham again doing the early-morning news on the radio. Somehow Wally and the Big Time were never on speaking terms for long.

"Yeah. You too? I've been up since they called me in at six to do a backgrounder on that rap singer who was arrested. I thought I'd done my bit with the anniversary piece on Dermot Keogh."

"Who?"

"Cellist. Very big with the long-hair CD crowd. Died a year ago, but still bigger than Big."

"Never heard of him. Should I have?"

"Cooperman, you live with your head under the covers. Keogh's more famous in death than he ever was in life. You may quote me on that." I assured him I would, but my curiosity had been aroused. I'm always trying·to patch my ignorance.

"What did he die of, Wally?"

"He drowned. Up north. Swimming. Far from the world's concert halls." Wally cast a wounded eye at the locked and barred door of the Di. Wally's shoulders were fragile and defeated. If I blew, he'd melt.

"So you were writing up his death a year after the event?"

"People are still buying his records, Benny. It's crazy. He's as dead as the Diana Sweets, but he keeps on making money. Hell, I made a few bucks off him this morning. Maybe you'll have a go this afternoon. Maybe you could prove he was murdered, Benny. There might be a dollar or two in that." Wally was not at his best when he tried to be sarcastic. I put it down to our common need for caffeine. He seemed lost without the Di to dive into for his morning fix. He twitched the collar of his coat, and passed his briefcase from one hand to the other. He looked me hard in the eye as though I was to blame. In Grantham, Ontario, Canada, we took our routines seriously. He moved on down St Andrew Street, muttering.

I had seen the same lost look on the faces of all the reporters from the *Beacon* who used to work with their cellphones at one of the Di's back tables. Bankers and lawyers were equally glassy-eyed as they stared at the locked front door, the naked interior masked with strips of newspaper over the windows. There was no easy equivalent to the Di; no obvious replacement. It was what we had instead of a town pump. This is where the gossip was retailed, the deals made, the plots plotted. It was central to the city's nervous system. The Di provided a sort of community dialysis—it laundered information and passed it on. Gossip is the life-blood of a town like ours. Until four weeks ago, most of it moved in and out of the now-closed door in the middle of the block down the street from my office.

When the Di closed, I should have known it was time for a change. Did I intend to be the last business to abandon St Andrew Street? What I needed, my friend and neighbour Frank Bushmill told me, was a change, a chance to rethink what I thought I was doing. Did I plan to die of old age after getting a chill standing in the rain trying to take a picture of an adulter-ous couple through a window of the Black Duck Motel on Old Number Eight? If I was going to die in harness, why should it be *this* harness? Did I want to give up and let younger men sweep me away with their body-mounted surveillance equipment? Why not? It was God's truth that I wasn't wired. In ten years in the business of following wives and husbands, tracing credit-card trails and even solving the odd murder case, I used sophis-ticated recording equipment only once, and I had to stand in the rain reading the instructions before I could turn the damned thing on. Collected an electric shock for my trouble. On the floor of my office stood a pile of computer components that had been given to me by various well-meaning friends: "This will simplify your life, Benny. You'll love it. It will put you in touch with the whole world." To cobble these elements together, I called upon a so-called computer guru, whose name I found in the Yellow Pages, after I found the right volume. (Even the Yellow Pages aren't as simple as they used to be.) The guru took four hundred dollars of my money to patch a few wires into sockets I hadn't tried yet and went away pleased with himself. From all those pieces, I still couldn't get a combination that simplified my life. I didn't love it. I was still not in touch with the world. After buying enough computer books to test the strength of my floor, I discovered that I was incapable of learning a new way of thinking. I got to hate the cheery, well-intentioned, yellow-and-black-covered books. They'll have to come up with something even dumber.

The computer nightmare quickly led to the Internet nightmare, about which I am not yet ready to speak. Far from "surfing the net," I was sinking like that English poet off the coast of Italy. Not Byron. What's his name?

"In life, boyo, you have to give *yourself* a break. Life itself won't do it." Frank was talking to me in his waiting room after the last of his patients hobbled down the stairs. A friend of long standing, Frank called himself a podiatrist. The sign outside still read "chiropodist." Go figure. We maintained offices on St Andrew Street, shared the same floor and bathroom in what was now known as "The Kogan Block."

"When was the last time you had a holiday at all, Benny? Think now. Can you remember that far back?"

"I was in Toronto house-sitting for my brother a year ago."

"A year ago! How are you?"

"Well . . . maybe longer than a year. I went to Vegas with a couple of the boys once."

"That was two years ago, Benny. I remember because you needed a loan to renew your detective licence when you got back."

"Investigator. Private investigator. Was it really two years?"

"You see? You need to get away, see the world, forge

something or other in the smithy of your soul. You're not getting any younger. And besides, isn't Anna going to be at some European university this year? Think about that?"

"Frank, you're the devil whispering into my ear. Of course, I'd love to get away. I like to have fun same as the next man, but, Frank, I've got responsibilities."

"Such as?"

"Such as my parents."

"They go to Florida for three months every winter."

"Well, who's going to look after their house? water their plants? They wouldn't want to trust that to a stranger."

"Benny, your parents got back from Florida three weeks ago. Let's keep the discussion relevant."

"So, now I have to drop in to see them every couple of days."

"What happens if you don't?"

"I've never tried that." Frank went to a cupboard and took out a bottle with his name on the label. He poured out two shots into the two glasses he kept for special occasions.

Frank was a sad character. He had helped me with a couple of my cases, but he remained a glum sort of Dubliner. An exile. With him came bad weather. He had known the writer Flann O'Brien in his younger days and got me reading him—which was a change from the Russians I was always nodding over.

"Frank, are you happy here?" He took a sip of the whiskey and looked out the windows.

"Benny, I'm different. I'm a hopeless case. I was a graduate student at Trinity when religious toleration was still incomplete. You see, I've been on the barricades, as it were, since I was in my teens."

"Are you saying that you peaked too early?"

"Maybe I am and maybe I'm not. But I find this a peaceable place, this town. It's like a fine, handsome head without an idea in it. And Ireland is an ugly witch of a shrunken head with ideas skyrocketing out her eyes and ears. It's a tree full of singing birds and a nest of stinging nettles. I'm a bit of a loser, you know. But that's not to be helped. Blame it on the steady approach of winter."

"But, Frank, it's April! April?" I had a sudden irrelevant thought: "What was that fiddler doing swimming in April?"

"What fiddler?"

"Dur-something Keogh. He drowned. Maybe it was down south. Florida's a good place to drown. No. I remember now: Wally said it happened up north."

"Dermot Keogh. Fiddler you call him? Damned fine cellist is what he was, Benny. I heard him once. God love me, that man could play!"

"Wally Skeat just wrote an anniversary piece about it."

"That was a damned bloody shame, that was."

"Tell me about him, Frank."

"Stop trying to change the subject. Never mind about poor Keogh. He's a year into eternity. It's not much, but it's a start. More to the point, boyo, you don't have to worry about your parents' house right now. They're back from Miami."

"I'm afraid of Ma's unspoken disapproval, Frank. She wouldn't say a word and the silence would kill me." He shook his head and for a minute I said nothing.

Frank Bushmill, as everybody knew, was gay. And a great reader; an educated man in a lunch-bucket town. I used to hope that he could go off and enjoy himself with his own kind, but Frank was unique. There wasn't anyone else quite like him. Oh, there were others of his ilk around, but Frank was either too fastidious, too shy or too cautious to get far in the local gay community. I once thought that in Grantham Frank *was* the gay community. Anyway, he blunted the edges of his lusts with Bushmills Old Bush, or any good single malt whiskey. He spent the worst of his drinking nights on the couch in his office, and appeared with dark-stained eyes the following morning. Despite this frailty, he had done battle on my behalf more than once. He had taken a few wallops on his head in my service, as he never tired of telling me. So, I mostly ignored what he called his "still small vice."

"Benny, we are different. You and me. I'm never going to light up the sky. I don't much care about it if I do or if I don't. But you, you're younger, and you've never been off the leash.

Time to break the silver cord. You should think about that, Benny. You'll be an old man before you know it."

I nodded my head as though I agreed with him. In part, I *did* agree with him, but I had a stubborn streak in me that kept me tied to the places I knew best. I didn't even enjoy reading the travel pages in the *Beacon* or the *Globe*. They made me car sick.

I didn't give Frank Bushmill a straight answer, but I had to admit that he had planted seeds in my mind and watered them with the care of my own good mother. I pondered the idea as I wandered the chilly street and looked for a restaurant that I might blight into insolvency merely by going in and sitting down. Indeed, as Frank once said, it was an incredible power I had.

I should have seen the writing on the wall.

CHAPTER **TWO**

◗ Another Tuesday

I don't know where the spring went. Some of it was eaten up in following a husband who had driven off in the family car without giving his estranged wife and joint-owner of the vehicle a forwarding address. After a two-week period in which he paid for his gas and oil in cash, he soon returned to using his credit cards. And that's how I nailed him. Bud told me—by now we were on a first-name basis—over coffee in downtown Buffalo that he'd suddenly realized he had been wasting his life in Grantham and that out there were Paris, London and Rome just waiting to be discovered. He recognized that his flight hadn't got him very far—less than fifty minutes' driving time from Grantham—but he said it had been Phase One of his plan. I could sympathize with the idea of flight, of getting away from it all, of escaping to one of the great places. But Buffalo?

When that was cleared away—it ended happily, by the way: she took the would-be world traveller back again—I cleaned up a few minor files, emptied the pencil sharpener, stapled down the carpet, which had been getting caught in the office door, and treated myself to summer hours. To fill the time, waiting for a challenging case to walk into the office now that the door was free to glide over the carpet, I read a lot of Tony Hillerman, Donald E. Westlake and Lawrence Block. Then I turned to William McIlvanney, the Glasgow writer, and to the titled ladies James and Rendell. Wally Skeat lent me a pile of Canadians: two Wrights, a Gordon, a Robinson and I can't remember who else. When I finished those, I got some more. I would have felt better if somebody's retainer was paying to support my reading habit, but beggars can't be choosers. With my usual two fingers, I wrote a few letters to Anna Abraham, the light of my life, who was tramping over Tuscany with two of her graduate students before going on to give a series of lectures in Paris. Lucky Anna. Lucky Paris.

In short, I was bored out of my mind. Until a knock at the door bade me put *The Papers of Tony Veitch* face down on my desk. I covered the novel with some papers of my own and walked to the door to open it.

Here stood, how can I describe her? A vision of loveliness? The woman of my dreams? All the clichés rolled into this particular five-foot-six package of earthly delights. The sort of woman you hope will walk into your office one day. For a moment I felt like Sam Spade, Philip Marlowe and Lew Archer combined. I took in her perfume, the cut of her suit, the silky legs, her dark hair and was just getting ready to go around again when I suddenly recognized her.

"Stella! My God! Stella Seco! I don't believe it!" I was taken up short by this. The vision had become flesh. It wasn't intimately familiar flesh, I hasten to add, but at least it was grounded to a terminal in my past. She was no longer an agreeable abstraction. It was as though the slinky model in a fashion photograph turned out to be the girl next door. Only Stella was never the girl next door.

"Hello, Benny," she said in that voice that melted steel. "It's been too long. How have you been?"

I didn't answer for a minute, I just kept looking. At last I cleared my throat and found some inadequate words. "You look terrific, Stella. Come in." She walked around me when I failed to clear the doorway.

Stella and I had been at Grantham Collegiate Institute and Vocational School together. Forget the fifteen hundred other teenagers. She was my first great love. She was the first great love of every male in the school. None of us, as far as I know, ever scored with Stella. There was a protective family watching over every step she took in her nickel loafers. Not that there was a scarcity of Stella-watchers. Truth to tell, Stella provided a lot of us with not only a richly imagined sex life, but with our chief incentive to stay in school. Where the challenge of French irregular verbs and the binomial theorem failed to ignite our attention, where the three results of the Persian Wars and the Keystone Clause in the American Constitution failed us, there was Stella walking down the aisle to take her seat. There are bankers and doctors today in this city who would have been clerks and technicians had it not been for Stella Seco's cool gaze and liquid walk.

Of course, the girls in the school hated her, as I discovered later on. They were as envious of her looks as the rest of us were of her good marks in everything from algebra to zoology. Girlfriends understood that their pinned dates' eternal devotion was subject to the possibility that Stella might nod in their direction. Stella was magic. Stella lit up the sky.

I remember one story of her sitting with some girlfriends in the Rec Hut, the coffee shop across from the school, when she saw a football player crossing the street. She asked who he was and then announced that he was going to take her to the next big school dance. And he did! It was typical of Stella's sense of herself and her power, which the senior girls ascribed to the near-drunken state certain adipose tissue can induce in the male. Some girls even went so far as to suggest that, in certain areas, nature had been assisted. From where I was standing, the results were still convincing.

"I'm on my way to a meeting with the head of the Shaw Festival in Niagara-on-the-Lake. I haven't been in Grantham in ten years. The old place doesn't change much, does it?" Her climb up my steep stairs added to the breathlessness in her voice. There was also a nervousness. I knew she'd get around to her reason for this reappearance in my life after an agreeable ramble. ". . . But this isn't a social call, Benny," she said at last, as though she'd been reading over my shoulder. "I'm in trouble and I need help." I pulled the best seat in the house from its normal place and brought it around behind her. We both sat down, but for Stella the act of sitting was a symphony for the eyes—my politically incorrect, unreconstructed eyes, anyway.

"Trouble," I repeated. "Tell me. Tell me all about it."

"First of all, I'm not Stella Seco any more. I've been Vanessa Moss for nearly fifteen years."

"I've heard that name somewhere. Recently."

"I married Paul Moss—"

"The disc jockey from the radio station! Deep voice, like roasted velvet. Yeah, I remember him."

"I was eighteen, Benny. I was on my own again when I was twenty." I nodded to show that I was keeping up with her. She rooted around in her bag for the cigarettes that, judging by her expression, she had recently given up. She found a candy mint, held it for a moment, then flung it back into her bag. I could sympathize with that. I had never discovered anything to replace my habit either.

"Life with Paul was very complex, even after I quit school. He taught me a lot about broadcasting, but in the end I couldn't hack it. Paul, I mean. Poppa made him give me an annulment. I did a catch-up year in Hamilton, then did a three-year B.A. in Toronto. You quit school too, didn't you, Benny?"

"I managed to hold on until I graduated. They didn't have to burn the place down to get me out after all. We missed you when you left, Stella. It was as if all the lights went from one hundred watts to forty. Did you know you had that effect on us?"

"Benny, that was *years* ago. And how can I answer that anyway? I know I have a certain effect on people, but I haven't worked it out to a science. I always knew I was a good-looking broad. The rest was—well . . ."

"Why 'Vanessa'? How did you get to 'Vanessa' from 'Stella'?"

"That was the doing of one of my mentors. I've had a few of those. He said it had something to do with Jonathan Swift. I've been climbing the rickety ladder called broadcasting, Benny.

I've already met all of the people I'm going to run into on my way down. But at the moment, I'm sitting pretty, except for . . . Let me finish what I came to say, Benny. We can talk about the old days later."

"Sure, Stella. I want to hear what you have to say."

"Since June last year I've been the Entertainment head at the National Television Corporation. I knew when I took the job that it wasn't going to be easy, but I didn't expect that they would be literally gunning for me."

"What do you mean?"

"Renata Sartori was an old friend of mine."

"Have I heard that name too, somewhere?"

"If you tune in on our channel. I used to live with her when I first came to Toronto. Two weeks ago, she was staying at my place. I was away. She was alone, wearing one of my dressing gowns. She answered the door and somebody shot her in the face with a shotgun. Both barrels."

"Jesus! *That's* where I heard your name: on the news."

"For a week, the cops thought that I was the corpse. *Me!* You can't blame them, really. It was my house, my dressing gown and Renata's face . . ." Stella winced, shutting her eyes for a moment.

"You can skip that part."

"The press outdid themselves: ENTERTAINMENT HEAD BLOWN AWAY! NETWORK CHIEF BLASTED! That kind of thing. When I came back into town—I was away at my place on Lake Muskoka—I walked right into the investigation. Even the cops thought I was a ghost."

"It's like *Laura!*" I said. "You know, the book and the movie?"

"I know, I know. Now I know what it's like to be Gene Tierney. It was a Preminger film; 1944 or '5."

"The heavy was—"

"'That venomous fishwife, Addison de Witt.' No, that was the critic, George Sanders, in *All About Eve*. This was Waldo Lydecker, played by Clifton Webb."

"The cop was Dana Andrews." I was glad to be able to make a contribution.

"You're right. I forgot. Anyway, this is too much fiction coming true for me. Somebody wants to see me dead, Benny. That's why I've come to you. I need help."

"When exactly did all this happen?"

"Renata was murdered two weeks ago yesterday, Monday night around ten, according to the forensic report."

"In the movie, the maid found the body. Who found Renata?"

"In the *forties* there were maids. I have a cleaning woman. And Lydia thought it was me. *Everybody* thought it was me. I've been dead on the front page of every Toronto newspaper, Benny. I had to call all my friends and relatives to say it wasn't true. Now that I'm alive again, I'm just as vulnerable as I was before Renata was murdered."

"Who do the police suspect killed Renata?"

"Me, for one."

"*You!*"

"Sure. They say I was jealous of her. She was moving up in the Network hierarchy. She'd been given more responsibility. She even had a show of her own. *Reading with Renata*? Sunday afternoons? She hosted it herself. It made her into a minor celebrity of sorts. The show played against all the football games in the world. It had an audience of one. Wait a minute: that isn't fair. She *has* built an audience. Not huge, in TV terms, but it's as big an audience as any book show gets outside France.

"It's true, Renata had come a long way from typing traffic reports and keeping the sports department within its budget, but she wasn't going to move up very far from the production level. That's what she knew about: making programs. That's where her interest was, too. She invented and hosted this cheap, but well-produced, show that saved our bacon when an American series bombed after two weeks. Before that she was a damned good unit manager. A bean-counter. Was that mean? I make the widgets around here, she tells me what they'll cost. She didn't want my job; she wouldn't know what to do with it."

"So the cops have you figured for a leading suspect—"

"Among a large supporting cast."

"They appear to have missed the point of Renata's being killed wearing your clothes and in your house."

"Exactly."

"Who's in charge of the investigation?"

"At the moment it's Jack Sykes. He's a sergeant of detectives. He was in charge of the Wentworth case at Rose of Sharon Hospital. Remember? Those kids with liver poisoning?" Stella, or Vanessa, was tugging on the clasp of her bag, clicking it in and out again. It may have relieved her nervousness but it added to mine. I was still having to reconcile all that she was telling me with the high-school beauty of my dreams. Light coming in through my venetian blinds banded her blouse and legs with agreeable stripes. Stella was still a member of the league of beautiful women.

"Stella, what is it you want me to do exactly?"

"I need your protection. That's what you *do*, isn't it? But, Benny, you've *got* to call me Vanessa. Nobody knows me as Stella any more and I like it that way. Understand, Benny? It's important." I nodded my head and held a quiet funeral in my mind for Stella Seco, girl of my dreams and nowhere else. But Stella, damn it, I mean Vanessa, went on. "I guess you'd say what I need is a bodyguard: someone who'll follow me around, check out security, and get me out of tight corners. Yes, I need a bodyguard until this thing blows over."

"Look, Vanessa, there are real people who do that. I mean for a living. I don't carry a weapon, for one thing. And if I did, I'm not a crack shot. What I'm saying is that carrying heat and doing all that secret-agent stuff you see in the movies is miles away from anything I know the first thing about." I could see right away she didn't like this line of argument.

"No, no, no, Benny. I don't want some rent-a-cop without a brain for anything but his next coffee break. I want you! I'm not what you would call a wealthy woman, Benny, but I pay better than the going rates. You will be provided for. You have my word on that." Here she removed an envelope from her bag and looked as if she was about to hand it over. My fingers got that twitch they get when I'm about to go to work.

"You drive a hard bargain, Stella." She caught my eye with disapproval. "Hell, I'm not going to be able to manage this 'Vanessa' thing! You'll always be Stella to me."

"That's sweet, Benny. I'm still 'Stella' to me, too. So that makes a pair of us. But, damn it, in *public*, I'm Vanessa. You got that?" Then, without a break, she asked: "When can you start?"

"I can get rid of these few files this afternoon," I said, lifting the paper litter above my McIlvanney paperback. "I can be in Toronto tomorrow afternoon."

"I'll book lunch at Dooley's. They've reopened it. I'll book my table for 12:30. After lunch I'll show you my office and get you started. Officially, as far as the network goes, you're my new executive assistant. That will open enough doors for you to get you started. Oh, and by the way, this cheque should cover your retainer and start-up expenses. If it's not enough, I'll fix things when I see you. Goodbye for now, Benny."

So saying, Vanessa was on her feet and heading for the door. Obviously, she didn't want to hear about the details of getting my smalls to the laundromat or about other similar banal but necessary chores. I liked her style, but I could already see that her company was going to be exhausting.

CHAPTER THREE

● Wednesday

The National Television Corporation occupied a large building on the west side of University Avenue in downtown Toronto. There was a weather beacon on the top floor of this skyscraper that tested the zoning by-laws regarding the acceptable height limits in that neighbourhood of hospitals, publishers and insurance companies. At the top of the beacon stood the familiar NTC totem, a big-eyed owl looking down at me. A nest of peregrine falcons, perched high under the beacon, kept the local pigeon population trimmed to the smartest and quickest of their kind. This was pure Darwinism, nature drenched in its own blood. Below, in the offices and studios of NTC, a sort of social Darwinism was practised. Here there was no job security. No forgiveness, no pity. Yesterday's boy genius was today's has-been. Budgets were quick to follow the wunderkind of the moment, along with suites of offices and charge accounts. All of this could be stopped without a word on paper. Here talented people grew old before their time. Heart attacks were as common as head colds. Only the locksmith was safe from the whim of the people at the top, who themselves were not safe. Any day could bring them down from their twentieth-floor offices. If they were lucky, they could then join the rogues' gallery of the formerly powerful along a corridor on the fifth floor where you could walk past their open doors one after the other, like Easter Island heads, familiar spirits of an earlier day. There they sat reading *The Globe and Mail* and *The New York Times* every morning, hoping that today would summon them upstairs, back into the Technicolor of power.

Of course, I knew nothing of this the first time I was ushered into Vanessa Moss's big office on the twentieth floor. Her secretary seemed sincere in her welcome. She found my name in the appointment book right where it should have been. Her offer of coffee or tea sprang from the pure joy of seeing me in the right place at the right time. Her smile and sympathetic manner, I found, went with the job. Sally was more or less connected to the floor and to executives at that level. If Vanessa fell from grace, which was what my research told me was about to happen, Sally would stay on to offer coffee or tea on behalf of her next employer.

Earlier that morning, I had driven around the west end of Lake Ontario and into the huge welcoming arms of the Megacity, Toronto. I found a cheap hotel on Bay Street, a sort of YMCA without a swimming pool, not far south of Elm, and unpacked. I turned the room, which had only one bed in it—unlike most hotels I've been in—into my headquarters. Everything I needed was spread out on the bed. When I was happy with the look of things, I walked over to Dooley's on King Street, about ten minutes before the appointed time, where the maitre d' informed me that I was being stood up by my client. In my business, being stood up is no great crime. Whoever writes the cheque at the end of the week carries a lot of clout. So, I swallowed my pride and had a sandwich at a place down the street called Quotes, where there were old movie posters under the glass of the tables and vintage cartoons on the walls. While I was waiting for my bill, I called the number Stella had given me. A polite but firm voice on the other end, Sally, as I later discovered, invited me to drop into "Ms Moss's office on the twentieth floor of the NTC building" at 1:30 and hung up. I shrugged at the cartoon on the wall and took a taxi to University Avenue. Leaning back into the plush back seat, and reading the *Thank you for not smoking* sign, I started to get the feel of living on expenses.

At NTC I ran into a SWAT team posing as security guards. They wanted to know what my business was and whom I had an appointment to see. They passed my wallet around among themselves, checking my documents, and finally laid a big sticky label on me with the word "VISITOR" in loud letters. Under the word was the warning that this label was to be worn at all times and was not under any circumstances transferable. I wondered whether in the case of fire, only properly labelled visitors would escape roasting. As I looked about me, I noticed that everybody in the place was wearing labels. They were custom-made labels, naturally, laminated plastic, but labels all the same. But we VISITORS were the conspicuous ones; both by our badges and by the humiliated looks on our faces. We had the expression of restaurant guests forced to wear house jackets and ties before being seated. Meanwhile, the security police were phoning everybody on the twentieth floor, including, I suppose, the murderer of Renata Sartori, to let the world know that Vanessa's most recent hireling was on the lot. I began to think, as I was finally cleared to go through a buzzing turnstile and frogmarched to the burgundy elevator, that maybe the people at NTC were not the creators of fun, entertainment and news coverage, but were guardians of the national hoard of gold bullion or maybe fronting for the CIA. It seemed to me that I had less trouble getting into the American Senate chamber in Washington. Anyway, I tried not to grind my teeth as I was wafted twenty floors above the sidewalk.

While I was waiting for my coffee, a skinny man with a nearly threadbare brown suit hanging on his bones came in and pestered Sally for a minute of Vanessa's time. He whispered to begin with and kept raising his voice a few decibels higher with every refusal. "But I've *got* to see her, Sally. She *promised!*"

"She's behind by thirty minutes, Mr Newman. And her next appointment is here, as you can see." Newman gave me a glance that tried to wither me, but it fizzled. Newman turned back to Sally.

"I'm not asking, Sally. I *need* this minute with her."

"Sorry, Mr Newman. Perhaps after lunch."

"Come on, Sally. I may not be able to get up here again. You know how it is. I *need* this favour. Do I have to *beg?*" Sally gave me a look, soliciting sympathy. I glanced at the flowers on her desk. How could she be so hard on Newman, an apparent old acquaintance, when she was so generous to me, a perfect stranger? The difference in our cases immediately became clearer. I was a newcomer, on my way up, in the good graces of Vanessa Moss, a first-magnitude star; I guess Newman was just the opposite. From the look of him he had no friends at court; he was reduced to begging.

Suddenly something clicked: Newman was Hy Newman, the ballet and opera director. I hadn't seen many of his TV shows, but was awake enough to be aware that he was known to be a national treasure. He'd won umpteen different awards over the years with his *Aïda* and *Carmen*. His *Nutcracker* was an annual Christmas institution. He was a wearer of the Order of Canada rosette in his lapel. How could this young woman be giving him a hard time? Hadn't his past work earned him sixty seconds of Stella's precious time? I got up and leaned over to speak to the secretary.

"Miss, I know I'm booked to see Ms Moss at 1:30, but I'm not in that great a rush. I'm sure that Ms Moss will spare the time for someone like Mr Newman here." Newman looked at me as though I had just spoken blasphemy; Sally, as though I'd just let my dog make doodoo on her carpet. Neither was amused. Of course, then it hit me. Sally wasn't being considerate of *my* time, it was Stella she was worried about. What I wanted was not much different from what Newman wanted. Newman's wants and mine were of no consideration to Sally, ever protective of her boss—beyond the offer of morning coffee to those temporarily in favour at court. Just let me try getting in to see good old Stella after I left the payroll. Newman and I could both die of old age trying to get in. I glanced over at Hy Newman, who was rubbing his chin. The flame that used to reduce the likes of me to stains in the bottom of ancient ashtrays had long ago burned out.

Stella—now even I could believe she was Vanessa Moss and not my dear Stella—exploded into the outer office like a thunderbolt. My Stella would never wear a charcoal grey pinstripe over a magenta blouse. The men with her, like chips around a newly calved iceberg, pocketed their notes and backed up to the elevator, nodding. "I want to see something on paper by next Friday, Len. *Len! Mr Cook! Are you listening?*"

"You'll see it, Vanessa, I promise. You'll get it if I don't go crazy like poor Bob Foley," Len quipped. The others paused in their retreat to the elevator to laugh. It was a cautious laugh, controlled and as far from hearty as Buffalo. Sally didn't smile because Sally was Sally.

"This network can't afford one Bob Foley, Len. Don't even think of going crazy. It's not in your contract," Vanessa said, moving away from the group.

While Vanessa was still talking, she caught sight of Hy Newman and me in the waiting area. "Hy, darling!" she said. "How *are* you? How is Phyllis? I was thinking about you only yesterday. We really have to do something new and exciting with the *Nutcracker* for Christmas. I keep getting the same old garbage fed me. You know what it's like. What I need is the Hy Newman touch. Will you promise to call Philip Rankin this afternoon? Tell him you were talking to me. Promise, now."

Newman stood dumb. He was disarmed and laid out. A touch of colour leapt to his cheekbones. Meanwhile Vanessa moved past his swaying body to grab me by the arm. I could feel her strength as she pulled me into her office and closed the door by leaning on it. "Give me a second, Benny," she called, scooping up the phone. "Sally? If I see Hy Newman up here again, we are going to have that unpleasant conversation that's been pending. Do I make myself clear? I feel sick enough today without having to run into the Ghost of Christmas Past on the way to my desk. You understand?" Now it was Vanessa's cheeks that were burning. Her usually warm grey eyes were on fire. "I don't give a sweet fuck what you tell him. That's your department. You be the heavy in this or I'll find someone who can." She slammed down the phone again and sat, or rather collapsed, into the big executive chair behind her large desk. It was probably Louis Quatorze the Fifteenth or something, but I couldn't tell.

The office of the head of Entertainment was everything it should be: windows on two walls, relentless interior decorating and hardly any paper visible on a flat surface. Labelled portraits of the founders of NTC, large and suitably framed in gold leaf, stood out on one wall, with smaller ones showing the founders of NBC and CBS for good measure. A portrait of Edward R. Murrow hung on one panelled wall and the familiar golden statuette given annually by the Academy of Motion Picture Arts and Sciences stood at attention in a niche. I wondered when she had had time to be in the movie business. A flotilla of golden and silver European and Canadian television awards shared another shelf. I noticed that with a respectable handgun I could get off a couple of good shots at the chair behind Vanessa's desk without moving too far away from the elevator. I wanted the desk shifted, just to make it harder for the opposition. If there was an opposition, of course.

"Benny, why do times get complicated and short? I'm late now for a taping. You'll have to come with me. It's a historic event: it may be our last in-house production. I've cut off people like Hy Newman because we are no longer producing our own series of entertainment shows. We've cut back to the late-night stuff, like *Vic Vernon After Dark*. Come on. We can talk on the way." She grabbed a big blond-leather bag and a buff suede coat and headed for the door without looking back to see if I was coming. People in the outer waiting room scattered. Sally held the door as we disappeared into the burgundy elevator. Here she reached into the bag, produced a compact and began adjusting her makeup. She knew exactly how much time she had before we arrived at the main-floor lobby. When the doors opened, the compact had been returned to its zippered compartment in her bag and Vanessa Moss, her smile in place, walked directly to the revolving doors.

Vanessa's custom midnight-blue Range Rover had been brought around, and a young man in a T-shirt and jeans pulled his forelock as he held the door open for her. "Get yourself a suit, George, and I'll see if I can move you up a notch or two before I'm out of here."

"Thanks, Miss Moss. I will!"

"Poor bastard," she said, as we pulled out into traffic on University Avenue, "he's been trying to get his toe in the door since I worked here the first time. And that was five years ago. He does something with computer animation. Supposed to be very clever. Don't know what he's doing around here. Yesterday I heard Bill Franks, the head of Drama—he's the house producer on Springbank's production of *Julius Caesar*—asking whether Brutus and Cassius couldn't be combined into one character for simplicity's sake. It's a wonder they still schedule Shakespeare. It only happens when we have to go before the CRTC to renew our licence once every ten years. But that's all slated to go now. And that'll include Bill, thank God. I can get the Mankiewicz *Julius Caesar*, if I'm ever insane enough to program Shakespeare. Of course, education's wasted on people like Bill. They're like potatoes in the sun: the light makes them poisonous. Do you have any aspirin?" I patted my pockets and shook my head.

The Range Rover gave us a higher view of the cars in front of us than I got in my Olds. It didn't do us any good, however; we still had to wait in line until the lights changed. Toronto drivers are in a bigger hurry than I'm used to. University Avenue looked like a street that had been laid out before the collapse of National Socialism. Albert Speer would have loved University Avenue. It was like driving through a graveyard of huge monuments. The boulevard between the northbound and southbound lines of traffic tried to take the curse off the prospect with flower gardens and fountains, but the dullness was ingrained. Order and discipline prevailed and endured.

"Benny, I've been thinking. You're going to have to tell the cops involved in this case that you're working for me. Tell Jack Sykes at 52 Division. Introduce yourself. Explain that you're running interference for me. Okay?"

"You're the boss."

"You're bloody right."

Vanessa looked impatient, checked her watch and slipped a package of cigarettes out of her bag. "Benny," she said, as she applied the car's lighter to the cigarette between her lips, "you never saw me do this. I gave up this filthy habit over a year ago. I can give you the date, if you need it." I nodded, and began worrying whether I would be able to refuse her offer of a smoke. I needn't have. She didn't offer.

"I have a lot of enemies at the network, Benny. They'd just love to know that I have bad habits on top of everything else."

"With a murderer loose, I shouldn't worry about lung cancer. When are you going to fill me in on what you want me to do?" I avoided calling her "Stella," but couldn't use "Vanessa" to her face yet. Some people have a heavy hand with a vocative; they don't believe in pronouns. Me, I just use a person's name when I find that for some extraordinary reason I've remembered it.

"Benny, all you have to do is stick close to me. You're my extra skin until I say stop. Okay? I need you and depend upon you utterly. You're an absolute angel for letting me take you away from dear old Grantham. Don't think I'll forget that. I know you're not supposed to carry heat up here, but isn't there a way around that?"

"Canadian law doesn't favour concealed weapons. I could get permission to carry a piece, but I'd have to dress like a Brinks guard."

"Just keep me from harm's way, that's all I want. If I can stay alive and hold on to this job for another six months, I'll die happy. All I need is to be able to quit on my own terms and not on theirs."

"I'll try to keep that in mind. One thing, Vanessa. I want to be able to nose around to find out where the danger is coming from. It's not a great idea just to wait for him to try again. Would you like to give me a hint about your own suspicions? Who should I be looking out for? An unbriefed bodyguard isn't much better than no bodyguard."

"You'll meet the lot of them as we run through the obstacle course that constitutes my day, Benny. First, we are going to meet a producer, Eric Carter, who is working beyond his competence. He knows it and I know it. He built a reputation doing six shows with Dermot Keogh, the cellist. We won awards for the network with Keogh. Now Keogh's gone, Eric is a leftover. He has the smell of failure on his clothes these days. I need him to succeed, while everybody else, who is supposed to be supporting him, wants to see him fall on his ass. They know I'm not well and they're taking advantage of the pain I'm in. That describes the sort of snake pit this business is: they want him to fail because it will reflect badly on me even though this production package has been pending for over a year. If it works, Nate Green will get the credit because he was my predecessor; if it fails, the shit on my heel is all mine."

"What happened to Keogh? I know he drowned, but how do you drown in April?"

"He was a scuba diver. A lot of string players are. He was diving some wreck up north."

"What a waste."

"I still think it's strange talking about things *happening* to Dermot. Dermot used to *make* things happen. He was never passive. You must have read about it. He was only forty and with a fat Sony contract and carte blanche around here. He could out-Casals Casals. Too bad, really. He was lots of fun."

It was Wally Skeat from the Grantham radio station who'd introduced me to Dermot Keogh back in April.

"Dermot's death was tragic, Benny. Tragic in the sense that we were taught to use the word in school." Vanessa's eyes were shining as she spoke Dermot Keogh's name. For a few seconds she was silent, then she announced, "I don't want to talk about it any more, Benny, not right now. Okay?"

I tried to change the subject: "Who's Len Cook, Vanessa, the guy you scolded before he escaped into the elevator?"

"Len's finished with me. Just working out the last weeks of his contract. He's the executive assistant you're replacing,

Benny. I think he'll turn up in News next. He hasn't ruined anything there yet. Next question?"

"What about Bob Foley, the guy who went crazy? Len Cook used his name to try to dissipate your anger." The remark that everybody in the corridor had laughed at still bothered me, because I wasn't in on the joke. If it was a joke.

"Foley is a senior technician assigned to the Vic Vernon talk show, *Vic Vernon After Dark*. Do you know it?"

I nodded. I'd seen it a few times without making it the regular end to my day. Vanessa hadn't stopped talking: ". . . Late night with visiting celebrities? We do it live from Studio Four five nights a week. Last night Foley walked off the show. He just got up and left, saying to no one in particular, 'I don't need this shit.'"

"What prompted it?"

"Oh, there was some wrangle going on about the sound quality. Vic Vernon is an egomaniac. You know, the sort of guy who remembers what he was wearing the day Kennedy was shot. Only he wasn't even *born* then. I don't know the details, but Vic was sounding off about his microphone. Said it gave his voice a tinny quality."

"Did it?"

"Who *knows* with Vic. Ten minutes earlier, he was unhappy with the lighting, which hasn't been changed since the last time he was unhappy with it. It's just the insecurity of the artist, Benny. If you expect somebody to let his entrails hang out in public regularly, you've got to expect him to demand a thing or two that might be unreasonable in normal adults. Anyway, Foley had had it with Vic's tantrums and said so. It was half a minute before broadcast, Benny! *Thirty seconds* to air, so Bob isn't going to find a job anywhere in the industry at the level he was working at. Even the people who hate Vic won't hire him. But he doesn't need to care. He's got the Plevna Foundation to administer."

"The what?"

"Later, Benny."

Vanessa pulled up in a small lot behind what looked like a car dealership on Yonge Street. "This is it," she said. "Studio

Seven is just about the last of our sound stages. We've been getting rid of them all over the city."

"Cutting down on the overhead?"

"Bill Paley said it years ago, Benny, we're not into real estate. We buy and sell programs. That's the way ahead. There's a lot of confusion, especially with the old diehards who like the smell of the greasepaint. But that's Dodo-land. That's ancient history."

I wanted to ask who Bill Paley was, but I'd shown off enough ignorance for one afternoon already. We walked past a protesting commissionaire and through a back door leading to a sound stage. Here dozens of children dressed in blue tulle and sporting silver halos and wings were pulling at the contents of three boxes of pizza. Walking around them were various floor managers and kid wranglers, carrying bags of knitting in case a dull moment should unexpectedly appear.

"Ernestine, you *can't* carry a wand if you're going to be an alto! The altos aren't carrying anything. It's just the little ones who carry wands, dear. Understand?" I out-grabbed a wedge of pizza from under the nose of a blonde, blue-eyed angel, who gave me a withering sneer. Vanessa led the way through the tulle to a control booth overlooking the sound stage. We walked in and closed the door behind us. On a line of illuminated monitors, I could see a band of brass players in grown-up versions of the costumes I'd already seen. The monitors blocked the view of the studio below from the right, and flats on the set obscured it from all the other directions. In fact, the eight or so people sitting closest to the glass could only see what was going on below through one or more of the monitors. Nobody turned around as we came in.

The angelic brass players were standing on steps rising towards a set of pearly gates. Highlights from the French horns, trumpets and trombones shone through the smoke or fog that was obscuring what was going on. One of the musicians was coughing into a red bandana that probably hadn't been cleared with the costume department.

The control room supported a gloom of its own. The monitors supplied the only bright spots in view. The rest of the illumination came from tiny points of red and green lights shining on control panels. Script assistants read by lights so dim as to imperil their vision. For a moment, nobody looked at us; then, when we were spotted, the producer called "Cut!" and everybody went on a five-minute break, while Vanessa and he had words in the suddenly emptied room. "Eric, I want you to meet my new assistant. Eric Carter, Benny Cooperman." Carter glanced in my direction and bussed Vanessa on both cheeks.

"I'm half a day ahead of schedule, Vanessa. In spite of the lighting trouble I told you about. The kids are going to be terrific. Just like you said. I can't believe this woman," Carter said to me, "she's right about everything. Even the effects! You said they'd slow us down and you were right, but I've got fifty replacement kids so I've cut down on the kiddy breaks. I just use different kids and keep rolling. Saved me hours and hours."

"When do you wrap, Eric?"

"Friday night we're out of here. I won't cancel our Saturday and Sunday booking just in case—"

"Sure, insurance. Use the time for publicity stills. Get somebody you trust to handle the turkey-shoot before you head for the hills of Caledon."

"Good idea."

"Eric's really a farmer, Benny. He's happy as hell with his quarter horses nickering for their lunch."

"When are you coming out again, Vanessa?"

Vanessa's eyes narrowed. "You know you're way over our agreed budget on this, Eric. I make it at least by three hundred thousand. That's including your saved half-day."

"Look at the film, Vanessa. You'll love it. You'll see it's worth every cent."

"Where can you save in what's left? I need this, Eric! Can you reprise anything? Think, love. You're too dear for this crapshoot."

"I won't have it savaged at this stage!" he said, pursing his thin lips and folding his arms in front of him.

"You'll come up with some cuts, or I'll get somebody else to finish it. You know I'm not kidding."

"Vanessa!"

"Eric, you're not Mickey Rooney and this isn't Judge Hardy's old barn! Get your ass in there and make the hard decisions. You've got the band on tape. Do you need them standing around on the steps? Anybody wearing one of those nightgowns can hold a trumpet. Extras cost less than the high-price help, darling."

"If I had time, I'd fight you on this!"

"You and everybody in town. Climb aboard. I want to screen this Monday morning. You hear?"

"It'll be on your desk, damn it!" Angry red spots had appeared under his eyes.

Vanessa turned and headed out into the light. Before I had the wit to follow her, I caught a monosyllable in my ear. To Carter, it summed up Vanessa and all other women in a word.

CHAPTER **FOUR**

Outside in the narrow lot, I tried to quiz Vanessa about her delicate health, while she foraged in her bag for car keys. "I may look healthy, Benny, but I'm desperately run down. My bones are dissolving. My doctors tell me that I need six months with nothing to do but watch geraniums grow. Some tropical paradise without e-mail. Oh, wouldn't I *love* it! Palm trees, bougainvillea!"

"Well, if that's what the doctors say . . ."

"There wouldn't be a designated parking place at NTC when I got back. Do you know how many names come off doors around there in a week, Benny?"

"But a needed rest for health reasons . . . ?"

"Sudden *death* is the only excuse they understand, darling. And even that makes them angry this time of the year. When Harry Cassidy suffered a fatal stroke, the brass were sure he'd done it on purpose. Look! There's a drugstore at the corner. Be an angel and get me some aspirin, Benny. I wouldn't ask unless I really needed something for my head." Vanessa pulled the car over into an empty space reserved for buses without waiting for my answer. I got out of the car and ran into the over-bright store to do as I was told. I bought a Kit Kat bar for myself, not knowing when Vanessa was going to call a halt to all this rushing around. When I got back, she ripped open the aspirin package while I wrestled with the top of the plastic bottle of mineral water I thought she might need to get the pills down. This accomplished, I continued to ask questions while she moved the car expertly through the heavy traffic.

"Do you suspect colleagues like Carter or Green of plotting against you? I mention them because their names are stuck in my memory."

"Of course I do. They and everybody else in the place. Bill Franks. He's head of Drama. Shotguns are his style. He likes to get a moose every fall. You know the type. But I don't think he's got the balls for it. And Nate Green's out too, of course."

"Why 'of course'?"

"He's dead, Benny. Don't you read a newspaper? He died of a nasty cancer. I don't even want to think about it."

"Hy Newman seems desperate," I offered.

"Hy is dead and buried like Nate, only he doesn't know it yet. He's an old man. The network isn't a home for tired artists, Benny. If it was, the floor would be littered with has-beens."

"That's a bleak picture, Vanessa. We all get to be has-beens."

"I've no time to worry about that. Let Human Resources deal with it. That's what they're there for. I'm not the Salvation Army, and Hy Newman's not my rehabilitation project. Let somebody else try to regenerate him. I've got to keep my ass moving fast enough so that I don't become the next victim of the system. Hy knew two years ago, long before I came aboard, that the network was getting out of producing its own pro-grams. Even the CBC's getting out of that. Hy knows it as well as I do. We are all looking for independent producers to pioneer ideas and create series. That's when I can be approached. We horse-trade and out of it come sweetheart deals. Everybody's happy. That's how it works today, Benny."

A Volvo ahead stopped abruptly at a stoplight. Vanessa was quick with the brake, but not quick enough to avoid bruising the bumper. The owner, a small, dark woman with curlers under a bandanna, got out and looked for signs of the impact. Judging by her sour expression, she could find none. Still Vanessa's knuckles were white on the steering wheel. She seemed to be bracing herself for the second impact of the trouble the woman was going to make. The woman didn't.

She returned to her Volvo, merely telegraphing a dirty look a moment before she slammed the door. By now, there was honking behind us. Vanessa leaned on her horn as well.

"How did television get to be so cut-throat? Why would anybody want to work in such an industry?"

"It's something you understand, Benny, or you don't. You either get off on the noise, the power games and the practice of cracking heads and breaking balls, or you get out. It's like mountain climbing and skydiving, you have to have a head for it."

"And you have?"

"Sure I do. One of the best in the business. Trouble is that I'm surrounded by memo-writers and button-counters. Like Ted Thornhill, the president and general manager. Ted's the big cheese around here. The CEO. He controls people by tripping them up with paperwork. He breaks up viable working teams because he has nightmares about them riding into power on a wave of public popularity. He dreads the idea that a newsreader or sitcom producer could replace him. What he really wants isn't big ratings or prize-winning programs, but quiet, drab, hide-in-the-corner schedules that nobody blasts or praises in the papers, the sort of programming the business community feels safe with."

I nodded, trying to reconcile this voice with the Stella of old. Who would have thought that under that tightly buttoned blouse of a former high-school girl beat a heart of such unfettered ambition. The thought made it hard for me to sort out material she was feeding me. I attempted to weigh the threat to Vanessa in what she said about her professional colleagues and adversaries. At the same time, I was getting a better picture of the background of the world she inhabited. What I didn't understand was "why?" Why did anybody put up with this kind of nonsense for thirty seconds? All the efforts of all these people came out the boob tube. So far I hadn't seen anything to convince me that that was a misnomer.

"You never did finish about Hy Newman, Vanessa. A burnt-out producer with a chip on his shoulder might be just the sort of villain we're looking for."

"Hy certainly could get frustrated enough. I hadn't thought of that. I don't see him making a mistake like that, though. He's so meticulous. He'd look first and then shoot. We're searching for someone who shoots without looking."

It was quiet in the car, which was filling up with smoke from the cigarette interposed between Vanessa's scarlet lips. When I rolled down my window, she shot me a look. "This isn't a criticism, Vanessa, it's just a need for air. Ever since I gave up the habit, I've become supersensitive."

The sharp look mellowed, and she grinned at me in a lopsided way that only Stella could carry off. "Benny, I always *could* talk to you. I'm glad to have you with me while this is going on." She patted my knee for a moment and then abruptly removed her hand to bang on her horn. "That son of a bitch! Did you see that?" A green Volkswagen I thought I'd seen before was still behind us after we'd been on the road for ten minutes. It distracted me from seeing a Japanese compact come up on the inside and pass Vanessa just as she began to move into the inside lane herself. It had been a near thing. The other driver looked scornfully over his shoulder and took the next right-hand turn.

This moment of excitement interrupted the beginning of a sobering reflection: in the past, Stella Seco had had so little to do with me that the idea of her always being able to talk to me, while flattering, was plainly untrue. But, as I said, the thought was interrupted and I didn't get back to it for some time.

"Tell me about your life, Vanessa. Away from the bright lights, I mean." She seemed to slouch over the wheel as though the helium in her balloon was leaking.

"My life, if you can call it that, is not much of a life. My everlovin' husband, Jeff Cutler, is effectively estranged, loving it and living in Vancouver. He takes time out in La Jolla because he adores the mussels at George's at the Cove on Prospect. He can't stand my company. That's not fair. He didn't see enough of me to decide that. And, as with most modern married women, my ambitions will never be satisfied by a lifetime of lowering toilet seats. Jeff never did understand this crazy business. Or the insane hours involved. Since he left, I live alone. The place is cleaned by Lydia, who also buys my groceries. She leaves cooked meals behind her in the freezer. She also looks after my laundry and sends the bills to the miracle accountant who makes my life possible. He handles all of my business affairs: taxes, parking tickets and charity. There's a woman at Holt Renfrew, Benny, who puts clothes on my back and looks after me in that department. If I say a word against her taste, I'm afraid she'll quit. She holds me hostage."

"She's doing a good job." I said it because Vanessa had paused to take a breath in her monologue. I meant it, too. She was well turned out for her job. But then, Vanessa provided the building blocks for Holt Renfrew to work with. And the accountant paid the bills at the end of the month.

"All that sounds organized and shipshape, Vanessa. Are there any complications in this arrangement? What about your family? Is all well there?"

"Poppa and Momma are both dead. Even with me newly back from the grave, my sister still isn't speaking to me. She thinks I did it to frighten her. We haven't spoken since Momma's funeral six years ago."

"I should get her name, just to check her out."

"Benny, you must be kidding! You think Franny's out to get me?"

"I'm just looking at the possibilities. Could you give her number to Sally for me? Anything I've left out? What about your private, unscheduled activities?"

"Are you asking me if I have sexual encounters, Benny?"

"Those aren't the words I would have picked," I said, feeling my collar growing smaller.

"Why, Benny, you're *blushing!*"

"Damn it, I have to know it *all* if I'm going to do my job. What's the use of telling me all this other stuff if you're withholding this . . . this other stuff." I was tripping over my words in some confusion. Vanessa kept her eyes on the traffic, but she was smiling at my awkwardness.

"You met that boy who brought the car around?"

"Yes," I said. "George, the animator."

"Doesn't he look a threat?"

"Ask me when I know him better. Does he come with a last name?"

"Brenner. Doesn't that ripple with muscle tone?"

"How serious is it?"

"He's ambitious and young, I'm well placed and not unattractive. It works out for both of us. Believe me, I have no long-term interest in George Brenner. We keep it simple. He really is a very talented computer animator, you know."

"But he won't gain anything at the network if you . . . uh, leave, one way or another?"

"No, he'll go on parking cars and making out until his looks go. He dreams of surfing in San Diego. Isn't that sweet? He is a dear, though, and very thoughtful."

"Could he be reporting to one of the heavies in your life?"

"About what? I don't discuss programming with him. We don't even watch TV together."

"Who's your boss, Vanessa? Who are you responsible to?"

"That'll have to wait, Benny. Here we are." She drove between the fat granite pillars on the curved driveway and the young animator was there to take the car underground. Vanessa slipped him a golden smile as he moved his lithe, athletic frame behind the wheel and was gone in a squeak of brakes and a belch of exhaust.

"Rule one," Vanessa told me, was "never talk in the elevators. They've got them wired. One reporter was fired on the spot for talking about the Blue Jays' selling a third baseman before it was announced."

"Is your office any safer?" I asked in a whisper as we headed down the corridor on the twentieth floor.

"Your guess is as good as mine, Benny. Of course, I don't trust Sally. She comes with the space, like the air conditioning. Her loyalties go with the twentieth floor. I don't know who she's talking to."

"I want you to get someone to move your desk, Vanessa. When your door is open, I can see you behind your desk from the elevator. Nice target. Nice furniture. What's her full name?"

"Sally's?"

"Who else have we been talking about?"

"Sally is Mrs Gordon Jackson. She lives in Richmond Hill, north of the city."

"Good," I said, making a note. Vanessa slipped out of her jacket and slid it over the back of her chair. "What's next on your schedule?"

"One hour and a half from now a meeting's taking place down the hall. All of the people under me will be there, except for those out of town or in a body cast. Wanna meet 'em?"

"I guess I'd better. What are you up to in the meantime?"

"I'm having a massage, and you're cordially *not* invited."

***

Before paying a courtesy call on the cops in charge of Renata Sartori's murder investigation, I phoned home, left word with my answering service and had a laugh with Frank Bushmill about where my much-needed holiday had taken me. At least it wasn't Buffalo. I gave him my number at NTC in case he needed to get in touch.

I had never visited 52 Division, City of Toronto Police, before. I was impressed by the brightness of the place: lots of glass and windows and overhead lighting. Glass brick from the sixties or earlier. The man at the reception desk looked more like a hotel clerk than a desk sergeant. I told him that I wanted to see Staff Sergeant Jack Sykes, who was in charge of the Renata Sartori case. I had my name taken and was shown where I could sit down and wait.

I had not researched many of last year's periodicals when I heard my name called in a brisk, metallic voice. I closed the magazine, immediately forgot what I had been reading in it and got to my feet. Watching me was a body that could have belonged only to a big-city policeman. He stood six foot two and was carrying about seventy pounds of extra weight around his waist, which even a heavy belt couldn't disguise. This effect was strengthened by his narrow hips and tiny butt. His hair was straight and sandy, tending to fall across his right eye. Blue eyes and a firm jaw set in a ruddy face completed the first impression. He held out his hand and showed a double row of even, friendly teeth.

"Mr Cooperman. Glad you dropped in."

"Staff Sergeant Sykes?" I asked.

"Boyd," he said and amended it to "James Boyd," giving me the feeling I'd heard the combination before. "Jack's on the phone; with luck he may be finished by the time we get there." He turned and left the reception area without looking over his shoulder. I followed him to a room at the back without getting a glimpse of holding cells or suspects in handcuffs. It must have been a slow day.

Sykes's door stood open. He was leaning back in a swivel chair, in some danger of overbalancing. He was still on the phone, but waved James Boyd and me into the room. In front of him lay a thick Toronto phone book, with "VICE" written in felt pen along the open edge. The desk was a mess of paper. I liked him already.

". . . Go look it up in the transcript of the trial. Don't ask me. Listen, Sheldon, I'm a working stiff, okay? Why don't you go down to the Police Museum and talk to Les Mayhew. He knows all that ancient stuff. He was *there*, which I wasn't." He cupped his hand over the phone and said he'd be with us in a minute. I could see that he had long ago grown tired of this call. "Sheldon, you get credit on the cover for writing your books, right? In your past three books did I see a word about the time I've given you? What I'm saying is go write your book. I told you all I know about the case." There was a long pause, while Sheldon tried to pin him to the line for another minute. Sykes held the phone away from his ear and sipped cold coffee from a cardboard container. When the dregs had gone, he interrupted his caller: "Sheldon, buy me lunch next week and I might remember something new, but right now your time is up. I got a desk full of problems and that's what I'm being paid for . . . Sheldon! . . . Shut up,

Sheldon! Call me at home . . . Mr Zatz, here's how it is: I'm busy Tuesday next week and Friday, but lunch is clear on Monday, Wednesday and Thursday. I gotta go." He banged down the phone and swivelled straight in his chair.

"Never agree to sit on a panel with writers. They get your name and you never breathe an easy breath again." Boyd sat down and I took the chair he'd left for me. I presented my warrant card to him, which he assessed, nodding. He passed it across the desk to Sykes, who let it sit there without picking it up. Sykes was a big man too, but he handled the belly weight better than his partner. His muscles hadn't begun their migration towards fat yet and he looked like he could throw me across the room if I asked him to help with a little plotting problem I was having. There was a patch of red fuzz above his forehead where his hair should have been. It looked like a dying plant in a shining vase. He was wearing a blue suit that had been tailored by a computer program that misfired. His tie looked like an enlarged tongue lolling on the right side of his green shirt. I figured that he was colour-blind and living alone. He didn't say anything for a moment as he settled his hands behind his neck and relaxed back in his chair. The chair wheezed like an expiring sea lion. I wondered why he'd bothered to take his hat off. Except for that, Sykes looked like a movie cop from the 1940s. Something out of Hammett or Chandler, Leonard or Ellroy.

"So, you're Cooperman," he said at length, disappointing me with the clichéd introduction. Sheldon Zatz, whoever he was, was on to something in Sykes. You could fill up a lot of pages just describing the way he sat there drinking his cold coffee. I nodded and showed some teeth.

"And you're in charge of the Sartori case," I said, moving things in the direction of my preoccupations.

He said nothing, but he was running me through his assessment apparatus. I could imagine him sucking a toothpick. "Jim, this is the guy from Grantham that Chris Savas is always talking about."

"Yeah?"

"He's the one who does the Philip Marlowe and Sam Spade bit in Grantham. Population 1,280, right? No offence, Mr Cooperman, but we've been getting whiffs of the legend from the Greek."

"Cypriot, not Greek, sergeant. He makes a good case for the difference."

"Whatever," he said. "You worked these mean streets once before too, didn't you? Something about a murder over a rare book?"

"That was a few years ago."

"Yeah. Up in the Annex. I remember it now; you assembled all the suspects in a bookstore and pointed the guilty finger. Chuck Pepper told me about that. Right out of an Agatha Christie movie for television. You like private-eye movies, Mr Cooperman?"

"Sure. Doesn't everybody?"

"Savas told me you answer a question with a question. How is he? Has he made inspector yet?" For two minutes I brought them up to date about Chris Savas and his present status in the Niagara Regional Police. When I'd finished, Sykes shook his head as if I'd just asked him a question. "You know," he said, "after all the shit going down in Grantham these days, I don't know why a freelancer like yourself gets in his car and drives to Silver City looking for work. You know what I mean? When those tapes turned up under the false ceiling in the Medaglia case, after the place had been searched a dozen times, I mean, don't you want to hide your head or something?"

"Are you making a soliloquy, Sergeant, or was that a question?"

"Don't get me wrong. You weren't on that case probably, being a rent-a-cop, but when there's that much shit going down, a little brushes off on everybody whether they're involved or not."

"Like you collected in the Wentworth case?" I asked. "Kids are always getting their livers poisoned, aren't they, when bad nurses are allowed to roam the floors of the Rose of Sharon Hospital at night."

"There's no crap on my boot, Cooperman," Sykes said, straightening and getting his motion seconded by a groan from the chair. "The inquiry cleared us completely, or did your lips turn blue before you'd read that far? The papers are never so happy as when they've got a cop to hang out to dry, peeper."

"Why don't you tell me how you manage traffic lights and colour-coded index cards? Party games tire me. Why don't we cut out the dancing around?" I got him with the colour-blindness: he blinked like a sports czar with his hand caught in the pension fund.

"What are you doing in my town, Mr Cooperman?"

"I've been hired to keep somebody from getting killed."

"Oh? So, you're a bodyguard now! Next week it'll be the secret service."

I turned to Boyd and asked, "Is it the audience that gets him excited, or is he always like this?" Boyd opened his mouth as though about to utter, but closed it when Sykes stood up, letting his height, looming above me, play the cheap menace trick. I tried not to look intimidated, knowing all the time that he could chew me up in little pieces and swallow me without choking. I tried to look bored. "Why are you acting the heavy in this, Sykes? Didn't I come to you? Didn't I show my credentials? Didn't I do the diplomatic thing? What do you want from my life? I'm just trying to make a living." Sykes and Boyd exchanged looks. I waited. In his own good time Sykes moved my credentials across the desk towards me. Taking my time from him, I put them away in my wallet.

"Okay, if you'll cut the crap, I will. I was just trying to see how you bounced. No offence. Saves time in the end. So, the Moss woman has hired you? You buy her story that she was the intended victim?"

"She hired me, didn't she? That must say something. She's scared that whoever killed Renata Sartori was really after her."

"Yeah. We're back in the movies again. But you could just as easily be a blind. You could be window dressing."

"I didn't come here to argue with you, Sergeant. You know a lot more than I do. This is my first day on the job. You've got a two-week hop on me and resources I can't even imagine. If you think she did it, you must have good reasons. Since she's not out on bail or in the lock-up, you can't make a charge stick yet."

"She had the motive, the opportunity, and we found the spent shotgun shells in her locker. Now, in my book, that puts the fancy wrapping paper around the package."

When your eyeballs suddenly leap out of your head, there is hardly anything you can do to avoid looking like an animated cartoon of a cat being hit on the head by a large mallet. I took out my handkerchief and blew my nose loudly. I tried to work it out. I wanted to think. I thought of England, remembered the *Maine*, to help my breathing return to normal. I was smart enough not to speak. I nodded twice to give a sage indication of the assessment Jack Sykes had just made of the evidence pointing to Vanessa's guilt. Of course, the whole scenario hit me all at once. Vanessa hadn't told me because I might not take on her little problem. Shotgun shells found in her locker! She was damned right I would have stayed at home cultivating my non-existent garden. I was blazing mad at my own stupidity and more than a little upset by my old friend Stella Seco. I attempted a smile.

"You'll have to convince me about the motive. She's looking for people shooting down on her from above, not shooting up from below. I've seen her in action. She can handle the little guys without resorting to weapons larger than a pink slip. Opportunity? I thought she could demonstrate that she was out of town."

"Conveniently out of town."

"And I'm the convenient dodge to put you off. She hires me to show that she couldn't possibly be the guilty party. Everything is looking suspicious because it's convenient for your suspect. It's one of those 'if you thought that I thought that you thought that I thought' routines. You can't collar her with ifs."

"You just see if I can't." He reached into the bottom right-hand drawer of his dull grey desk and lifted out a plastic freezer bag. Inside lay two used red shotgun shells. He threw the bag at me, and I picked it up. To me one shotgun shell looks like another, but I tried not to show it.

"You found these in her locker, right? Where do they get off having lockers in fancy offices like hers?"

"I wondered that too. She says that there are sensitive documents that need overnight protection a little stronger than your average filing cabinet or desk. I know that a locker closed with a—" Here he paused long enough to retrieve a second plastic freezer bag from the same drawer. "—combination lock isn't Fort Knox, but you have to admit it's safer than—"

"Where you keep your evidence, for example," I said.

"During working hours, Cooperman. During working hours." Again he tossed the bag towards me and again I examined it through the plastic. It was an ordinary combination lock that, by the look of its broken shackle, had been cut off by powerful bolt cutters.

"You've tried the combination of this lock against the combination you got from your suspect?"

Sykes looked me straight in the face and said, "Sure we did." It was one of his little white lies. I could read that much in his partner's face. Boyd didn't say much, but he provided lots of information without troubling his vocal cords.

"Where did all of this take place, Sergeant?"

"You better call me Jack like everybody else or they won't know who you're talking about. You're Sam, is that right?" For a minute I thought he knew about my brother who works across the street from NTC in one of the hospitals.

"'Ben' or 'Benny' will do nicely. And you get 'Jim,' is that right, Sergeant Boyd?" I asked, turning towards him. He nodded. The three of us took a breath and waited for the second act to begin on an even keel. Only it couldn't start yet, because I had to hurry back to NTC to meet some of the possible villains in this case. And I wanted to speak to my damned client about omissions in her story.

CHAPTER FIVE

The meeting on the twentieth floor was a blur of names and faces. There was a balding six-footer sitting across from me called a comptroller, but what the two women bracketing me did, I never learned. I couldn't begin to sort them all out. I counted the bodies, divided them into men and women and promptly forgot the result. There were about half a dozen women, maybe, and twice that many men. The men affected a studied casualness in their dress: leather jackets gently cupping generous bellies, sweaters from the Outer Hebrides and Irish tweed over Gallagher shirts. The women had adopted more conservative pant suits and tailored skirts, both real and imitation top labels. I patted my pocket for the Kit Kat bar. I'd left it someplace. I could only hope that there would be coffee and biscuits.

Printed smiles cut through the serious look around this monumental table. Such were the junior executives answerable to Vanessa. Here were some of the rivals for her job. All of them looked worried under the template of affability, anxious to impress Vanessa and each other. One of them, Jack McKellar, head of the children's section, I think, tried to trip Vanessa up when she mentioned *Gambit*, a CTV program that she'd seen.

"Why were you tuned to CTV, Vanessa? *Gambit* is opposite our *Unprivate Eye*." He tried to look bewildered.

"I'm moonlighting at CTV, Jack, because they don't surround me with idiotic, back-stabbing yes-men. They pay me more into the bargain."

McKellar wasn't altogether clear that Vanessa had made a joke. Nor were half the others at the table. They tried to show expressions that could be read either way. Later on, Vanessa dropped in a homily explaining that part of her job involved knowing what the opposition was up to, that there was more to running her department than enforcing the No Smoking rules. McKellar was unconvinced.

Vanessa kept to an agenda. She listened to all of the section heads as they gave their reports, or what they called "the actual," and kept the meeting rolling when it bogged down into generalities or—and I was surprised at this—gossip. I was amazed that these paper-pushers were in awe of the actors, hosts and anchor-people they had placed before their cameras. It was as though they had forgotten the parts they had played in making these faces so well known.

She introduced me at the beginning of the meeting. There were no smiles of welcome. No drums, no trumpets, no cheers. Executive assistants come and go too rapidly to pay much attention to the incumbent.

Vanessa asked for a progress report on "the proposed" from each of her section heads. Each, after his or her fashion, tried to bamboozle Vanessa into believing that progress had been made since last time. Vanessa was very clever in finding out which projects had made progress and which were standing still. Her idea of a meeting wasn't just to rehearse the status quo, but to shake things down and slip through or around the bottlenecks. There were attempts at levity initiated by a few of the more secure people at the table, but they were killed off with a hard look from Vanessa. Even references to crazy Bob Foley, the independent runaway technician, couldn't find a smile in the room.

"We're still dangling on the Plath-Hughes special, Vanessa. The agent just isn't returning my calls. It must be chaos over there." This from a bright-eyed youngster who leaned back in his chair to the balancing point.

"Rod," Vanessa said, staring anywhere but at him, "that's where things stood last week and the week before!"

"I know, but you know the Brits."

"Who have you got in London?"

"In London?" He was stalling.

"That's the city we're talking about. Who are you talking to there?"

"Vanessa, I'm—"

"Rod, your place at this table is under review. Do you understand me? Now get up to speed. There are no Jonahs on this ship. Audrey, since Mr Sinclair is unable to help us, what can you tell me?" And so it went, on and on. Vanessa was critical of everybody. Even the few who could report progress had, according to Vanessa, missed a percentage of their advantage. I started to think how glad I was not to be working for her, when it came over me with a chill that I was. Was I staring at my future as I surveyed the smiling, unhappy faces opposite me?

The final item on the agenda was finding a replacement show for *Reading with Renata*. Vanessa gave credit to the producer who had thrown together a tribute show for the coming Sunday. But now it was time to find a permanent replacement. All around the table, it was thumbs down on another book show. Rod Sinclair may have saved his bacon when he told Vanessa about a fashion-show pilot he'd just seen.

"Okay, Rod. You run with it. But keep me informed."

Afterwards, when the meeting broke up and Vanessa's minions went to check whether their names were still printed on their doors, I got the feeling that I'd been through a document shredder. And they weren't even aiming at me. After a washroom break, Vanessa sat me down in her office for a chat. While Sally went for fresh coffee, I thought I'd better clear up the unpleasant business of the omissions in my first conversation with Vanessa.

"Vanessa, I can't be much good to a client who isn't straight with me."

"What are you talking about?"

"At 52 Division, I caught up with the story of the spent shotgun shells found in your locker. Did you think that if you said nothing the fact would blow away?"

"I can *explain* that. You're not angry with me, are you?"

"You're bloody right I'm angry. Do you have any idea how important those shells are?"

"They might have cleared me if it wasn't for those god-damned shells!" She stopped there, as though she was measuring the importance of other things she'd saved me from knowing. "I was going to tell you, Benny, but we never got back there." She moved a hand to rearrange a tress or two that had fallen over her forehead. "All right, they found the damned shells in my locker and say that they're like the ones that the murderer used on Renata."

"Were they yours?"

"Of course not! I've *never* owned a gun. And these shells didn't have my fingerprints either. There were no fingerprints. Or at least, that's what they say. Benny, tell me that you're not going to be cross at me. Right now, the way I feel, I couldn't bear that."

"While we're at it, why did you keep a metal locker in your office? That wasn't picked out by your friend at Holt's."

"It was part of a pressure play. I'd ordered a proper safe for important papers, but Ted Thornhill was delaying things. You'd think a CEO would be above that kind of pettiness, but you'd lose your bet. I bought the locker myself, for practical reasons and to embarrass Ted. The week before Renata was shot, Ted spotted the locker, and I saw by his red face that I'd won the round. There, Benny, that's the whole truth."

"You'd better tell me the whole truth from now on. If you want to stay alive, that is. Maybe you have other plans?" She made contrite noises and underlined them all with body language, knowing that that was the sure way to distract me. Then she began to berate me about neglecting her. I reminded her that I'd been out of her sight only a couple of times, notably when I was checking in with the police working on the case. Then she told me to leave the solving of Renata Sartori's murder to the cops; my job was keeping her, Vanessa, alive. She was no longer the supplicant asking for another chance, she was back in the driver's seat, not a motion wasted.

"But," I argued, "finding Renata's killer could be a shortcut to the same end."

"Yeah, and the cops are working that corner, Benny. Don't crowd them. You stick with me. Watch my back. That way I've got two strings to my bow, and I might still be alive in September."

"Okay. I hear you. But, there are a few avenues I'd like to try out on my own, Vanessa. I know how to stay out of the way of the official investigation. They'll know all about me anyway." I saw the smile fade from her face. I was sinking into the same quagmire of disapproval that had caught Rod with his pants down. I knew I had to talk fast or I was going to line up with the other losers. "Look, Stel—" I did that on purpose to under-line our special relationship. "You have told me practically nothing about what happened. I don't know where you live, who knew you lived there, how long you've been in the neigh-bourhood or anything else. I need to know more about Renata: who her friends were, who your friends are. All that stuff. Where is your place in the country? when did you drive up there? who saw you? when did you get back? where did you buy gas? where did you stop to eat? Your life may be hang-ing from a thread woven from your full and unedited answers."

She was angry at me now. Partially because she thought she had reached a position where nobody could talk to her like that and partially because she knew I was right.

"Okay, Benny, get out your notebook." I grabbed a pad from my new desk. "I live on Balmoral Avenue. That's two south of St Clair, off Avenue Road. The place is owned jointly by me and my husband. I've been there for five years. Every-body at CBC, CTV and all the other places I've worked knows the place. I like to give big parties. Everybody in this building knows the house, the garden and maybe even how to get into the backyard from the cemetery at the rear. All of those people you met in the boardroom were at a party two months ago. I gave it to encourage our efforts before the sweeps. Talk about business losses."

"What are the sweeps?"

"Benny! Your innocence is astonishing. It's like not knowing what's at the end of the Yellow Brick Road," she said, smiling indulgently. Then she cleared her throat and began again. "The sweeps are the audience surveys run at fixed times of the year. Independent head-counters measure our audiences for a test week. Our advertising rates for the next season are based on the numbers they come up with. Part of our job is to make sure that our best efforts go into those important time-slots." I scribbled all of this on the pad I balanced on my knee, and hoped to be able to translate my shorthand afterwards. She kept right on going.

"I found the place at the lake through Ed Patel, a small-town lawyer and an old friend of my Poppa's. They used to hunt and fish together. The cottage is in my name; I have eight years to go before I renew the mortgage. It's not a big place, just seven acres with only seventy-five feet of lake frontage. The lake is Muskoka. The nearest big town is Bracebridge, but Port Carling is where you go to buy charcoal and milk. Are you getting all this, Benny?" She didn't wait for an answer, but kept larding on the facts and details. "The place is called *Puckwana*, and, no, I don't know what it means. Probably Ojibway. The house replaced a log house dating from the turn of the century. The frame house is only fifty years old. I go up there to be by myself, although that's getting harder and harder to do since Hollywood people like Peggy O'Toole and Goldie Hawn discovered Muskoka. Apart from the cellphone I leave in my car, there is no e-mail, Internet or fax up there. There *is* a phone, but it's in the name of the former owner. It never rings. The lawyer I mentioned, Ed Patel, my nearest neighbour, lives an eighth of a mile away, but he's in the Bracebridge hospital, so he didn't see me while I was there. Nor did his secretary, Alma, because she electrocuted herself in the bath. Am I going too fast?

"I was in the bookstore in Port Carling, but I don't know if I created enough of a stir to make your life easy for you. You might try the Esso station on the town-side of the lift lock. I filled my tank there and got the attendant to wash my windshield. I didn't stop to eat on my drive back to the city; I just nibbled on the things that would perish if I left them in the cottage fridge and planned on a good dinner when I got home, a dinner I never got to order, because I walked into the arms of Sergeant Jack Sykes and his merry men in blue sitting in my living-room. How am I doing? What have I left out?"

"When exactly was that, Vanessa?"

"I arrived home about noon on Monday, the twenty-second of May. The long weekend, remember? I wanted to avoid the mob scene on the highways later on, and I did."

"So, Renata was killed on Monday, the fifteenth."

"What a brain! You want more about Renata? I met her when we were both nobodies, just starting out. We lived on next to nothing at 410 Jarvis Street; it was a flophouse run by an old radio actor who'd lost both his arms. That was close to the CBC in those days. Hamp Fisher was still setting up NTC. He was switching from newspapers to TV." She stopped talking when she saw that the name had changed my expression. "Ah, you've heard about him? Hamp Fisher's the chairman and controlling shareholder of NTC. Owns about forty-two per cent of the voting shares. Nice for Hamp. Renata, on the other hand, worked her passage up from the mailroom and typing pool. Mostly at CBC. She did time at CITY and Global too. Back then, you moved fairly freely back and forth between the networks looking for somebody who'd let you try out new things. She knew about numbers, so she came out the other end here at NTC as budget manager of different shows."

"Friends? Enemies?"

"She dated two budget chiefs—I can give you their names—an actor or two—*they'll* give you their names, and for a brief moment she was the lover of the one and only Dermot Keogh. Remember I told you that her book show had one lis-tener? It was Dermot. He watched it wherever he went. But their affair didn't last long. She started as his bookkeeper and worked her way through from the office to the bedroom. I thought she'd made the gravy train at last, but it didn't stick. It never did with Dermot. Of course, this time it was his death that got in the way."

"How long was it before he drowned?"

"Oh, they were at it hot and heavy for about two months. He died in the last week of April last year."

"Which lake did he drown in?"

"Muskoka. What other lake have we been talking about? Benny, a lot of people around here have places in Muskoka. Have you ever heard about the Bradings Trust?" Her face was about a foot away from mine by now, and she had been talking a mile a minute.

"Tell me about it."

"Ernest Miller Bradings left a huge property on the lake to a trust, which has, for reasons I don't think are relevant, sold off pieces to people in the industry."

"TV people, you mean?"

"Closer than that. Many of the top people here at NTC have bought lake lots from the trust. It's not exclusive, of course, but the Bradings properties are worth avoiding if you're trying to get away from it all." She got to her feet. "There, Benny, that's all for now. We can have another go when your writing hand stops tingling."

"Could you ask Sally to give me a list of the people I saw at that production meeting, Vanessa? And if there's a rundown on each of them, I wouldn't mind seeing that as well." I tacked on this request as a bid for elbow-room.

"I've already instructed Sally to get you anything you want—short of old videos of movies from the forties. (This isn't a joyride, Benny.) You may find Sally reluctant to be your pal on things. Just tell me if she drags her heels or gives you excuses. She'll try that, but don't take it from her. I mean it. If you say please too often, you'll never get her to find you a postage stamp."

"You seem skilled in the ways of the Sallys of this world."

"Yes, the Sallys, the Jack McKellars, the Rod Sinclairs and the rest of them."

Vanessa was still standing up under the pressure of a non-stop day. Her Armani suit was looking a little wilted around the edges, but I guess that's part of the look. She shot me a wan smile and sat down to work again. She asked me to leave the door open. I was dismissed.

Someone had set up a dull wooden desk in a corner near one of the windows. It had a black leather inlay on the top surface and nothing in the IN and OUT baskets. The drawer offered paperclips in metal and colourful plastic. There were a couple of pink erasers and a clutch of sharp yellow pencils. When I worked briefly for a lawyer, a cousin of mine, he issued new pencils on an "as needed" basis: show him a stub shorter than one and a half inches, and he would replace it happily with a longer one. The same scene-shifters who had brought my desk had moved Vanessa's out of the line of fire. It made the whole deal more sporting.

A fresh noise exploded in the corridor. It came with the sound of the elevator doors opening in a sort of cushioned groan. I heard the sharp crack of Vanessa's coffee cup hitting wood and the name "Devlin" hissed through her set teeth, as though the name unlocked a chestful of pestilence. Vanessa jumped up behind her desk. Sally's eyes were wide. She was on her feet and ran into Vanessa's sanctum sanctorum. They both came out a second later, shoulder to shoulder, to meet the man in a grey suit with a hat, a briefcase and his topcoat over his arm. He was accompanied by a dark, curly-haired man half a head shorter. There was no mistaking which was the bishop and which the clerk.

"Raymond! Raymond, you shouldn't have!" This was Vanessa as she came within bussing distance of the newcomers. He kissed her soundly on each cheek without even noticing that Sally stood next to her. "I would have sent the contracts down to you by courier. You didn't have to come all this way."

"Vanessa, I don't trust people. When I want something done, I do it myself. That's the only way to survive. Besides, with all these changes in the air, I thought I'd better get the ink on the paper as soon as possible. By the way, you know Roger here, I think."

"Changes? What changes? What are you talking about, Raymond? Do you mean our revised fall schedule? Revising is what we do best around here." Vanessa smiled broadly, but I could tell that she hadn't liked what Raymond had blurted out. Raymond, too, was now looking like a child who had said too much and now was being badgered to say more. Raymond took the fatter of the two briefcases from Roger here, and began a paperchase with its contents. Roger here stood by and watched.

"Oh, I must have thought that you'd be taking some time off now. Because of the shooting, I mean. By the way, I called Ted and Whatshisname, you know, from your plant department, or whatever you call it, to sign for the engineering side of things." At this point, Vanessa introduced Sally and me to Raymond Devlin, who was acting as though that name was better known than it was. Roger here turned out to be Roger Cavanaugh. Even with a last name, he remained the acolyte of his boss. Sally passed a man with a bald dome and black-rimmed glasses as she went out in search of beverages. He turned out to be Whatshisname.

"Oh, here you are, Harry." Vanessa introduced Harry Parlow, head of Plant and Services, whatever that meant. The bald head bobbed, almost bowing, over handshakes.

Devlin boomed, "Glad you could make it, Harry. I don't have long, so I'm glad you're on time."

"Raymond's legal firm is the executor of Dermot Keogh's estate, Benny. Thanks to Keogh's estate, NTC is building a new concert studio and Raymond has generously allowed us to use Dermot's name. He'll remain as a consultant on the sort of things that the studio will be used for. We hope that it will rival the CBC's Glenn Gould Studio."

"Rival? Hell, Vanessa, it will make the CBC hall look like a swill bucket to this Limoges tureen we're putting up." Raymond Devlin looked like a young Henry Kissinger, with jowls poised to start sprouting after his next corned beef sandwich.

Fussiness was written all over him. He fairly quivered with fastidiousness. His eyes drank you in and spat out the seeds, leaving your innards on his hard drive for later use. His weight was doing damage to an expensive, well-cut suit. He managed to make it look like he picked it up off the rack in a "Reduced to Clear Sale." Roger Cavanaugh gave me the look he'd learned from his master. He was out for learning.

Sally arrived back not with coffee but with proper drinks. There was an array of bottles on a trolley and a nearby credenza yielded biscuits, glasses and napkins. While she was working on the refreshments, Vanessa was laying out four copies of the contract for all to sign. Raymond Devlin brought out a package of cigarettes. Menthols. "I don't suppose that here on the twentieth floor we are free from the prohibitions that obtain elsewhere in this building?"

"You'll have the security squad down on you in a minute. And you'd better not take it up with Ted Thornhill when he gets here. He's a former smoker, Raymond, so you'll be dealing with a convert. You know what they're like."

"The world is conspiring against smokers, Vanessa. The only way I can fly these days is Air India, and you'd be surprised at the places where Air India doesn't fly. Why, in my own office I had to install a vent through the window. The owner is still furious at me, but we do rent the whole floor."

Vanessa told me that she'd need Sally and me to sign as witnesses. When I asked her what this was all about, she told me to play along; she'd explain later. Just as we were about to make the papers immortal, someone introduced as Ted Thornhill, the CEO of NTC, came through the door with a photographer whose camera was already loaded and poised. Introductions were not attempted. I was the only odd man out. I could see that Harry Parlow was feeling good about it; he didn't get to meet the top dogs every day. Vanessa was on her toes, playing hostess. Raymond didn't sweat, but his brow showed a certain tension. His donation of Keogh's hard cash gave him points and he knew it. Roger came into his own, pointing out small changes, places to initial and so forth. When we had had a go at examining the four copies, passing them around like it was a game, criss-crossing and twice getting mixed up, Raymond plainly relaxed. Ted Thornhill supervised all of this, glancing down over a cascade of double chins. His eyes were small but alert, his mouth the thinnest part of the whole anatomy. His suit showed the wear and tear that a large body can give to the best imported serge. Sparse blond hair betrayed a recent attempt to comb it with water. I found that likeable.

For a quiet, informal gathering, the signing itself was accomplished with sober deliberation. The principal pen was picked up and handed to all the signers by Ted Thornhill. All eyes watched as the ink moved along the paper. The pen was a Montblanc. It fairly blushed from black to grey with the weight of the honour entrusted to it. "There!" said Thornhill with a flourish after all the signatures had been applied. "We make a little history every day. The public event will be next . . ."

"One week from today. Wednesday at 4:30 in the library, on the mezzanine floor, southwest end of the Royal York Hotel." Vanessa stepped in to help the forgetful Thornhill.

"Of course, I remember now. There's a press conference to begin with. Right? I'll call on you, Ray. You knew Keogh better than anyone, except maybe Philip Rankin. Not many speeches, just what's necessary to hit the right celebratory note."

"And then the drinks," said Devlin. "I hope you've not ordered those bits of coloured cheese, Ted?"

"Cheese?" He looked puzzled. "I don't ordinarily see to the catering, Ray. We might have better receptions if I did. Vanessa, will you look into that? We want the announcement of Dermot Keogh Hall to be a major cultural event. The usual cheese and crackers will not do. Not in any way. Please see to it." Vanessa smiled one of those pasted-on smiles, the sort you get in opera when the clown's heart is breaking.

"It has a good ring to it, that name: Dermot Keogh Hall," mused Devlin. "The hall will seat five hundred, with ample backstage and lobby space."

"We've got a logo that uses his signature, Ray. It will be on all stationery and, of course, above the doors. I've got a firm of architects working on it now. I want you to be pleased with this every step of the way."

"Good. I knew you wouldn't sell me out. This is a red-letter day for the Plevna Foundation."

The name Plevna stabbed me in the ear. I'd heard the name earlier in connection with Bob Foley, the independent-minded technician.

This sideshow didn't last long. Nobody really drank more than a sip of his drink—Sally and I were excluded from the libations, by the way. Roger grabbed a drink when Raymond wasn't watching.

"I don't mind saying that I'm uneasy with even an *uns*igned document in my safe," Raymond said. "Having the fully executed documents will plague my sleep, Vanessa. You keep those two copies and I'll take the other two."

"Why don't you leave the original and all the copies here and I can get two of them matted and mounted for framing. I'll send your copies over by courier. They should be ready by Monday or Tuesday. Lots of time before the reception on Wednesday."

"I hate to let things get away from me, Vanessa. The world around us is fragmenting in every direction. I can't do much about that. But I *can* try to keep a few things in order."

"Don't be a fusspot, Raymond. I won't lose them. When did I ever let you down?"

"Vanessa, a man isn't safe in your hands. All right, keep three copies. I'll take one along with me. But you keep the others under lock and key."

"I'll put them in my new safe. I just got it this morning." Vanessa shot Ted Thornhill a look that coloured the flesh over his cheekbones. He cleared his throat and didn't meet Vanessa's eyes.

"I don't blame you for worrying, Raymond. I'll personally see to it that nothing happens to them. But remember this: it's not every day that NTC commits so much of its resources to one big project. We're in this together. There'll be glory enough for all." Raymond thought that this was the cue for an informal embrace, which caught Vanessa off guard. She entered into the momentary entanglement in a lively spirit, then extracted herself without a hair mussed.

I missed the moment of Ted Thornhill's departure. It must have been right after the photographer, who'd changed films at least half a dozen times. Thornhill had that rare skill of being able to retreat silently without taking away the feeling of his presence in a room. He and Raymond both made you feel as though you'd just witnessed the signing of a major peace accord.

"Now, tell me," Raymond said, his voice in another register, and following Vanessa to a free couch, "how are you making out since this horrible murder? Are you all right? Are the police giving you the protection you need?"

"I'm fine, really I am. If I can only escape north again for a long weekend, I'll be completely recovered."

"Oh, I don't know about that. No, no, no. I should think that you'd be more vulnerable at the lake than here. Have they let you go back to the house yet?"

"I don't want to go back just yet, Raymond. I'll go when I'm ready. It's not for the police to decide. They've finished taking the place apart, I'm told. But I'm not up to putting it back together again."

"It's a Humpty Dumpty situation," I volunteered.

"What?" said Raymond Devlin, examining my face as though it were turning purple. He seemed to be not so much at sea in Mother Goose as he was surprised that I had uttered at all. "What?" He looked at Vanessa with a quizzical expression. For a moment I thought that my remark might have made it necessary to sign the contracts all over again. But it was only my own craziness. He soon packed up his briefcase, watched over by Roger Cavanaugh, and began shaking hands with the remaining principal signers. The witnesses got a half-smile just before he turned and walked briskly to the elevator. Harry Parlow's exit was less dramatic and took place not two minutes later. His expression showed a picture of the back room he was returning to.

I sat there for a few minutes, watching the rooftops below me. Time and place had been distorted by this meeting. It made me jumpy. Vanessa went from her valedictory posture near the entrance directly to Sally.

"Damn it, Sally! How was he able to get up here without my knowing it? Isn't that why we have security? I want you to find out who's responsible for the slip-up. I mean it. I want to see the name. Do you hear?" Sally immediately picked up the telephone.

"Commander Dunkery, please," and waited.

"I hate surprises, Benny," Vanessa said, checking the polish on her fingernails. "I didn't want Raymond Devlin walking in on me unprepared. I'm lucky it went as well as it did. But I should have been warned."

Soon Sally was explaining what had happened to the security chief. Meanwhile, Vanessa used the time to return telephone calls that were waiting for her on top of her desk. From the blur of blue message slips, she selected three, dumping the rest into the recycling bin. I tried to follow what she was talking about and make a note of the name of the caller. She used a slightly different voice with each call: Vanessa the repentant procrastinator, Vanessa the wheedler, Vanessa the straight-talking manager, Vanessa of the walking wounded, carrying on under difficulties and against doctor's orders, Vanessa the neophyte seeking professional help. When I couldn't take any more, I mimed my departure from the door, and she acknowledged it with a wave of coiled telephone cord.

Outside, there was Sally. Sally who wouldn't be my pal. Sally who had to be watched. Sally whose loyalty lay outside this office. I wasn't up to asking her for favours just then, so I skirted her desk heading for the burgundy elevator and the outside world.

CHAPTER SIX

Much later, in the dying minutes of rush hour, Sykes and Boyd were sitting opposite me in a Second Cup coffee place across the street from 52 Division on Dundas Street. The kid behind the counter, the one with the metal rings in his ear and nose, knew the cops when we came in, and gave me a look that tried to guess whether I was a suspect in a bank hold-up or a serial killer about to be brought to book. Boyd was still taciturn, Sykes still suspicious. I warmed my hands on the coffee mug and pulled at a Danish pastry contributed by Boyd. In the back of my mind, I was reviewing my last meeting with the official police team. I wondered whether this conversation would lead to another awkward confrontation with my client.

"Have you been talking to those people over in TV-land?" Sykes asked, licking his fingers and shaking his head to tell me that he had been as bewildered by them as I had. "I don't know how they get off being so full of themselves. It was like every one of them imagined he was being photographed and recorded all the time. Like they were being chased around by a film crew. Like they lived under a follow spotlight. I can't believe it."

"What do you honestly think of Ms Moss's theory that someone is trying to murder her?" I looked at Boyd, challenging him to offer a theory, a word, a grunt.

"Like in that movie? Dana Andrews and Jennifer Jones—"

"Not Jennifer Jones!" Sykes said with more passion than I'd expected. "It was what's-her-name: Gene Tierney!"

"I think it's what it sounds like: right out of Hollywood," Boyd said, proving that the gift of speech was his when he wanted to use it.

"I don't like the bounce on it," said his partner.

"But, as you said, we are dealing with professionals at make-believe. To them there's not much difference between a real villain and reruns of *Law and Order*. You know what I mean?"

"Yeah. I know."

"What's your stake in all this, Mr Cooperman? Tell me again so I'll get used to the idea."

"I was hired to guard Vanessa Moss. Whoever it is out there probably has more shells for that shotgun. If it was a mistake the first time, he may try again."

"What the hell can you do? You don't carry. Maybe you're a karate hero and we don't know about it. And what the hell are you doing here? Your client could be dead four or five times while you're shooting the shit with us."

"That's something you can take up with her. She's within her rights. If she needs her head examined, that's her lookout. Besides, I had to make contact with you guys. You knew I was here, so I had to drop around as soon as I could, or I'd be in deep trouble whenever our paths crossed later on, right?"

"Right. So you think we've got inside help?"

"How else would you know I was in town? I just got here and you knew all about me. It figures that you've got a snitch inside NTC."

"Snitching's a dirty job. Nobody loves a snitch. Does that hold for PIs, Benny?"

"I didn't go looking for this job any more than you did. It's all in a day's work with me too. And frankly, I can use the business. She's paying a good dollar plus expenses. I tried to talk her out of it. She thinks I'm a hotshot. What am I going to do about it?"

"Okay, so you're the hotshot from Grantham, watching over a suspect—hey! That's another movie, isn't it? The one with the 'Bell Song' from *Lakme*, right?"

"It was from *Lakme*, but not the 'Bell Song.' It was a duet. Two women, like the two men in *The Pearl Fishers*. Close harmonies."

This contribution came from Jim Boyd. Next he'd be ordering vodka martinis, shaken not stirred. He was full of surprises.

The conversation shifted to internal police talk of retirement, pensions, holidays, dental plans and other collective benefits. I watched Boyd and Sykes. They weren't excluding me, but there wasn't anything I could add to the discussion. Still, they were having it in front of me, which might be seen as a sort of acceptance into the Toronto Police Grousing Society. I started counting the bubbles in my cup and collecting the crumbs of my Danish with moist fingertips. When I retired from doing private investigations, it would be because I'd found a less stressful way of making a living.

"Consultants aren't worth shit," Sykes was saying *apropos* of something I'd missed. "When you press them for the stuff that led to their findings, they won't show them to you, because in most cases those findings don't exist. Then they'll tell you off the record that their findings were concocted on the basis of what they thought we wanted to hear. The customer is always right."

"Depends on the outfit you use," Boyd protested. As for me, I got up and went to the john. When I got back, they were arguing about something of more interest to me than portable dental plans. They were going over the evidence in the two freezer bags.

"Art Dempsey told me that these things haven't been made since around 1935. Used to get them through the English Army and Navy Stores in London. After 1935, they went in for a different style. Same half-brass base and cardboard case, but different powder and printing. The wadding that went with the pellets into the victim came from the shells we recovered in her boss's locker." Boyd was muttering this to Sykes, who was listening with his eyes half shut. I took my chair and tried not to make it squeak as I sat down.

"That sounds right up your alley, Benny. If the shells were that old, we are looking for an antique weapon. Isn't that the sort of thing private eyes in books are always running into? Indonesian stilettoes, bejewelled Tong daggers, Thug axes, antique sporting guns?" Sykes eyed me with a single open eye under a raised eyebrow.

"Sure," I said, "when we can't get murder by tiger whiskers in the stew or icicles rammed into the victim's heart. Why, only last week, I solved a case of murder involving a gun that was fired automatically by a string tied to the door knocker. Killed three Girl Guides in a line. He did it for the cookies, I figure."

Boyd laughed, and even Sykes cracked a grin.

"Week before that, I uncovered a mad archer who replaced her deadly arrows in the victims with icepicks when nobody was looking. She had me fooled for about thirty seconds."

"Okay, *okay!* Enough's enough. Chris Savas is right about you, Benny: we can't bullshit you into going back home, can we, Jim?"

"Welcome to Toronto, Benny." Boyd passed the sugar, which had been lying just beyond my reach. I took it as a peace offering.

Twenty minutes later, we were sitting in Boyd's car outside a house on the north side of Balmoral Avenue. It was in an area of modest to big houses, sandwiched between main north-south streets. Sykes said that it was about a fifteen-minute drive from here to NTC. An old Catholic cemetery ran along the back of the house, Boyd told me, leaving a skimpy garden behind to match the one in front. The three-storey brick house was attached to the two neighbouring houses, leaving a front door, still decorated with torn scraps of yellow "Crime Scene" tape, as the only access from the street.

The two cops rolled their bodies heavily out of the car and lumbered up to the house. Sykes had the keys to it and to half a dozen other places; these he slowly excluded from his selection. The door opened inward into a narrow hall, useful for storing a few overcoats and a snow shovel. A second frosted-glass door introduced us to the rest of the house. The opening side of this had been peppered with stray shotgun pellets, and a blackened smear in the same area reminded me why we were here. To the right were heavily carpeted stairs going to the second floor and, to the left, a passage to the kitchen in the rear. Someone had placed a plaid blanket over the bloodstained broadloom; otherwise it was impossible to go anywhere in the house without walking through the darkened gore.

The rooms on the ground floor had recently been painted; the lush carpeting looked less than two years old. The decorations and furniture were a credit to whomever Vanessa relied upon completely for this sort of thing. Besides a baby grand piano, there was every electronic media device known to man, mostly ranged in a black metal stack against one wall. The results were not uncomfortable, but there was a prepackaged feel to the effect. I tried to imagine the faces I'd seen a few hours ago around the boardroom table relaxing in these surroundings. No, the decor discouraged relaxation. There was a hint of the principal's office about the dark wood accents and bookcases. If Vanessa herself relaxed, it was not in the front room.

The kitchen was white, bright and contemporary, with refrigerator notes held up by magnets disguised as tiny bunches of cauliflower and broccoli. I looked over the notes for something that would introduce itself as a clue. There were a couple of *New Yorker* cartoons with a media theme. One showed a bunch of groundskeepers sweeping the sidewalks and patios of New York's Lincoln Center with witches' brooms and gnarled wooden rakes. The caption read something about using only original instruments.

Whenever I looked at Sykes or Boyd, I caught him looking at me. Did they expect me to uncover in a minute what their whole team had missed for two weeks? That's all I needed to cut the fragile bond of co-operation completely.

"Okay," I said after an interminable silence, "what do you know about the terms of the victim's stay here? Was she a guest, a tenant or what?"

"According to your client," Sykes said, using both hands to make quotation marks in the air on either side of his head, "Sartori called Moss and asked to stay for the weekend of the thirteenth. Moss told her that she was going out of town and that she could stay the week if she wanted."

"Renata had a good job at NTC. Didn't she have a place of her own?"

"She was living, without benefit of clergy, with Barry Bosco, a lawyer, until she decided that she'd had enough of him. We got that much from Bosco himself. I gather that it was mutual."

"Sure it was. Now tell me how come Vanessa Moss is your prime suspect and not Barry Bosco?" Sykes smiled at Boyd like I'd just delivered the straight line they were waiting for.

"Bosco was giving a speech to the Junior Chamber of Commerce in Orillia at ten that night. Twenty-six young businessmen say he was there. He's not much of a speaker, I gather."

"Let me repeat the question. Lake Muskoka's farther away from Silver City than Orillia. Or it was the last time I looked."

"Look, Benny," Sykes said in an even voice, "if we were satisfied with our suspicions, your client wouldn't be driving all over town in that Range Rover of hers. If we were sure, she wouldn't have gone to see you in Grantham yesterday on her way to Niagara Falls. We're watching her, sure, but that's all we're doing right now: just watching."

I hate it when clients lie to me. I can live with it, but I don't like it. Vanessa told me she was going to Niagara-on-the-Lake to see the head of the Shaw Festival. That's a fair hike from the city of Niagara Falls. Either Vanessa was fibbing, or these guys should take a refresher course in geography. I decided not to say anything lest they haul Vanessa's sweet ass to Dundas Street to answer some more questions.

I got up and headed for the front hall, stepping over the plaid blanket. "What were the lights like when you got here on Monday night?"

"It wasn't me or Jim. We weren't on the case until the next morning. But, if you believe what was passed on to us, the house was dark except for a light in the bathroom upstairs, a light over the bed, a lamp in the downstairs living-room and the hall light up there."

"What about the porch light? I saw one coming in."

"It wasn't on."

"Have you been here after dark?"

"Yeah. The hall light was behind her all right. The only light coming in was from the streetlight down the street. And that's not enough to see bugger-all."

"So? What are you saying?"

"What I'm saying is that the physical evidence here isn't at variance with the mistaken-identity story. That version is consistent with the facts as far as we know them."

"'Consistent.' That's one of those hedging words you hear a lot of these days. What about the wounds? I've only heard that she took both barrels of a shotgun in the face at close range."

"That's it. She was dressed for bed and wearing one of Moss's dressing gowns." I thought about that and hoped that Sykes and Boyd didn't see my involuntary twitch when an image of the crime in progress shot through my brain. I felt a dry retch coming too. I fought to control it, thinking of Las Vegas, for no reason I can explain.

"Okay. So it is *possible* that the murderer shot the wrong woman?" I tried to look Sykes in the eye.

"That's one interpretation. One line of thinking, yeah, sure."

"The other is that Moss did it herself, hoping that all of you remembered the same old movie," I said.

"That's *one* other line, yeah. We've got others."

"Such as?"

"I thought the lady was paying you to find out about that sort of thing?"

"I never pass the free lunch, Jack. You never know when you're going to be hungry next." The detectives exchanged a glance. They were feeling superior and safe. Just where I wanted them. "Okay," I continued, "so there are aspects that you aren't ready to talk about. That's fair. I can live with that." I wasn't happy about it, but what could I do? Argue? I thought that maybe they weren't that far ahead of me in the investigation, and this "other line" thing simply created a wholly imaginary lead suggesting that all systems were go and that these two were on top of every aspect of the case.

A buzz sounded close by. Both cops reached for their cellphones. It was Sykes who was being summoned. Boyd put his set away slowly, as though this wasn't the first time. He checked the pager on his belt.

"Yeah!" Sykes said, and then he repeated it a few times with different inflections before folding up his phone and putting it away. Both Boyd and I were looking at him. "The mystery begins to thicken," he said with a grin. After a suitable dramatic pause, he announced: "They just discovered the body of Robert Foley of NTC in his Sackville Street house, stone dead, it would seem, from an overdose of sleeping pills and strong drink. You knew this guy?" he said, giving me the eye again.

"He's a senior technician on the Vic Vernon late-night talk show. Last night he walked off the set saying, 'I don't need this shit.'"

"Looks like he didn't need any." I didn't laugh and Boyd only showed a few teeth to be friendly. "The office just let me know because of the NTC tie-in. At the moment, they're treating it for what it looks like. Or maybe you think it's some kind of fancy murder, Benny?"

"Look, Jack, my life's complicated enough right now without trying to match the plots of movies and TV series. If you'll settle for suicide, that's good enough for me."

"Who's looking into it?" Boyd wanted to know. Me too, although I tried not to show it.

Sykes mentioned two names. Boyd winced. Sykes answered him with a shrug. I gathered that this was not the A team. "I'm going to call in and get a parallel investigation going. With everything else going on, this should get the 'suspicious sudden death' treatment. I want another team from Homicide checking this out."

"Those guys you mentioned?" I asked. "They're as bad as that, eh?" I didn't get an answer.

"Are you all done here, Benny?" Sykes wanted to know. "You want to check out the second and third floors?"

I didn't, but now I was determined that I would go through every drawer and turn up all the mattresses, just to show them. It took the next twenty minutes or so, and when I'd finished, I didn't have anything I didn't have when I got up that morning. If it was a moral victory, I was surprised how low I'd sink to collect one.

CHAPTER SEVEN

A hotel bed may be the ideal place for many things in this life, but sleep isn't one of them. At least not in the New Beijing Inn. The traffic on Bay is slow to die, and it gets started again about the time the early edition of *The Globe and Mail* hits the street. Nearby construction also gets up with the pigeons and sparrows, most of which were camped outside my window.

I had ended my first day in Toronto by having dinner in the Treasure House, a downstairs Chinese restaurant that Sykes suggested, not far from the bus terminal on Bay. The steamed rice was good for a stomach that didn't travel well or often. It was a friendly enough place and bargains were pasted up along the walls in Chinese characters. I got the idea that if you could read the language, you could dine for next to nothing. But I was on expenses, so I didn't let it worry me. From there, it was a short walk back to the hotel. A small crowd had gathered outside the Chinese Baptist church just off Dundas. I walked closer. While there were several Chinese faces, most of them were non-Asian. It seemed a strange time for worship—it was pushing 9:45 p.m. When I saw the coffee urn in the hands of one of the women, I knew that I'd blundered into an AA meeting. I continued on the go-home trail. Every step seemed to be taking me farther away from the bright lights and wicked deeds of the Ontario capital. Two hours before midnight and Silver City was letting me down.

I bought a paper and a *TV Guide* and spent some time in my room watching the NTC late-evening shows. Spread out with my paper on the bed, with the TV blaring, I felt as though the colour was draining out of my life and finding a new home through some electronic transfusion in the box. Everybody on the tube seemed to be having one hell of a fine time. Even Vic Vernon, the talk-show host, was in good form. He was interviewing a diplomat just back from Albania, while a strongman from a circus was having a cinder block broken on his chest through the agency of a blonde, leopard-skinned body-beautiful with a sledgehammer.

Vic took a moment, with his face close to the camera, to pay a solemn fifteen-second tribute to the late Bob Foley, a friend to all and a brother to everyone on the show. Then, without a wasted second, he grinned to the camera and announced that he would be right back. When he returned after what seemed to me an endless stream of commercials, he talked to a young actress who had just played a young man in a movie. On the face of it, it was unlikely casting. The conversation didn't touch on playing a particular character, it lingered on the cross-dressing aspect. I yawned and switched off the set. I'd given my pint for today, I thought, and picked up the paper.

It was sometime after that when I dimmed my light and discovered the problems of the bed and the bedding. The bedding made a good first impression: it was white and wrinkleless, smelling of Bounce, but on closer acquaintance, it proved to be sleep-resistant. I could make no lasting impression in the pillows, punch them as I might. At least the moving shadows on the ceiling were a distraction. If I got any sleep, they probably paved the way.

 Thursday

I was in the office before Sally Jackson had changed out of her walking shoes into her sitting-behind-a-desk shoes. She wasn't particularly happy to see me. She told me that Ms Moss never appeared before ten, as though this were a natural phenomenon comparable to the tidal bore on the Bay of Fundy.

"By the way, Mr Cooperman, you had a call a few minutes ago." She handed me a blue slip that was covered with numbers.

"What kind of call is this?" I said aloud, although I hadn't meant to.

"Overseas. Would you like me to get it for you?" I nodded vigorously and handed back the paper. In under a minute she said my name. I picked up and said "Hello" without much conviction.

"Benny? Is that you?"

"*Anna!* Where are you? How'd you find me?"

"Rapolano Terme. It's near Siena in Tuscany. I checked your answering service and then had a chat with Frank. He gave me your Toronto numbers."

"I thought you'd be in Paris by now. How's the weather?"

"Glorious. We're pushing the season a little, but at least we're ahead of the crowds."

"'We,' who's 'we'? You're not on a tour."

"Oh, I met Andrew Moser on the plane when I was bumped up to First. He's a mushroom grower from California. He's been sort of looking after me."

"Nice," I said through my teeth.

"I'd forgotten how charming some wealthy men can be."

"Nice. Are you seeing your fill of the galleries?"

"More than that. Andy loves food and we've been on a food orgy, on a high level, you understand. We've run down a few great spots. It's like Bloor Street in Toronto. This place is a famous spa, although I haven't taken more than a sample of the waters."

"Nice. When will you leave for Paris?"

"My first lecture's not until Monday, the twelfth, in the old place I told you about on the rue d'Ulm. Remember?"

"I miss you."

"I'll be home in a couple of weeks. You can tell me what you're up to in Toronto when I see you."

"Right. I'll be talking to you." Anna said goodbye, and I started wondering what that was all about. Was it an announcement of some kind? It would be a little after lunch-time in Italy. I wondered whether she'd eaten yet or whether her mushroom millionaire had left her waiting at the hotel. Maybe he was planning a late supper that evening in some out-of-the-way hilltop village. How do I know he's a million-aire? Is this *my* day-dream or yours? I thought about the morn-ing coffee I hadn't had yet. Sally was at the door. It took me a moment to recross the Atlantic. I squeezed the bridge of my nose to force my concentration.

"Do you know where Vanessa's staying right now, Sally? Since the murder, I mean."

"If Ms Moss wants you to know, I'm sure she'll tell you, Mr Cooperman. I have instructions not to tell anyone."

"Good point," I said, and began sifting through some pages in front of me on my desk, like I was busy at something. When I looked at them, actually focusing, I saw that they were the rundowns I'd asked for yesterday.

On top was a name and phone number: Frances Scerri. Ah, yes: Vanessa's sister. The one she's not on speaking terms with. I put it in my pocket. Under that I found a hierarchical chart that divided the page into several boxes. The first box on the left had *Chairman* written at the top. His name was Hampton Fisher, and he was NTC's controlling shareholder, owning forty-two per cent of the A shares. Hampton Fisher and I had never met, but I had known his wife, Peggy O'Toole, the movie star, about ten years ago when she was making *Ice Bridge* in Niagara Falls. I got to know her fairly well, now I come to think of it, but her standoff-ish, germ-fearing husband so rarely came out in public he was being accused of being Howard Hughes back from the dead. He had surrounded himself with flunkies in Niagara Falls, rented a whole floor at the Colonel John Butler Hotel, and watched people's comings and goings through a series of TV monitors. If he and Peggy had had any children, I never heard about it. Yet they stayed married, which was an improvement on Hughes. Fisher had not scrimped and saved to make his fortune, nor had he beat his way to the top pushing less dedicated entrepreneurs out of his way. He was born into a successful newspaper family.

It was his grandfather who'd done all the pushing and shoving. Hamp simply inherited it all when his father died. For that reason, many tried to write off Hamp Fisher. He was easy to put down: the drinking water he had flown in from California, the thermometer he carried at all times, his peculiar diets. All this gave reporters from opposition papers a field day whenever he threatened to take over another group of dailies. To tell the truth, Fisher had weeded and trimmed his garden of papers, pruning the unproductive ones and fertilizing the promising. His grandfather would have been proud of him. More recently, having put the papers in a holding company, he had been buying up television stations and setting up the newest of our TV networks. I guess it beat collecting stamps.

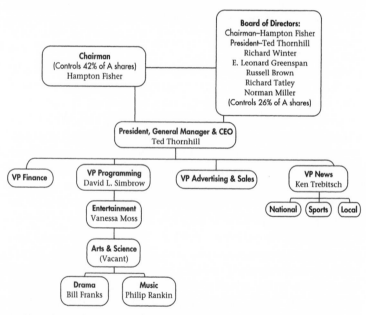

Two lines had been drawn from the *Chairman* box. The top one ran to a box marked *Board of Directors*. On it, I would find that the members, friendly outsiders, plus the chairman and the president, owned another twenty-six per cent of the A shares. The names of the friendly outsiders didn't light up my sky at once, but on a second reading I recognized the name Ted Thornhill. Hell, I'd even met him! He was the guy who made a guest appearance at the signing of the Dermot Keogh Hall contracts, the man who'd arrived with his own photographer. He was the president and general manager, the chief executive officer of the whole shebang. Not only did his name appear in a list of the Board of Directors, but it appeared just below it in a box all his own, joined by a line to the *Chairman* box. A vertical line ran down from the *President, General Manager & CEO* box to a horizontal line from which depended several boxes: *Finance, Programming, Advertising & Sales, News*. All of these were vice-presidents. Again, the names here meant nothing to me.

I tried to remember what I once knew about shares in limited corporations. The A shares were voting shares, the preferred shares held by a few insiders. The B shares were publicly traded. The insiders were allowed to own only five per cent of the B shares, according to what my paper said. That left twenty-seven per cent of the remaining B shares widely owned in small batches. I put this page away for future reference after checking to see that Vanessa's name turned up in a box of its own directly under David L. Simbrow, the vice-president of programming. She was designated *Head of Entertainment*. Her name had been inserted where that of Nathan Green had been removed.

I called out to Sally, "What happened to Nate Green, Sally? Where did he fit into the frame of things?" Sally looked at me for a good deal longer than I thought necessary to prepare an answer.

"Mr Green died three months ago, Mr Cooperman. Cancer of the oesophagus. Very sad." As soon as she'd said it, I remembered Vanessa telling me on our first official outing together. Meanwhile, Sally had gone back to her reading, once she'd passed on her news. Again I abruptly pulled her attention away from the copy of *Billboard* she was clipping.

"But Ms Moss has been here for a year, more or less. What department was Mr Green moved to?" I was plainly annoying Sally now, and she slapped down the paper on top of a stack of out-of-town newspapers.

"He had several titles: first he was vice-president of Arts and Entertainment for a time, switched to become a senior assistant to Mr Thornhill, then he was made vice-president of Arts and Sciences. That was his title at the time of his death."

"I see. Who's the vice-president of Arts and Sciences right now, Sally?"

"There isn't one. I don't expect there will be."

"So, it was created for Green and died with him?"

"That's one opinion, Mr Cooperman."

"Do you have another?"

"The charter of the National Television Corporation has always insisted that we have a mandate to keep the arts and sciences within our purview. Some think that we have been lax in this area. Having a vice-president in charge tended to defuse that criticism."

"So, the ailing Nate Green helped quell the charge of programming for the lowest common denominator."

"Mr Cooperman," she said, colouring just a little, "we program to a wide popular audience, not to the lowest common denominator."

"You believe that?" I asked, but was destined not to get an answer, for at this moment Vanessa Moss thundered into the room banging down a full briefcase on the broadloom. Once again, she was beautifully turned out, thanks to her friend at Holt's. This morning she wore a navy pinstripe with a white collar open at the throat and pointing down towards the sort of cleavage that should never be worn by applicants for junior positions at NTC. Boards are notoriously puritanical.

"Where the hell have you been?" There could be no mistake about who she meant.

"I could be dead and buried by now and you wouldn't know about it until you saw the noon news. Come on, Benny. Get with the program!" I told her that I'd spent the late afternoon with Sykes and his partner, examining the scene of the crime and checking over what measures they had taken to see that no harm comes to her. "And?" she demanded.

"And, yes, the cops have taken steps. They are tailing you day and night. I might have checked in with you, but you didn't leave me with an address or phone number. They also told me you were in Niagara Falls the day before yesterday, not Niagara-on-the-Lake. Funny how they get these things wrong, isn't it?" She lowered her guns, and tried to smooth things over.

"I can explain about that. It was a secret meeting with the Shaw Festival artistic director. He suggested we not be seen too close to his present employers."

"But you failed to tell me the truth, innocent as it appears to be."

"Coffee?"

I nodded. Sally got up to go fetch. "By the way, Sally, did you get the things I asked you to get for Mr Cooperman?"

"They were waiting for me on my desk when I got here an hour ago, Vanessa."

"Good," Vanessa said through her teeth, without looking up, and Sally stalked out on her morning mission, her trade journals left unattended on her desk. Vanessa began sorting through the newly arrived paper in her IN box. "The daily hell," she announced. So, after frowning for five minutes, I started telling her about my meetings with Sykes and Boyd. When I stopped talking, she said, "They think I did it. They *still* think I did it!"

"Not necessarily, Vanessa. Sure, they're watching you, but that's at least partly to see that what happened to Renata doesn't happen to you too. To tell you the truth, I don't think Sykes himself knows what he thinks happened. All he's doing is hedging his bets. That's the best he can do. He's also making sure that Bob Foley's suicide is properly gone into. Foley may have been pissed off at the Vic Vernon people, but even Vic Vernon doesn't drive everybody to suicide. What do you know about him?"

"Vic's an egomaniacal—"

"Not Vernon. You told me about him already. I mean Foley."

"Bob? I don't know. He was a good technician. One of the best, so I understand. I don't deal directly with the grips, riggers, lighting and sound people, Benny. The job just won't let me. I know that there are cameramen, and I recognize most of them, but that's out of my realm. Bob Foley I know by reputation. He was good at what he did. So good that Dermot Keogh got him to do all of his last Canadian recordings. Wouldn't work with anybody else."

"Yesterday in the car you mentioned a foundation. Raymond Devlin spoke of it too."

"Oh, yes. Bob was one of the trustees of Dermot's foundation. Under Dermot's will, Raymond set up the Plevna Foundation. Don't ask me what Plevna means. The foundation basically establishes bursaries for brilliant but poor music scholars, and thinks up new ways to spend Dermot's posthumous earnings, which are considerable."

"How did that happen? Dermot was a well-known, world-famous celebrity; Foley a fine, but obscure, technician. Wasn't there some social and economic distance between them?"

"Dermot was many things, Benny, some of them maddening, but he was not a snob. He and Foley, in the course of their recording work for the last two years of his life, grew close to one another. Dermot attended Foley's father's funeral. Foley had keys to Dermot's downtown studio. He drives Dermot's old Jaguar. I heard—this is hearsay, because I didn't get it first-hand—that Foley once complained that working with Dermot included walking his dog, staying up all night and moving furniture from Toronto to Dermot's summer place. Dermot loved the diamond in the rough, Benny. He introduced me to amateurish ivory carvers with no talent, a virtuoso bubblegum artist and a charming panhandler who made his home at the corner of Bloor and Walmer Road. Outside, on the street."

"How old was Foley?"

"Oh, I don't know. Ask the cops," she said, unbuttoning her jacket. Here I was treated to what every male in my class at Grantham Collegiate Institute and Vocational School would have killed to see: a little more of Stella Seco than Stella noticed was on display. When she saw my expression, she made an adjustment, clucking her tongue. "Benny, won't you *ever* grow up?"

"If taking you for granted, Vanessa, is mature behaviour, then I hope to stay in short pants forever."

"I suppose that's very sweet, but from over here it's boring."

There was something calculated about Vanessa's sudden unbuttoning of her jacket. She knew the effect it would have on me. Was she trying to change the subject?

"What does Vanessa Moss have planned for today?" She looked at an electronic appointment book and snapped it shut after a few seconds' study.

"Yesterday, you met the junior executives trying to boot me from my Entertainment throne. This morning, you'll meet the senior executives equally dedicated to the same noble purpose."

"How is it you manage to make all these people mad at you?"

"I don't take shit, Benny. Not from incompetents below me or above me without making damned sure everybody knows about it. I chose to come into broadcasting a long time ago. In my way, I care about it. I'm not going to carry the can for those bastards who can't see higher than the bottom line. That's my answer. You'll have to get Sally drunk some night and pump her for her version. Sally's separated, by the way. Do you think you can melt such frosty, unmalleable clay? I'd like to see it, but not on my time. You hear?" I loved the way Vanessa could make a subversive suggestion and, a moment later, accuse you of thinking it up on your own.

The meeting of top executives took place in the boardroom at the end of the corridor on the twenty-first floor. It was a big room that tried to look impressive. Until you recognized the sober-faced portraits on the wall as set decorations from everything from *Martha O'Malley's Children* and *The Bartletts of Oak Street* to *The Blue Team* and *Northern Cross*, you might have been taken in. The books on the beautiful dark wood shelves were more studio cast-offs. Fake books. Just the spines showed. My respect for this bunch was quickly going downhill. The centre of the table, which was an amazing bit of woodcraft, was reserved for the CEO of NTC. The table must have been built here from a kit of some kind. It certainly didn't come through any of the doors I'd seen. Ted Thornhill, too, would have had difficulty getting through some doors. But here he could be sure that there were no living or inanimate obstacles between him and his high-backed black leather chair. Apart from the abundance of Ted Thornhill and his pink, wagging chins, I could see that he moved with a certain balletic grace. When he stood, it was with a boxer's firm stance; when he sat, it was an act of will, not the passive subsidence of one-eighth of a ton of flesh and bone.

He was soon surrounded by his fellow board members and the vice-presidents. As head of Entertainment, Vanessa almost counted as a vice-president, but not quite. Except for me and a stenographer in Yves Saint-Laurent glasses, Vanessa was the lowest life form present. All the others carried voting stock totalling just over a quarter of the voting shares. But this didn't look like that kind of board meeting. None of the four women present had had their hair done for the occasion. Only Thornhill sported a boutonnière and it looked like a leftover from an earlier event. Once more, Vanessa tried to introduce me to her colleagues and no one looked up. Papers were exchanged across the table. The steno distributed photocopied pages all round. Even I got a set. I wondered whether all boards were like this.

When it came to Vanessa's turn at bat, she described her fall line-up of programs: which of the old ones were coming back and on what terms, what new series were coming and from which production house. "We've finally rung the knell on *The Newton Street Mob*. After three years of decline, I've washed my hands of it."

"You told Christopher Hodges that he was *fired?* I don't believe it!" This from the dark man with a moustache sitting next to Thornhill. He liked to quarrel with everybody.

"That's your scenario, Ken, not mine. I made him a low offer and he declined to accept it. There was no blood on the floor. As a newsman, you should get your facts straight."

And so it went, on and on. Vanessa kept her mouth shut unless she was addressed by name. One fellow kept chirping up that in cases like this—I forget what "this" was—justice must not simply be done, but it must be *seen* to be done. I figured him for the idiot son of a wealthy family. Thornhill's skill in handling a meeting was on a par with Vanessa's, only, if anything, Vanessa allowed a little more expression. Nobody tested Thornhill's loyalty to the firm. Nobody was shocked when he referred to a program carried on a rival network. I remembered that at Vanessa's meeting, one of her underlings saw such a reference as a heresy. After hearing his comments on the reports of several of his vice-presidents, I could see Vanessa's point about Thornhill being a bean-counter and not from show business or broadcasting. His closest approach to greasepaint came from sitting in an aisle seat two rows away from the orchestra pit. When I think about it now, he seemed like a good interim head, but not an enterprising, go-ahead sort of leader. Hamp Fisher could do better than this conservative heavyweight.

I asked Vanessa in a whisper who the fellow called Ken was. He seemed to be the only one in the room who wasn't a yes-man.

"That's Ken Trebitsch, VP of News. That's the most powerful job. He pushes the rest of us around. Especially Entertainment. He's always trying to steal time from us for news specials. Then we never get the time back again. He's practically the only real broadcaster in the room. No, that's unfair, I'm forgetting Philip Rankin over there." She indicated a sloping chin I'd hardly noticed across the table. Philip Rankin wore a dark bird's nest of a wig, cut to look fashionably silky and shaggy, a conservative grey suit and an unlined, slightly bewildered face.

"What's his department?"

"Music. He's head of all music heard on the network."

"That can't be a lot," I offered.

"More than you think. He's head of the large recording division of NTC: NTC Music, NTC-CDs. It's a vital and growing department, Benny, trying to struggle on with a structure that is hopelessly outdated. There will have to be big changes here, but whether Philip is the man to inaugurate them is a matter for debate."

"You said he's an old-timer?"

"He came here from CBC Radio, where they do a lot of music programming and recording. He built up that whole department. Now he—well, you saw that Christmas show yesterday? He's ultimately in charge of all of that."

"Why didn't his name come up then?" I asked.

"Because we were in the studio; Philip never goes near the studio if he can help it. Do you collect CDs, Benny? Philip started NTC in the recording business in a small way about four years ago. Now, we're right up there with the top labels." A look from Thornhill ended our conversation.

I wasn't getting much out of this meeting. I'm not even reporting on it very well: so much of it flew over my head. Thornhill managed to keep a regal distance from his vice-presidents. The vice-president of Programming, Vanessa's immediate boss, seemed like a cipher. He had nothing to say and let Vanessa do his talking for him.

When the meeting broke up, I followed Vanessa and the others into an adjoining room, where plates of yellow and orange cheese were laid out like a corpse on a white tablecloth. Two or three bottles of domestic and Californian wine stood at attention, daring anyone under the rank of vice-president to pour a glass in front of his betters. A few other senior executives, who were not at the meeting, were allowed in to take some light refreshment. Soon the room was crowded with beaming faces and the noise level was raised high enough to endanger good crystal. Luckily, there was none around, just heavy-duty glass that probably had come with the cheese and the toothpicks. Philip Rankin came over to say hello to Vanessa, who introduced me as her assistant. He grinned as though he and Vanessa were sharing a joke about the length of my stay on the payroll. Ken Trebitsch joined us. I noticed grey in his black hair, and the fine moustache sheltered a very youthful smile, spoiled only by dark, hooded eyes.

"I was thinking of you yesterday, Ken," Vanessa said. We all tried to look intrigued. "I saw on the news that our one-time CBC colleague, Bert Russell, has set up a digital communications empire in Pasadena."

"I heard about that. He was always a whirlwind. Of course, Bert was treated miserably by the CBC when they got rid of him. Remember, Philip?"

"Yes, axed from above. He didn't suspect a thing until his keys wouldn't open his door. And after all he'd done for the Corp. He must have reduced staffing there by thirty-five per cent during the years of budget cuts."

"He was the best salesman for public broadcasting they ever had," Ken observed.

"NTC invited him to take on just about any department he wanted five, six years ago, but he wouldn't have it."

"That's how loyalty gets paid off." They went around again, Ken and Philip Rankin exchanging comments on the ill-done-by Bert Russell. When it looked like he was about to run out of steam, Ken turned to Vanessa in a teacher-like way. "Did you ever know Bert Russell, Vanessa?"

"I introduced his name into this conversation not five minutes ago, Ken. Are you losing your memory?" There was an attempt at laughter, then Trebitsch wandered into another conversation group. Vanessa held on to me and engaged Philip Rankin in further chit-chat. "Philip, what's Bob Foley's death going to mean to your Plevna Foundation?"

"Why, nothing, dear girl. At least I don't think so. I haven't thought about it much. There were three trustees, now there are two. That's all."

"Philip's on that Dermot Keogh foundation I was telling you about, Benny."

"Oh, yes. The cellist. From what I hear, he was a remarkable man."

"Understatement, Mr Cooperman." He grinned at me with the misty eyes of a true believer. "Everything about Dermot is an understatement. Apart from the two books about him that have already appeared, I know of three distinguished writers who are working separately on biographies. There are more of his CDs out now, since his death, than there were last year or the year before. Cut-out limbo doesn't exist for Dermot Keogh. People can't get enough of him. Not since the death of the great Glenn Gould has there been such a musical phenomenon."

"And you knew him well?"

"What? Goodness, did I know him? I *brought* him here to NTC. Oh, yes! We recorded a series of half a dozen shows and were committed to do another six. I met him at the CBC originally. In the Old Building. He was just twenty, but already reorganizing the music department there from the inside. A year later he made his break-out recording of the Bach *Suites for Unaccompanied Cello*. That sold a million copies worldwide in the first six weeks on the shelves. It went platinum within the next month. Oh, I could go on and on about Dermot, who was, along with his genius, a wonderful human being. I keep having to remind myself that I was privileged to be counted as one of his friends."

"You must be excited about the building of Dermot Keogh Hall."

"Indeed, I am. It will be a memorial worthy of its subject, Mr Cooperman. And glory enough in it for all concerned." It seemed to me I'd heard that phrase before.

"Were you around at the time of his death?"

"Me? Oh, not me. I detest swimming in cold water, and when I do swim, I stay on top. I could never understand these snorkellers and scuba-diving types. Seems unnatural somehow. Know what I mean?"

"I think I do. I stay away from most vigorous exercise. I want my body well rested when the crisis comes and I need all my physical resources at short notice."

"Good man! That's the spirit." Philip Rankin grinned at me, showing a mouthful of teeth in need of urgent attention. It was the face of an adenoidal carp. The smile seemed warm enough, but I wasn't quite buying his "Good man!" and his "wonderful human being." I was going to have to pick up a little more about Keogh as I went on with my body-guarding responsibilities. It would help me bear the tedium, like a side bet made to keep an edge on my interest.

Meanwhile, the body I was supposed to be guarding was talking to Ted Thornhill himself, while the CEO of NTC chewed on a handful of crackers and cheddar.

"Well, are you still having fun with it, Vanessa?" he was saying through a fine mist of expelled cracker crumbs. Vanessa was holding a glass of white wine, which she tasted and abandoned on the edge of a table as she spoke.

"I love the pressure, Ted. I get off on the problems, and crow over the rewards. That doesn't mean I'm not looking forward to getting away as soon as I can put a normal long weekend together."

"Yes, you should, you know. What's happened to you wasn't in your contract. This murder thing is killing us in the papers. Naturally, they delight in all of our difficulties. Particularly that Turnbull woman at the *Star*, and of course our old friend Carver at the *Globe*. Are the police coming up with results, Vanessa? The sooner the murderer's put away, the sooner we can read the papers again without wincing, eh?"

I heard my name being whispered a few inches away from my ear. It was Sally, the usually glum receptionist. Only now she was almost smiling. "You're wanted, Mr Cooperman," she said.

"I am? Who wants me?" I tried not to look startled. Nobody knew I was here.

"The police," she said, looking me straight in the eye for the first time.

EIGHT

The police, announced so dramatically by Sally Jackson, turned
out to be Jack Sykes and Jim Boyd, as I should have guessed.
They were waiting for me in that part of Vanessa's office that
was sacred to me. Since I had seen them so recently, I wondered what brought them up to the twentieth floor this close
to lunchtime. Could they be buying, I wondered?

"We gotta car downstairs," Sykes said simply. From his tone,
I decided that they hadn't come all the way up to tell me this
without my going down with them to see it for myself. So we
did that. When I started questioning them in the elevator,
they shushed me, like Vanessa had warned them about talking
in the elevator. On the way out the cops had to hand in their
paste-on VISITOR passes to the SWAT team at the security desk.
"This way," Boyd prompted, as though I didn't know my way
through a revolving door. Outside, with its lights flashing but
without the noise, stood a cruiser with someone sitting in the
back seat. I glanced through the window, while I tried to open
the back door.

"Hello, Benny. How have you been keeping yourself?"
Damned if it wasn't Detective Sergeant Chuck R. Pepper, the
cop who worked on that rare-book murder investigation I did
six or seven years ago. It's a story I haven't told many people
about yet, but I might one day. Chuck looked about the same,
with a military look to his short-cropped iron-grey hair. There
were red mousetracks on his cheeks that spoke of the good
things of life. Underneath, he was grinning in a controlled

way. Chuck never went overboard while on duty. Behind me, Sykes and Boyd were taking it all in.

"Chuck! How are you? Damn it, it's good to see you!" We shook hands after I managed to get the door to open. Out of habit, Boyd clapped me on the head as I ducked under the door frame.

"Much better now I've seen you. I might make it to my pension after all." The other two piled into the front seat, and with a squeak of rubber Sykes moved the car away from the ABSOLUTELY NO PARKING signs and into traffic on University Avenue. Sykes turned around, smiling.

"I should have brought my camera; I wanted to catch this reunion for posterity, but I forgot. Still, I thought that you might want to know that Chuck's now in charge of the questionable death at 518 Sackville Street."

"Bob Foley?" I asked, and counted three nods. "Is it still questionable, or has it been downgraded to a tropical storm?"

"It's only the circumstances that are suspicious. The suicide part looks real enough," said Chuck. "But I reckon it won't hurt to have another look around. Would you like to come along? We were thinking of going for dim sum afterwards. You haven't eaten, I hope?"

"No, I haven't eaten. They're serving plastic cheese up on the twenty-first floor. My client never eats and I could starve to death on this job. What's dim sum? And thanks, I'd like to tag along." Boyd explained about the Chinese tea lunch and Chuck warned me that I should say little and keep my hands in my pockets on the far side of the yellow plastic tape. Good old Chuck Pepper: he hadn't changed a bit.

The late Bob Foley's house at 518 Sackville Street looked like its neighbouring houses, 520 and 516. It wasn't much different from lots of rowhouses and semi-detached houses in that part of town: a rather narrow, three-storey brick structure with a bay window and a gable roof. From what Sykes said, I gather that the neighbourhood had sunk to the status of a genteel slum between the wars, but was now up again, showing off big brass house numbers on sand-blasted brick. Sykes parked on the "no parking" side of the street. He seemed to have a built-in contempt for traffic signs.

Bob Foley had had a comfortable life, judging from the downstairs rooms. One wall in the living-room had been stripped down to the brick, which set off a couple of good-looking watercolours of barns, farmhouses and other farm buildings. There was a woman's touch in the furniture and curtains, but the general messiness of all the flat surfaces suggested that she was no longer in residence. A half-eaten box of pretzels stood near the TV set. Two old sweaters were draped around the backs of chairs. A smelly sleeping bag covered half of the couch, doubling as a blanket. The basement was a fully outfitted recording studio. Fancy recording and editing equipment, giant speakers, controlboards with dozens of sliding keys all looked ready to go to work. Racks of used and unused magnetic tapes stood handy, as did a dusty computer under a plastic cover. Much of this stuff was new to me.

On the second floor Chuck led the way to the bedroom. The bed had been stripped. Six empty bottles of Molson's Export beer were sitting in a cardboard carton. An equal number of empties were lined up on a bedside table. A bottle that had once held Cutty Sark stood behind them. Pepper turned to me.

"There was an empty vial of sleeping pills on the table with the bottles, Benny. That's gone to the lab. Dr Melton, who took a look, gave me to understand they were the sort that are not recommended to be taken with booze. I'm not talking about him not driving or moving heavy equipment, I'm saying that mixing alcohol and that stuff was dangerous for him even if he was only lying there watching *Seinfeld* reruns. He even had a last cigarette. There was a long ash and a stain in the bottom of an ashtray, also taken from the bedside table."

"May I speak?" I asked.

"Yes," Chuck said the word so that it carried its own warning.

"I saw a package of Nicorettes downstairs. Had he given up smoking?"

"He had. It was too much hassle at work, I was told, so he gave it up with a prolonged struggle two years ago, about the time Jean left him."

"That *Mrs* Foley?"

Chuck nodded.

"So, he revived the habit as a last defiant gesture? Is that how you see it?"

"Unless the three of you can see some element that isn't consistent with suicide."

"Don't use that word. 'Consistent' makes me want to have a smoke myself. Where's the pack the cigarette came from?"

"It had fallen under the bed. A throwaway lighter was there too. They're both downtown."

"Supposing Foley had had a visitor. The visitor could have got Foley drinking and then slipped the pills into his drink when he was nearly drunk."

"Yes, I thought that as well," Chuck said. "But we found only one dirty glass on the bedside table. It had Foley's prints on it."

"Did you check out the glasses on the drainboard in the kitchen? There may be prints on them. Or inside the yellow rubber gloves by the sink."

Chuck turned his mouth down, to indicate the remote possibility that I was right. He looked like Robert de Niro playing an older man. "I'll try it. I'll try anything that looks the least bit phoney."

Then I thought of something. "Your gang has kept this place secure since it was labelled a suspicious death, right?"

"Yes. Why?"

"Well, look at the floor over by the bed, and over by that chair. It seems to me there's a lot of cigarette ash around. How many smokes were gone from the pack you sent to Forensics?"

"Just the one."

"And you say the ash from that was nearly intact?"

"Right."

"Well, either you have a dead cigarette package in the garbage, or somebody took the rest of the deck away with him when he left Foley unconscious in his bed. The prints on the glasses or rubber gloves, if they exist, will help tell us who did the dirty deed."

"There's half a grapefruit peel, coffee grounds and eggshells in the garbage. No paper, no cigarette package."

"I think we just got lucky," Boyd said.

"Not until Forensics tells us we have. But, we have got some hope, and that might be worth something."

"If our suspicions here are supported by Forensics," I said, trying not to sound fatuous, "might I suggest that you let Foley's death remain on a low level of suspicion. As far as the media are concerned, I mean. I don't think it will help with the Renata Sartori case if we insist that there is a thread linking the two cases."

"It's less than a thread at this point," Sergeant Pepper said, expressing what the four of us were probably thinking. "But you're right. It would be bad policy to see a link between the cases before we know there is one."

"Right now, the only link is the fact that both Foley and Sartori worked at NTC. How many people are on the payroll over there? You see what I mean?"

"Let's go to the Kowloon," said Sykes. "I need a *shiu mai* fix." At first, nobody moved, and then we all did. Chuck carefully restored the yellow plastic tape and turned out the light as we went out. While this was going on, I took a look out the back window. There was a small yard with a shed against the back fence, near the gate leading to a lane running behind the houses.

"Anything in the shed?" I asked Pepper.

"There's a fine glory hole if you like antique wheels."

"That's too small for sportscars."

"There are three old bikes in there. Motorcycles. An Indian Roadmaster, a Crocker—real old one—and a Brough. Must be worth from seventy-five to one hundred thousand, I reckon. Easy."

"Where's his car?"

"Kept it on the street. Parking permit. It's the one with the parking ticket under the wiper. He should have changed sides of the street this morning. It's the first of June."

"How's a dead man to do that?" Boyd asked.

"Send it to his widow," Sykes said, trying to sound cynical and succeeding. "They were still legally married."

"Is his car a Jaguar?"

"Yeah. How did you know?"

"I heard that it once belonged to Dermot Keogh, the cellist."

"It's still registered in Keogh's name. Ontario licence number BWV 988. I reckon it still belongs to the estate," Chuck said.

"Can I see the shed for a minute? I won't be long."

"I'm starved," said Boyd. "Let's move."

"I'll buy," I suggested. That did it. Pepper handed me a ring of keys, and I let myself out the door at the rear of the kitchen.

The shed was a well-built structure with a stout door to it. The gate leading to the lane was equally substantial and showed signs of being improved within the last few months: fresh two-by-fours had been added along with a new and unrusted lock. I found the right key, and the shed disclosed to me the bikes that I'd been told to expect. I'm no expert on motorcycles, new or old, but the three here could awake the hidden collector in most riders. They were protected by plastic and revealed, once I pulled it back, a good dollar's worth of motorcycles, oiled and polished to perfection. The shed also contained paint cans, a lawn mower, rakes, a workbench, metal and wood-working tools. The workbench had a grinding wheel mounted at one end. A cascade of metal filings had collected on the floor below it. Did Foley sharpen skates in his spare time? Next to the wheel rested a rubber ferrule, like the kind you see on the ends of crutches or canes. This one was smaller, as though it had been made to fit over the end of a chopstick. For the motorcycles, I wondered, or for what?

A two-drawer metal filing cabinet was parked on the workbench. It didn't belong there, so I looked around for its previous home and found it at the back of the shed, where four pieces of wood were fixed in the gravel floor, to raise the cabinet off the ground. Nobody likes rusty filing cabinets. One of the drawers was slightly ajar, the one below it was shut. Foley, or someone, had fixed hasps to the side of this cabinet so that it could be secured with a padlock of some kind. There was no such restraint visible so I opened it first.

Inside I found a collection of fine electronic solderers, long-nosed pliers and the makings for the insides of computers: transistors, commercial cards with their printed spider-tracks and other hardware that has names to those who know about the electronic bric-à-brac that make this modern age possible. Under this mess were papers, business cards from car dealers, real-estate agents, marina operators and contractors. I thought that there might be an important clue here some-where, but I was too hungry to write down all these names and addresses. I remembered that I had good intentions, because I had taken a notebook and pencil from my pocket, but I was distracted when I dropped the pencil. In retrieving it, I noticed pencil marks on one of the uprights supporting the corner of the shed. It was near where the filing cabinet had been, so there was lots of room to get close to the writing. It read, "R x 2 to 25, L x 1 to 11, R to 39."

I made a copy in my notebook and pocketed it. I could hear the cruiser at the curb gunning its motor with impa-tience. I closed up the shed, locked the kitchen door and made sure I heard the front door click behind me as I pulled it shut. Sykes kept revving the motor.

The Kowloon restaurant is nestled in a block of stores and restaurants on the south side of Baldwin Street, near where it ends at McCaul. A woman with a shiny broad face grinned a greeting to the three cops and showed us to a table in the "no smoking" zone, under some flashing Christmas lights that had been left blazing to see in the spring and summer months. A waiter, who looked like a Chinese Charles Bronson, gave Sykes a printed order form, which he began to fill in with the pro-vided pencil without looking back at us or asking questions. The order form was separated by the waiter into its compo-nent sheets, one of which was left with us, while the other made its way to the kitchen. We could hear aggressive cooking sounds: bangs and crashes, interrupted by the regular tinkling of a bell. If I didn't know better, I'd guess a Chinese mass was being celebrated back there; the accompanying incense was delectable, sensual, not inspirational.

"Where are we on this thing?" Boyd wanted to know as he began doodling on a piece of lined paper. "We've got two cases that may be linked. And again, they may not be linked. We've got Renata Sartori, murdered because she was Renata Sartori. Or, again, she might have been taken for Vanessa Moss. We've got a suspicious death, which might be murder, and again it might be what it has always looked like, suicide. Have I left anything out?"

"You don't have a murder weapon in the Sartori case, but you have shells found in Moss's office at NTC." I added this to help rid the air of the notion that I might be biased in favour of my client. Perish the thought.

"What we don't have is the big picture. What ties Sartori to Foley?" Nobody answered. Boyd watched his ballpoint as it doodled a sketch of a hangman's noose, Sykes stared at the aquarium of lobster and crab near the front window, Chuck watched the changing patterns in the string of coloured lights. I stole a secret glance at my watch. Even an untrained assassin could have claimed Vanessa six or seven times since I saw her last.

That got me thinking of my client's tawny hide and I asked Jack if he could have a talk with NTC Security about stationing an extra man outside Vanessa's office.

"With their system," Jim said, "it can't help."

"It can't hurt," I said.

When it came, the food was impressive. Served in wooden and metal steamers or on saucers, the dim sum was an assortment of nearly bite-size items wrapped in noodle, a lotus leaf (I was told) or a steaming bun. I watched the others to see what to do. Sykes and Boyd were moving items from the steamers to the bowls in front of them with chopsticks. Chuck was using a ceramic spoon. I stabbed a noodle-wrapped object, which looked like a small scallop shell, with one of my set of chopsticks and dropped it in my tea. I'd been aiming for my bowl, but it was not to be. I abandoned it there, hoping that nobody saw. Then I tried a pancake-wrapped, half-moon-like object with a spoon, getting it to the bowl just as a waiter arrived with a fork to help me out. My friends exchanged nods and I tried to ignore them. I mused upon the idea that in thousands of years the Chinese civilization hadn't stumbled upon the chopped-egg sandwich. I decided to be charitable, and tried something else. It looked hot on the end of my fork, but I had manoeu-vring time in case I found it not up my street. Admittedly, it was a far cry from my usual lunch. I grinned and bore it.

Lunch continued, I ate, mostly enjoying the food, and, between mouthfuls, we continued to push the case around the table. But, except for the food, which disappeared rapidly, nothing new developed on the problems at NTC.

Later, about an hour later, I ran the gauntlet through NTC Security, pasted on my pass, and made it, via the no-talking bur-gundy elevator, to my corner of Vanessa's office. Sally Jackson was finishing the last crumbs of a paperbag lunch on her desk. She looked up at me, and gave me a smile that showed she was really trying to be the sunbeam that Jesus would have her be.

"They didn't lock you up?"

"No, they took me to lunch instead." (In spite of my offer to use my plastic, Sykes had paid the shot at the Kowloon. I could catch it next time, I was told.)

"I should be that lucky," she said, making a moue, if people still make moues.

"Next time, I'll invite you along." I told her where we went and began to describe the food.

"Dim sum may be unknown in Grantham, Mr Cooperman, but we in Toronto have had it for nearly forty years."

"How lucky for you." I paused a second and looked at her. Sally looked as tense as a rock band on their first gig. "Look, Sally," I said, "for some reason you and I got off on the wrong foot. If it was my fault, I'm sorry. Maybe we can start over. What do you think? Can you take time off to have a cup of coffee with me?"

"Mr Cooperman, somebody's got to look after this depart-ment. You may not know it, but next to News, Entertainment is the most important department at NTC. Somebody's got to be here while her ladyship is off buying up the pills in the neighbouring drugstores. Vanessa's only going to be here for another season, but this is *my* department. It has been for six years. And I hope it will be for another six. I ran it with Nate Green. Now I run it in spite of Vanessa Moss."

"Hey! Don't take it out on me! I'm on your side. Come on! Let's let the place run itself for five seconds. Show me where the coffee lives and I'll bring us back two cups. What do you say?"

"The kitchen's three doors down the corridor to the left. You should . . . Oh, to hell with it. I'll show you." Sally got up and I followed her. She opened a door into a tidy, tiny kitchen, where you could make a Christmas dinner for ten if you watched your elbows. Instead of showing me, Sally banged the cupboard doors herself and soon the coffee was dripping through the filter. As she returned to her place running the department, she gave me a grin that was intended as a peace offering. I accepted it and swore I'd bring the coffee and fixings as soon as the Braun stopped gurgling. True to my word, I did that.

I didn't expect to find out much from Sally. Our truce was too new to be tested so soon. But I did manage to discover that she was no longer living in Richmond Hill, that she was staying with a girlfriend in the City Park apartments near Maple Leaf Gardens, and that she was free to have a drink after work. She knew a place where the NTC people never went after five. As she said this, she smiled and clicked her coffee mug against mine. What more assurance does a guy need to start living on hope?

CHAPTER NINE

When Vanessa barged in twenty minutes later, she found me at my desk, reading up on the latest pocket biographies of her NTC colleagues supplied by Sally. She stood mutely over me, so that I could, if I was up on such things, identify her perfume, or imagine her wrath, which could be something biblical when she needed it. "Where were you for the last three hours?"

"Doing my duty with the officers investigating Renata's death."

"That's right! And the fact that I'm still standing here, instead of lying dead in the morgue, doesn't bother you at all, I suppose?"

"Well, if you want to give me credit for it, sure, go ahead, but, Vanessa, even murderers take time out. Maybe our guy has a day job just like you and me." I could see her eyes darkening and a squall coming, but suddenly it subsided. A lot of her bite was straight histrionics, worked out in advance with the weight of the audience figured into the total effect. It was all calculated to within a centimetre of where she wanted it to be.

"Would you like to tell me where you went after the reception, Vanessa? Through the Khyber Pass and back?"

"Now, Benny, don't *you* start. I had a bad enough time with Ted. He wants to split up Entertainment into three independent sections with me at the top."

"Well?"

"Well, that's like inviting me to leave. He wants me out of

here, Benny. How many times do I have to tell you? He does; they *all* do."

"I don't see . . ."

"Look, once it's divided among three hungry underlings, what is there for me to do? All I can do is sit on policy and keep my hands off the all-over good of the department. I *won't* let him do this to me."

"But, Vanessa, aren't the sections we saw at yesterday's meeting independent?"

"God no! I keep them all on short leads. They all do exactly what I say or they're out of here. He wants to tie and gag me. Under Ted's arrangement, I wouldn't be able to veto anything. I couldn't make a suggestion and have it taken seriously. I'd never see a pilot or meet a producer. I'd be making sure that their pension-plan contributions were being deducted properly. Damn it, Benny, I'd rather be shot at than reduced to a cipher. I'd much rather clean out the fridge."

"Okay, okay. Simmer down. Catch your breath. Let's take things one at a time. What do you have to do for the rest of this afternoon?"

"Let me think. Oh, yes, I've got to go over to Studio Three where they're shooting a pilot I'm interested in. Then I should send another thunderbolt to Eric Carter. You remember, the Christmas show you saw in production yesterday? I just saw what that butterball turkey he's cooking is going to cost. I'll have to stop there again on my way home."

"Vanessa, remember that fellow who was here that first day? Hy Newman?"

"Yesterday. What about him?"

"Why don't you get him to do a lot of your running around for you? He's an experienced producer. You could make him your personal emissary or something. Eric Carter wouldn't be able to fool him about his wasteful ways."

"Don't be an idiot, Benny! Newman went out with the A-line, the cha-cha-cha and canasta."

"Yes, but he's been in this business since geese first went barefoot."

"You let me look after Entertainment, you look after *me!* You hear?"

"Yup. You want me tagging along with you?"

"That's what I'm paying you for." While she was talking, she was winnowing the phone messages and faxes with a deft hand. "Oh, by the way, thanks for the 222s."

"The what?" Here she lifted up a fresh package I'd never seen before.

"The Frosst 222s. You know how I depend on those things."

"Vanessa, I bought you some *aspirin* yesterday. I didn't get you any 222s."

"Well, I wonder . . . ? They were on my desk. Funny. Oh, never mind. The main thing is that I've got them."

I jumped up and grabbed at her arm. A blue telephone message slip floated to the carpet. "Vanessa, let me see them!"

"What? The 222s? Whatever for?"

"You don't know where they came from. That's reason enough. Get them and put them in—in—" Here I reached for a big manila envelope. "—in here."

"Benny! what sort of melodrama are you acting out?"

"Trust me, Vanessa. I just want to be on the safe side."

Instead of accompanying my client on her late-afternoon rounds, I took a taxi to 52 Division with my manila envelope of questionable medicine. The driver didn't seem to understand the need for speed, and I lacked the courage to tell him to hurry.

Boyd was sitting in Sykes's chair wearing a bright yellow straw hat. He was reading a computer monitor. He looked up and gave me a friendly grin, then returned to the screen for another two minutes. I moved my weight from shoe to shoe. At last he squeaked his chair away from the screen. I explained what I had found and he said that he'd see that somebody had a look at the vial. "Who touched it besides Ms Moss?"

"Nobody that I know of," I said. "Not me, anyway."

"Well, that's a good start." He loaded the envelope and its contents into a plastic freezer bag, typed information on a stick-on label and attached it. He did this carefully and without comment. Then he made a note on his calendar.

"Jack taking the rest of the day off?" I asked, to fill in the silence.

"Naw, he got a call from College Street, the Chief's office. Probably has to explain his expenses. It happens. What can I say?"

"Well, I hope they don't deduct it from his take-home pay. You want to talk about this now?" I asked. Boyd looked at the freezer bag.

"Naw, it'll keep. No sense talking until we find out whether there's anything to talk about. It may end up being the usual aspirin-caffeine-codeine concoction. If it is, we can talk about old movies or how the Jays are shaping up."

I could see Boyd was right. Cops in Toronto are bound to remain calm in every situation. Grantham cops tend to be less worn down by the rigours of the work. The result is that they get excited on one occasion and are oyster-calm on the next. It's harder to figure. So, I made my retreat past the desk sergeant and the glass-brick walls to the outside world, where the warm spring day continued to give delight to all who stopped to notice it. Not many.

As I decided what to do next, one of those new Volkswagens pulled away from the curb. Its green matched the young leaves on the trees in a playground across the street, where swings, slides, climbers and sandpiles waited for the ringing of a bell. The Volkswagen was still in sight as I rounded the corner on University Avenue and headed south.

When I got within sight of the big NTC owl, I began to hunch down mentally, ready for the renewed onslaught of Security. I was wondering whether Vanessa might let me do my business from the New Beijing Inn and thus avoid running the gauntlet here every time I wanted in or out. I had just nerved myself to the ordeal, when two men in wool jackets moved in on me. "Mr Cooperman?" It was the tall, curly-headed one who spoke. "Mr *Benny* Cooperman?"

"That's right." I tried to feel in my pockets for anything that might, in a pinch, be used as a weapon.

"My name's Alder. Jesse Alder. I'm one of the techs here at NTC. So's Ross."

"Yeah, Ross Totton, Mr Cooperman. Glad to meet you." They both fumbled to take my hand, which I delivered as soon as I could drop my car keys back in my pocket.

"We heard that you were here, sort of working for Ms Moss and all. And we just wanted to buy you a beer and tell you what's going down around here."

"There's a pub around the corner, if you've got a few minutes. Sort of a technicians' hangout."

"Where did you say you heard about me?"

"There's not much going on at the network that we don't hear about. We thought you might need an introduction to the characters you're going to bump into."

"Fill you in, bring you up to speed, that sort of thing," Totton added.

"Wouldn't that tend to prejudice me?"

The men looked at one another, then grinned back at me, nodding vigorously. Unopposed, they led the way to the Rex, a busy pub on the ground floor of an old hotel building not far from where we were standing. It was a lot like the old Harding House back in Grantham, with waiters balancing trayfuls of draft beer and giving change in a sustained balletic feat to the music of conversation and heavy metal. Alder and Totton led the way to a table in back, far from all but the most unrelenting beat of the music. There were four others already seated there, to whom I was introduced. I didn't catch more than their first names. Like Jesse and Ross, they were all technicians at NTC. Jimmy, who looked the most senior, called the waiter, who set down a tray of brimming glasses in my honour. Over the rim of my first glass, I asked Jesse a question: "Why are you doing this?"

"You seem like a nice guy."

"Come on. Or I'm out of here."

"We all liked Renata. She was a sweetheart to work with and didn't pass the guff she got from the twentieth floor on to us. She was a pro and all the techs knew that."

For the next hour and a bit, the boys took turns in telling me everything they knew about NTC except why. This was a view from below stairs, as it were. This was broadcasting beginning with the roots and underpinnings. There was no room here for the airy-fairy shenanigans I had been seeing since I arrived in Toronto. The boys knew which of the producers were worth their pay and which they had been covering up for. Some had the sensitivity to do the job, others had only their ambitions. While I was there, Ross Totton took out his pipe and fired it up a few times. He was the only pipe smoker I've met who spent more time smoking his pipe than cleaning it. I liked the smell of his tobacco. Two other technicians joined us and listened in. Three of the earlier members of the group left together after consulting their watches. The newcomers added to my store of information.

"They can't get rid of Ken Trebitsch because he's been collecting personal information on everybody he's ever worked for. He knows where the dirt is. He has a couple of junior producers collecting it. Talk about an enemies list. Trebitsch's looks like a roll of fax paper."

"Besides, his sister's married to a cousin of the prime minister."

"Yeah, and that's not the only sweetheart deal around. Your boss makes big demands on outside producers before she'll let them do a pilot. Talk about kickbacks!"

"But that's normal in Entertainment. Life is short there. You have to make your bundle before the axe falls."

"That's right, but in the meantime she has lots of money to spend outside the network. That's why there are so many Moss-watchers."

"Have you met David Simbrow? The Moss-boss? Vice-president of Programming? He's so stupid he couldn't get work selling raffle tickets. But his father's in the provincial cabinet."

"And Ted Thornhill, the CEO, doesn't know what to do about it. How can he reorganize Entertainment without booting Simbrow out?"

"Did you know that we're doing more 'sustained' programs than ever before?"

"What are they?"

"When you can't get the advertising, you underwrite them and hope nobody notices. It's only a step away from lowering the advertising rates."

"Have you met Philip Rankin yet?" I said that I'd had the pleasure. "Proper gentleman, isn't he? Well, he couldn't produce fleas in a zoo. Jesse and Ross and lots of us used to save his bacon regularly. That was a long time before Bob Foley came along."

I tried to get them to continue talking about Bob Foley, but all attempts died on the vine.

"You see, Benny, Bob was never really one of us. We got tired of his stories about the Great Man. You know, Dermot Keogh. Bob talked as if we never worked with headliners more than once, twice a year. The brutal fact is that between us we know just about everybody. Hell! I've stuck a mike up Anne Murray's shirt more times than . . . you know? That stuff doesn't mean anything. We do it all the time. How many times have you arranged the lights for the Queen, Ron? See what I mean? I had coffee with the prime minister one time, killing time between appointments. So why would we suddenly get excited about Bob becoming Dermot Keogh's gofer?"

"He had us up to a summer place in Muskoka one time. He was trying to lord it over us like he invented the place."

"Yeah," agreed Ross. "Remember how he treated that Paki lawyer? I just wanted to fade into the woods."

"That's right. And he'd tear up and down the roads on that borrowed chopper."

"Didn't mind *that* so much. I like choppers."

"The Moss tried to call the Provincial Police on him."

"Jesse, is Vanessa Moss doing her job?"

He thought about it, pulling at his earlobe and watching the flickering images on the TV set high above the bar. "Is she doing her job? Hell, Mr Cooperman, *nobody* can do that job. It'd be like trying to agree on guidelines for an orgy."

"That's the truth," Ross Totton offered. "She'll last another season, then they'll find someone else. That's the way of the beast."

I figured that besides enjoying the beer I'd had, I'd been given a backgrounder to the network I couldn't have found elsewhere. In the end, I thanked the boys and tried not to trip over my feet on my way out of the Rex.

———

At 5:30 p.m., I sat in the bar at the Hilton hotel, a few short blocks from NTC. It was a generous bar of dark mahogany, with gleaming brass in all the right places. The crowd was hard to figure. The customers were well-dressed frequenters of steak-houses, dapper account executives buttering up clients from Calgary or Edmonton with a taste of the *real* Toronto, before heading off to the hockey game and who knows what else.

Sally Jackson came in wearing her high-heeled walking-out shoes, which made her just an inch taller than me. "Sorry I kept you," she said, finding her centre of gravity on the tall bar stool.

"What can I get you?" I tried to read her mood. Why had she decided to join me?

"Is the season well enough advanced to order gin and tonic?"

"Sure." I passed the order along and sipped at my rye and water. The ice had melted. For five minutes or so, until her drink came, I tried to make small talk. I discovered that she knew little about the Blue Jays' recent performances at the SkyDome and less about the delayed Stanley Cup playoffs. In general, her eye was more often on the door or the mirror over the bar than it was on me. Even the bartender gave her a look that, in my reading of it, said, "This dame ain't gonna run a long tab." I tried to think of how I could make things easier for Sally.

"You seem a little nervous, Sally. If this wasn't a good idea, just say the word."

"To tell you the truth, Benny—may I call you that?—this is the first time I've been out with a man since I left Gordon." She was fiddling with the plastic wrapping from a pack of Benson & Hedges. She stopped short of taking one out and lighting it.

"Life can't stand still," I suggested. "When we can't go back, we have to move on."

"You don't understand, Benny. I left Gordon for my good friend Crystal Schild. I've been living with her for three months now."

"Oh," I said, clearing my throat and swallowing hard.

"Does that shock you?"

"*Me?* Of course not. There's a lot of it going . . . Some of my best . . ."

"There, I *did* embarrass you. I'm sorry. I keep forgetting that you come from Grantham. Here in Toronto—"

"Look, dear Sally, Grantham's not that backward. We've got the railroad; the bus service is going fine; we've got cable TV and even the World Wide Web has come along to show us what we're missing. There's not much going on in the world that could shock somebody on St Andrew Street in Grantham today."

"What about you? You look a little pink around the ears."

"Well, I'll admit, it was a little unexpected. I was unprepared. I mean it hadn't entered my mind." Part of my mind, the most primitive and least defensible part, was pondering whether this constituted getting a drink under false pretenses.

"Well, now you know. And now you know why I have to be so careful around that place."

"Who else knows, and why is it such a big secret? And why are you telling me? Why, only this morning I thought that the sight of my bleeding corpse wouldn't spoil your day. Now you volunteer this. How come?"

"I don't know. You've got a good face. I hate the way Vanessa orders you around. Maybe it was the sweet way you tried to make peace this afternoon. I don't know."

I still wasn't sure I trusted her, but, at least, she'd put up an unusual defence against the moves I had been plotting for later in the evening. She reminded me of my basically predatory nature, which I try to control, and of Anna, whose absence I was feeling in my bones.

"I assume that Vanessa knows nothing of this?" I asked.

"As far as she's concerned, I don't exist except as a source of coffee and treachery. I don't think she worries much about people's sexuality. She uses her own charms to manoeuvre men—she's a past-master at that, as you may know—but apart from that, she's not very observant about people and where they're coming from. She divides the world into two groups: those who can help her and those who want help from her."

"Is there anyone at NTC who knows?"

"Nate, Nate Green knew I was going through hell living with Gordon. He was a dear, sympathetic man, even when his own health started to preoccupy him. Unless he told somebody, then you're the only one, apart from one or two of the women there that I trust."

"Why don't you want it to get out? I can think of several reasons but what are yours?"

"Benny, I just want to get on with my job. From where you sit, it might not look like much, but it's all I've got right now, except Crystal. I don't need complications."

"But they can't fire you for what isn't any of their business, can they?"

"No, not any more, but it wouldn't endear me to some of them either. Three years ago, a man got shunted around because it was thought there were too many gays in his department. Because of some idiot's idea that a 'quota system' was needed in Audience Relations, he was sent back to writing local news and weather." She paused long enough for me to register her point, and then took the first sip of her drink.

The bar was beginning to fill up. It hadn't looked particularly empty when I came in, but now the contrast showed. Little silver bowls of peanuts, olives and shrimp chips had appeared. The bartender was talking to an elderly man in a string tie at the other end of the bar. I drew a happy face with my finger in the wet ring where my glass had been sitting.

"Did anybody come looking for Vanessa while I was out this afternoon, Sally?"

"Only about three or four hundred came in raising hell."

"*What?*"

"I mean it was business as usual around there. You've seen it, but you haven't seen the traffic when it gets bad. Multiply Hy Newman by fifty and you'll begin to get an idea of my job."

"You feel sorry for Hy, don't you?" She stared into her glass. Droplets of moisture forced their way through cloudy condensation on the sides.

"Hy was part of NTC from the beginning. Now he can't get past Reception most days. Security has his picture and orders not to let him in."

"Does he run amok? Does he threaten people? What's the problem?"

"Hy reminds most of them where *they* were when Hy was the best producer of big shows that the network had ever seen. He hired some of them and promoted others. Hy's the sort of person who makes up for all the times we fail, or don't measure up to who we should be."

"You take this very personally, don't you, Sally?"

"Benny, somebody has to." I quite liked Sally then. And I believed her. There must be a lot of people on the payroll who aren't trying to make the worst programs possible, people who feel a responsibility to the public, who are aware of the lightweights they have been delivering over the years.

"What brings you to NTC, Benny? You're not a broadcaster." I considered telling Sally the truth and then I took another sip of my drink.

"I know Vanessa from a long time ago. She's in a bind and I'm trying to help her. I suggested that she get Hy Newman to sort out some of her production muddles for her."

"That was a great idea!"

"She didn't think so."

"Give her a day or two. I've seen her take suggestions of mine a couple of days after she told me to mind my business. It is a good idea, Benny. So, she found you in Grantham at loose ends?" I could see she was pumping me, but I didn't see the harm. I could use it to reinforce my cover story.

"Yes, I was just waiting around to go on a European holiday. She got me at the right moment. Tell me, Sally, did you know

Renata Sartori at all?" I watched the reaction to the question in her eyes. She was suddenly guarded. I'd lost yards by trying to get too much too soon.

"Not . . . too well, Benny. She'd worked here for a long time, but it's a busy place. We used to have coffee together occasionally. I liked her. She did my income-tax returns for two or three years until I started doing them myself. She was clever with figures. She could have been a certified accountant if she troubled to take the exam. She did the books for a lot of people around the network."

"So I've heard."

"Well, she was so good at it."

New people were filling up the empty spaces behind me, crowding the bar and raising the din, so that it was becoming harder to hear Sally without leaning close, which I didn't mind a bit.

"Getting back to Renata: did she really look all that much like Vanessa?"

"Well, they weren't dead ringers. From the back they could pass for one another: same height, proportions, hair colour and length, but from the front, Vanessa has finer features. Renata had brown eyes and used heavier makeup. I guess in the dark it might be hard to tell them apart. The papers said she was wearing a dressing gown of Vanessa's. The murderer would have an expectation of seeing Vanessa answer her own front door."

"Didn't she have a man in her life? A lawyer?"

"Renata had been seeing Barry Bosco. He's with Raymond Devlin's firm. But I don't know that it was a burning passionate affair. It may have been. Don't get me wrong. I just don't know the details. She didn't talk about him at all when we had lunch that last time. They went out together; that's all I know for a fact. He had a sports car as well as other cars and she liked that. I don't know whether Barry felt as casual about Renata."

"How do you happen to know Bosco?"

"He's a fraternity brother of Gordon's. He was on the fringe of a crowd I used to know better than I do now." She sipped her drink thoughtfully. "Barry is hard to figure. He has all the charm in the world, but he can't be pinned down on anything. He's a strange sort of lawyer, now that I think of it. He hates to sign things. Can you imagine it? A lawyer who hates to put his name on the dotted line. Raymond is just the opposite. He'll get you to sign a contract just for coming in to keep an appointment. I've never seen anyone who was so paper-bound. Well, you saw him in good form yesterday, Benny. He probably gets the kid who cuts his grass to sign a contract. He had kids of his own: they died in a car accident when they were teenagers. But when they were eight and six, Ray made them draw up wills!"

"Is he married?"

"Technically. He's been separated from his wife for over ten years. She left him a year after the accident; moved to Julian, California; opened a second-hand bookstore."

"How do you know all this?"

"Barry did some legal work for Vanessa, and Raymond took me out twice, before I married Gordon. I've been a Raymond Devlin watcher for years. He tried to get me up to his cottage once, but I out-foxed him."

"At the meeting, this morning, I met Philip Rankin and Ken Trebitsch. Where would you place them on Vanessa's enemies list?"

"That's hard to say. I haven't had much contact—"

"This could be important, Sally. Renata was murdered, remember." Sally's mouth stood open for a few seconds. Some sort of mental process was going on behind her well-shaped brows. "Tell me," I said quietly.

"Like the rest of the people in that boardroom, Ken and Philip are ambitious. Both would like to add some of the clout Entertainment has to their own empires. Entertainment has the squeeze on prime time. They both want a bigger share. Ken, at least, isn't subtle about how he goes about things. If he likes the apple on your desk, he'll grab it. If you catch him at it, he was 'only fooling.' Philip's not as easy to read. While Dermot Keogh was alive, Philip Rankin was a somebody, as they say in the muffler commercials. Recently, he's had to work harder, do more scouting around to find talent. Dermot's death really shook Philip. He hasn't got over it yet, I think. Whenever I overhear him talking, he's telling stories about the old days. He shared Dermot's passion for antique cars and rare wines. The only thing that Dermot collected that Philip disapproved of was motorcycles."

"I can't picture a cellist on a chopper."

"Neither could Philip. Thought it was too dangerous. Also, he didn't run after women the way Dermot did. He just didn't have the looks or the glamour for it. But you should have heard his eulogy at Dermot's funeral. There wasn't a dry eye in the church."

"Does everybody call him 'Philip'? Isn't he 'Phil' to anyone?"

"Philip's rather particular about his name. Actually, he has a string of initials he uses in writing, plus his degrees, both the earned and the honorary ones. Plain Philip Rankin is as simple as it gets. The whole name is something like Philip Ross Gardiner Rankin, F.R.C.O., D.M., R.A.M., R.C.M. Shall I keep going?"

"Was part of his value to NTC his closeness to Keogh?"

"Naturally. Philip could get around him, get him to agree to do the promotion necessary to ballyhoo his shows. Dermot believed that the programs sold themselves, that his name sold them. He hated to appear to be pushing or giving a sales pitch. You could never catch him bragging, although he was on first-name terms with all of the greats of the musical world. Philip once said that he dropped in on him, this must have been five or six years ago, and the Three Tenors were making salad in the kitchen. Dermot was boiling potatoes. Apart from his playing in public, he was really rather shy without Hector to lean on."

"Hector?"

"That's what he called his cello. It was a Stradivarius, I think."

"What happened to Hector?"

"I guess it was swallowed up into the estate. Ask Philip, he'd know. He's one of the trustees of the foundation."

"Is Philip Rankin all that approachable?"

"Are you kidding? If it has anything to do with Dermot Keogh, his door will open wide."

"Great!"

A beefy man with a brown moustache, suit and hair sat down on Sally's other side. At first she didn't see him and then she turned, unpleased by what she saw.

"I thought I might find you here," he said, with just the suggestion of a Scottish accent.

"*Gordon!* What are you doing here? Have you been following me again?"

"I need to talk to you, Sally. I've got to."

"Gordon, this is neither the time nor the place. Remember what the judge said. You have to keep to what he says. Especially 'watching or besetting.' Section 381, Gordon. You know that." I may have been imagining it, but now I could sense heather in Sally's voice too. Nervously, she introduced us. Jackson looked at me with a face so troubled it could not even muster an unfriendly glare. We didn't shake hands.

"I said I needed to talk—"

"Not *now*, Gordon. I'll join you in the lobby in five minutes."

"What I've got to say can't wait five minutes. I was outside your office all afternoon. You don't know the—" Again she cut him off.

"Not here, Gordon. Are you *listening?* In the lobby. Five minutes." Gordon Jackson got to his feet. For a second, I thought he was going to do as he'd been told. But, as soon as he had gained his balance, he grabbed at Sally's arm, pulled her off the stool so that it fell over into me and then down to the carpet and rolled into a startled waiter.

"*Gordon, you can't—!*"

"Hey! Watch it!" My efforts at mending things between the Jacksons were foolish and badly executed. I reached out and tugged at his lapels, trying to get him away from the struggling Sally. He couldn't punch me—he was too close—but I could see it in his eyes. Meanwhile Sally started moaning. I don't think he'd hurt her, but the pain was real nonetheless. The farther away I got him from his wife, the greater were his opportunities for striking out. He missed me twice but landed a good one on his third try. I ended up sprawled next to the fallen stool, with a flailing sort of wonderment in my brain: This can't be happening! Not to me!

Suddenly, I couldn't see anything but legs. My view of everything was cut off by a crowd of my fellow tipplers. I heard Sally still crying out, and by the time I got up and pulled a few bodies out of my way, I could see them leaving the bar together. Sally was walking on her own, but Gordon was holding her arm behind her back. As I caught up to them, I called out Sally's name. When I'd cleared the bar entrance, still coming along as fast as I could, Gordon turned and let me walk into the fist on the end of his extended right hand. I went down again to the carpet in an explosion of colours and stayed there.

CHAPTER TEN

There have been a few times in my career when I have had to pick myself up off the floor. *Ignominiously* is the word that Frank Bushmill adds to my telling of these tales. An educated man, he should know. I merely pass the word on, as I remembered it, lying there, thinking of those other times. This time I reached up and found a warm hand and grabbed it. It remained calm while I pulled myself up on it. I held on with a good strong grip. I was on my knees, rising almost into the lap of a woman with wheels. It was a motorized wheelchair she was sitting in. She had curly red hair, was wearing plaid slacks and was grinning at me.

"I missed the beginning," she said. "Could you push the replay button?"

"There were three of them, right?"

"Oh, at least. Your nose isn't bleeding. I don't see any loose teeth. But your eye, your poor eye."

"Who are you?" I asked, loosening my grip on her and starting to brush the carpet fuzz from my jacket.

"Barbara," she said. "Barbara Turnbull."

"Well, Barbara, thanks. Did you get his licence number?"

The remarkable thing was that nothing was spilled. No blood on the rug, no fallen drinks weltering in their own ice cubes. No broken furniture. Nothing. And, apart from having to meet the gaze of the manager and the assistant manager, a florid face and a grey one, I was in fairly good shape, thanks to Barbara Turnbull. She watched me as I scanned the room for my former poise and sense of purpose. A woman with a green dragon clasp on her dress offered me tissue from her purse. A tall young man with a Walkman plugged into his ears held out my fallen keys, notebook and pencil. The assistant manager presented my bar bill. It only took a zip-zip of my credit card and I was free to leave. The whole incident had been quietly encapsulated, purged and forgotten by the hotel regulars as quickly as a chewed olive pit. My right eye felt better when I kept it shut.

The evening air hit my face like a slap in the eye, and the figure of speech knows what it's talking about. I tried opening the eye and it took in a fuzzy image of the traffic on University Avenue and of the monument to something or other in the middle of the boulevard. I hadn't been blinded. So I needn't seek medical help right away. Judging from what I'd been reading in the papers, they wouldn't get around to treating my eye for six or seven hours at the handy array of emergency departments in nearby hospitals.

"May I get you a taxi?" It was Barbara, now putt-putting after me from the hotel.

"Thanks, but I think I need to clear my head."

"Sure?"

"Yeah. I'm really okay. I'm just out of practice."

"Well, I think they're giving a course in barroom brawling at George Brown College. They might let you go directly into the second-year program."

"Thanks a lot!"

"Well, if I can't be of further help, I've got to get back to the paper. See you." She backed her chair up, executed a deft turn and headed off down the street.

I wandered back to Bay Street and the New Beijing Inn. With my wonky vision, the city looked like a badly executed set for a low-budget movie. The panhandler, reaching for loose change, had exaggerated colours on his face as I passed his dark form leaning on the corner of the bus terminal. There seemed to be faces on the windshields coming towards me as I crossed the street. Their eyes followed me home.

"I've got to get back to the paper," she'd said. Barbara Turn-bull, my rescuer. How did I know that the paper was a news-paper and that the paper in question was the *Star*? The answer didn't hit me right away, but I assigned part of my head to work on it.

The night clerk scarcely lowered his Chinese newspaper as I rounded his desk on my way to the elevator. I shut out the outside world when I snapped the various locks behind me. Eight floors should distance me from irate estranged husbands and all other physically demonstrative creatures. Looking out the window and without checking my watch, I tried to calcu-late the time of day. The sunset was reflected in the windows of the office building opposite my hotel. I hadn't intended to fall asleep, but, without any direction on my part, that's what happened. Dozing, I made a better showing in the fistfight my subconscious dreamed up for me than I had earlier. In the future, I'll confine all my scraps to the Beijing Inn. The Hilton's bad news when it comes to mixing it up with the Mar-quess of Queensberry's rules.

It was the ring of the telephone that brought me around. I was lying aslant the bed, still fully dressed even to my shoes. I could feel the strength of my heartbeat in my right eye. There was a throbbing in my head that wouldn't go away until I lifted the phone from its cradle.

"Benny?"

"Yeah? Who wants him?"

"Benny, I've got to see you." It was Vanessa. For once she sounded scared. I hadn't heard it in her voice when she first hired me, and I hadn't noted it any time after. Fear puts humanity back into the most outrageous people. I liked Vanessa Moss sounding just a little as though she was caught up in the tangles of her own life. Fear was the right sensation for her to be feeling. It kept her human. Unless, of course, it was all fakery, acting for my benefit. If it was that, it sounded like she deserved an A in the course.

"Where are you?"

"Belmont Avenue. Number 365. You know where that is?"

"Don't worry; I'll find it."

"What did the cops say about the 222s?"

"I haven't got their report yet. Make sure you don't dip into anything you can't personally vouch for."

"Okay, *okay!*" she said with irritation.

"Vanessa, does Barbara Turnbull work for the *Star*?"

"Yes. She's been covering the murder investigation, and the network hasn't 'scaped whipping. Why do you ask?"

"Tell you when I get there. I'll see you in twenty minutes." I hung up and took a quick shower. While under the water, I heard the phone ring again, but I thought I could live with an unanswered phone once in a while.

Forty minutes later I was leaning on the bell at 365 Belmont, a small, quiet street just off Yonge. There was still the purplish afterglow of dusk hanging about. The dark hadn't taken hold of the night completely. An unwashed elderly red Volvo was parked across the street. For a moment, it looked as though there was someone inside. Since when are rusty Volvos the unmarked cars of choice used by the boys in blue? I tried to brace myself for whatever surprise Vanessa had in store for me. I could hear footsteps in the hall as the light above the door went on. She didn't ask who was there, which, in the circumstances, might have been a good idea.

"Why didn't you ask who it was?"

"Through the door? But I wasn't expecting anybody but you."

"And who was Renata expecting?"

"Oh, Benny! I see what you mean." Her fingers momentarily tightened on the edge of the door, before throwing it open.

She was wearing a blue dressing gown; her hair had been brushed one hundred times. It glowed in a soft way that I had never seen before on Vanessa or on anyone else outside the movies. It certainly was not the Stella of the Grantham Collegiate Institute and Vocational School or the Vanessa of the National Television Corporation. "What happened to your *eye?*"

"It's all included in the service, Vanessa."

"Seriously, Benny. Have you been in a fight? I don't think I'm paying you to get involved in barroom *brawls*."

"You should have spelled that out back in Grantham. Anyway, this barroom brawl couldn't be helped. I was collecting information." She stood aside so that I could move past her through the hallway and into the tiny house. There were stairs leading up to a second floor, where lights were burning. In fact, the whole house was ablaze with electric light. She followed me into the hall at the foot of the stairs, then led the way into a living-room, which suited the Vanessa I knew as well as this new hair-style.

"This house belongs to a friend, Benny. The cops said I could go home, but I'm still too upset to go back there. The owner of this house is travelling in Tuscany, so she let me have it until my place gets back to normal. Nice, isn't it?"

"Why is everybody travelling in Tuscany this year?" I was thinking of the fair Anna Abraham and her mushroom millionaire. Vanessa didn't bother with my question.

The living-room was done up in off-white walls and hangings with chrome and glass furniture, and expensive architectural magazines on the glass-topped coffee table. Lighting in the room was provided by three halogen lamps slung low over the backs of the couches and chairs. Large watercolours of lighthouses and wharves with lots of clouds showing broke up the walls with a calculated effect. It wouldn't have been my mother's way of doing a room. I suppose it told a lot about Vanessa's friend, but I didn't have time to decode the message.

"Vanessa, when you called, you said you had to see me in a hurry. Okay, what's up?"

"I was going crazy, Benny. Too many people know I'm here. I *tried* to keep this place a secret, but I keep telling people. I can't *help* myself. I don't think it's safe any more. Besides that, I feel so lonely on my own." If she was frightened, why didn't she pay more attention to whom she opened her door? Vanessa was determined to prove a paradox. Or was it just another one of her games?

"Nobody's *ever* told me about the chill factor of raw fear before. I'm cold all the time." She hugged herself to illustrate the chill. The gesture also pushed some cleavage through the top of her dressing gown. It was this part of the gesture that told on me, a mammal from the cradle.

"So, there've been no new developments? No pills you can't account for? No threats, shotguns or frightening phone calls?"

"Not in that way. No. But I'm scared, Benny. And that's real enough. I'm still getting used to the idea that maybe my 222s were drugged or poisoned in some way."

I tried not to look too relieved. She'd hold that against me. From what she said, after announcing that she was trying to organize a cup of coffee for me, I gathered that she had been living here since soon after the police finished questioning her about the murder at her house. I followed her into the kitchen, where she squinted at the places where coffee might spring from. I found a kettle and plugged it in after filling it from a tap that gave me a choice of every kind of water but tidal. While that was coming to the boil, I found the instant in a cupboard. I took two mugs, brown and browner. Vanessa watched me pour out the instant powder like she'd never seen coffee made before.

"Vanessa, have you given my phone number to anyone?"

"Of course not! You mean at your hotel? No, I'd never do that. Maybe it was one of your police friends."

"I don't remember giving it to them either. Did you call me back after we talked the first time tonight?"

"No. I'd have remembered that. Are you sure I can't give you anything for your eye?"

"Such as?"

"There's a steak in the freezer, but I don't think it will do any good until it thaws. I'll take it out." She did that, laying a slab of meat on the counter with a clunk.

"When your office door is locked, Vanessa, who has access?"

"In theory, nobody. In practice, there are a few keys about. Ted has a set. I suppose Security has another. Why?"

"I was thinking of the used shotgun shells found in your locker. Who else knew the combination to your locker?"

"Nobody had access."

"Are you sure you didn't have it written down someplace just in case you forgot it? I know I have a combination pasted to the bottom of a stapler in my office in Grantham. Usually, I remember it, but I've had to fall back on the stapler solution from time to time."

"Well, there's nothing wrong with my memory, Benny."

"Before I leave, remind me to get the combination from you."

"But the cops cut it off!"

"I still want to check it out." By now I could fill both mugs with boiling water and stir up the powder.

Seated again in the living-room, sipping coffee, we pulled at a few more of the strands hanging from this bird's nest of a puzzle. Most of it was repetition. I did what I could to reassure her that the villains hadn't traced her here, that her enemies were not gathering on the porch and that I was on the job. It seemed to calm her, which was good, because both nervousness and fear are contagious.

"What happened this afternoon?"

"I think Thornhill intends to carve up the department."

"You told me that already. I thought he was just playing with the idea."

"You can't trust that son of a bitch for five minutes. He's famous for turning the vaguest, the filmiest of ideas into boilerplate with no further discussion."

"Maybe he'll turn it back the other way round just as fast?"

"Dream on. He wants my guts for garters, and I can't figure out how to keep what I have. It's only this murder thing that might slow him down. He knows that everybody's watching. I don't think he wants a shake-up in Entertainment until I stop being the Victim of the Week." She had argued around in a circle. I was about to point that out when I noticed it had a mild calming influence. So I left it alone. "You were going to tell me about Barbara Turnbull, from the *Star*."

"I just ran into her."

"Don't tell her a thing about me or about the department. You can't trust newspaper people."

"I haven't lost my grip yet." I didn't bother telling her of the incident in the lobby of the Hilton, or that my relationship with reporter Turnbull did not involve Vanessa or NTC. She might not know how to take it.

Vanessa leaned back against the eggshell white of the wall, flattening her body, trying to make a smaller target. When the wall failed to enclose her, she shifted her weight and came over to the couch where I was sitting. She moved slowly, giving me a sense of her perfume, and sat next to me. I wondered where George, the car jockey and computer animator, was at this time of night. When she started to get close, I let her. Anything to calm her down. It's funny, I mean, I'd always been attracted by Stella Seco, even though I'd put it on hold for a dozen years or so. Now that she was Vanessa and my employer, I thought of what *she* needed before consulting my own usually healthy appetite. I thought of Anna, off in Tuscany. I thought of all she meant to me. I thought of Tuscany and the peanut-grower from California. Mushrooms. What the hell?

She had allowed her dressing gown to fall open both at the neck and again lower down, so that there was a fair amount of Vanessa on display and in the most beguiling way. I decided that what she wanted was a hug. Where's the disloyalty in that? It was the least I could do. We all need hugs from time to time. Especially when we're scared. Possibly good-looking women don't get their fair share. Men are easily discouraged in a face-to-face encounter with the object of their desires. A pretty face, in spite of a come-hither look in those beautiful eyes, often has the effect of forcing a strategic retreat on the timorous seducer. So, I didn't get either flustered or my hopes up. It was, as I said on my way in, all part of the service. While I was still seeing myself in terms of the steadfast little sentry at the door, the hug developed into something more serious, and the brave sentry could hardly abandon his musket at a time like this. Besides, the steak for my eye was still thawing in the kitchen.

ELEVEN

◖ Friday

Staff Sergeant Jack Sykes shook his head sadly. He fussed with paper on his desk.

"You've made some powerful asshole mad at you, Benny."

"What are you talking about? I told you, I walked into a door. It can happen to anybody. You can hardly see it."

"It's not the eye I'm talking about, Benny. It's your making free with the division offices and your fraternization with two of its finest officers."

"Somebody's been on the blower, Benny," Boyd added, just to make me feel good, "and he or she's been complaining."

"For crying out loud, I don't even *know* anybody in Toronto. I've only been here since Wednesday." Now he was nodding, agreeing with me, as though that made a difference.

"I know. I know. But I have my orders. I'm sorry, but I can't have you dropping in here any more."

"What do you mean?" I was leaning over Jack's desk, trying to keep my eyes off the word FRAUD, written on the open edge of the Toronto phone book. The last one said VICE. He just couldn't help swiping things. He was also busy trying not to look me straight in the eye. Jim Boyd was sitting off to one side, attempting to look neutral, still wearing that silly summer hat. He, too, was not big on eye contact.

"I shouldn't even be seen talking to you. That's how bad it is. The way I see it is that somebody in NTC has raised a stink about you being so close to the investigation, and you working for one of the leading suspects in the case. You haven't been passing out your professional cards down there, have you?"

"Vanessa Moss is the only person who knows. Except—"

"Except for all the part-time snoops that run around like laboratory mice from office to office, telling tales out of school. One of them thinks he can pick up the phone and complain. I don't like getting pressure from College Street, which just happens to be the source of most of my headaches, but in this case, I have to agree the Chief's got a point."

"The Chief!"

"Yeah. For a snoop from Grantham you've been making big waves."

"So, let me get this straight: we're no longer co-operating? Is that it?"

"That's right."

"Wait a minute! When were we co-operating anyway? I paid a *courtesy* call. That's all."

"I'm not going to argue with you, Benny. I've heard the word from on high. When does a plain cop get to be so independent he can ignore a straight order?"

"You're not going to tell me about those 222s, are you? And I'll never hear about the combination lock on Vanessa's locker either."

"Of course not. That would be a direct contravention of my orders. What do you think, Jim?"

"Oh, yeah. The order says all contact must stop at once. No more free lunch, Benny." Jim was trying to free a piece of his breakfast, lodged between molars, with the corner of an official-looking piece of bond paper. Then he looked over at his partner. "Jack, my mind's going soft. What was it Art Dempsey said about those pills? Refresh my failing memory."

"How many times . . . ? Jeez! Twenty-five of the thirty-eight pills were a powerful anti-depressant. Among its listed side effects are drowsiness. You wanna stay away from machinery, especially cars, unless you're riding in the back seat. Take some of that and you don't want to be behind the wheel of a Range Rover. Not even in Grantham. You want to know the name? Desyrel. One hundred milligrams. Little devils look like 222s if you don't look close."

"Well, thanks at least for that."

"For what? I wasn't even talking to you."

"Right. And thanks for . . . for . . . giving me street directions to the YMCA."

"Okay, always happy to help out the tourist trade, but that's the end of it."

"Have you checked out that lock yet?"

"Get out of here! What's with you and that goddamned lock, Benny? I swear to God I think you think the killer's hiding inside the lock like a—a—troll."

"Imp?" I suggested.

"Sprite?" Boyd said. Both were better than *troll*.

"Will you get out of here? Until I see how this bounces, Benny, I gotta watch my ass. In the meantime, don't walk into any doors on your way out."

"Sure. See you fellows around," I said lamely, and backed away from the desk and out the open door. Slowly—because I didn't want to outrun them—I walked down the echoing corridor and out into the marble halls of the lobby or whatever they call it. The desk sergeant looked at me, and I read into his expression that he too had been instructed to give no help. I thought of asking him for directions to the art gallery next door, but I felt too bad to be playful. The Yellow Brick Road to Paranoia was stretched out before me. I knew I had to get a grip on myself. I felt like the fat man in Shakespeare, the one who gets shafted by the young king. Falstaff! I thought, Yeah, Jack will call me tonight. He's only going through the motions. That wasn't Jack Sykes talking. That's why the door was open, in case someone was listening.

Over coffee at the Second Cup across the street, where I'd had my first long talk with Jack and his partner, I pondered the changes in my position. The cops held all of the hard evidence in both the cases I was interested in. I'd even been some use to them: helping them to justify linking the two deaths and being on guard about the appearance of suicide in the Foley business. I wondered whether Sergeant Chuck Pepper was included in the ban. The Chief might not know about the Cooperman-Pepper axis yet. That might still be a live connection, but not one I cared to try out until the dust settled. Even as I went over the ground, I still half-expected Sykes or Boyd to walk into the café and pick up the tab like last time. But they didn't.

Back at Vanessa's NTC office, I weathered Sally Jackson's painful apologies for the way our quiet drink ended. She was very kind about my eye, which had turned an impressive purple with a rim of pale yellow reaching through green for blue. She reported that Gordon had gone off meekly into the night almost as soon as Sally had explained who I was. This kind of behaviour, she reported, was new to Gordon, and probably wouldn't happen again. "He tried to sleep in his car last night, parked across from Crystal's apartment, but he was made to move on by the cops. Now he thinks I called them. I know, because he was on the phone in the middle of the night. I'm at my wit's end with that man, Benny." Sally was looking a little wilted this morning. She'd taken extra care dressing and making up her face. The results showed more about her rough night than her voice did. I wondered whether Ken Trebitsch gave her a little extra on the side for being his snoop in Vanessa's kingdom. I was guessing that it was Trebitsch who called the Chief.

"Where's her ladyship?"

"Closeted with Mr Thornhill. He called early; she had to reschedule two meetings."

"What does Mr Thornhill want?"

"Hard to say. He's been on her back all week. He wants changes in the department. I know that. She's not giving him an inch. She's fighting him on the changes. So far, there are no winners."

"Is Mr Thornhill in this alone, or does he have allies?"

"Oh, Ken Trebitsch has his hands in that pie too. A bigger bite of prime time might make him smile. He might even take me to lunch without pumping me for information. Ken's an empire builder of the old school. Thornhill likes him, because he knows the type. He's easier to understand than someone like Ms Moss." This sounded like a confession. My black eye was paying off in spades.

"Do you trust Trebitsch?"

"As far as I can throw a baby grand. He's had people in here measuring the floor space. How's that for undermining the opposition?"

Before I could answer, Vanessa was suddenly standing there in the doorway. "Undermining what opposition?" she demanded. Her eyes looked as though she wanted to hit somebody. Anybody.

"I was asking about Ken Trebitsch."

"That son of a bitch! He's got more clocks on the wall of his office than CBS, NBC, ABC and Switzerland put together. He's the sort of newsman who's just bursting to yell, 'Sweetheart, get me rewrite!' The only trouble is that he wouldn't get the joke. You have to recognize a cliché before you can see the fun."

"You've had a rough morning," I said, trying to change the subject.

"*All* my mornings are rough, Benny. You should see some of them. They dump their slag on my afternoons, which are worse." I thought that after last night she might have lowered her gunsights. I never figured out why I was the favourite target for her black humour. Almost everything she said suggested that she was the only one who did any work at NTC. I don't know what she was complaining about. She was still alive, wasn't she?

Vanessa was wearing a charcoal grey pant suit with a white shirt that aped an Oxford button-down. She wore it open at the neck without a tie, just the way I like it. Her hair had abandoned the loose, newly combed look of the previous evening, and was now severely bound by an unforgiving silver clasp. "You're expected to attend me this afternoon, Benny. My afternoons are dillies. Friday afternoons are the worst of the bunch. Especially now that this damned Dermot Keogh Hall is in the works."

"How does that make it worse?"

"Where to start?" She took a breath. "Raymond Devlin is looking after Dermot Keogh's estate. You know that. Since he decided to give a big whack of that money to us, he has been demanding first-class treatment from Ted Thornhill. Well, big, brave Ted has passed him on to me as often as he could. Ray needs a lot of hand-holding, Benny, and I've been elected to do most of it. After all, he can still back out if he wants to."

"What about those papers I witnessed in your office?"

"That's just for the building. He's got I. M. Pei to do the design. Did I tell you? He's the best. The big money will come later to sustain programs and endow concert series. Ray wants to keep a continuing interest in the Hall, even after it's been launched. We're going to see a lot of Ray Devlin around here in the next few years."

She rested a small briefcase on the edge of Sally's desk and opened it. She sorted some papers and left three with Sally. Then she added, as though it had just occurred to her: "Benny, I'm off to L.A. tonight. I'll be there for four days, maybe longer. I'll be back Tuesday at the earliest. I have to see the new man at Universal to get something solid in the way of deadlines and delivery dates. I've got to take a meeting with Max Winkler at Warners to settle the fall schedule. You got all that?" She was relaxing a little behind her rapid-fire stream of talk.

"I'll pack a bag," I said.

"What for? Nobody on the coast is trying to kill me."

"But, where better to nail you?"

"Your job is *here*."

"But, *Vanessa!*"

"I've thought it through, Benny. I can look after myself in L.A." There wasn't any point in arguing further.

"I'll unpack," I said. "Do you want me to drive you to the airport?"

"George is driving me, Benny. Now he drives as well as parks. He's moving up in the world."

Later, just when I was getting tired of moving from floor to floor, maintaining radio silence in the elevators and being dragged limp from meeting to meeting with Vanessa, I discovered that Vanessa kept up communications between appointments on her cellphone, which she used as she walked down the corridors. Once she emerged from the Ladies' with the phone to her ear.

"Mark, are you listening to me, Mark? I want no more monkey business from you. I want the first six episodes, as you promised, on the agreed date. No ifs, ands or buts. So fix it up and get the six shows to me *on time*."

Then she was in a wrangle with another outside producer. "*Yesterday's Headlines*, Frank, is a *game* show. Why show it to Ken Trebitsch, sweety? Game shows are Entertainment, not News. Yesterday's news is history, Frank, and that's Entertainment. *Capisce?*" She lowered the cellphone and dumped it in her bag.

When I found a clear moment, I asked her more about her place on Lake Muskoka. While we waited in a very empty boardroom, between meetings, she filled me in on the details of how to get there and where to find the keys, which were kept hidden in an old barbecue under a lean-to with other half-discarded junk such as paddles, broken oars, folding chairs and old sun umbrellas. She didn't question me about what I was planning. To tell the truth, I don't think she cared much. She had already moved out of Toronto and its problems; she was already in Los Angeles defending NTC interests against the moguls at Universal and Warners. When I bugged her to give me numbers where she could be located, she said she'd leave them in an envelope with Sally. We got through the whole afternoon without once looking into one another's eyes. Last night was already in a sealed box, dropped overboard, only leaving me with the knowledge that she slept with a loaded gun under her pillow.

I don't know what to say about that part of the night before. As I said, it began with a hug, but it quickly got out of hand. I have been with a few women in my time, but never have these encounters had so much violence and passion and so little personal feeling. Vanessa was good in bed, but scary. When the gun came out from under the pillow, it did nothing for my ability to concentrate. After she had pressed the muzzle into my groin, I tried to get it away from her, tossing the bed-clothes around, and she fought, biting and kicking, until I'd thrown it across the room. She tried to retrieve it, but I held on to her. I've got scratches on my back to show that she didn't like being handled this way.

When I'd showered and dressed, I found that she'd thrown a blanket and pillow on a couch for me. The bedroom door was closed.

At one point in the afternoon, the producer Eric Carter joined us just long enough to gloat over the fact that his Christmas show was in the can, on time and less than fifty thousand dollars over budget, which was almost like being under budget, judging from his grin. Vanessa took the news soberly and sent him off with some scripts for series pilots to look at over the weekend. Was that a way to say thanks in television land? I wasn't sure.

While Vanessa dictated a string of letters to Sally, I went digging in the kitchen for something to eat. I found a brownish orange and half a lemon, nearly turned to stone. I tried these with boiling water and some sugar cubes and promised to treat myself better next week.

"Oh, Mr Cooperman!" The voice came as a surprise as I strolled the corridor away from the Men's. I looked behind me. At first the hall looked empty of all but the usual traffic on the blue broadloom—people with letters to photocopy, coffee mugs to return and reports to rewrite—then I saw an arm waving from an open doorway. As I walked back towards it, I tried to recall the fruity voice that hailed me. The answer came a moment before my eyes confirmed my guess. It was Philip Rankin, Music Department. Puffy face, like a fish drowning in air. One of the people trying to get Vanessa to leave NTC. I nearly laughed out loud as I tried to imagine him holding a shotgun.

"You've had a merry thought," he said, waving me into the darkish room. I was surprised that my face was so legible.

"Just surprised that you remembered my name, that's all." Rankin's office was one of the larger kind, with a door leading to a receptionist or secretary, the usual way of gaining entrance to this holy of holies. But Rankin kept his private door open from time to time to catch the traffic coming and going. I couldn't make myself believe that he was on the lookout for me particularly.

"Take it as a compliment, dear boy. They don't come around that often that you can ignore them. Accept them, grapple them to your heart and cherish them. But, be on your guard, my dear fellow. These corridors are crowded with spies and deceivers. Take care." He placed a canny finger alongside his nose.

"I thought a 'merry thought' was a wishbone."

"I'm serious, Mr Cooperman. This place is as packed with false friends as a piñata."

"Why would anyone bother? In the short time I've been here I've learned that the executive assistant is the lowest form of life."

"Nevertheless. You are close to a hotly contested area."

"Entertainment?"

"Exactly! The world revolves. Things are happening."

"I haven't heard that Vanessa Moss has been eclipsed. When was that announced? Her name was still on her door ten minutes ago."

"While you are right to question the accuracy of what I've just said, I fear that the truth—that she's not been sacked yet—is a mere quibble. But that doesn't mean the blades are not being sharpened, my boy. The wagons have been circled, and the wagonmaster has a bee in his bonnet about that woman. Well, it's only a matter of time."

"I like your openness. It's good to know where we stand."

"You see, it's only the commercial interests that have saved her this week. The CEO is trying to gauge the reception of our unloading that baggage with the murder thing still unresolved."

"Are you saying that the advertisers are calling the shots? That NTC is run by snake-oil salesmen?"

"Oh dear! What a low opinion you must have of the medium, Mr Cooperman. What I meant to say is that they are still trying to see if she fits their definition of a liability. If she's not a liability—and that has to include all of the publicity she's garnered both for herself and the network—can she be described as an asset? I think not."

He must have read an uncomplimentary expression on my face.

"You know, Mr Cooperman, we have a book of advertising standards that spells out the rules for acceptable commercials. Toilet tissue, for instance, must stress absorbency and softness, but without showing the product near anything made of porcelain. I think snake oil is banned no matter what the approach. We have recently gone in for brand-name companies taking a high-toned institutional approach. 'The following concert by the late Dermot Keogh was recorded in Madrid with the support of the Morgan Armstrong Corporation and Bix-a-bix Cereal Products.'"

"You knew Dermot Keogh well. I'd forgotten that. I know people in Grantham who have all of his recordings."

"Yes, dear boy. And he keeps on selling. Luckily, we have a great deal of him on tape and on compact discs. His reputation will not stop growing for another ten years."

"I remember one summer, up at Dittrick Lake, I was staying with friends and he was giving a radio concert. Warm night. Stars. We turned the radio up loud inside the cottage and listened to the music on the patio where we could look out over the lake. The house became a kind of sounding board for his cello, so that we felt that we were right there at the concert. I'll never forget that." It hadn't actually been Keogh I'd heard, but the adapted anecdote fit the situation.

"That would have been the summer *before* last. There were no concerts last summer, of course."

"You said that there are half a dozen biographies about him in the works. Why aren't you writing one of them? You knew him better than anybody."

"Too sadly true. I don't think I'm ready to ride his coattails into the *New York Times* best-seller list, thank you very much. I'll not repay his friendship in that way. Why, during his lifetime, someone approached his father—old Michael *was* still alive then—asking him all sorts of questions about Dermot's childhood. When he heard about it, Dermot was fit to be tied. 'If you want to know about *me*,' he said, 'ask *me!*' Oh, that wasn't a good day to be close to him. No, indeed!"

"Was he unforgiving?"

"He was generosity itself in most things. I've never known a more liberal spirit. But, on the subject of his own life, especially of his past, he demanded and insisted on holding a tight rein on all the options."

"A control freak?"

"Something of that. The real mystery is why would he bother. His life was as ordinary as could be. His father was a streetcar conductor and his mother was a kindergarten assistant in a private school. They were neither rich nor poor. Apart from his genius, he was a nobody. I think it was a matter of control for control's sake. Ray should have known that."

"Ray?"

"Oh, a friend of his. He went too far." Rankin wet his lips with the end of his tongue before going on. I made a guess and I was right. He *did* change the subject. "Mr Cooperman, it has come to my attention that your work here is at least partly a matter of security. Am I misinformed?"

"I've been trying to keep a low profile," I said.

"Oh, yes, I can appreciate that, dear boy. Does that mean that we are all under suspicion? I just want to be clear about that."

"Mr Rankin, the detectives over at 52 Division are in charge of the list of suspects. As for me, I'm still trying to figure out who reports to whom around here and why nobody talks in the elevators."

"In order to understand this place, Mr Cooperman, I suggest you arrange a tour of the CIA facilities in Langley, Maryland. It will act as a primer for operatives in these corridors."

"I'll remember that. I always like to see the bad guys get punished in the last reel."

"Oh, I can see that you are going to have a great success around here, Mr Cooperman."

Just after five o'clock, I picked up the information Vanessa had left for me, wished Sally a good weekend and headed out into the streets of Silver City without a care in the world.

For dinner, I wandered up to the Annex, and took my pick of the places that had survived my last stay in Toronto. There was the edge of audacity about my being in this neighbourhood: Sam, my older brother, lived here, and I saw him seldom enough that he would have insisted on my staying with him while I was in Toronto. Not that he enjoyed my company all that much, but he knew the right thing to do even when it killed him. I thought it might be better for me and my work to hold on to my independence and risk running into him on the street. But, avoiding Sam meant that I couldn't call my parents in Grantham. I knew that Ma's first question would be, "Have you called your brother, Sam, yet?" So, ignoring my brother was a double headache, one of those family kinds that nag at you whenever your mind clears of other things.

After my pasta and Italian coffee at Via Oliveto, I wandered the bargain-book bins at Book City. I bought a book with maps of what is called "Cottage Country." I tried to outfit my planned expedition, but beyond what I've said, my imagination let me down. I refused to believe that somewhere north of here I might find it difficult to buy certain things. I couldn't imagine what they might be. I wasn't going to the source of the Nile, after all. I had no need for gun bearers or cleft sticks. To be on the safe side, I bought a two-litre bottle of mineral water and some dried apricots. You never know. After walking along Bloor Street, past the poor of the city sitting in doorways begging the price of a night's peace, whether that was a mickey of rye or shelter, I began to feel weary. In spite of them, I felt snug in the heart of the great city. I looked in the windows of the stores on both sides of the street, nearly gave in to a sudden urge to visit Sam a few doors up Brunswick Avenue, but contained it by walking through Book City again with a vagrant mind. Well, not completely vagrant. Part of it at least was back on Belmont Avenue, where I had spent the night waiting for a steak to thaw on the kitchen counter and learning that love play can include the handling of a loaded gun. I was over-whelmed by the beauty of the covers of the books on view. I drank in the titles and authors' names. They all made a good case for their claims on my attention. Recent memories and the unpurchased delights before me rendered me useless for planning ahead. Only my stomach twisted with guilt as I saw all I had yet to read outweigh the little I had. I bought a paperback biography of Dermot Keogh to still the inner voice. I'd lied to Rankin earlier about having read the book. I'd only flipped through the pages. Here was a way to make my fib come true.

Outside, I wandered past the hungry and homeless, paid the pavement tax when I could think fast enough and moved off.

"Any loose change, mister?"

"Sorry, I've run out."

"There's a guy in that car wants a word with you."

"*Huh?*" A green car was parked at the curb.

"You heard me! Keep walkin'." Before I could turn to get a better look at the source of these marching orders, I felt my arm grabbed hard and a push from the rear propelling me off the curb.

"What the hell are you doing?"

"Shut up, Mr Cooperman." I'd been shoved into the back seat of a small car. It looked new enough and small enough to make this ridiculous. I'd been thrust tightly against the feet of a man already sitting in the back seat, when the man with his hand on my arm came into the car after me, slamming the door as the car moved out into traffic.

"What's this all about?" I demanded, not knowing what to expect by way of an answer.

"I said, shut the fuck *up!* I'll ask the questions."

"Okay, I'm not hard to get along with. Ask."

I tried to take inventory of my new-found playmates. There were three of them: the driver and the two beside me. None of them looked like he could take punishment from Mike Tyson on a good day. They didn't look like Moose Malloy in *Farewell, My Lovely*. They didn't look like dancers from *The Phantom of the Opera* either. They were youngish, with their hair short except on their faces, which were masked with carefully attended stubble beards.

"When are you going back where you belong, Cooperman?"

"As soon as I can. I've got business here, but I'd rather be fishing. Know what I mean?"

It was the driver who was doing the talking. He leaned over the gap between his seat and the passenger seat as he moved through the sluggish traffic. He was wearing a plaid shirt with a gold medallion hanging in the V opening. "It's not that we don't like your company around here. But your timing's bad. You wanna try it again, later?"

"Yeah, in about another ten years," added a voice from my left.

"Shut the fuck up, Sid!" said the man on my right. "Let Bernie do the talking."

"The both of you shut up!" I leaned forward, and before I quite knew what I was doing, I reached out and made a snatch for the steering wheel. The two in the back seat grabbed me fast, but the driver turned the wheel to correct for the spin he thought I'd given it. But I'd never reached the wheel, and the car went careering into a car in the outside lane. There was a back-jolting shock as we stopped, the crunch of metal, the sound of a horn and some unexpurgated expletives from the other three men in the car. I collected a punch from my two neighbours. Then a horn or two from the rear brought the driver of the car with a newly folded fender out into the street to bang on Bernie's window.

"Shit!" he said, opening his door. "I'll deal with you later!" he added, turning to me.

Traffic was stopped and other motorists came to offer their versions of what had happened. Traffic on Bloor Street was backing up. There was a group of four or five pedestrians crowding our car when I said a polite "Excuse me" to my captors, pushed forward the passenger seat and took to the street. Apart from more expletives from the bearded trio in the green car, I didn't hear another thing.

TWELVE

◖ Saturday

Dark and early the following morning, I paid my hotel bill and forced my way, against the grain of incoming traffic, north, out of the city, up the big highway to vacationland. Slowly, the six-lane freeway lost the city's strong gravitational pull. First to go were the fire hydrants and curbs, then the glimpses of parking lots and streetlights, and finally, I left the cement of shopping plazas behind. Grass and fields were a good exchange. Soon I was driving by cows watching me from under trees and horses running by white fences. With a stop at a place called Webers, where I ate the nearest equivalent to a chopped-egg sandwich—a hamburger and fries—I began enjoying my sudden freedom from Silver City. Two hundred kilometres north of the big city! Here TV was something you turned on when you felt like it, not a world that consumed you. If I told the kid flipping hamburger patties on the grill at Webers that Renata Sartori may have been killed so that somebody could move a little higher on the TV ladder to success, he'd say I was crazy. But crazy or not, here I was driving north to find hard evidence that my client was in fact at her cottage while Renata was being murdered in Toronto.

On the far side of Bracebridge, which stood exactly halfway between the Equator and the North Pole, according to an official plaque, I began seeing signs at the side of the road for a place called Norchris Lodge. I needed a place to stay on Lake Muskoka and Norchris Lodge was on Lake Muskoka, just where the Muskoka River empties into it from the highlands of Algonquin Park. I drove off the two-lane road I'd been on since Bracebridge, followed the signs and at a moderate speed made it to the gravel lane leading to the office. This was housed in a large log building with, as I later discovered, a monstrous stone fireplace. Through the boughs of trees and bushes, I could see glimpses of the lake, a beach, a water slide, docks, boats and a lawn with rustic bright red wooden chairs lined up to point out the view. It was early, the season hadn't properly started yet, so I couldn't see many guests looking at the lake.

Christopher McArthur and his wife, Norma, ran the lodge. They were a friendly young couple with several youngsters of various ages. They were all making last-minute repairs to window screens, door hinges, motorboat gear and sailboat rigging. I could hear a boy's voice calling: "Stuart! Renée! Abigail needs you!"

"That's Winston," Norma said. "He likes organizing things."

I told the McArthurs what I needed, and they told me what they could provide. Across the lagoon formed by the outlet of a creek into something they called "The Cut," Norma pointed out a cottage called "Nova" or was it "Scotia"? Here I could cook or not cook as it suited me. The main dining-room of the lodge, she explained, wasn't open for the season yet. I took a look at the cabin, which was luxurious compared to what I had been expecting. The shingles on the roof were partly covered by fallen pine needles. I could imagine what the place must look like under the falling leaves around Thanksgiving. I made a mental note.

Chris helped me get my stuff from the car. He was amazed that the Olds was still holding together. I guess there aren't many cars of that vintage still operating on the forty-fifth parallel. The bed was comfortable, the bathroom well appointed and in working order. Through my windows, I could see a rack of red canoes and kayaks of yellow and blue. There were paddleboats, and motorboats for the more ambitious. A cream-coloured float plane was moored to a dock just at the edge of my vision on the right. A Japanese-inspired bridge joined together the land cut in two by the lagoon-like harbour, which ran behind or in front of several of the cottages. I also had a clear view, not only of the lake, but also of a most inviting hammock strung between massive pines. I was beginning to like this job.

In the hammock, less than twenty minutes after signing in, and looking at my pale, bare toes, I opened the paperback I'd bought at Book City about Dermot Keogh. It was a slim volume with pictures reproduced from magazines and newspapers. It had the look of a book flung together in a hurry on a computer, or several computers, judging from the many changes in font. The author was described as "a sometime critic and music lover." The chapters carved Keogh's life into convenient phases. From childhood and youth, we went on to triumphs in London, Moscow and New York. I saved the part about his untimely death for later, like it was the icing from my birthday cake. I was beginning to feel guilty about the hammock. This Cooperman had no real aptitude for relaxation. I knew in my heart that I had to get back to work.

A plan began to form in my twisted little mind. I would locate, if I could, Vanessa's cottage. Inside, I would try to find some proof that she had been there within the last two weeks or so. I'd question the neighbours, speak to the gas-station attendant and otherwise try to place my client away from Toronto on the date of Renata Sartori's murder.

I drifted into a thoughtful reverie, and from there slid into something more dream-like. I was back in my car, driving through a pine forest, which surrendered to tundra and then to icefields. I kept checking the road-map to see whether I'd come too far. Whatever I saw on the map, it didn't convince me to turn the car around. The icefields became a frozen river, the right of way marked out by empty oil drums. There was a shimmer to the ice and snow, and I couldn't see the road properly even with sunglasses. There was no other traffic on the single track now over a bleak frozen lake. I tried to turn the car around and managed to get stuck in the slush and ice at the edge of the frozen highway.

I was awakened from this suddenly by the sound of a steam whistle. Was a ship caught in the ice? Was a boat crossing the frozen lake? Then I saw my white toes at the end of the hammock. I looked up to see several people along the waterfront watching a long, narrow steamship moving at a steady pace through The Cut. Built low to the water, without being wide in the beam, white-hulled, she cut across the background of trees. As Cary Grant used to say, she was yare: nimble, lively, trim and gorgeous; everything a steam yacht ought to be, with lots of dark wood and brasswork gleaming even from where I was lying. She let out another whoop as she began her turn into the mouth of the river.

"Beautiful, isn't she?" Norma McArthur was shielding her eyes from the sun to get a better look. "During the season, she puts in here, and you can go for a ride. She's chartered now. Private charter."

"What's her name?"

"*Wanda III.* She was built for Lady Eaton. You know, the department-store family."

"They still run her?"

"Oh, no. There were three *Wanda*s. I'm not sure about their history. If you want accuracy, there's a book inside. Let me see, the first was sold after she failed to get a kid to hospital in time to save his life. Very dramatic story. *Wanda I* raced from Port Carling to Bracebridge at twenty knots, but it wasn't fast enough for a burst appendix. The second *Wanda* burned in a fire at the time of World War I."

"Who owns number three?"

"The Muskoka Steamship and Historical Society. Local. But she's chartered right now to Hampton Fisher, the TV and newspaper tycoon, and his movie-star wife, Peggy O'Toole."

"*Peggy O'Toole?* I'd heard that she was up here somewhere."

"You're a fan, then?"

"Isn't everybody?"

"I've seen a few of her pictures. She was terrific in *Deadly Intent II*. Did you see that?" I told her I agreed, but didn't add that a few years ago, when she was still a young actress, I'd met her on location in Niagara Falls. She used to call me "Pistachio" for some reason. But that was many summers ago.

"Well, you just missed seeing her in the flesh. They say she loves running about in *Wanda*." Norma had the blonde good looks of her kids. When they stood together, which wasn't often, they looked like a set of pan pipes with a thatch of blond hair on top. Their skins already had the beginnings of a deep summer tan. Their mother quizzed me about my knowledge of Bracebridge. She recognized near complete ignorance when she tripped over it and proceeded to fill me in on where to buy everything from gas to worms. I knew that if the assignment up here threw me a curve, I could depend on Norma to help me out.

The opportunity for this came sooner than she might have guessed. I got her to go over the map with me, to fit Vanessa's instructions into the real estate and lakes at hand. I watched while she charted my course from the main road that passed by the lodge to Milford Bay. From here, she abandoned my map and found one of her own, which showed the shoreline in greater detail. "The place you're looking for, Benny, is not really that far away either by water or by car. Are you renting a boat or keeping your feet on terra firma?"

"I'll take the car this time. How long a drive is it?"

"Not more than half an hour. Forty minutes at the outside. The road is fairly good. It'll take you to the turnoff to Millionaires' Row. The road after that isn't much. I hope you're carrying a spare tire."

"Bad as that, is it? I'll watch myself. What's Millionaires' Row?"

"That's where the first families from the south, both Americans and Canadians, built their rather glorious summer homes. Mowed lawns down to the docks, white-painted rocks, big verandahs and probably antique tickertapes under bell jars in the studies. Lots of them were top executives of big corporations.

They'd come by train to Gravenhurst and be met by their private launches."

"Like *Wanda III*?"

"Like *Wanda I, II* and *III*."

"Interesting piece of local history. Thanks. Sorry I interrupted your instructions. After I pass the turnoff to Millionaires' Row?"

"You're looking for Evans's Marina on this bay where the fold crosses. You see the red square? That's Ifor Evans's little goldmine. He spells Ivor with an *f*, for some reason. He services most of the boats on the row and winters the boats that don't have their own boathouses. The ice up here after Christmas is murder on anything built on the water, Benny. Most of the people on the row lift their boats out of their slips with a vertical hoist, then lower them to rest on beams placed across the slips."

"Like placing a casket above an open grave, with tapes laid out for the lowering."

"Huh? Why, yes. Yes. I hadn't thought of it like that. Have you been up on Lake Muskoka before this, Benny?" She was naturally and warmly curious about people; I didn't get the impression that Norma had taken a course in public relations, even when she was trying hard not to look directly at my black eye.

Thirty-five minutes after the maps had been re-creased and returned to a plastic waterproof pouch, which she lent me, I was parking my car at the marina in Segwin Bay, looking across at the long promontory known as Moosehead Point. Ifor Evans, if that was he, was sorting out a package of stale worms with a large ruddy-faced man in a red plaid shirt and khaki shorts.

"Well, I'll talk to them, Mr Prendergast. I will. They're sold to me as fresh, and if they ain't fresh, that's a fraud plain and simple. Here, let me get you your money back. No sense paying—"

"You hang on to the money, Ifor. You know I've got no complaint against you. I've known you for over twenty years."

"That's right. I remember your father and mother very well, Mr Prendergast. Often think of 'em, yes, I do."

"Dad was like a hound in rut every spring, Ifor. Couldn't talk straight about anything else. 'Is the ice out of Segwin Bay yet, Ollie?' 'Do you think the old roof held up through that bad patch of heavy snow in late February? Maybe I should call Ifor just to be sure.' Oh, he loved these rocks up here something terrible." Mr Evans was eyeing me over the ample scarlet back of Ollie Prendergast. He was a tall, skinny man with wet grey hair plastered over a bare dome and large, almost pointed ears. His narrow chest looked as though it needed a smaller T-shirt. Both the cap on the counter and the shirt broadcast the name of a Texas oil company.

When Prendergast had stepped back into his mahogany open launch and puffed a few billows of yellow smoke towards me, Mr Evans waved a bony hand, then looked at me. "What can I do for you?" he said.

"You know Vanessa Moss?" I asked. Abruptly, Evans shifted from my side of the counter to the business side.

"Oh, there's a lot of people come in and out of here, mister."

"I'll bet. Norma McArthur says you've got a good thing going here."

"Norma McArthur's not starving either. You can tell her that from me. She doesn't have an empty cabin from July to October and that's a fact." He hadn't moved during this sudden, viper-like attack, but continued to study my face like it was a chart of a dangerous passage.

"About Vanessa Moss," I said, trying to look relaxed. "I work for her, and I'd like to rent a canoe to get over to her place."

"She give you keys?"

"I know where she keeps 'em." He was still sizing me up and not worrying much about being subtle. My knowing about the keys was a mark in my favour. He didn't show that I'd passed a test, but he wasn't watching me so closely after that. "You have a canoe for rent, Mr Evans? I won't need it for more than a couple of hours."

"You're not staying the night, then?" Information is power, and information is formed from trifles such as this.

"No, I don't think I will this time. Maybe later in the summer. How's the fishing been?" I didn't know much about fish, but I was able to affect an interest for Mr Evans. His monosyllabic answers to my questions suggested that he hated the slippery subject. One carton of bad worms could do it to him. Or maybe he just didn't want to waste his breath on a customer who only wanted to rent a canoe. He slipped his cap over his bald head and headed out the door.

"This way," he said without turning around. I picked up the pack I'd slipped my maps into and followed him to the side of the marina building, the part that faced away from the dock. "This thing passes for a canoe. She leaves it here. You know how to run 'er?" I could feel that he was going to have fun with me about my naval skills, but he was only going through the motions. There was no audience. As he lifted the green shell with its yellow interior, I could imagine him with an audience of cronies at his back. "You wear shoes like *that* when you go boating, boy?" The bite was there, but it was only—what's the word?—perfunctory. Evans didn't seem to enjoy his work the way Norma McArthur did. What was a strayed puritan doing in vacationland?

While he was feeding the length of the canoe out into the water beside his low dock, I slipped out of my shoes and pulled off my socks. I placed the paddle across the gunwales and placed one foot after the other into the centre of the craft, kneeling with my butt supported by one of the thwarts. I thought that by not sitting in the sternsman's seat, by play-ing the rules I remembered from Camp Northern Pine, I might score points even with Ifor Evans. Of course, he'd be the last person in the world to be impressed.

It had been several years since my knees had felt the ribs of a canoe cutting into them. I didn't try to put a date on it. I still remembered how to twist my paddle stroke at the conclusion of each stroke to keep me going in a straight line. But which straight line? I was heading towards the middle of the head-land in front of me, when I heard a shout behind me. Evans was standing on the end of the dock, his cap had been pulled off his head and he was pointing much farther to the right. I waved my thanks and corrected my navigation. I must have got it right, because the next time I looked back at the marina, Evans had vanished.

There wasn't a lot of water to cut across. I probably could have walked through the woods and got there in about the same time, but this was fun, and there isn't all that much fun in what I do, so I grab the moments when they appear.

I was on the water for less than twenty minutes. A proper canoeist could have done it in ten, and a powerboat could have sliced half of that time away. I took my heading on a brown inverted V I could see half-buried in greenery. As I got closer, it grew into the sort of cottage I had been expecting. I tried to remember the name she had called it; something with an Indian flavour. A few moments later, I could see a sign: Puckwana. It was painted in fading white on the side of a short cliff on the east end of the property. Between it and a small wooden dock lay a sandy beach. I headed the canoe there and gave a few strong strokes to bring the canoe as far up the beach as possible. I still wet my feet in the chilly sand. I pulled the bow higher out of the water and considered turning the thing over. I didn't bother: Ifor Evans couldn't see this far.

The cottage looked about eighty years old, but it was hard to judge such things this far north, where the winters are severe and the maintenance is neglected. It stood about twenty metres back from the shoreline, with bush around all sides, and about the same distance above the lake. I climbed first up that forty-five-degree slant on a path cut into the red soil and marked by whitewashed rocks, and then up rickety steps to the screened-in porch, which wrapped around three sides. I remembered where the keys were hidden and found them without having to send up an S.O.S. flare. Inside the screens, chairs, all high-backed, and some of them rockers, invited the visitor to relax to watch the way the light hits the water from this height.

Inside, I found all of the things that go with a summer cottage in Muskoka. In the large kitchen, there were a leftover ice-box and a kerosene refrigerator as well as an electric one. Three stoves told a similar history. The cupboard was as bare as Mother Hubbard's. The main room, which was bigger than the outside dimensions of the cottage suggested was possible, appeared lined with book-filled shelves running up well above my head. A fine old library ladder was asking to be rolled effortlessly along the wall. I tried it, and it coasted back to where it had been. I hadn't noticed the canted pine floor. The books bore the imprints of vanished publishers. A stack of early *New Yorkers*, pillars of *National Geographics*, ghosts from another era such as *Colliers, Esquire, Vogue, Life* and *Look*. There were three bedrooms. Two were made up, one topped off with a patchwork quilt, the third stripped, with the mattress rolled at the end of the bedstead. In short, as I said to begin with, this was a very cottagey sort of place: comfortable and without pretension. I liked it. If I wasn't under the pressure of work, I could easily have settled in. Here, at least, I had all of the books I lacked at the hammock back at the lodge.

The kitchen seemed to be the cottage's centre of gravity. I could imagine people sitting around the wide pine table discussing the ills of the world over mugs of hot chocolate on a chilly morning or settling the NTC fall schedule over a glass of lager on a balmy day in August. The fridge was clean but, except for a bottle of Smithwick's beer, empty. What I needed was a bag of milk with a date stamped on it. There was nothing to help me confirm Vanessa's presence here at the time Renata Sartori was being shot. The foot-pedal garbage can was empty, already lined with a new unsoiled bag. A telephone hung from the wall near the door. There was a dial tone when I lifted it. Nearby, a piece of cardboard had been stapled with names and numbers. I made a note of these and pocketed my jottings. Also nearby, hanging from a finishing nail on the edge of a cupboard, dangled several sets of keys, all very helpfully labelled. One set belonged to a cottage marked "Ed," others indicated "boathouse," "generator" and "Johnson 55."

Outside, I found a few paths. One led to a disused outhouse, which had been modernized in every way except in its plumbing: a citified toilet seat, a vase with dried flowers, even a David

Hockney reproduction on the back of the door. Another path led to the boathouse mentioned on the ring of keys. It was high and dry, half hidden in the new spring growth, with a spidery window that looked in on a small fibreglass hull and motor. A low grey structure of peeling paint and cobwebs hid a Delco generator under stunted cedar shrubs. All of the keys but the bunch marked "Ed" were accounted for. On a hunch, I pocketed them. After a last longing look at a couch inside the screened-in porch facing the lake, I walked down the hill to my canoe.

Back at the marina, Ifor Evans was peering into the dark, oily secrets of an outboard motor. I know he heard me coming, but he didn't turn around. I leaned my back against a warm wall and waited. When he finally looked up, he said, "I thought it would be you."

He went back into the motor with renewed interest. I picked up a rag and handed it to him the next time he tried to reach for it. I don't know why I try to be ingratiating, but I'm aware of doing it. It knocks off the rough corners of relationships. Sometimes, it puts me in the way of attracting more business. He took the rag from me and handed it back when he was through with it. I felt a little like an operating-room nurse, trying to outguess the surgeon on what he'd be needing next. I saw the hand reach out again and put the rag back in it.

"Wrench!" he said, in a tone that declared me a fool or an idiot. I obliged from the tools laid out on a board running between us. He took it from me, used it, and slapped it back into my hand again, like he was thinking of the operating room too. After ten or fifteen minutes of this, he looked up and out at me. He didn't say "Thanks," or anything as gauche as that. For a moment, he didn't say a thing, then: "That Faulkner kid just about ruined this new motor. Took him only an hour and a half doing doughnuts in the lake. His father should talk sense to him. Kid doesn't respect anything, least of all a good motor. Comes from a good family too. His people've been coming to the lake since my uncle Russell ran this place. We've been up here since the fall the S.S. *Waome* went down up by Beaumaris, coming out of Port Carling. I was a youngster. Nineteen and thirty-four." I wasn't surprised to discover that Evans was a bit of a moralist. The lake had its rules, and you disobeyed them at your own risk. Evans was a watcher and a judge. I could imagine him, when sufficiently moved, doling out summary justice to repeat offenders. But, I could be wrong. Maybe I was just tired of waiting for the moment to ask my questions. Before I could, he ploughed into me with one of his own.

"Why are you sticking your nose into this?" I caught my breath.

"Vanessa says she was up here when Renata Sartori was killed. I just had to see that what she said was true. Frankly, I haven't found her all that truthful in other things."

"Takes after her father. Always tellin' fish stories."

"Was it a fish story when she said she was at her place on Monday the fifteenth of May?"

"Oh, she was here all right. Took a briefcase in with her and some bread and cheese. Frozen dinners. She never could look out for herself proper like."

A second chance for a question of my own finally came when we were both holding Cokes from the big cooler on his dock.

"Who's Ed?" I asked.

"Ed? Which Ed do you mean?"

"I mean the one you thought of first. The Ed that gave his keys to Vanessa for safekeeping."

"Oh, *that*'d be old Ed Patel. Lawyer from town. His place is at the end of the path that the road peters out into." Here he indicated a direction with his right hand, vaguely in the direction of the parking lot, which was the official end to this spur of the highway.

"Why would Ed Patel give his keys to her?"

"What are friends for? Ed was like an uncle to Stella while she was growing up." He smiled to himself at the picture in his mind. Then his face darkened. "Ed's been in and out of hospital for the last year. He's in a bad way. Vanessa told him she'd see to his place."

"She doesn't take the time to see to her own place. How is she going to look after his?"

"You don't miss much, for a . . ."

"She hasn't had her boat out this year yet. There's not much in the cupboards."

"Don't I know it. Oh, she came with a few groceries when she was up a few weeks ago, even bought bread, cheese and juice from the marina like I told you, but she didn't bring any of the basics, you know, flour, soda, sugar, onions, potatoes. Just frozen stuff and a few boxes of Kraft Dinner was all she carried with her. She usually treats herself better than that."

"So, you've been looking after Ed Patel's place as well as hers?"

"Had to be done. A place can go to wrack and ruin in short order here at the lake. If I hadn't kept the roofs of both places cleared of snow last winter, by now there'd be nothing you could salvage from either place. Ed found this place for Mrs Moss and acted as her lawyer for the conveyancing. He's got an office in town."

"Which town would that be? Port Carling? Bracebridge? Gravenhurst?"

"Ha! Funny you said that. Ed used to keep offices in all three, but he's closed the ones in Port Carling and Gravenhurst. Even the one in Bracebridge's closed most times I go by. Now that Alma's gone."

"Who?"

"Secretary."

"Oh. He's that sick, is he?"

"You don't go home again when you're as sick as Ed is. I go see him once a week. We play cribbage. You know."

"Hard?"

"Oh, he's game. Yes, he's game, but failing. Nothing left but the spirit holding him together."

"Bracebridge hospital?"

"N'yup. Good little hospital. Had my gallstones out there. Dr MacGruder."

"Vanessa says there are other NTC people, you know, television people, up here on this part of the lake." Then I remembered something. "There was a block of property. I forget the name, but the estate sold cottages on this lake to NTC people."

"You're talkin' about the trust Ernie Bradings set up. Aye, Ernie let in the TV people with a vengeance. We got all sorts. Most of them bought their places. Others have long leases. Some don't know the sharp end of a boat from the round end. Some do. Fellow named Trebitsch has three boats and he keeps them in good condition. Has cellphones in 'em. He tells me he's an important man in Toronto. Says he's a *newsman*. I guess he is; I see his picture in the paper. But I don't hold much stock in getting your picture in the paper. I think if you set your mind to it, it can't be too difficult. Think Mr Trebitsch learned about watercraft from Dermot Keogh, the cellist. Dermot's boats were always well kept. Bob Foley knows his engines. But those friends of his, like that Mr Devlin and Mr Rankin, they're worse than both the Faulkner boys put together."

"How did Devlin get a Bradings Trust property? He's a lawyer, not a TV person."

"His father bought a place not too far from here after the war. No connection with Bradings, except when they went fishing together. Should be a law who can run a boat. The way I see it, the lake's the same as the highway. You obey the rules or the Provincial Police'll run you in. That's funny about Mr Devlin too, because I heard from Dermot that he's a keen sailor. Has a yacht down in the city. I wouldn't have guessed it. For a time there, Mr Devlin was ruining a motor every time he came up to visit Dermot. But then—that Dermot Keogh was a smart feller—he cut Mr Devlin off. Wouldn't have him at his place any more. Didn't much like Rankin either there for a time."

"When would that have been, Mr Evans? Dermot Keogh died a year ago last April. When did Devlin and Rankin become scarce around the lake?"

"Well, let me see . . ." Ifor pulled at his chin a minute to see if he could get his dates and tourists straight. "It would have been in the late spring of the year before last. Around June, I'd say. Didn't see Mr Devlin or Mr Rankin on the lake after that." He thought a minute as though checking on his facts a second time. Then he shook his head: "Mr Devlin never did know how to dress up here. I think he's the only man been up here wearing a three-piece suit since Mr Eaton died." Ifor Evans was not given to laughing at his betters, but he came close as that vision flashed through his head.

After that, he seemed to tire of giving away so much information. He leaned into me with a few questions, which I tried to answer as honestly as I could. He knew about the murder of Renata Sartori, and seemed to accept the theory that Renata had been killed by mistake, that Vanessa had been the intended target. "She was a very nice woman, that Renata Sartori. She loved it on the lake when Dermot drove her up for a weekend. Mr Keogh told me he might just marry that girl. That's what he told me sitting right where you're sitting. 'I could do worse,' he said. 'I could do a great deal worse.' Pity about that woman. She wasn't very old, was she?"

A few minutes of this went by, with the professional questioner answering all of the questions, and the amateur resting his hands at the back of his head. At last, I placed my empty pop can in the barrel designated for bottles and cans and took my leave, jiggling the keys to Ed Patel's place in my pocket as I headed up the trail a piece.

THIRTEEN

The road I followed from the parking lot was less than a road but more than a path. You could call it a lane. The trees arching down around me from above were very lane-like, and the twin ruts that made their parallel way through the bush were rather road-like, but the bumps, roots and outcroppings of rocky Precambrian Shield made it hard to imagine anything not on tank tracks making its way up and down this stretch of whatever it was. The birds didn't seem to mind it. Animals kept me company, just beyond my actually seeing them. I could hear them all right, off in the bracken or among the trees, and the sounds were scaled small enough so that only once or twice did I think I might be in trouble from a man-eating chipmunk or a rogue rabbit.

The trail led through a grove of dense white pine. It must have been second growth, but it looked substantial, even commercial. My path ended, to my complete surprise, at the back end of a beautiful, dark blue, antique Bentley. I nearly fell down and worshipped. It was sheltered under a rustic lean-to with a covering that was half canvas and half blue plastic. I would have been less surprised to have found a sleigh and eight tiny reindeer. But, on reflection, I thought I *am* less than a few hundred metres, as the trout swims, from Millionaires' Row. I shouldn't be surprised at anything seen in these latitudes.

The cottage, painted a forest green, lay just beyond the lean-to. Like Vanessa's, it was screened in along three sides, which tended to show the varmints out there who was boss. The key

I'd taken from Vanessa's kitchen turned smoothly in the Yale lock, and I found myself in a brand new way to define what a Muskoka cottage ought to be. There were only four rooms, two of them bedrooms. The kitchen, a dark, gloomy hole, had been added as an afterthought, but it had made up for that in being used to capacity. There were signs of years of cooking at high temperatures. Under the counter I found gadgets for storing pot lids and drying tea-towels. Out a rear door, I found large cooking pans that had been placed outside possibly for the wildlife. I could imagine that a family of raccoons licked many a platter clean of congealed or carbonized fat and grease.

The biggest room was a comfortable one, filled with wicker easy chairs, couches and low rattan tables. The small shelf of books was dedicated to old law reports and to ancient novels of the Book of the Month Club, featuring *Forever Amber, Leave Her to Heaven* and *The Sun Is My Undoing*. A couple of philosophical volumes such as *Meetings with Remarkable Men*, by G. I. Gurdjieff. There were a few others, more modest in size, written in Hindi or Urdu, featuring blue-faced ladies serving platters of sweetmeats to lounging young men wearing robes of office or of pleasure. The focus of the room was a fieldstone fireplace of monumental proportions. The large opening was buttressed by a pair of massive andirons. The ashes from the most recent fire were cold; the remaining scrap of newspaper that I found bore no date. So much for detection, I thought. And what was I doing here anyway? Ed Patel wasn't a suspect. Did I still hope to find a gas receipt with Vanessa's signature on it? And why here? Just because Vanessa had keys to the house? Patel's name had come up too often and from too many directions for me to ignore it without losing sleep. Vanessa knew him. Jesse, the technician, said that Foley knew him. One likes to be thorough, I muttered through clenched teeth.

I stood up and heard the snap of my knees. A familiar voice whispered his familiar refrain in my inner ear all about age and futility. This fireplace was as free of clues as Vanessa's across the lake. I cursed the fireplace silently as I steadied myself on the rough wooden floor. But then I smiled. My powers were more acute than I realized: above the fireplace hung an old gun. It was a shotgun of some kind. Twelve gauge, I thought. At that point I felt an itch at the back of my knees that has been in the past, if not infallible, at least a fair guide to what was going on. I was suspicious enough to look for something that might not smudge fingerprints if there were any. A plastic shopping bag served the purpose very well. I took the gun off the wall, keeping the plastic between me and the gun. A dog owner would recognize it as a variation on pooping and scooping. I smelled the twin barrels. They smelled like the barrels of a shotgun. I couldn't tell whether it had just been fired or if it fired the last shot in the First World War. Certainly, it looked old enough to have been fired in that war, if shotguns weren't banned by international agreement.

Since I needed a bigger plastic bag than the one I'd first hit upon, I looked into a low cupboard to the right of the fireplace. In addition to a big Mountain Co-op bag, I discovered an old cardboard box containing eight live shells for the gun. It had originally held twice that many. I slipped the gun into the larger bag, and slipped the box of shells into the one I'd been using instead of rubber gloves. As I brandished these trophies, I thought, These might earn me some slack with the Toronto cops. They couldn't throw me out on my ear if I handed them the murder weapon, now, could they? Of course, maybe Muskoka cottages abound in displayed firearms. I don't know. I'd have to wait to see whether their eyes lit up when the tests came back from the Forensic Centre.

Beyond the gun, I didn't find much of interest in Ed Patel's cottage. I saw where he kept his car keys. I found another set with the name Dermot Keogh on a piece of cardboard attached by a string. What were they doing there? I wondered, as I wandered from one of the bedrooms into the other. Patel was a lawyer before he took sick, wasn't he? I tried to remember. Offices in three towns to begin with, now dwindled down to one. I decided that I might remember better if I stretched out on one of the beds and closed my eyes for ten minutes. I did that. Then I kept them closed for another twenty minutes, and awakened with a start when a clock in the big room went off, sounding the hour, which was just four o'clock when I checked it with my watch.

I felt better for the nap and closed up the cottage, taking my pieces of evidence with me through the bush back along the path to the marina parking lot and my car. Ifor Evans wouldn't hear of my paying him for the use of the canoe, and I left the marina promising to see him again before the summer was over. Driving back to the lodge, I decided on a detour to Bracebridge to buy a bathing suit. I had been moving around this planet without one for several years and I thought it was time to end that situation. The huge shopping malls on the highway going into Bracebridge swelled with promise under the afternoon sun. My greed for camping stoves, jackknives, sleeping bags and tents was tested by the reality that these delightful objects were all too readily at hand. I only hoped the stores contained the solution to my more modest request, a bathing suit in my size.

The parking lots on both sides of the road were nearly full. Business was good for Canadian Tire, the beer and liquor stores and the supermarket. I found a pair of black trunks, paid for them and wandered out on the steaming asphalt grinning to myself. I liked swimming, but I hardly ever made the opportunity.

"*Pistachio!*"

"Huh?" I looked in the direction of the voice. A pretty woman was walking towards me. Her smile opened out and overwhelmed me. There's only one person who calls me that.

"Pistachio! Don't you *remember* me?" My mind was still churning, trying to fit the memory into the right channel. By now she was stopping in front of me, blonde and, well, beautiful. In a moment, the smile would begin to lose its lustre if I didn't show signs of recognition. She took off the large sunglasses so I could see her eyes.

"*Peggy!*" I said, the thing hitting me at the last possible moment. "*Peggy O'Toole!* How are you?" It was my dear Peggy from the case I'd helped work on in Niagara Falls some years ago. I'd hoped to run into her, but since the great north woods don't work the way streets in Grantham do, I'd pretty well given up any hope of running into her at the intersection of Beaver Meadow and Muskrat.

"Gosh, Benny, it's so *good* to see you! I can't get over it. You *remembered* me! I was just a little girl when you saw me last. It gives me goosebumps just thinking about all that time that's gone. Remember? Niagara Falls and all the trouble we had making *Ice Bridge* with Mr Sayre. You remember *Jim Sayre*, I hope? The director? He, Mr Sayre, is coming up to see us this summer, Benny. Will he be surprised to see you!"

"I hope I'm still around, but it looks—"

"You'll just *have* to be around. You're *family*, Benny. Even if we hardly ever see you. Even my mother asks about you. And Mr Sayre, why he thinks . . . You look wonderful, Benny!"

"You look wonderful yourself, Peggy."

"Go on. In this light? I look . . . well, frankly, I don't care how I look. Gosh it's good to see you!"

"You've grown up fine, Peggy. I've even followed your career. I boasted to my mother that I knew you when."

"What did she say?"

"She reminded me of when my father sold his original shares of IBM. I guess she thinks I let you get away."

"You'll never get away from me, Pistachio. You can tell her that from me. But, what are *you* doing here? You can't be working on a case. Not *here*."

"You'd be surprised. I'm only here for another—"

"Benny. What are you doing now? Right *now?*"

"I'm talking to—"

"I don't mean that. You have to meet Hamp! You've never met him, and I've been talking to him about you for years. *My God!* Is it *ten years?*" It was more than ten, but I wasn't going to tell her. The years had been good to her. She not only looked as lovely as she is in the movies, but she even looked happy. I was glad of that, because I remembered her as a troubled young woman when we'd first met. But that was before her marriage to Hamp Fisher and all of his eccentricities.

The upshot of the conversation in the parking lot was a short walk from where I'd parked my car, following the white wraparound hem of Peggy's skirt to where she'd parked her Range Rover. It was like Vanessa all over again. In no time, together with my newly purchased bathing suit, I was sitting beside Peggy as she shifted her gears up and down the highway that ran from Bracebridge to her cottage somewhere beyond the point where I'd earlier turned off the road to Evans's Marina. Only about half of her gear changes were absolutely necessary, but it was nice to see that she took her driving seriously. There was also a fair amount of Peggy's tanned legs visible as she managed the gears and adjusted the outside mirrors on both sides of us. Further, there was a kind of paralysis in my breathing when she turned to check the road behind her for rivals to her mastery of the road. The strain on her buttons tweaked my masculinity by its nose, or something. I was feeling guilty about looking, since I'd just been made a member of the family circle, but my hormones are always speaking out of turn. They have no sense of decorum. I sometimes think that my sexuality is like having an idiot brother who follows me around. I make excuses for him, I apologize for him, but there he sits, drooling. I try to ignore him, attempt to engage the female of my acquaintance in elevated chat, but his demented leer gets in the way when she so much as breathes or leans over to improve the position of the Rover's floor mat. He is so incorrigible at times, I've considered sending him away, but most of the time I think with kindness and understanding he can still be managed at home.

An hour later, I was aboard *Wanda III*, taking a short spin around Lake Muskoka. Well, not really a spin. *Wanda III* doesn't spin. She's a lady, and she takes things more calmly than the powerboats and motor launches we could see coming up and down a narrows on our right.

"This is Millionaires' Row," Hamp said, pointing at the huge summer homes of the wealthy of another age. I tried to remember what Norma McArthur had told me about Millionaires' Row back at the lodge. Funny that Hamp should be pointing it out. His cottage was as large and as impressive as any of these hundred-year-old follies. "That's where Sir John Craig Eaton built his summer house. He kept the lawn in front cut as though he were in the city. Over there, behind the white boathouse, lived Sir Wilfred Chambers. I hear that he had to blast away a small mountain to put in a tennis court back in the 1920s. Next to it, with the green gingerbread, is the house of Ettie Cohen. You know, the *Titanic* survivor? Ettie went into a lifeboat only when Captain Smith insisted. She wrote a book about it. This place was built for her by an admirer from Seattle. Lumber baron. Now look up on the hill beyond the point. There's the place where General Fields, the breakfast cereal man, and the heiress of his chief rival built a secret love nest with twenty rooms. They thought nobody up here in Canada would know that they were not—what's the phrase?—legally united."

I remembered hearing that Hampton Fisher was a bit of a prude years ago. He was a lot of other things too, including being the closest thing to a genius to enter the boardrooms of newspapers he controlled. He had always been a paradox: a guy who hated germs and shunned society, but who went swimming under the polar ice cap and climbing in the Himalayas. I remembered that Vanessa had told me he set up the NTC network himself and still owned a controlling share of the voting stock. Years ago in the Falls, I never got a good look at him because he never went out. Once, I was watching Peggy shoot a scene in front of the American Falls. When I turned around and looked up, there was Hamp Fisher watching the same thing from his penthouse balcony. It struck me then as a little eerie, but I could never figure out why.

Fisher had aged well. His hair was too long for a boardroom. Still, the grey temples reminded me of the old "Men of Distinction" ads I'd seen in ancient magazines in people's summer cottages. His yachting outfit was immaculate too, like another page in the same old magazines, but he brought the effect off with panache. He didn't look as though he had his drinking water flown in from California any longer. Maybe he never had. At the moment, he and Peggy were sitting together in white wicker chairs, like the one I was sitting in, at the rail of *Wanda III*. We were shaded from the afternoon sun by a canvas cover of stretched blue duck, through which *Wanda's* smoke stack protruded into the air. We were in the open air, too, of course, sipping drinks from a table set up aft of the funnel. Hamp was drinking Perrier, Peggy, coffee from a tall silver Thermos, and I, ginger ale in a crystal tumbler with the name of the ship embossed in the glass. There were others aboard, too, although I had only seen one of them when I came up the gangplank.

After hearing about the rich and famous of Millionaires' Row, I heard about how they loved Muskoka, how they were thinking of building a cottage when the lease on the one they had expired. Hamp made an attempt or two at asking me about me, but I couldn't get up enough steam. Peggy kept interrupting me and buttering up my past. She kept quizzing me about the case I was working on. After a while, I sketched it in for them in broad outline. Of course both had heard about the murder, and Hamp knew the people at NTC. Peggy recognized the parallels with the movie *Laura*, and moving to it was as good a way as any to get away from the more obscure facts of my investigation. Peggy launched into an appreciation of the face structure of Gene Tierney. "It's her jaw, really. Any good orthodontist could have spoiled all that."

When I got the chance, I wondered out loud about their presence on the lake. "Isn't there a need for both of you to be elsewhere? Aren't the boardrooms and the sound stages crying out 'Where are they?'"

"Let 'em holler," said Peggy, and Hamp grinned his endorsement. "We both worked flat out this winter, Benny. I did two movies, back to back, no rest in between. And Hamp has been trying to step back and let his organization run things. What's the use of setting up a big structure if you don't stand back and see whether it works or not? Oh, I've brought up a few scripts with me, but, to be honest, I haven't read one of them. Hamp sometimes reaches for one of his boxes, but he knows better than to do it when I'm around."

"You see the tyranny I live under, Mr Cooperman. Not a minute to call my own."

"But you have had time to do some scuba diving, I understand."

"Not this year. Last year's experience rather spoiled it for me. Oh, I've made a few small dives, just enough to keep the McCordick brothers happy. I get my diving gear from them over in Bala. But last spring, at the end of April, I dived a wreck here on the lake."

"The only wreck I know about is the S.S. *Waome*, which sank coming out of Port Carling in the mid-1930s."

"That's the one! She sank in a freak squall in the fall of 1934. It was like a water spout. Came out of nowhere. *Waome* heeled over to port, water rushed in through the mooring chocks. She lies in eighty feet of water. I've seen her. By the end of the summer, I expect there will be few serious divers who *haven't* seen her."

"Why all the interest?" I wondered out loud.

"I expect it has to do with Dermot Keogh's death. There are morbid sensation hunters even among skilled scuba divers, Ben."

"I guess you're right."

"She looked a lot like the *Segwin* that still plies the lake. But *Waome* was built with big glass windows and large freight doors close to the waterline. When the squall heeled her over, the water rushed in faster than I can tell it. Three were lost, the captain suffered a heart attack, the rest of the crew swam to a nearby island. In the summer, the steamship would have had twenty, maybe fifty passengers, but this was early October, so there was only one. One of the ship's officers, a man named Thompson, tried to rescue him from the saloon, but the door was closed on them by the water and both were trapped. The company called on divers from Prescott, on the St Lawrence, to get the bodies. When I saw her, she was still in one piece, lying right side up. Hadn't let the cold, dark waters break her up."

"Was Dermot Keogh on that dive?"

"It was his idea. We planned the dive summer before last when Peggy and I were staying with him, while we were looking for a place last summer."

"It was horrible," said Peggy. "I get goosebumps just thinking about it. We had to go to a hotel in Bracebridge, just to get away from the media. Some holiday."

"Were you in the water with him when it happened?" I watched Hamp Fisher look straight at me, as though he was trying to figure out how much of this I wanted to hear. Then he looked away in the direction of the funnel and sipped his Perrier.

"Dermot was a good diver for an amateur," he said. "He had been checked out on all of the equipment we took with us. The McCordick brothers know their equipment and are careful who they rent it to. I hadn't leased *Wanda III* yet, so we were using a Sea Ray 200 with two inflatable rafts. There were six of us: two to stay topside and four divers. Dermot and I were teamed up, and Jeff Hetherington and Penny Freeman were buddies."

"She's about five seven," contributed Peggy, "with short brown hair. She still has traces of an English accent after thirty years in Canada." I nodded to show that I was appreciative of the details.

"Hetherington is a young fellow we met that summer," Hamp said. "He's a student, or was one, in Niagara Falls. We met him at the marina when I was renting the Sea Ray. He had learned scuba diving on a holiday in Belize, but hadn't tried Lake Muskoka yet."

"I met Penny just about where I met you this afternoon, Benny. My shopping bag split and I had apples and lemons rolling all over the asphalt. She repacked her things and gave me one of her plastic bags and helped me load up the car. I brought her back for drinks. She learned her scuba diving in Alberta of all places." Peggy was smiling at the memory.

"So, the four of you were pretty experienced?"

"I don't know whether Penny or Jeff had ever worked at that depth or had to carry their own lights before. The waters near the reefs off Belize are very clear, Ben. You can see for miles. But here. Ha! It's black as deep outer space down there."

"How did you know where to dive?"

"The wreck's had a buoy marking the spot for years now. Once we'd tied the boat and the rafts together, we lowered a long anchor line as well. We used the rope attached to the marker as our guide rope. Again, I can't emphasize the blackness of this water once you get down a few feet."

"And Dermot Keogh was okay all this while? No problems?"

Hamp Fisher laced his long fingers together around a knee as he picked his words. "We'd been down nearly twenty minutes before he started having trouble. We'd found *Waome* on her bottom, still in one piece, as I said. We did a survey from stem to stern. We located one of the open freight doors, and taking turns in pairs, we went inside. Jeff and Penny went first. When it was our turn, I followed Dermot into the ship. We went down through the freight door and through the lower saloon to the companionway leading to the main saloon. It was hard getting through the stairs, so again, I followed Dermot. When I got there, that is, in the upper saloon, I found Dermot had spit out his mouthpiece."

"You mean there was trapped air inside?"

"No, Ben, we were both under water and at about eighty feet. You understand, for an experienced diver, the sight of your buddy with his mouthpiece out isn't as immediately frightening as it might seem. We learn to make adjustments and to hold our breath while doing them. The air supply is always ready and waiting. But that wasn't what Dermot was trying to do. He was trying to unhook his tank, his weights, everything. I went over to him, caught up his mouthpiece and tried to help. That's when he lunged at me. I say lunged, it was more like fending me off, a warning to keep my distance. I swam around behind him. Again, I found his breathing tube and held it in place. This time, he couldn't reach me with his hands, but he was wilder now, more frantic. Somehow, he pushed me away again and the diving mask came free. And he'd unhooked the main belt. Thinking there might be something wrong with his air supply, I took off my own and tried to fit it over his mouth. He beat me off again. That's the part I never could understand. His brain must have been confused. That's when I started to panic myself. You see, we were swimming free. Apart from the buoy line and the anchor rope, there was no contact with the diving raft. Dermot was smaller than I, but I wasn't able to fix the mouthpiece in place again, and he was breathing out what air he still held. I couldn't think of what to do. The other pair were at least a minute and a half away from me, if they were still hanging around the freight door. I tried again to approach him. I shouldn't have come at him from the front. He got an arm around my neck even before I could find his air supply. Once he got me around the neck, I dropped the light I was carrying and it left us in relative darkness. Using my feet, I was able to free myself. I rescued the lamp and kept on swimming until I reached the outside of the hull. I indicated that Dermot was in trouble, gave the danger signal, and we swam back inside. By that time, Dermot had passed out. He was floating under the ceiling of the saloon. He'd jettisoned his tank and weights. At least we didn't have to fight him any more. We got his air going again and strapped the tank back on his back. As quickly as we could, we evacuated him, got him out of *Waome* and back up to the raft. It could have been as much as three minutes in all. As soon as we got him on the raft, Jeff started the usual resuscitation routine. We took turns. Meanwhile, the boat crew called through to Bracebridge for an ambulance. We kept up the artificial respiration until the paramedic team relieved us. By then, we were back in harbour at Port Carling." After saying this, Hamp was still. His eyes scanned the far side of the lake.

After nearly a minute, I asked, "He never came round?"

Hamp Fisher shook his head.

FOURTEEN

Hamp Fisher's account of the death of Dermot Keogh quite dampened conversation for a good ten minutes after he finished. While looking at the wooded headlands alongside *Wanda III*, I thought of Wally Skeat, the Grantham TV broadcaster, from whom I'd first heard the name of the cellist at the end of April, the first anniversary of his death. I watched Hamp as he refilled my glass. I watched him with Peggy and got a good sense of their relationship through small things like the way he refreshed her drink and cleared away crumbs on the sun-dappled table with his napkin. Small things, but they penetrated to the heart of his affection for her. Peggy remained a little aloof from this, but I didn't doubt her attachment to him. Again it was little things: when he pulled on a sweater, the way she tucked the label in at the back.

It was a big, comfortable navy blue sweater from Cornwall. I saw that much before the white tag was tidied away. I was wishing that I had brought something warm with me. A rank of dark clouds had come between us and the sun. It looked temporary, but my shoulders and back felt the chill. I began rubbing my elbows, I thought with some subtlety, but Peggy got up and returned with a white Aran sweater and another for herself.

"You mentioned the two divers who went down to the wreck with you and Mr Keogh. Were many of his friends chosen as casually? I gather that they went on the fatal dive simply because they were in the right place at the right time."

"What you say was certainly true of them. They just happened to be passing through. Diving that early in the year doesn't often find dozens of enthusiasts to choose among. But, in general, you're right too. Lots of Dermot's friends were just ordinary people he happened to like."

"Oh, Hamp, Dermot had other kinds of friends too. There were people he met at NTC and from Sony in the States, sure, but there were other musician friends, architects, painters, horse-breeders—you name it. But, usually they came up later in the year. About this time. Just when the weather is perfect and the last thing you want to think of is a sound stage."

"What people from NTC?" I asked.

"There was quite a colony here last year and the year before that." Hamp covered his chin with both hands, as though that helped him to see the faces from those vanished summers. "Let's see, let's see."

"Philip Rankin came up a lot our first summer, although we didn't see much of him." Peggy was adding a plastic nose guard to her sunglasses. "He says he's allergic to the sun."

"Yes, and Ken Trebitsch comes up regularly. He rebuilt an old boathouse and lives above a small fleet. Remember, he introduced that lawyer, Ray Devlin. Dermot took quite a shine to Devlin. In the end it worked out to be an important relationship. Devlin's firm handled all of Dermot's contracts in the U.S. and in Canada. Eventually, Ray designed Dermot's will."

"When would that have been?"

"Oh, well before the spring three years back, I'd say. Yes, Ray was on the scene quite a bit then, but not here the following summer. Old Evans at the marina thought Rankin and Devlin should be banned from operating boats on the lake."

"Oh, Hamp, Ray was lots of fun, once you got him to shed that bogus courtroom manner of his. You couldn't ask him to pass the salt at first without being cross-examined." We laughed at that.

"Yes," Hamp said, nodding his head. "We missed him the summer before last. He wasn't around really. There are always other people. One forgets. I will say this, Dermot thought him a very likeable chap."

"But you didn't warm to him, Hamp?"

"*Me?* Oh, I'm still a bit stand-offish, you know. Habit of a lifetime. I have to work at it. I work hard, and I've got a good teacher." Peggy took Hamp's hand. They smiled at one another and then both, a bit sheepishly, at me.

"We thought we'd drive to the Inn at the Falls for dinner, Benny. I hope that you'll be able to join us." I tried to make an excuse, but it was torn away before I'd fixed it firmly to the mast. Hamp knew that the kitchen at Norchris Lodge wasn't in operation yet and that if I wasn't going to eat with them, it was because I'd chosen to eat elsewhere alone. When he put it like that, I accepted. What else could I do?

But first, we returned to the cottage. "Cottage" isn't really an adequate word for this mansion in the woods. It was made of squared logs with fieldstone and other masonry at strategic intervals. The massive fireplace had openings in four rooms. The interior was simply furnished except when you examined the pine closely and discovered that even the kitchen chairs were Early Canadian antiques. While wandering about on my own, according to my hosts' invitation, I discovered a series of rooms in the back. They were filled with electronic equipment —phones, fax machines, computers, e-mail, the Internet—all manned by three men in shorts and T-shirts. Hamp's empire was awake and active, even while Hamp was cruising in *Wanda III*.

After a swim, the inaugural swim in my new suit, off Peggy and Hamp's dock, I opened the Dermot Keogh book where I'd folded down the page. I let the strong, late-afternoon sun dry me as I half-dozed on a white deck chair. Later, as soon as I'd showered and dressed, I excused myself for an hour or two while they read or napped. I told them I was going off to "explore." I didn't know exactly what I was going to explore, but I was feeling a growing connection between pieces of what I had been learning up here. It was the sort of exploration I had to do, or I wouldn't be able to sleep. I'd been there before. There may have been no connection between the deaths I was hearing about, but I knew I had to exhaust the possibility. Peggy offered me a butterfly net to aid me in my great work. More practically, Hamp let me borrow his sleek black BMW, since my car was still back in town.

The marina in Bala was less rustic than Ifor Evans's establishment on Segwin Bay. The paint on the clapboard siding was fresher, the sheds for stored boats looked more permanent. It was the same lake, of course, but the highway passing through Bala carried more traffic. A large sign advertising a big American-built outboard motor dominated the cedar-shingled roof of the boathouse. It eclipsed the older and much more modest sign: McCordick Brothers' Marina. There were extensive docking wharves, most of them empty on this sunny afternoon. There was a sense of languid bustle, of sun-fried picnic hampers, of children smeared with sunblock, of orange life preservers and of the faint smell of gasoline on the wind. Sun reflected from glass, chrome and water as the remaining flotilla in the slips moved with the breeze off the lake, metal rings sounding musically on the tall masts. I parked where Hamp's car could be seen and walked into that back part of the marina sacred to scuba diving. Here were tanks and suits, regulators, masks, fins and other paraphernalia of the deep. I asked a sun-bleached blond kid in cut-off jeans who was in charge of the underwater gear.

"I'll get Stan," he said, and off he went like Peter Rabbit through a cabbage patch. He didn't come back, but he sent along a lean six-footer in a white T-shirt with the printed slogan "Charles Wells, premium bitter" sitting over his heart. He was tanned all over, as far as I could see. From the look of him, you'd have thought the McCordicks would put him on the pink cabin-cruiser runabout detail. He couldn't miss with the ladies.

I was frank with him to start with; gave him my name and calling. What the hell, I thought, maybe he'll enter into the spirit of my investigation. I gave him a short version of what Hamp Fisher had told me about the dive to the S.S. *Waome* a year ago. He remembered the whole thing, of course, from the coming of the Provincial Police to the exit of the reporters and TV trucks. Stan relived the event as he'd experienced it, and, what the hell, I let him. Then he asked me some good questions, which I tried to answer precisely.

"If the equipment was rented from us," he theorized, "then maybe we've got a record of which items went along with them to the dive site." I gave him the date of the dive, which Fisher had mentioned, and he went to a log attached to a slanted desk, about chest high. It was mostly a record of reservations to rent and appointments for dives using McCordick boats, rafts and other equipment. He turned backwards from the half-filled page that was open, flipping back and back again towards the front of the book.

"Here it is," said Stan with his finger in the middle of the page. "Yeah, it was quite an expedition: two rafts and four sets of wet suits and tanks. Mike, who was here then, wrote this. Mr Keogh made the order, let's see, three, no four days before. He was picking up the tab for everybody. Vern and Will McCordick thought the world of Mr Keogh."

"Who ended up paying? After the accident?"

"There's a note written by Mike. 'Paid by cheque: B. Foley.'"

"Bob Foley? Dermot's man of all work. So, he was up here for the dive on *Waome*."

"On most dives they take a crew of people to work the topside. If they had a boat and two rafts for four divers, one topside person would be the minimum. Two would be better. Let me see if I can get ol' Mike on the phone. He's waitering this summer at the King and Country. That's a pub outside Port Carling." Stan started on the phone, and I began examining swimming masks and fins, all of which were new to me. The marina carried professional equipment, with only a few items intended for small fry. I'd missed underwater sport when I was young enough to wear the equipment with no self-consciousness. The sun through the big window looking over the lake was lower than it had been, although I had been there only a short time. Its effect on the boats and wharves was still strong, daunting even. I could feel the sweat in the creases of my arms. I'd have to invest in sunblock, I promised myself.

Stan wasn't gone long. When he came back, he said, "Bob Foley was Dermot's chief boat wrangler on the *Waome* dive. The second person was Keogh's girlfriend. Mike remembers her as a stunner. Says her name was Renata Bowmaker."

"Are you sure about the last name?"

"That's what the man said. He said that. Called her 'my little Bowmaker.'"

"Good and thanks, Stan. Tell me, if I wanted to sabotage somebody's dive, how would I go about doing it?"

"You planning to murder somebody?"

"Remember I told you I was a private investigator? What I didn't tell you was that in my spare time—and there's a lot of that—I write detective stories. On the side, you know. You may have seen some of my stories in *Ellery Queen* or *Alfred Hitchcock*. And there are the novels: *Haste to the Gallows, The Glass Key, The Dalton Case, The Lake of Darkness* . . ."

"Oh, yeah. I've seen some of them!" I was glad to see we were both liars of about equal skill.

"Well, in my new plot, the murderer wants to do away with his victim by tampering with his aqualung. I try to keep my fiction as close to the truth as possible. Is there some way that my murderer could alter the mechanism of an aqualung and get away with it? It can't be something that the cops would find."

"Yeah, yeah. I see the problem. Let me think. I guess he could fill the tanks with carbon monoxide."

"Where would he get it?"

"Good point. The cops wouldn't miss something like that. He could send him down in a tank that was nearly empty."

"How can you tell the difference between a full and an empty tank?"

"A full tank is a lot heavier than an empty one. Air has weight. A lot of people forget about that."

"But would you send out an empty tank from the marina?"

"Not on purpose. Or maybe the murderer opens the valve and lets the tank empty as he and his victim head for their dive site."

"Wouldn't that hiss? How could the heavy—the villain in my story—hold the tap open?"

"You're right. It's a demand valve, so that there's no leakage from just having the main on/off tap open. Yeah, and an experienced diver would feel the difference in weight. Hey! What about this: your murderer could tamper with the O ring in the regulator."

"The what?"

"The O ring is a black ring made from neoprene or hard plastic. It balances the intermediate pressure in the regulator. Yeah, you could do it with a screwdriver. You see, there's a balance chamber in there. It prevents the diver getting air at a pressure that isn't right for the depth he's at. O rings wear out like anything else. If the cops looked at it, they might catch it, but again, they might not. It could look like ordinary wear and tear."

"Does that mean I'll have to make my murderer a marine engineer?"

"Naw. Anybody who can read a manual could do it. Wouldn't take long either."

"Could he do it with others around, say in the boat on the way to a dive?"

"Look, let me show you." Here Stan gave me a lesson in the fine art of sabotaging a perfectly good aqualung. All in the aid of crime fiction. He was right. It wouldn't have taken a man like Bob Foley more than a few minutes to "fix" Dermot's tank. But how could he be sure that Dermot would use it and not one of the others? Stan had an answer for that too. Using the *Waome* dive as an example, he pointed out that Dermot always rented the same tanks. They were made of an ultralight alloy and not the usual steel. "Your fictional victim could use special tanks too."

"Yeah!" I agreed. "That would make it easy."

I promised Stan that I would remember him in the acknowledgements to my next book. Before I drove away, he asked for my autograph. I wrote Sheldon Zatz on the lined paper he held out to me.

"Could you make it 'to Mike Coward,' Mr Zatz?"

"I thought your name was Stan?"

"It is. I was thinking of giving it to a friend. Is that okay?"

"Sure."

"And didn't you say your name was Cooperman?"

"That's right. But I write my books using a pseudonym, a *nom de plume*. Got it?"

A charming waitress in a long skirt, obviously a student enjoying a working vacation in Muskoka, cleared away the wreckage of a dinner of ribs of beef and Yorkshire pudding from our table and carried it from the dimly lit patio and into the main building of the Inn at the Falls. We had been talking about all sorts of things, Peggy, Hamp and I. Hamp described his expedition to the Queen Elizabeth Islands to dive through the Arctic polar ice cap. "We were supposed to be testing winter equipment for the army," he said, "but that didn't stop us from having fun. You may have seen our pictures in *National Geographic*. It's an eerie world under the ice, I don't mind telling you."

"That was Hamp's second polar dive, Benny. He went the first time before we were married."

"Peg, that was off Cape Hooker on Baffin Island the first time. Scarcely within the Arctic Circle. Last year's trip took us—"

"*Not me!* I was in Arizona with Nic Cage and Michael Douglas," corrected Peggy.

"Yes. Of course, dear. *Aaron's Run* kept you busy for three months. By 'we' I meant 'the expedition.' This time we were off the Disraeli Fiord at the top end of Ellesmere Island. We were on the site for nearly a week." I nodded my interest from time to time, turning my head back and forth. Finally, Hamp forced me to pull up my end of the conversation with an account of some of my cases, beginning with the one in Niagara Falls. When I'd finished with an exaggerated version of a case that took me into

the north woods in search of an evangelist who had "disappeared," I took a sip that emptied my glass of red wine. That was
when Hamp outlined the case of an American explorer who
died mysteriously in 1871 on a dash for the North Pole.

"It was a badly run show from start to finish. Lots of fights
and rows. The leader's body was exhumed from the permafrost
nearly one hundred years later. It was perfectly preserved, of
course. The body proved to be full of arsenic. Now there's a
puzzle for your enquiring mind, Ben."

"In history, everybody was poisoned by arsenic," I said,
remembering something from a few years ago. "Take
Napoleon."

"Yes! A very interesting case!" said Hamp, shortly before
Peggy excused herself to walk down to see the falls before the
light was gone. That killed it. And about time too. There is
something about Napoleon that either turns you on or turns
you off. There's no middle ground. We got up after a few minutes and, at a distance, followed Peggy down the steep and
twisting path to the river. On the way, he quizzed me about
the investigation. I talked as we walked.

"A vexing case, I'd say," Hamp said, his hands thrust deeply
into his pockets. "A veritable three-pipe problem."

"Excuse me?" Hamp waved his hand to show that it wasn't
important.

"May I ask who keeps you informed, Hamp?" I was tempted
to call him "mister," since the familiarity, which worked quite
well with dinner, had now hardened into the old routine of
my being professionally nosey.

"Ted Thornhill is my main source, but there are others too.
I'd prefer to keep their names to myself, if you don't mind.
Unless it becomes important later on, I mean."

"Not at all. Can you tell me how Vanessa Moss came to
NTC? She seems to have collected a number of business rivals
and, well, enemies since she arrived. I don't know whether any
of them would try to advance himself over her dead body or
try to remove her opposition to dividing up her empire."

"You think that her enemies are that dedicated?"

"Well, at least one of them could be. As you know, someone shot and killed Renata Sartori. She was staying in Vanessa's house, wearing her dressing gown."

"Yes, I see. I see. I don't know quite what to say to you, Benny. I first heard of Vanessa Moss a little over a year ago. She was still with CBC then. Her name came up twice in two separate meetings. Same day. I mentioned this to Ted Thornhill as a curiosity. Nothing more. A few weeks later, I heard from Ted that he was negotiating with the CBC to buy up her remaining contract."

"I know you're not kidding."

"No, I'm not. Ted should have been warned by the eagerness with which the CBC entered into negotiations. I try not to meddle at that level. People learn from their mistakes. Perhaps I'm a teacher at heart. Although what I could teach Ted Thornhill about bad decisions is moot."

"Why do you keep him on, then?"

"He is just that much better than his nearest rival. I swallow his imperfections. He'll do until another comes along. People are so ambitious, Benny, they unmask themselves. No eighteenth-century French court official ever got more mail from the colonies than I get from ambitious time-servers at NTC. I hear about their rivals' stupidity, their duplicity, their petty dishonesties, their ignorance. Oh, don't get me started. I am sometimes forced to promote liars and swindlers to high positions, Benny, simply because the alternatives are even more disastrous. I'll leave you to imagine the rest."

We had come to the riverbank, where the Muskoka River ran swift and black in front of us. Peggy had walked to her left, upstream and under a series of high bridges that criss-crossed the river at the waterfall. The sinking sun caught Peggy's silhouette as she traced the edge of the stream back to the falls, which could now be heard more and more clearly.

"She's lovely, isn't she?" Hamp Fisher said out loud.

I wasn't sure whether it was meant for my ears or not. I took a chance: "Yes, I've always thought so."

CHAPTER FIFTEEN

Sunday

For the rest of the weekend, I was content with my view of Lake Muskoka from the hammock at Norchris Lodge. I finished reading the Dermot Keogh biography, which left me with a clearer notion of the man. It reminded me that if I wanted to know more about him, I could catch his posthumous doings on the Internet. I made a mental note. In the hammock with my toes lined up against the view of pines and birches, that seemed like enough work for one day.

In front of the fireplace in the lodge on Sunday evening, I had been reading up on the history of Muskoka, the Muskoka Lakes, the summer cottages of the Lakes. There was a book about poisonous mushrooms that tempted me. I saw myself becoming the only private investigator in the Niagara Peninsula who could detect mushroom poisoning. Norma invited me to look into the photo albums for pictures of summers gone by. Judging by the smiling faces, I'd been misspending my summers for some decades. Norma told me that Chris, her husband, was on a fishing trip with his brother. When I'd finished with the albums, I returned to the mushrooms. By the time I was ready to go to sleep I could tell an *Amanita phalloides* from an *Amanita verna*. It's a start.

I heard the city beckoning. I knew that should Vanessa return from Los Angeles early, she would expect to find me on hand to defend her against sudden death in whatever form it took. While thanking the McArthurs and paying for my short stay at Norchris Lodge, I got directions to the hospital in Bracebridge. I headed there after a bite of breakfast in town at a Chinese-Canadian restaurant, where I tried to memorize the creatures of the Chinese zodiac from a paper placemat.

The hospital was small, but busy. Orderlies, nurses and doctors were running through the halls as though they were on film that was being played at the wrong speed. The calm centre in all this was a woman in a crocheted sweater behind a glass marked "Information."

"Why is everyone running around this morning?" I asked. "Has there been a big accident on the highway?"

"Welcome to the New Ontario," she said with a mock grin. "We practise no-frills medicine these days. What may I help you with?" I told her and she looked up the room number. "Mr Patel's a pet," she added. "Doesn't get many visitors since Alma died."

"His wife?" Then I remembered.

"Alma tried, but Ed could never see anyone after Lilly passed on. Alma ran his office and bought his neckties. Down the hall to your left and then turn right beside the stairs."

I followed these instructions to the letter and came out in a small cafeteria. Reversing engines, I got back to the main corridor and asked an orderly for the room I wanted. This time I ended up in a new wing that had been attached to the main building as an afterthought. I walked past the nursing station and entered the small room, trying to decide which of the four men in the room was Ed Patel. I decided that the grey-faced skeletal figure by the window was the best candidate. The name, posted in masking tape to the wall behind him, confirmed my diagnosis. He was dozing over a copy of *National Geographic* balanced on his blue hospital gown. I saw that it was open to a picture of Lawrence of Arabia dressed in his flowing Arab costume. Ed Patel opened one eye and stared at me. Then his other eye opened, and they both examined me for a full thirty seconds. The magazine slipped from his chest to the edge of the bed and then to the floor.

"I haven't seen you before," he said. "Which agency sent you? Are you Community Care or Centra? I told them I can't go home yet. My house's been sold and the apartment's still unfurnished."

"I'm not from any agency, Mr Patel. I'm just a visitor."

"What church sent you? I don't hold with churches nowadays. I've tried them all."

"I'm a friend of Vanessa Moss, whom you probably know as—"

"I know, I know, I know. Is Stella at the cottage?"

"No, she's in Los Angeles. She asked me to see how you're getting on," I lied.

"Well, that won't take long. They keep telling me that my time here's run out; they want to move me, but I can't see how they can do that with all of these tubes running in and out of me."

I couldn't argue with that. He didn't look as though he would ever travel again. His brown skin was as grey as death itself. I didn't want him to read that in my face, so I stooped and retrieved the magazine. I put it down on the moveable table that straddled the bed.

He glanced at the magazine cover. "I once went to visit his house at Clouds Hill in Devon," he said.

"Whose house?"

"Lawrence's, of course. Tiny, nearly windowless place, hardly room to feed visitors. He sat the G. B. Shaws outside and fed them alfresco. Fed all his visitors that way. Okay for Shaw and Charlotte: they could munch on carrots. But what about Churchill? I can't see him putting up with the muck Lawrence lived on. Lawrence couldn't stand the smell of cooking. He sustained life on tinned fish, I think. But the Shaws knew better than to expect a banquet. I met the lad—one of the lads—he died trying to save, you know."

I tried to show some interest. As he talked, he was rubbing his blanket between his thumb and forefinger. Perhaps there was a lurking memory of real blanket fuzz. He wouldn't find any in these blankets. Ed Patel continued with his story: "There were two of them, on bikes, riding abreast even though they were told not to. Lawrence came on them as he reached the top of a hill and ran his Brough off the road to avoid hitting them. Saved their lives at the cost of his own. He lingered for nearly a week, never regained consciousness. That's the way to go, eh?"

"I guess it is," I said lamely.

"Not like this with all these pipes and tubes showing what's not working inside."

"Is there anything I can get you?"

"I don't suppose you have a copy of *The Seven Pillars* with you? Or even *Revolt in the Desert*, I reckon. Oh, well. What about a Perry Mason mystery? There aren't many of them I haven't read. But now my memory's so poor, I can read them all over again. What did you really come for? I won't remember your name, most likely, but you might tell me just to humour me."

I did that, and he nodded while trying to boot his memory to receive and store the information.

"Is Stella in trouble? What can I do?"

"She thinks that there might be somebody trying to kill her," I said.

"And she's made a heap of enemies at that city job of hers."

"You don't miss much."

"I've got the mentality of a small-town lawyer because that's what I am. In other words, I'm a snoop. But I'm getting behind. I used to enjoy being in the thick of things. I once had *four* federal cabinet ministers at my dining-room table. Bet you don't believe that. It wasn't planned, it just turned out that way. My cottage was always like that, especially when Lilly was alive. Everybody loved Lilly." He seemed to drift into a reverie, thinking of the absent Lilly, and I let him.

"Stella's dad and I were fishing buddies. Saved my life at least twice. Both times in fast water."

"What do you know about Dermot Keogh?" I asked. He blinked at the change of subject.

"Fine gentleman. A bit wild, maybe, but solid, if you know what I mean. He could separate the serious from the frivolous when he had to."

"What was he to you?"

"He was a neighbour. For two years I didn't know he was famous. He'd never tell me."

"He shared your interest in old motorcycles, I believe?"

"He was a collector. Had a fine Brough. And a Crocker. They're getting scarce."

"Would you know all the Brough collectors?" He nodded, quickly. There can't have been that many. "Does the name Bob Foley ring a bell?"

"Foley? Foley? Yes-s-s. He used to drive Dermot around. Only man Dermot would allow behind a wheel. Stella had no use for him. She'd wince when his name came up. Scared of him, I think. He had an appetite for bikes, though, but he didn't own any. He was just hungry. Collecting bikes is not a poor man's game. Not any more."

"What happened to Dermot's collection?"

"He left 'em to a British collector name of Horwood. Sir Harry Horwood. Very fine collection. It's all spelled out in the will."

"How did you meet Dermot Keogh? You said he was a neighbour?"

"Neighbour, friend, fellow music-lover. Fellow at the marina introduced him to me. He invited me to dinner that same day. We exchanged books and drank a lot of Scotch together. Also Irish, bourbon, rye and a few other things. Once we canoed down the Indian River singing 'I Am the Walrus' at the tops of our voices. Damned silly that he should be dead, I'll tell you. It's a great loss. I liked the man, Mr— See, I told you I'd forget."

"Cooperman," I prompted. "Did you do any legal work for him?"

"Not much. That city fellow, Raymond Whatshisname, did

all the fancy stuff. I wouldn't know where to begin on those complicated recording and film contracts. No, I stick to the simple staples of a small-town attorney's practice: conveyancing of real property, wills, torts and a little domestic work. It's provided me with a good living for over forty years. I can't complain. I've enjoyed the work. Setting something going that would get out of bed and turn itself on in the morning. Know what I mean? Like that palliative care unit I set up. It'll still be doing good deeds when I'm gone too. Once set up a puppy farm too. Manitoulin Island. Wonder how it's getting on."

"When did you give Vanessa the keys to your place?"

"She's got my keys, and I have a set of hers. We look after one another up here, young fellow. Evans at the marina, he's got keys too. He sees to our roofs in winter; gets 'em cleared if the snow's heavy. Alma had keys too, just in case."

"Alma?"

"Alma Orchard. My secretary. Runs—I should say *ran*—my offices for me. She met with a tragic accident this spring. And I couldn't even get out of here to go to Croft's Funeral Home, and it's just across the street from here. Big house on the corner. Lots of big houses end up as funeral homes in a town like this. Dying's a thriving business. That and used cars."

"When would that have been, Mr Patel?"

"Call me Ed. Everybody does now, now that Alma's gone. Could never get her to ease off on formality. You'd think that formality was the only thing that kept that woman hooked together. She died second Monday in May. They didn't find her until Wednesday. Poor Alma. All those years of filing and writing the numbers of cases in a ledger."

"Does the name 'Bowmaker' mean anything to you?"

"Not a thing. Unusual name, though," he said, trying to lift himself higher on the bed. I helped him. He weighed nothing at all.

"What about Renata Sartori?"

"Ah, the murder victim! Yes, I knew Renata. Dermot was very close to her. She would have been good for Dermot. Now they're both gone. And I linger on, temporarily."

I could see that I was beginning to tire him. That note of sentimentality wouldn't have crept in normally, I suspected. I made leaving noises, scraping my feet and making the chair squeak on the linoleum. I promised that I would send him a few Erle Stanley Gardners when I next found myself in a bookstore. He waved me off with a forced smile. I navigated my way through the confusing corridors and found my car where I'd left it.

As I swung the Olds out into traffic, such as it was, the first thing I saw was the sign on the front lawn of the corner house: "Croft's Funeral Home Since 1913."

On a whim, I pulled into the lot connected to the chapel and parked next to the only other car. I got out and went through the glass doors that had been added to the side of the big white clapboard house. The quiet inside hit me. It was just the quiet of an empty house, but there was an extra hollowness underlying the silence. Then a man in a grey cardigan came through from a room at the back.

"Mr Egan? I'm Henry Croft. We spoke earlier on the phone." The welcome that began as friendly as you please wilted as he came to realize that I wasn't Mr Egan at all. I quickly explained who I was, that I had just been to see Ed Patel across the street and that he had told me about poor Alma Orchard. The sound of those names warmed him up again. "Oh yes, Alma. She was quite a character around town. Everybody liked Alma once they got on to her little eccentricities. Did you know her, Mr Cooperman?"

"I didn't, but Ed Patel was just talking about her and feeling sort of powerless because he couldn't come to the service you held for her."

"Yes, indeed. He was missed. But, under the circumstances . . . It was very well attended. The service, I mean. Alma was local, you understand, and there weren't many in these parts she didn't know. My grandmother and hers were great chums when they were young. She'd been keeping Ed's practice going after Ed took sick. Couldn't take on new work, but kept up to date on what was there."

"Was she an elderly woman?"

"Coming up to her retirement. Was worried what she'd do once she shut down the last of Ed's offices. One here in town, I mean. It was a great shame about Alma. She was a healthy woman and a careful one. Not like her to take a radio into the bathroom with her."

"Nasty way to go," I offered.

"Closed casket, of course. They didn't find her, you know, for some days after it happened. I told her time and time again about living alone in that big old house. It just goes to show you. Naturally, it tested our professional skills out back. But I think we made the best of it. Got her all dressed up in her Sunday best. Mrs Croft is a licensed female embalmer, you understand."

"Of course."

"Yes, she'd just taken off a clean outfit for a bubble bath with the radio perched on the corner of the tub. That's what Sergeant Hoffmeister told me. The Provincial Police took an interest for a few days. There were things that puzzled them. Things puzzled a few of us."

"Like what, Mr Croft?"

"Well, I never speak ill of the dead, Mr Cooperman. They're my bread and butter, so to speak. But Alma was never all that fastidious about herself. And I wondered what she was doing all dolled up in clean clothes *before* she took her bath. Most times you find discarded dirty clothes and linen in the bath or bedroom, but not in this case. She was all dressed up to go out to the church bake sale that Monday when she stopped to take a bath. How do you like that?"

It was nearly noon when I hit the highway back to Toronto. It was a perfect day for travelling in an air-conditioned car. Unfortunately, none of the former owners of the Olds had thought of installing air-conditioning. The present owner hadn't the initiative either. So he fried, even with the back windows open. Through the windshield, which had by now acquired an impressive collection of dead insects, I could see Canadian Shield granite following me back to town. It quit only as I neared Orillia, where I missed the overpass to Webers hamburger stand. Feeling that lapse keenly in the pit of my stomach, I pulled into the city of Orillia at the first suggestion from the highway signs.

Orillia was a borderline sort of place. For those driving north, it represented the gateway to vacationland; for those moving back to the city, it represented the first touch of urban civilization. Here you were reintroduced to fire hydrants and sidewalks, curbs and parking meters. You were once more in the iron grip of the city. From the highway, shopping plazas and large, flat areas devoted to parking took the place of outcroppings of rugged granite rock. Names such as IGA and Zehrs and Century 21 led the way into the town on Lake Couchiching. In saying that Orillia was the tunnel through which you re-entered civilization, I don't mean to bad-mouth all of those towns north of there. Places such as Gravenhurst, Bracebridge and Huntsville can all boast of curbstones and parking meters, but they are inside the inescapable context of being *north*. At least to a southerner like me, they are north. So, for me, driving back to Toronto, Orillia was the gateway to the south.

Orillia was squeezed between the eight-lane highway and the south and west shores of Lake Couchiching. Part of the town spilled south of the lake, filling the gap between it and Lake Simcoe, which hooked up with the smaller lake at The Narrows. Like the great city of Rome, Orillia seemed to be built on seven hills as well, with streets climbing away from you towards the highway or sloping away from you towards the docks of the port. A large information booth that was set up here for tourists was having a busy day. Men and women in shorts or cut-off jeans were filing in and out carrying maps and brochures back to their cars as though they spelled the way to ease from earthly pain. I spotted a restaurant between two stone buildings that must have gone back to the early years of the community.

The meal at the Town and Country wasn't exactly gourmet fare, but while I scanned the menu, I was watching a living diorama of busy Orillians taking their ease.

"I've had that car on blocks for two years, Lyal, and I don't dare fill them tires without a damned good reason." Lyal was wearing a grey T-shirt, blue pants, a heavy brass bracelet and yellow work boots. His pal wore a peaked blue cap, a light-blue shirt and running shoes. He'd hung a blue-on-blue wind-breaker on the back of his chair.

"You got no call to talk like that, Bert. I only asked if she ran, is all."

"You know as much about cars as you do about livestock."

"The hell I do!"

"You couldn't breed rabbits, Lyal. You *know* that!" said Bert with finality.

The restaurant was furnished in reproduced captain's chairs, with captain's stools next to the bar, where a Molson's Export sign winked at the thirsty. A big Coke cooler filled the part of one wall that wasn't occupied by the kitchen hatchway.

"What can I get youse?" This last was a red-headed waitress with a blue butterfly tattooed on her bare arm. She wasn't chewing gum nor was there a pencil stuck in her hair, but her apron and salmon-pink uniform were starched and pressed as though they came from a roller mill.

"What's the soup today?"

"Too hot for soup," she announced flatly. I moved my fin-ger further down the menu. I placed my order and tried to move my ears away from the discussion.

At another table, what looked like a small-town lawyer was eating a piece of apple pie, his chin nearly touching the plate. He was wearing a worn brown tweed jacket. Pens and pencils filled his shirt pocket beside a greasy necktie. Next to him, his briefcase threatened to explode, sending tattered pieces of writs and processes around the room. When my chopped-egg sandwich on white bread came, I tried to think of what awaited me in Toronto when I got back. Vanessa was probably still in L.A. and might be there for another day or so. That would leave me free to continue my digging. I would mend my fences with Sykes and Boyd by giving them the shotgun and shells. If that didn't work, I'd try something else. I didn't know what that might be, but I knew that I always thought of something.

Back on the street, I found a second-hand bookstore, where I saw a clutch of Perry Masons. For five dollars, the clerk agreed to send them on for me. Before I'd quite got back to the street, I returned to change the instructions I'd given: I'd written Ed Patel's address as "care of Croft's Funeral Home."

Next, I headed for the newspaper office on Colborne Street and found it in the block between Peter and West. This was a busy block, containing the fire hall, the police station and a Tim Hortons restaurant.

The office of the *Orillia Packet & Times* was busy that noon hour. A man in an old-fashioned straw hat, carrying a tuba in a case, was filling in a subscription form. A woman in pink shorts and a sweatshirt reading "It's not ale if it isn't Charles Wells" was waiting for him to finish. Was Charles Wells beer and ale taking over the Canadian market, I wondered, or were two sightings of advertisements on clothing just a coincidence? I'd have to be on the lookout for another appearance.

The capable woman behind the counter had sculptured jet-black hair with a shock of white at the front. She was trying not to nibble the temple of the glasses she was holding near her mouth. She was short and buxom and was grinning at something interesting going on inside her head that had nothing to do with the *Orillia Packet & Times*. A photograph of what I guessed were her grandchildren stood on the desk to which she returned from time to time. When I came to her notice, I explained that I wanted to see copies of the paper going back several weeks, to May, in fact. I was looking for the write-up of a talk given on the evening of the fifteenth of May.

"Aren't you on-line?" she asked.

"I beg your pardon?" I looked around to see if there was anyone in line who might claim to be ahead of me.

"The information is obtainable on the Internet." She said this as though explaining quantum theory to a six-year-old.

"Oh!" I stuttered. "I don't have my laptop in the car."

"You'd better come around and let me set you up. Clarence won't be back until after lunch. If I hadn't packed a lunch this morning, I'd close up this place for an hour. And just let *anybody* complain." She lifted a flap in the countertop and showed me into an office that sported a framed poster of an old-fashioned reporter hollering into a telephone: "Make it snappy, sweetheart, and get me Rewrite!" I thought of Vanessa's description of Ken Trebitsch, the hot-shot head of News at NTC.

I was sorry not to meet Clarence, but I did find the story I was looking for as I flipped from screen to screen.

> The Junior Chamber of Commerce, meeting jointly with the Orillia Bar Association, was treated last night to the keen wit and interesting comments of Barry Bosco, a lawyer with the Toronto firm of Devlin and Devlin. Meeting in the library of the Leacock Museum on Brewery Bay, and introduced by Cam Millar, the curator of the museum, Mr Bosco thanked the audience for coming out on a rainy evening. Reading from a prepared text, but illustrating his points with anecdotes, he kept the room with its 24 listeners enthralled for almost an hour. He talked about five of his interesting cases, which had caused a stir in legal quarters in the Ontario capital. Most interesting was his account of the baby deaths at Rose of Sharon Hospital. In thanking him afterwards, and in the act of presenting him with a T-shirt commemorating the incorporation of the town of Orillia as a city, Ernie Moffatt expressed the sentiments of most of those in attendance when he said, "Hopefully, we hope that you'll come back and see us again before too long." The deputy mayor, Harry J. Torgov, seconded the motion to adjourn to the next stage of the evening's entertainment. Tea and cookies were served, with special thanks to Mrs Halpern and her committee. The speaker informally chatted with his audience afterwards.

When I pulled myself away from the back issues of the *Orillia Packet & Times*, I saw the woman with the shock of white in her black hair explaining to a newcomer that she couldn't guarantee anyone the size of a photograph that would mark the winning of Sunday's regatta. "It's expensive to run a picture more than two or three columns, Carla. Besides, pictures is another department. Talk to Clarence when he's finished drinking his lunch over at the Rendezvous." Carla went out in a hurry. My friend behind the counter knew how to get Clarence back to work when she wanted him. Before I left, I asked her if any pictures were taken at the time of the Junior Chamber and Orillia Bar meeting at the museum. She opened a drawer on her side of the counter and came up with a grey manila envelope.

"Clarence took these, but as you know, we didn't run any of them. These are hard times in the world of print journalism." She said this last in a sad, breathy voice that showed how much recent economies had hurt her personally. I took four glossy pictures out and looked through them. There was Barry Bosco being introduced, there he was giving his talk, there he was accepting the T-shirt, and there he was posing with some of the others, "informally chatting with his audience." The only trouble was that Barry Bosco wasn't Barry Bosco. The man in the photograph was Roger Cavanaugh, the man Raymond Devlin brought with him last Wednesday to sign the contracts for Dermot Keogh Hall. Roger Cavanaugh may not have had the most prepossessing of faces, but here on these glossies, he cut quite a dash. I could almost hear the sound of an exploding alibi as I grinned idiotically at the prints. The first thing I learned when I started in this business was to check everything. This was one of those times when it paid off.

I paid for one of these photographs, collected a receipt and found, on locating the Olds, that my parking meter had expired, but that no parking ticket had yet been placed under my windshield wiper. I was at least half an hour over-parked and within spitting distance of the police station. After that, I won't say a bad word about Orillia again, ever.

CHAPTER SIXTEEN

Tuesday

Once more, I was installed at the New Beijing Inn on Bay Street, not far from Toronto's Old City Hall. Although the floor was different—they'd moved me up to the ninth—the view from the window was unaltered. After showering and sorting my laundry, I called Sally at the office.

"Benny! Did you have a good weekend?"

"From the sound of your voice, I take it that Vanessa's not back yet from sunny California?"

"You've got it. Rumour has it she'll be home late today. But I'd put my money on Wednesday. She *has* to be here on Wednesday."

"You know her pretty well, don't you?"

"Benny, I'm just guessing. She's never here when Ken, Mr Rankin or Mr Thornhill are on the phone every ten minutes. All three of them have called at least twice. They're still after her head. After all she's been through."

"And all she's put *you* through."

"Well, that's show business. Are you coming in?"

"I'll be there in about half an hour, Sally. You want me to bring you a Danish?"

"Why didn't I meet you years ago, Benny? I like the gloopy kind. Bring napkins and—oops! I've got another line flashing. 'Bye."

Last night, as soon as I had got back into the steaming city and applied calamine lotion to the few itchy places on my legs, I got dressed in my remaining clean clothes and found a bite to eat at a deli called Yitz's on Eglinton Avenue West. Here the service was crisp and speedy. Here I could afford to branch out from my diet of chopped-egg sandwiches and try a little chopped liver and a corned beef sandwich with sweet lemon tea. Just the way I like it. Still, I missed Orillia's Bert and Ernie, or whatever their names were. I thought of Orillia again as I removed a parking ticket from my windshield. With the threat of starvation once more in check, I drove down to 52 Division on Dundas Street. Kids were climbing into the holes in a gigantic bronze sculpture at the corner outside the art gallery. They were having a wonderful time, while their parents looked as though they thought the holes might be better employed if they were filled with useful, necessary clocks.

I didn't stay in the cop shop long. I just delivered my plastic-wrapped package addressed to Sykes and Boyd. My name appeared on the label, but I had to fill out a form that duplicated what already existed clearly printed. I got the feeling that all parcels were regarded as bombs until proved to be innocent bags of laundry or forgotten lunches.

Not too many blocks from there and a good night's sleep later, I bought a couple of fat Danishes and two large coffees and walked down University Avenue, past the *other* TV network on the street, to NTC, with its big rooftop icon looking down on my progress. Near the front doors I saw George Brenner, the talented car jockey, sitting on the edge of a cement flower bed, sipping a coffee of his own. I parked my carcass on the same planter, hoping to find some useful conversation. He was wearing a white T-shirt and jeans. As far as I could see, there wasn't a pack of Camels or Lucky Strike tucked under either of his short sleeves. Nor was there an ad for British ale on his T-shirt. After a few thoughts about the continuing warm weather and some philosophical remarks about city living as opposed to life in the wild, we went on to more interesting things. "Vanessa Moss tells me that you're a very clever computer animator."

"I used to be. Worked for George Lucas for six years. That makes me an old man in this business. A year ago I left. Now I need a job here, but I can't get back in."

"In? In where?"

"Inside. Through the door behind you. Back under the two big eyes of the NTC owl. That 'in.'"

"Why's that?"

"You working for her now, right?"

"Started last Wednesday. She's kept me hopping. I've got a lot to learn."

"She said she could do me some good, but I don't know . . ." He was sipping his coffee through a hole in the plastic cover.

"She told me a little more about you than about your computer skills."

"Yeah? She digs my bod. I know that. Not many around here keep in shape. You understand? It turns to jelly if you don't work it. One time I kept in shape surfing in San Diego. The waves burn off the fat. But I can't afford that any more. I worked myself hard in the joint for eighteen months. When I got out, I ran into a brick wall. The people around here don't want an ex-con getting back in. Oh, they let me handle cars, but they won't cut me any slack about getting into the Art Department. She brought you in as her bodyguard, right?"

"Where'd you hear a thing like that?"

"Drop it. Everybody knows you're a P.I. Everybody except Security, that is. They don't know it's raining out until they have a meeting about it."

"What were you in for?"

"It was drug related. The boys in blue can't tell the difference between personal use and trafficking. You understand?" I nodded encouragement, and he went on. "Fellow upstairs in the Art Department says there's nobody like me in computer animation except for a guy out in Vancouver, who's already got as much work as he can handle. But this guy upstairs I was telling you about, he can't get me past Security. And Security has an ass-breaking hold on things. I can't even use the john inside. Have to find my own crapper, except when I've parked a car down in the parking garage. Sub-sub-basement. They've a toilet down there that Security hasn't heard of yet."

"Have the cops hassled you about this murder thing?" I was glad I remembered "hassled." Hassle was a good word from the sixties.

"They talked to me. Local cops. Yeah."

"Has anyone else been asking you questions about Vanessa?" I thought my use of her first name would suggest that I was on his side. He took another sip of his coffee to think on.

"Ken Trebitsch, uh, you know, from News: he's been asking about her. He knows about us getting it off together. You know how he knows about that?" He looked honestly puzzled, as though a toy had come apart in his hands and wouldn't go back together.

"He lives on information, George. He can't get enough of it. He's an information junkie. It's his armour against finding himself barred from the twentieth floor someday."

"Can't come soon enough for me."

"Oh?"

"Yeah, Security didn't come bothering me until Trebitsch knew I had a record. Then it didn't take long. There's a news producer, Bernie Something, works for Trebitsch. He sat down here one day last week and asked me to tell him the story of my life. So I told him. Half of it was taken from Kerouac. But he'll never know. I told him lots of shit including the time I was inside. Then that same night I caught him following me home in his Punchbuggy."

"His what?"

"He drives one of those VW bugs. His is bright green. He should know better than to come after me in that Punchbuggy."

"How often have you spotted him?"

"Few times. There's another guy in a rusty red Volvo. Spells him off maybe. Can't be sure he's Trebitsch's man or whether he's legging for somebody else."

"Why all the interest, you think?" George gathered his shoulders in a shrug while making a face with a down-turned mouth. As a gesture, it was pretty broad, but it gave him time to choose what he was going to say next. He seemed to be talking to himself with the sound turned off.

"Yeah. That was another dumb thing. I get a little high shooting my mouth off. It makes up for parking the Mercedeses and BMWs I don't own. Ms Moss is the only decent person I've met on this job. Sure, she takes it out on me, but I don't go yellin' harassment in the workplace now, do I? She's a treat most of the time. I don't have any reason to hurt her. Besides, I think the cops checked me out and I came up clean. I told 'em I was at the movies that night, and they got me to tell them the story of the picture. I must have got it right."

"You weren't at the movies, then?"

"Shit, I don't know where I was. Like the man says, I fell among evil companions that night. I don't remember much about it." I grinned and nibbled a corner of my Danish.

Thirty seconds of silence dragged by and I didn't try to punctuate it. I kept listening.

"Most people buy Ms Moss as the intended victim at the shootout at her place. I know for sure she's scared shitless. She sees guns aimed at her, all kinds, pointed from right around the compass. She don't entertain any doubts on that score. That's where you come in, I figure."

"Go on." George was getting thoughtful, for George. The words came out more slowly and with long pauses in between the phrases.

"Well, the people around here want Moss out on her ass pretty damned quick. It's only natural to figure somebody took steps to see her out of the way."

"You mean with a shotgun?"

"Sure. It figures. But if she wasn't the intended target, then you gotta ask new questions. If she's mixed up in the murder, like it looks, then they wanna know about it fast."

"Who wants to know, George?"

"If the gunman meets her, Trebitsch wants to know about it right away. He's shooting for a bigger piece of prime, man. He wants it so bad you can read it in his sweat."

"You ever fire a shotgun, George?"

"Now you're askin' *their* kind of questions."

"Whose? The cops'?"

"Well, I don't mean NTC Security. They're too busy searching people for stolen pencil stubs."

"You've got a good hate going on that bunch, haven't you?"

"You get off on that shit? Hell, I *smoked* more Bible than Dunkery and his bunch, and he calls me 'unsuitable' while waving the Holy Writ in my face. See how you like it around here this time next week. It's the same thing in the joint: Security's a power trip. Little people get big on it. Security makes fascists. That's all it's good for."

A small-sized Buick rolled up to the entranceway. Ken Trebitsch put on the emergency brake and got out. He was carrying a fat briefcase. He nodded at George but kept on going through the revolving doors and into the lobby, which I could just make out through the glass doors. I thought of all these people dependent upon the whims of executives such as Thornhill and Trebitsch and Vanessa Moss. George put down his coffee. "I gotta go," he said.

I gathered up my food parcel and Styrofoam cups and headed through the doors to the security desk. I set my burden down and dug out my plastic card. "This is no good without a picture, you know."

"What?"

"If you're going to be a regular or even a semi, you gotta get your ID and picture."

"Where do I get that?"

"Speak to your supervisor."

"She's in Los Angeles, and the coffee's getting cold."

"Well, I'll let you past this time, but you *need* that photo-ID."

"I'll remember that, and God bless you."

"You got attitude, Mr Cooperman. You want me to call *my* supervisor? There are four supervisors above him, so your coffee could be good and cold by the time this is straightened out. You hear me?" I bowed to acknowledge I'd been beaten. I'd been hoping to catch Ken Trebitsch in the elevator, but he was long gone now. Speed didn't matter any more.

SEVENTEEN

Philip Rankin's chubby hand waved at me as I passed his door with my coffee and Danish. "Dear boy, so good to see you!"

"Why do I suspect that you mean the opposite?"

"Oh, you *are* learning our ways. Excellent progress in such a short time. How was your weekend in the untamed northland?" I must have looked surprised. "Yes, dear boy, the little northern brooks have been babbling."

"And so early!"

"Early's not a dirty word in network television. Has your boss come home to roost?"

"I thought you'd know that already. She's still in L.A."

"She's going to miss all the fun. Pity! Trolleys of boxes headed for Central Records. That's what we have instead of a morgue. They'll have her stash of secret ashtrays packed and ready to go by noon."

"If you're wrong, are you going to help put her things back where they belong?"

"Mr Cooperman, I try to make all allowances for your unfamiliarity with our ways. And for your innocence in general of the great wicked metropolis. I was a new boy myself once. But you aren't paying attention. Why, at this very moment the CEO is closeted with the people most concerned with the future of your employer. Your fates are entwined, I expect. You should follow what's going on out of self-interest at the very least."

"Then why are you here and not with Thornhill and the others? Ken Trebitsch just arrived a couple of minutes ago. He hasn't been closeted with anyone all morning. Maybe he knows that the meeting isn't as important as you seem to think it is. He has a private information-gathering service, you know."

"Oh, you know about *that?*"

"And a bit besides."

"Ken once operated under a sign that read 'When I hear the word culture, I reach for my gun.' I think he's a retarded National Socialist, a strayed member of the Third Reich. His favourite composer is Wagner. He marches briskly to the tune of the 'Horst Wessel Lied.' They moved him to News because he frightened the writers and idea people. News people are made of sterner stuff. You've met some of Ken's associates, I take it? The young men with long hair and a regulation three-day beard? I often wonder how they keep the three-day look. Have you?"

"That green car's easy to spot. I hope they are better producers than they are thugs."

"You exaggerate. They're not thugs, just some of his yes-men, his disciples."

"Does he have a dozen? That's the usual number."

"Mr Cooperman, it's instructive to watch a man's paranoia work its way through an organization like this. Have you observed that Ken never goes anywhere by himself? He attends meetings with a phalanx of supporters. I think he likes the sound of all those leather heels sounding on the terrazzo in unison. I wonder if he sleeps with the light on. What do you think?" Rankin shot me a look with an arched eyebrow. I pretended to catch it. He thought a moment and then went on. "I shouldn't be too hard on the poor boy. We are still all in shock after Renata's death. Dreadful! Dreadful! Look how her boyfriend's taking it. He knocked on my door the other night, wanted to talk."

"Barry Bosco?"

"Very good. You *are* keeping your eyes open. Yes, Barry Bosco. He's taken a rather personal interest in the murder of his inamorata. I don't think his legal firm will be happy about this if it continues beyond the end of this month. He's a clever lawyer and all, but no Greenspan or John J. Malone. You might do worse than trying to have a word with him yourself."

"I'll remember the suggestion." The smile Rankin gave me was dismissive. His eyes returned to other things. Just to bug him, I said, "I read a paperback biography about Dermot Keogh over the weekend."

"Enterprising. What did you think?"

"It was a fast job, not very good. Looked like it was a collection of write-ups and reviews from the papers."

"That's exactly what it was, Mr Cooperman."

"I'd give another thought about writing your own book on him."

"Mind your business, Mr Cooperman."

Sally came out of the office to meet me when she smelled the aging victuals I was carrying.

"Your senses are in terrific tune. Good morning. I'm afraid that the Danish has become cold and soggy and the coffee cold with a cardboard aftertaste."

"I'm well acquainted with both. Which are mine?"

"I was waylaid by Philip Rankin down the hall."

"Yes, he poked his wobbly chin in here too. I don't know what he's so worried about. Music can't win a bigger piece of Entertainment than it already has. Maybe it's just habit."

"Any further word from our chief?"

"She's in La Jolla, meeting with Winkler from Warners."

"I thought that Warners was in L.A.?"

"Right now, if you ask me, Warners is wherever Winkler is. He has a house on Camino de la Costa. Doesn't that sound delicious?"

"You've tried out his pool?"

"No such luck. I remember typing the address on an envelope. But I can imagine the Pacific across the street whispering to them as they contemplate those three outstanding series that he has yet to deliver for our fall line-up."

"Has Ted Thornhill been in touch with her?"

"Not yet. He's still at the message-leaving stage."

"So the department is still in one piece. The moving vans haven't arrived."

"As of this moment, but the day is young. Here, let me get you a napkin before you get cherry jam on your other cheek as well." Sally jumped up and with a few well-choreographed motions delivered a few paper napkins to my sticky fingers.

We munched in silence for a few minutes, during which time I gave her the once-over: her seams were straight, her eyes unlined, her makeup minimal. She'd had a good night, and Gordon was leaving her alone. Good. I hadn't even thought of my black eye this morning. It must be doing well too.

"Sally, do you happen to know what Barry Bosco's specialty is at Raymond Devlin's office?"

"Mostly putting deals together, I think. He put together the Reliance Cable deal with Northeastern. He was in charge of the legal side of Global's acquisition of anchorman Garth Walsh's contract from CBS. Remember that? He was Mr Devlin's right hand in putting the Dermot Keogh Hall project together. He had to keep an eye on his boss, who is the executor of Keogh's estate."

"Ah, yes, as one of the senior executives in the big board-room keeps saying, 'Justice must not only be done but be *seen* to be done.'"

"*Oh, him*. He never saw any justice around here. And he was one of the founders. Anyway, these days it only must *seem* to be done."

"Sally, is there any way of getting a peek at Dermot Keogh's will? The Keogh Concert Hall is being set up under the will, isn't it? Is there a copy around?"

"Sure. It's attached to the file. I'll put it on your desk. We only had to have the pertinent sections, but I think they sent the whole thing from— Oh, that reminds me, I have to send the matted copies of the contracts over to Devlin's office by courier. Raymond Devlin likes his trophies framed." Sally stretched to find a piece of pink paper on which she scribbled a note to herself.

"I can take care of that. I was on my way in that direction anyway," I fibbed. "And I've been looking for an excuse to butt my nose in there."

"Wear your sunglasses. All that chrome and glass is too much for the normal unprepared human eye."

"I'll remember. Barry Bosco is still handling the Dermot Keogh Hall stuff, right?" Sally nodded, and I said, "See you later." I collected the wrapped bundle of matted contracts and put them under my arm. Downstairs, the security people were of two minds about whether I should be allowed to leave the premises with a parcel. While they were arguing, one of them remembered that it was time for an eleven-o'clock coffee break. I slipped out before they did.

———

The offices of Devlin and Devlin occupied a full floor and were situated in a tower that cast a long shadow over Bay Street. The green copper roof of the Old City Hall could be seen from the reception area, which also showed painted portraits of Mr Charles Devlin and Mr Raymond Devlin. The senior partner was pictured in vigorous middle age, wearing his gown and tabs. A notice on the wall beside the portrait told me additionally that he had been referred indefinitely to some higher court beyond the jurisdiction of the Supreme Court of Canada. Raymond Devlin, lucky stiff, was left with the whole shebang, aided and abetted by two dozen juniors who had not yet got their names insinuated into the partnership's legal and official style and form. When I'd attracted the interest of the receptionist, I asked to see Mr Bosco. I gave my name when asked and said that I was from Vanessa Moss's office at NTC. When this information was repeated into the phone, I was requested to take a seat. I was on my way to do this when I caught my still-blackish eye in the chrome-and-glass space divider that shielded the entrance into the sancta that lay beyond. With very little movement on my part, I could change my reflection into a funhouse distortion of myself. I was occupied in this way when I was summoned into the inner chambers.

Barry Bosco sat behind a huge glass-topped desk and lent me five fingers without doing great damage to my right hand. It wasn't a boneless handshake, but with work it could get there. My first impression of him was that he looked like a private schoolboy. It might have been the haircut, no clipper marks, and his rosy, unmarked face. He was tall, willowy even, with a big head that gave the impression of being concave. I tried to see where the impression came from: a big chin and a pronounced forehead without much nose to speak of. The eyes, partly hidden by round glasses, were blue. I couldn't read them as either warm or icy, yet. He'd cultivated that. Naturally, he didn't look anything like the Orillia photograph.

"I'm Ben Cooperman, working with Vanessa Moss at NTC," I explained, as though the receptionist hadn't already filled him in. I handed over the package with the signed contracts inside.

"That's good of you to drop by with this. I could have got the messenger service." Having said that, he now felt that he had to offer me coffee, which would lift my personal service out of the class of paid go-between. He tried to make small talk, but not with much skill. He examined his watch only once before the coffee arrived. "I hope you take your coffee unabridged. I didn't think to ask if you'd prefer decaffeinated." I assured him that I took my vices at full strength.

He asked about NTC's plans for the official press conference and reception scheduled for Wednesday. I told him what I remembered and admitted that Vanessa was out of town.

"You're Vanessa's executive assistant, isn't that right?"

"That's what she calls me. I'm still learning the ropes."

"Come, now, Mr Cooperman, you're being too modest. I suspect that that befuddled manner of yours proves very useful on occasions." I hadn't expected that, and I couldn't wait to hear what I was going to say in response.

"You're well informed, Mr Bosco. No sense asking who your moles inside NTC are, I guess."

"You know as well as I that a blown mole is no mole at all, Mr C. Now why don't you tell me the real reason for this visit. Does it have anything to do with the agreements represented in these contracts?"

"You know the answer to that. Maybe it has to do with a red Volvo, somewhat the worse for wear, that keeps turning up like a dirty penny. Maybe it has to do with a photograph I have of Roger Cavanaugh accepting a T-shirt from the friendly people of Orillia a few weeks ago."

Bosco looked stunned. It wasn't a passing expression that flickered across his face. When it hit him, it stayed there, unfocused, poleaxed. He'd known that it would come one day, but he hadn't expected it to come today, and not from me. "Let's get out of here," he said, getting to his feet. Without looking back to see if I was following him, he hurried down the corridor and around the bend to the waiting area, where he told the receptionist to hold his calls and reschedule all of his meetings for the next two hours.

"But, Mr Bos—"

"*All* of them!"

"What about Ms Slopen? You invited her to lunch!"

"Send her a dozen long-stemmed roses. Make it two dozen. Tell her I'll call as soon as I can. Tell Mr Devlin—"

"What should she tell Mr Devlin?" Raymond Devlin had stepped out of his office into the reception area. Bosco looked like he'd been goosed. Then, recovering, he smiled at the senior partner.

"I'm stepping out of the office for—"

"For two hours. I heard you loud and clear. What's this about? Hello there, Mr Sugarman, isn't it? From Vanessa Moss's office?"

"Yes, Mr *Cooper*man just brought over the matted contracts from NTC."

"Good of you, Mr Cooperman. Sorry about your name; I still have some ragged edges left over from when this was a one-man operation. Back then, I was something of a fire-engine chaser. But I wasn't very good at it because I couldn't remember names. People told me I should settle for a less adventurous brand of law. I think they were right. Anyway, what's this all about, Barry?"

"Just a few minor glitches in the details of the reception tomorrow, Raymond. The hotel had a few logistical problems. Security; things like that. We'll be able to sort it out over coffee around the corner. I think it's important that things should run smoothly tomorrow."

"Well, better you than me, Barry. I'll see you later. Good afternoon, Mr Cooperman." He was about to step back into his office, and Barry Bosco had recovered a little.

"I'll speak to you as soon after five as I can, Raymond. The Cluny and Lorringer files are on my desk. We have to see Mr Murphy about the Levitt business. Could you be free next Thursday after lunch?" Devlin emitted a golden smile and waved five fingers as he retreated to his desk. The young receptionist, however, was obviously flustered and Bosco saw this. "Esmé, don't bother to cover for me. Go to lunch; let the machines do the work."

"Yes, Mr Bosco."

Fifteen minutes later, Bosco and I were seated in a booth in a Chinese restaurant called the Champion House. It specialized in serving Peking duck and announced the coming of each duck from the kitchen by sounding a gong. Although the restaurant looked tidy and comfortable, the patrons repaid the good food and service by writing their thanks on the wallpaper. On the wall behind Bosco, I could make out: "Greeeeaaat duck!! You did it again. Blessings and thanks, Alabama and Stan, Mel and Lorne, Port Alberni, B.C." Bosco ordered a plate of Chinese vegetables and some sliced duck. The waiter brought a big pot of green tea.

"Okay, let's have it," Bosco said. "I want to know what you know. Then tell me your price."

"I'm not buying or selling. I'm collecting the facts, just like old Joe Friday on TV."

"You've talked to Roger? Shit! You can't trust anybody!"

"Look, if we're going to get anywhere, let's not cut the ribbon before we build the bridge. No, I haven't talked to Roger, but I recognized him in the Orillia photographs. He must have been crazy to stick by the alibi he provided for you. I've never heard of a more harebrained scheme. I mean, talk about stupid. The pair of you. You both could lose your licences. Hell, with the murder, you could both be facing prison. How did you shut him up when Renata was murdered?"

"Like everybody else around here, he wants into the charmed circle. He's a good trial lawyer and will be an asset to the firm, so I'm not introducing dead weight to the partners."

"Save me your rationalization. I just want the why and wherefore."

"I've felt like a hit-and-run driver since it happened."

"So you got him to cover for you on the night of the murder."

"It didn't start out as the night of the murder! It was just a Monday-night talk. Christ, you have to *see* that." He moved a hand through his hair, checking to see that it was all there. "All he had to do was drive to Orillia and read my speech."

"But how did you keep him quiet when they found Renata dead? Suddenly it had become more complicated."

"Promises. I made him promises, just as I said."

"Okay, now the big one: where did you go that night?"

"I could lie to you."

"Yeah, and you could stand mute. But I have a hunch that you want this thing cleared up. You went to see Renata, didn't you?"

"You're leading."

"Didn't you?"

"Yes. Oh, yes; God, yes!"

"Tell me about it." He looked at the ceiling, then around at the three remaining diners in the place. Nobody was looking at him.

"I got there at eight. She cooked dinner. We ate it. Do I have to tell you this? We made love in her room. Is that what you want to hear? You want to know what it was like? Sorry, Cooperman, but you're pushing me, and I don't like it."

"Just tell me."

"Later, we did the dishes, you know?—and talked. We had a lot to talk about. About us, I mean. Things hadn't been going all that well."

"Did you arrange to meet her or was it the other way around?"

"She phoned me at the office; said she *had* to see me. It was important, she said."

"Did she get to the subject?"

"No. She *did* say that she thought she was being followed. She was nervous. We'd gone from the kitchen to the living-room; she was leading up to something she wanted to tell me. I could tell, but before she could get launched, the doorbell rang."

"Go on."

"She got up, said that she'd be back in a minute. Before I could pick up the paper, I heard Renata's voice. At first it was indistinct and then it built into a scream. I can still hear it in my head. I won't ever get that sound out of my head. Then I heard the gun go off. Just the two blasts, one right after the other. Almost at the same time. It couldn't have been more than a few seconds after she left me sitting there."

"You heard the scream and then the gunshots, right?"

"Yes. I thought I'd said that."

"What did you do?"

"I'm ashamed. I'm so *ashamed!*"

"I'm not your priest. Just tell me."

"I hid behind the couch. I thought he was going to come into the room and get me too."

"You were sure it was a man?"

"At the time I was. I don't know why. I guess it *could* have been a woman."

"And you forgot that he or she had to reload the gun after firing both barrels?"

"I didn't see the gun. It could have been a pump action. But I wasn't thinking straight. I hid, sitting on the floor. Behind the couch."

"Okay, okay. I probably would have done the same thing. Look, I'm no hero either. What else? Did you hear anything?"

"Nothing until the door closed. I must have stayed there for another five minutes before I realized that the murderer had gone and wasn't coming back."

"So you got up to see what had happened?"

"That's right. What had happened was that Renata . . . had . . . You know. Don't take me through that again. I turned on the hall light. Just for a second. I had to turn it right off again. I couldn't . . ."

"Okay, you saw that she was dead—that she was beyond saving, anyway. What else?"

"What do you mean, 'What else?'"

"Did you think for a moment that you *might* call the cops?"

"I went into the bedroom with that in mind, but before I reached the phone, I saw how bad I'd look. I'd be perfect casting for the murderer. I'd set up an alibi so that I could show I was a hundred miles from the crime scene. Why would I do that if I didn't have some sinister purpose?"

"But, Mr Bosco, you *did* make those arrangements."

"That wasn't to provide an alibi! I got Roger to spell me off for the evening. He'd do the talk, and I'd see what Renata wanted. It only becomes suspicious in the light of what happened to Renata."

"You're lucky Roger's so ambitious."

"He's nearly come unstuck twice. Don't get me started on *that*."

"Back to the scene of the crime. Besides Renata lying there, what else did you see?"

"Nothing. Nothing but the two spent shells from the gun. The ones they found later in Vanessa Moss's locker. I can't figure that one out."

"The shells were left in the hall by the murderer? Is that what you're saying?" Bosco nodded. His lank hair was falling over his eyes, and he brushed it back with his hand unsuccessfully. "You could have told the police that it was Renata and not Vanessa who'd been killed. You kept quiet. For a whole week. *Why?*"

"I don't know. I must have been in shock. I tried to think of a way to let them know, but everything I thought of brought the cops to my own front door. They'd have finished me. Ray runs a very tight ship, Mr Cooperman. There's no room for second chances."

"So, instead of doing something useful, you've been playing Sherlock Holmes on your own. I hope you have a couple of prime suspects?"

"That fellow George Brenner, the parking guy at the network. He knew where Vanessa lived. They've been having an affair. He may have seen me arrive at Vanessa's house and mistaken Renata for Vanessa."

"The old jealousy dodge. Who else?"

"Well, Bob Foley was looking good for a while. It might be the reason for his suicide."

"Why'd Dermot Keogh choose him as one of the trustees of the Plevna Foundation?"

"They were friends. Foley was Keogh's gofer. He saw to Dermot's laundry, licence renewals, boat and car maintenance, electric bill, you know, all the stuff a genius hasn't time to look after."

"You're not impressed by genius?"

"It's all right in its place. But Dermot's affairs have transformed our firm. It should be renamed Dermot Keogh Enterprises. The whole of his estate is operated out of our office, and the balance between criminal and corporate law, which used to exist, is way out of whack. I haven't been in a courtroom for six months. That's a long time, Mr C. I love trial work and I'm good at it. But the firm's interest in that end of the business has been distracted." The waiter dropped two hot, wet washcloths in front of us. I scalded myself in two places before catching on to the operation. Bosco handled his cloth better, but he wasn't looking well.

"I'm still not thinking straight, Mr C. Give me a break, please? I can't talk any more. I touched the hall light switch. I must have left a print. Since that night I've been jumping every time the phone rings. I have heard the voices of the cops asking if I could come downtown to clear up a few things."

"Just one more minute, Mr Bosco: how did you leave the house? The body and the shells were in the hall. Was the door open?"

"I think it was closed. Yes, it was closed. But when I left, I know that I left it open. I had an instinct to go back and close it, but I couldn't make myself. I fled. That's the only word for it." He looked at me with his eyes watering, searching my face for the answers to questions I hadn't the skill to ask. They were washed-out blue eyes now, like the colour of a chalk drawing on a rainy sidewalk.

Most of the vegetables and meat had grown cold over half an hour ago. Neither of us had eaten much. The tea was cold. Bosco paid the bill and left, miming a parting word. I cracked open one of the two fortune cookies. It read: "Your problems will vanish if you have patience." I never found out what Bosco's said. He didn't open it.

CHAPTER EIGHTEEN

After Bosco left, I sat with the green tea until it was bitter as well as cold. I couldn't think of anything witty enough to write on the wall. I was asked if I wanted more tea. I did, but I thought a walk through Chinatown would be even better. There were some things on my mind that had been rattling around without my having time to see if any of them stuck together. The walk along Dundas Street to University Avenue wasn't a long one, but just the right length to get my thoughts straighter than they'd been. I reminded myself of a visit from my Uncle Nathan from New York. He took one look at my father's dress store and complained, "Manny, you've got inventory all over the place. You must be crazy overloading the shop like this. A man can't live on inventory alone." He was right. And an investigator can get facts so stuck in his head that he can't read them any more.

There was a big grey truck backed up to the entrance of NTC's main entrance. The back doors were open, and a wheeled ramp led from the truck-bed to the top step of the entrance. As I approached, I saw a security guard holding visitors back from the dismantled revolving door. Three men in grey shopcoats were running a pair of digital editing machines through the lobby in the direction of the truck. Another mover was holding a padded blanket to help ease the hardware through the tight squeeze of the glass doorway. I waited my turn. They looked like professionals. The man in charge, with a redoubtable beer belly, supervised the manoeuvres without putting his hands on metal. When the first two

machines had been loaded, I saw that a second pair was waiting just inside the door, with a security guard keeping visitors
well away from adding their fingerprints to the shiny blue-
grey metal surfaces. How did I know that they were digital
editing machines? To be honest, right then, I didn't. They
could have been egg hatchers or baby incubators as far as I was
concerned. The only thing I thought about them then was the
fact that I was coming and they were going. I was between a
dismantled revolving door and a hard place to get into.

A couple of familiar technicians I recognized from the pub
around the corner were watching the loading procedure. They
looked at one another, wearing curious, light-hearted, knowing expressions. It took me a while to learn how to read them.
When I looked for them a few moments later, they were gone.
The usual crowd of smokers hovered in a group, like exiles,
just beyond the door.

"How long is the door going to be blocked?"

"You can get through in five minutes," one security guard
said, sizing me up. "Or you can go around to the side door or
you could come back later. They'll be through here in ten minutes at the outside." I was about to follow the latter advice
when I saw an opening between the first two pieces, and
grabbed it. I could feel the weight of the machine pressing
against me as I sucked in my breath and forced my way
between the quilting and the doorway.

Once inside, I found myself in the midst of another break in
the routine. A bandstand had been assembled in front of a
huge map of Canada cut into a massive screen of illuminated
glass, and a jazz band was playing its heart out while NTC regulars went about their business without giving them more than
a shrug of notice. The lobby hadn't been designed to encourage
music, and the glass entranceway and marble interior offended
it with a hostile bounce, repelling the Dixieland riffs as though
they were an embarrassment. Whoever organized this noon-
hour concert had forgotten the plugged doorway. The boys in
the band were playing for the converted. There were no
strangers within the gates. The musicians paid that no mind;

they were in a groove and enjoying themselves. The lead guitar was pushing a modern version of an old prison work song:

> It's a long John,
> He's a long gone,
> Like a turkey through the corn
> Through the long corn.

The few trapped visitors or regulars who noticed were impressed. In a corner were huddled the forms of a few more unreformed smokers, taking advantage of the circumstances to steal a few puffs in the lobby, buttressed by one another against the momentarily divided attention of the guards. I paused to listen for a minute or more, waiting for the courage to run the gauntlet of Security. The other guitarist and the bass now joined in the chorus:

> Mister John, John,
> Old Big-eye John,
> Oh John, John
> It's a long John.

You could hear the work-song origins pulsating through the lines. You could hear axe blades or railroad hammers striking with a rattle of prison chains as they finished up their take on this old jazz classic.

"Ruth Pierson! Hey, baby, what are you doing here?" It was one of the musicians. He was addressing an attractively turned-out woman, who looked as though she was enjoying the music.

"Hi, Josh! They won't let me out of here. I'm trapped until they clear the doorway." Ruth went over to the bandstand and began talking to the drummer in a quieter voice.

I wandered through the lobby watching the people. Are there types who frequent TV network offices? Are there shy geniuses with bright ideas? Hucksters looking for a sucker? I wandered and eavesdropped. Two attractive young women with the glitter of metal in their ears and noses were talking about a party. ". . . It was billed as this terrific *event*. But there weren't any *real* movie stars there. Not even *real actors*."

"Apart from the drinks, it was hardly—"

"Oh, there *was* that female midget from *Total Recall*. She was there, but she's not anybody."

"She did some guest spots on *Seinfeld*. She was on a few times."

"We thought that they'd have people from the *movie* or some production people or at least those robots . . ." I left them with their disenchantment and disappointment.

Security this afternoon was a bored face with rimless glasses. She examined my pass, made me sign in and instructed me to go directly to my assigned floor without stopping to gossip in the halls. When she caught my expression, which I'm afraid echoed my heart, she turned on me with a stony look. "Commander Dunkery knows about you, Mr Cooperman. I'd be on my best behaviour if I were you."

"Who's your Mr Dunkery?"

"What? You don't know *Commander* Dunkery? That is a surprise. I suspect you're having me on."

"I suppose I can look it up. If I remember."

"You should get your picture on that pass, you know. It's as good as my job if I let you through here after a week. You see to it, now."

I found the burgundy elevator and let NTC in all its corporate ugliness settle down around me again.

Sally put down some complicated-looking schedules she was working on. Television requires a lot of work to keep it as bad as it is. Armies of talented people work their hearts out about whether to broadcast a series about a Martian who has imprinted on a gas pump earlier or later in prime time than a series about a straight guy pretending that he is gay in order to continue living with four scrumptious college girls. I'd seen them all, adults, every one of them, get depressed because a series had slipped from sixth to seventh place in the ratings game. And what was the series about? A show about an analyst who's trying not to fall in love with two of her patients and who's allergic to a third.

"Benny! *She's* been asking for you."

"You mean, she's *back?*"

"She just called from the airport."

"Good. I thought she was yelling for me here." That gave me a little time.

I must have looked fretful or indecisive, because soon Sally asked, "Where are you going now?"

"How did you know I was going anywhere?"

"You get this *look* when you've been in one place too long."

"But I just got here!"

"Doesn't matter. Gordon used to get it. It's a *man* thing, maybe."

"I'll try to watch out for it. I was thinking of going over to News, to bother Ken Trebitsch for a change."

"Watch your back."

The News Department fairly vibrated with activity. There was a sense of purpose in the air as three dozen people moved like a human tangle of multicoloured wires about their business in the large newsroom from computer monitor to chalkboard, from chalkboard to duty desk and from duty desk back to monitor. There were enough clocks on the wall to tell you the time anywhere on the globe: Los Angeles, Tokyo, London, Rome, Moscow, Beijing, Washington. There was something self-important and comic about the bustle and the serious faces that managed to avoid eye contact as I came through the door. Trebitsch, in shirtsleeves, was leaning over a huddle of backs at one computer monitor. Obviously, he was a manager who stayed close to the action, not a dull administrator. "We haven't got a story if we can't get film on it."

"We've got file film, Ken."

"Yeah, with Tito leading the parade. You're going to have to do better than that. See if Humphreys at CBC can feed you anything. He still owes us for Kosovo." He disengaged himself from the clutch of news people and was heading into another huddle when he saw me. "Mr Cooperman! Are you still here?"

"I'll bet you thought I accepted an invitation to go home to Grantham."

"You'd be surprised at the amount of good advice that gets ignored. But there's no reasoning with some people."

"What's your part in all this?" I asked. "Do you see an enemy behind every bush and stone?" He looked at me in a peculiar way.

"You just don't get it, do you?" For the first time his eyes had lost their hooded, snake-like look. They shone with innocence.

"I came here hoping to learn something."

"If you don't know now, you won't learn in a thousand years."

"You want to run all this?" I moved my arms to suggest that there was a world beyond News.

"Not just *this*, but—never mind. I haven't the time to explain. But you need an education, and I think you're going to get it."

"You're talking hard knocks?" He didn't answer directly, but looked over a pair of shoulders into another monitor for a minute, made a suggestion, then turned back to me.

"As you may have noticed, I'm a hands-on type. I like to know what is going on around me."

"And what happened to Renata Sartori is outside your grasp. Not in your schedule? Is that it? How's that different from a plane crash or a hurricane? You're in the dark, and your friends aren't very good at turning on the lights."

"Go home, Cooperman!"

"That was the message you tried to deliver the other night."

"Don't know what you're talking about, but it makes sense. Take it to heart. You'll live longer."

"Sounds like a threat."

"Forget what it sounds like; grab the sense of it and go!"

"Your boys with the green car aren't much good. They could get into trouble negotiating a stoplight. I'd get them out of sight, if I were you. They could be an embarrassment to a man on the move like you."

"I said I don't know what you're talking about. But there are a lot of heavies around here if you need them. There are always new bodies to take the places of the fallen."

"Yeah, and the Third Reich will last a thousand years. Can your world takeover be stopped with Raid?"

"Look, Cooperman. You're *persona non grata*. Need a translation? I don't like it when there are too many players on the floor. Even the cops would be happier if you went home. I know that for a fact. Why don't you just do that?" I shrugged. It only irritated him. "For God's sake, this isn't some sort of game! This is my *life* you're playing around with. My fucking *life!*"

"This isn't a life. This is a delusion. You think you're delivering the news. You're a pap merchant. At least be an honest one. It's not all the news that's fit to print; it's all the news that fits. It's not news if you've got no pictures. A two-week war is a week too long. It needs editing."

"You'll never understand what we're trying to do here."

"Right, because I won't smoke the stuff you're smoking. Writing the news is honest work. But you puff it up like it's a blast from Mount Sinai."

"I want you gone, Cooperman, and gone fast. This place is filled with serious professionals. We know our business. Why don't you mind yours? If you don't, as I keep telling you, you could get hurt. You'd be surprised how little that would bother me."

"For a newsman, you're behind the times. Things have been happening under your nose in the last few hours. You've got some catching up to do. There have been some moves since you stopped watching the board. See you around." I turned to go. I was sorry I couldn't get more from him. Just for the hell of it, I turned to see him still watching me as I headed for the door. I called across to him, "At the sound of the tone, the time in Tokyo will be exactly four, seventeen and a half." For a moment the only sound you could hear in the newsroom was the sound of electric clocks.

I left him intrigued, I think. Trebitsch was the sort whose shoes pinched when he wasn't in the race. I didn't want to tell him that shortly the cops and I would be talking again—that would only prompt another call to the Chief's office—but it gave me a good feeling to see him looking just a little uncomfortable.

It proved to be a little premature for me to feel smug about the tenuous hold I had over Trebitsch. I discovered this as I reached the halfway point between News and my office.

"Mr Cooperman!" It wasn't a greeting, a sign of recognition, but a command to stand still. I did that. When I turned around, I could see three men in uniform coming along the corridor after me on the double. For a moment, I thought of running for it, but I gave up the idea. This wasn't my own briar patch. I was certain to find a dead-end corridor or try to cut through a broom closet. If I was to get the better of these three, it would have to be through other means.

"Mr Cooperman, you'd better come with us." The trio in uniforms marked NTC Security blocked my passage. There was nothing to do about it but to shrug and go with them. At least they weren't the Horsemen. I tried to engage them in chat, but it didn't work. One guard pushed the elevator button with a deeply concerned brow, as though it signalled the destruction of civilization as we know it. Inside the elevator, I got no answers to my many questions. I made a reference to Mr Dunkery, which made one of them blink. So, I was guessing right about who wanted to see me.

They led me down a trail of turns and ins and outs until we entered a room clearly marked SECURITY on the door. At least they weren't trying to keep that a secret. I was left seated on the civilian side of a counter for about five silent minutes—I was getting used to silence—and then I was told that Commander Dunkery would see me now. My three playmates saw me to the door, where they were dismissed by a nod from the man behind the desk.

Dunkery's office was designed to intimidate. It was part war room and high-command post. I thought of officers being briefed, and smoking if they liked, and synchronizing their watches, and not having any questions. There were more photographs of Dunkery shaking hands with well-known figures than you'd ever want to see. Citations and diplomas covered what was left of the wall space that wasn't given over to floor plans of the NTC building. A big brass globe with the network's owl on top sat on a shelf near his right hand, so he could stroke it maybe if he started feeling insecure. An abridged Bible, not printed on smokable paper, lay open on the desk blotter. Several of the texts were underlined in colour. I thought of George trying to get past the Commander. Dunkery sat behind his desk, which was lifted up on a platform of some kind, so that I sat below him looking up. For a moment I thought I'd try the play from *The Great Dictator* and sit on the edge of Commander Dunkery's desk, staring down at him, but I decided against it.

"Well, Mr Cooperman! So, we finally meet. You should have come to me a week ago."

"I didn't know you were looking for me. You know where I work?"

"Yes, and we know who you're working for and why."

"That makes it unanimous, I guess. What can I do for you?"

"You can get the hell out of here and let professionals deal with what is clearly none of your business." I nodded at this, as though giving it serious thought. On the subject of my getting out of town, this silly network was a bloody theme park.

"What gives you the monopoly at NTC? I saw local cops on the twenty-first floor last week. Maybe there are Provincial Police on the third or Mounties on the sixteenth. Are you planning to tell them to shove off too?"

"I won't answer that or any other foolish questions. I want to see the back of you, Cooperman, and I want you gone this afternoon."

"Sure you do. And when Vanessa Moss gets shot because you won't put a man on her door, you're going to look terrific.

Especially when they find out that you chased away her babysitter. I can't see that I'm queering your pitch, Commander."

Commander Dunkery was a brown man. I'm not talking about skin pigmentation, I mean he was wearing a brown suit with a military cut to it, his sparse hair was brown, and his shirt and tie looked brownish as well. A brownish moustache tried but failed to underline his authority. His face was florid. I guessed that he was having trouble with blood pressure as well as with unwanted private investigators. "This afternoon!" he repeated.

"Just how are you going to arrange that? I'm working on the staff of Vanessa Moss, head of Entertainment. I guess she can hire whom she wants. Or are you going to limit her to the grandsons of Desert War veterans?"

"You're being irrelevant, Cooperman."

"Sorry. Ms Moss wields a lot of weight on the twentieth floor. She usually gets what she wants."

"Not for much longer. She's nearly finished at this network." I got the feeling that he wanted to go *thwack* with a swagger stick against the side of his boot.

"But, alas for you, not quite yet. I understand that she will be back in the building within the hour with all of her titles intact. If that's so, why don't you tell me what's *really* on your mind. You must have seen rent-a-cops before? You probably have hired quite a few in your time."

"You have been insulting to my staff on several occasions. It has been reported to me, and I will not stand for it!"

"I don't like wearing stick-on labels, Commander. They're hard on my clothes."

"You were told to get proper identification."

"I've been too busy trying to stop Vanessa Moss from getting murdered."

"Nobody's trying to kill Ms Moss."

"Can I quote you? What about Renata Sartori? Were you looking after her too?"

"That happened *off* the premises. I'm not responsible—"

"That does sum it up, doesn't it? Now, if you'll—"

"Listen, Cooperman! You don't get to this office without building a network of trust. There isn't anybody here who doesn't owe me. I've been a useful fellow to know for the last ten years. I'm owed favours on the twentieth floor. If they don't start flowing by themselves, all I have to do is rattle their chains. Do you follow me?"

"And you'd call in all these favours just to get rid of me?"

"I have broken better men than you, Cooperman. You make me sick. I've got a good system going here, and it works as long as everybody plays the game. You and your sort never play the game, do you? Not in my experience. Can't stay in line. So, my advice to you—"

"Before you break some important blood vessel inside your head, Commander, I'd like to report a breach in your system."

"What are you talking about? *My* system?"

"Yeah. A couple of thieves have just driven off with a truck-load of recording equipment belonging to NTC, if I'm not mistaken. Looked brand new. But what do I know? That comes under your responsibility, doesn't it? Your people were holding the doors open for them when I came in here half an hour ago. The crooks were wearing shopcoats, and the truck was unmarked, except for the licence. Do you let that happen often, Commander? All part of the system? A man could get wealthy on that sort of thing with just one or two truckloads a month. Of course, there might be criminal charges if anyone was caught in the act. There were at least two witnesses besides me. Maybe they got the truck's licence number too."

"Why you . . . !" He stood up at his desk. It was the first time I'd seen him standing. He was right to place his desk on a riser. He was shorter than I am by two inches. I would have got up myself just then, only I had never been asked to sit down. I turned and walked out of the office of the head of Security and caught an elevator back to my office on the twentieth floor. I left the Commander sputtering behind me.

NINETEEN

I could tell that Vanessa was back. There was a crackle of static electricity as I rounded the corner to her office. She *did* something to the way people moved by her door. My suspicion was confirmed when I saw Sally: trade papers and draft schedules in sight, no coffee mug sitting near her.

"Who's with her?" I asked.

"Thornhill was waiting for her. They've been in there ever since she arrived."

"Is she going then?"

"Benny, she hasn't had a second to tell me anything. It's been non-stop since she walked in the door. Philip Rankin's there, of course. He's always been 'Mary, Mary, quite contrary.' He watches to see how his garden grows and grows. Wants Music to become NTC Recordings, Benny. A whole division under him. Oh, and Ken Trebitsch is in there now. Wouldn't you guess? He'll come out with pie all over his face even if he gets only another thirty minutes of prime."

The thought that Vanessa had been dumped opened a leak in my system. I could feel myself deflating like a party balloon that has been lost behind some furniture. I hadn't realized the extent of my partiality for Vanessa's empire. Maybe last Thursday night meant more to me than I suspected. In spite of the obvious ways in which I'd seen her manipulate people, ways that seemed crude as well as self-serving, I'd been pulled in with the other suckers. I was a consumer of Vanessa's magnetism, and I hadn't suspected it until that moment.

Suddenly she was there. With Trebitsch, Rankin and Thornhill. She was radiant; Ken Trebitsch was glum. Like he'd been run over by a campaign bus. Even the three flunkies he travelled the corridors with were glum. Stella had beaten them! Rankin sputtered like a beached flounder. Thornhill looked confused. His little eyes strained to find focus. No wonder: he couldn't figure out what had just happened to him. I wouldn't hear the details until later, but their faces couldn't have told me more.

"Thank you, Ted. I appreciate your help on this. Good morning, Mr Cooperman. So nice of you to drop by."

Her face was tanned, and Armani was keeping his side of the bargain. She looked younger, more poised and healthier than when I last saw her only four days ago. Thornhill and Trebitsch shook my hand without emotion when Vanessa reintroduced us, then headed off in other directions, neither daring to speak to the other as they went. She was secure enough of her position to wave the visitors on their way, as though it was she who'd called the meeting. After they'd gone, she collected some message slips from Sally on her way back into her private office.

"Benny," Sally said, breaking in on my sudden infatuation with my client's presence, even in her absence. "Here's a copy of that will you were asking about." I must have had a stupid look on my face as I stared at the closed door to Vanessa's private office, because Sally repeated what she'd just said. I said some calming words to myself and cleared my throat.

"Thanks, Sally, I won't keep it long." I retreated to an unoccupied corner and sat in the mock shade of one of those indoor trees with trunks that look as if they've been woven from the trunks of three or four smaller trees. The leaves were narrow and pointed and didn't really give any shade. The lighting in the office banished shadows of all kinds. I sat down on the edge of the window ledge.

The will was long and complicated. It had been drawn up by Raymond Devlin on the kind of paper that is made from royal bedsheets. After a number of small bequests, including the gift of his cello to the University of Toronto's Hart House collection of stringed instruments, the bulk of the estate was divided among several trusts. There were sections on the setting up of the Plevna Foundation. Both Bob Foley and Philip Rankin were named to it. Its direction and the direction of the rest of the will were left in the capable hands of the sole executor, Raymond Devlin. The will was dated March second, three years ago. It was witnessed by two women, whose names appeared again with affidavits that they had indeed witnessed the signing of the will I was holding. I looked at the scrawled signature of Dermot Keogh in all the places where his signature was supposed to appear. The bottom of each page was initialled. It looked as legal as hell. I couldn't argue with it. But, there was nothing about a palliative care unit on any of its fifteen pages. Nor had he disposed of his collection of motorcycles. That left me something to chew on.

It was nearly five when Vanessa finally sent for me. She was seated behind her desk, but got up and walked around the desk to greet me with a double bussing until my cheeks shone with gratitude and pleasure. "Benny, you know, I often thought of you during the weekend. You mustn't let it go to your head, but you were missed." She sat on one of the couches that flanked a glass-topped coffee table and indicated that I was to join her. I did. "Now, tell me what you've been doing while I was on the coast."

I gave a fair rendering of my activities as far as seemed best. I held back a few things that I thought she shouldn't know about just then. I didn't want to hamper my own investigation by having too many people know as much as I did.

"You've been busy," she acknowledged.

"So have you, Vanessa. I'm all admiration."

"I was playing dirty pool in L.A., Benny. I got Warners and the others to sign contracts with a clause that lets them off the hook if I'm suddenly no longer head of Entertainment. They didn't like it, but they could see that that would give them the power to go on dealing with me for a while. Nobody down there wants to break in a new head right now."

"Is that legal?"

"They signed it, so it's legal. Irregular but solid enough to put them off trying to break it."

"What's next?"

"I need to clean off this desk. It'll take me a few minutes."

"So, you don't need me for the next half-hour?"

"Benny, I'm Vanessa Moss, and I don't *need* anyone. I survived a coup right here in this office ten minutes ago, and I was *terrific!* You should have seen me! Oh, Benny, I *was good!*"

"That translates as follows: you can spare me for thirty minutes. I read you. Over and out."

"Cooperman, you have a leaden soul. It will never rise. Scram. But I want your trim ass back here in an hour. Then we'll celebrate."

I wasn't sure where I was going, but where I ended up was the Rex pub around the corner on Queen Street. I didn't know whether the blaring TV would help me think or not, but the idea of a cold glass of beer had been growing within me, and I was happy to see its reality being set down at a table in front of me. Before I'd finished the first cool draft, there was a hand on my shoulder. It belonged to Jesse Alder, the technician I'd met the other day.

"You want to join us? There's a gang of us at our regular table in the back. You're welcome any time, Mr Cooperman."

"Thanks, Jesse, I'd like that. But first, I want to talk to you for a minute. You mind?"

"No, go ahead. I'm on break. My time is your time." Jesse sat down facing me.

"The other day when I was here with you, I asked about Bob Foley. You know that I'm a private investigator and that I'm trying to keep Vanessa Moss from getting killed the way Renata Sartori was."

"Sure. I know. Everybody knows."

"What I wanted to ask you is why did everybody at the table dummy up when I brought up Foley's name?"

"He has never been popular with the guys, Benny."

"I guessed that much. And his sudden rise under the banner of Dermot Keogh didn't add to his popularity, did it? But there's something else. I feel it itching the backs of my knees. My knees tell me when I'm close to something. Never fails."

"Just a minute." Jesse got up, revisited his table long enough to retrieve a glass of beer and return in less than twenty seconds. He took a long drink before he spoke. "Look, before Bob Foley came along, I did all the gofering for Dermot. We were friends over at the CBC long before Bob got out of Ryerson with his Radio and TV Arts degree. I'm talking about the ten years before I introduced Dermot to Bob four years ago. I mastered all of the recordings he made in Toronto except for maybe half a dozen that Bob did. I liked Dermot a lot, but I couldn't go at his pace any more. Nobody could. And my back was giving me trouble. So I introduced him to Bob, who is really a good technician. He's got a good ear and he's learned to read music. The boys know this, and they think it's unfair that Bob should have figured so big in Dermot's will, and I got left out altogether."

"I could make a good case for your being an aggrieved character. If Dermot was murdered, you'd stand high among the suspects."

"*Me!* Look, Benny. You don't understand how it was. I was Dermot's friend. I mean, he told me about his life: his time with Casals in Prades, his classes with Rostropovich in Moscow, his tiff with Von Karajan. All that stuff. But even more important, I got to do that work—before, I mean. I recorded him, did all the editing and mastering. *Nobody*, not Bob, not Rankin, not even Dermot Keogh himself can take that away from me."

"I hear what you're saying."

"I did the work. You couldn't buy that from me. So not being remembered in the will doesn't bug me all that seriously. I still got those crazy phone calls from him late at night, and he'd tell me what was going down. Yeah, he'd tell me how Bob was ripping him off in small ways and we'd laugh at that, because Dermot didn't care that Bob was getting his laundry done in Mississauga and charging him for a forty-mile drive. He told me that he charged him for going to buy his special unsalted, raw cashew nuts and arrowroot biscuits in Oshawa and charging him the mileage."

"Wait a minute, I don't get this. How could he charge back the mileage?"

"It happened like this. Dermot lent Bob the money to buy that house in Cabbagetown. He lent him the *cash*. Bob was supposed to be paid for the odd jobs he did for Dermot, so Dermot got him to keep track and mark off these expenses against the total loan. Of course he was paying him for the work he did in Dermot's studio, over at 18 Clarence Square, you know, in the corner, south of King, off Spadina?"

"No, I've never been there."

"Well, nothing's been changed. It's still there. All of Dermot's Canadian and American recordings are there. So is all of Dermot's recording equipment."

"Has the estate been paying rent on that place?"

"*Rent?* Hell no. It was Dermot's. They only have to pay the taxes, water, sewage—that sort of stuff."

"I'll remember that." I took a sip from a new draft set in front of me. "So, *you* brought Bob Foley into Dermot Keogh's world four years ago, and that effectively pulled your plug."

"Yeah, you could say it like that. But, like I told you, Dermot and I still kept in touch."

"Right. Now, was it Bob who brought Ray Devlin into Dermot's affairs?"

"No, I think Ray was always working for Dermot, doing contracts and what have you, all the legal stuff that an entertainer needs. Not the management stuff. He looked after most of that himself or delegated it to Bob. Early on, he had a guy in New York, but Dermot got rid of him. Yeah, Dermot was always complaining to me that he could never get Ray on the phone when he needed him. It pissed him off royally. Or as Dermot would have said, it 'peeved' him."

"Did he ever mention the creation of a palliative care unit to you?"

"How did you hear about *that?*"

"He did, then?"

"Sure. Dermot was always a health nut in theory, but he really never looked after himself. He loved to eat and drink and, you know, fool around. But, the year before he died, early in the new year, Dermot's father got sick. I mean really sick. Dermot knew that he was dying, and he did die about a year later. That's when he started talking to me about setting up a unit that would deal humanely with hopeless cases. That's the way he was. He hated to see anything suffer. He was always bringing home stray cats to Clarence Square, and I had to tell him that the cat hair was no good for the computer equipment. 'Screw the equipment,' he'd say. That was Dermot."

I paused, hoping that Jesse would continue without prompting. He looked at his watch, took another swallow and picked up the story.

"The last time I talked to Dermot, he woke me up at three in the morning to tell me as a surprise that the unit was a reality. He said it was fully provided for. His old man was still alive then, so I thought good on Dermot. But nothing came of it. Not while Dermot was alive, not after his father died and then not even when Dermot's will was read. Something's funny, I used to say to myself. You know what I mean, Benny?"

I told him that I thought I did. Together we walked over to the other table and joined the other technicians. We downed a few rounds before they had to return to their assignments. I was left with my share of the tab and sat there trying to get a time sequence straight in my head.

TWENTY

I had something on my mind and I thought Chuck Pepper was the one to fix it. I called him from the pay phone near the front of the pub.

"Pepper." His voice on the phone sounded the way a cop's voice ought to. I trusted that voice.

"Chuck, it's Cooperman. How's it going?" I'm sure he could hear and recognize the din behind me. Still, he didn't say anything. Sykes or Boyd would have.

"The forensic people want you to join up, Benny. Your suggestions on the Foley case paid off. Far too much cigarette ash for the number of butts and packages. They even went further: they say the ash was new; it wasn't mixed in with floor dust enough for it to have been an accumulation over time. I reckon that makes you a happy camper, Benny?"

"What's it got to do with me? I was just being helpful. But, while we're on the subject of forensics, what about the glasses in the kitchen and the yellow rubber gloves?"

"You hit a nerve there too. They aren't as happy about that; think they should have thought of it themselves. There's one good print inside the glove. But they don't have much to compare it with. It wasn't Foley's. Not his ex-wife's either."

"Could you do me a favour, Chuck?"

"What else have I ever done for you?"

"I need to know—no, wait a minute—*you* need to know the combination of the lock that Jack and Jim had cut off the locker in Vanessa Moss's office. I've been bugging Jack about it since I first met him a week ago and he still hasn't found out, or if he has, he hasn't told me. But then, I've been made Out of Bounds by the Chief. You heard about that, I suppose?"

"Yeah, Jack called me. The Chief put his head in the microwave. Nothing he could do about it. But what's this about locks?"

"I've got a half-baked idea, Chuck. But if it turns out to be better than that, it could be important, and I don't want to be connected with it any more than I have to. You want a clean chain of evidence, and I don't want to foul it for you."

"I'll call Jack about it. I won't mention your name. I'll say the half-baked idea was all mine." I heard a blurred sound. Chuck left the line for a moment. When he came back, he asked if I could meet him for breakfast in the morning. We arranged a spot near my hotel, and we both went back to work.

I got no flack from Security when I returned to NTC. I was whizzed through like I was wearing Commander Dunkery's own identity card. Vanessa was standing in her office with the door open, looking down onto University Avenue. An amateur gunman could have got off a few rounds at her without stepping far from the elevator.

"Are you trying to get yourself killed?" I said, closing the doors behind me. "You can't go on exposing yourself to danger."

"Benny, you really still believe that I'm in danger?"

"Of course I do."

"I survived four days in L.A. without getting shot, didn't I?"

"Renata was killed right here in Toronto. In L.A. you get killed breathing the air. I could have gunned you down from the elevator without getting out, Vanessa. Maybe I'm being dramatic, but—"

"You're being a mother hen and ridiculous."

"What are you talking about?" I told her about the 222s I'd taken from her. I wasn't planning to tell her things that would upset her. A Vanessa innocent of the threats to her life was easier to manage than the one with a loaded gun under her pillow, and, besides, she seemed stronger since she got back from the coast. The buzz of having defeated Ted Thornhill was still with her, adding to the high she was experiencing. She threw a few papers into the wastebasket and handed me the jacket she had been wearing. I held it as she slid into the silky sleeves.

"There! That's all the damage I can do for today. Tomorrow is another day. God, I hope so! How about taking me out for a drink, Benny? I think I deserve one."

We left the building, getting not a breath of criticism from the guard at the security desk. He noted our passage in a log as we crossed to the revolving doors. I made a mental note as I stood back while Vanessa's long legs moved her quickly through the whirling glass. She hailed a taxi and was sliding into the back seat before I could get the door of the cab open. I recognized that I was not good at this, or that I was as good at it as I was going to get.

The top of the Park Plaza never changed, she said as a smiling waiter with silver hair led the way to a table overlooking the city. "It's not even called the Park Plaza any more, but it's too much of an institution to change with every change of management. The Park Plaza was the first steel and concrete building this far north. Bloor Street was almost Toronto's northern boundary when it went up." I asked Vanessa what she wanted to drink, and when she told me, I placed an order with the waiter for a single malt and a rye and ginger ale. When he returned with the drinks, he referred to Vanessa's as her "usual." For a minute I stared at my drink while she looked into the pinpoints of light in the darkness.

"Vanessa, I want you to answer some questions."

"Benny! Lighten up! Relax for thirty seconds. What kind of questions?"

"You phoned me back last Thursday night. Why did you say you didn't?"

"You don't know that I did."

"Let's try to keep things simple. Nobody but *you* knew my number. It had to have been you. Why did you call?"

"If you *must* know, I had a presentiment of how the night would end, and just for a minute, I got cold feet."

"You're entitled."

"I'm glad you came, Benny. I don't know how I would have got through the night without you. And I *did* have all the best intentions about your poor eye."

"Never mind my poor eye. Tell me what you know about the gun you keep under your pillow?"

"*Benny!*"

"Don't pull that shocked, innocent look on me, Vanessa. It's just another kind of smoke-screen. I'm not acting the scorned lover. I just have to know, that's all. Where did you get it?"

"George gave it to me."

"You know he's got a record?"

"Yes, I know. I don't know where he got it. The gun, I mean. He said I needed it for protection."

"You weren't using it for protection last Thursday night."

"*Damn it, Benny. That's private stuff! Nobody* has a right to probe that. You certainly didn't bring it up at the time. I don't recall your being at all curious about where it came from then. We could have discussed it, only the question never came up."

"Okay, okay! I'm only human. My feet of clay are the best in town, rival all others. I didn't say anything because right then you didn't need questions. You needed something like a hug, and that is what was going on until it took a turn that had nothing to do with good intentions. I can't and won't say I'm sorry it happened, Vanessa. But I sure didn't want it to complicate things. So all I need from you now are good clear answers to my questions."

"Honestly, I don't know anything more about the gun, except, as you know, I've found it exciting."

"Okay, tell me . . . tell me about Bob Foley."

"I thought we were having a relaxing, after-work libation. Can't you forget the office for half an hour? I was telling you about this hotel. It's crooked, you know. I don't mean the management; I mean structurally. There's an underground stream below the street and that gives it a list to starboard. Or maybe to port. Don't be cross."

"It doesn't matter what I am. I'm just the working stiff trying to keep you alive." She didn't say anything for a moment.

She was looking at caricatures of local literati in a big frame on the wall. I watched her hands on her glass. She was rubbing a finger around the rim, but it made no sound. She shifted her weight, she pouted, she leaned into her blouse with a full breath, and that didn't work either. Not tonight.

"Oh, all right! What do you want to know?"

"You told me you hardly knew Foley, but that's not the truth, is it?"

"I knew him. I'm quite the authority on Bob Foley."

"Let's hear about it." She picked up her drink and took a sip, mopping her lips with one of those undersized napkins that are useless for almost everything.

"When I first came to Toronto, I worked at the CBC. I was the gofer in those days. I was trying to learn the ropes. Bob Foley was a technician. One night in Studio L, I was cleaning up some tapes, getting ready to go back upstairs, and Bob Foley groped me. He was all over me like a rash, pulling and— Anyway, I struggled and got away from him. I was terrified, violated, embarrassed. The lot. I didn't tell anybody. But the next time I was in a studio by myself, Foley was there again. Same thing. After that little adventure, I complained to my supervisor. The upshot was that while I was a recently arrived, untrained, expendable female production assistant, Foley was a highly trained, valuable senior technician whose work was beyond reproach. The Engineering Department decided to ignore my complaint. He represented a bigger investment in corporate resources than I did. They did *nothing* about him. Bob went on his merry way and the women he ran into kept having to cross their legs whenever they were booked into a late-night studio alone with him. After all, there would always be more of them than there would be trained technical operators. Benny, I once mentioned the experience when talking to a former CBC vice-president. This was years later, and I didn't mention Foley by name. He knew I was talking about Foley. *Everybody* knew that about Bob Foley."

"Wow!"

"I left CBC for a while and worked other places. I've been with all of the Canadian networks. On the whole, the technicians are a great bunch and we have always got along well, but Bob Foley was the rotten apple, Benny."

"That, as shocking as it is, Vanessa, is ancient history. What recent contacts have you had with him?"

"I've checked up on him, Benny. Quietly, and without briefing my informants beforehand. I wanted to be fair."

"And?"

"Foley was up to his old tricks. He never changed. I got the names of four different women that he had . . . had . . . importuned."

"Fancy word, but it's the same old groping Bob Foley. Did he know that you were trying to get him fired?"

"Who told you that?"

"I'm getting to know you, Vanessa, and I'm good at guessing."

"He knew. He also knew that he was just as safe from dismissal from his highly skilled job at NTC in this century as he'd been at CBC in the last. So much for all the recent legislation. It doesn't mean a thing when money's involved."

"I hope your experience with Raymond Devlin was less stressful?"

"I knew him first years ago. He did some legal work for me out of his tiny office off Bay Street. Not too far from where he is today. But that first place was more of a shoebox than an office. Of course, I've had to work close to him since the Plevna Foundation was set up. The Dermot Keogh Hall deal has taken a lifetime of work, Benny, not all from me. There are a lot of people working on it."

"Do you like him? Do you trust him?"

"He needs a lot of looking after."

"I know; you told me about that. What else?"

"He's a good lawyer; he's thorough, dependable. Solid from a business standpoint."

"You don't like him?"

"I don't *dis*like him. I have no *reason* to dislike him. I know,

I know. Okay, let's stick to facts. I have nothing against him but a feeling. Can you deal with a *feeling?*"

"It's a start. Did you ever visit him in Muskoka?"

"He tried to lure me to his cottage one weekend, but he did that to everybody. Everybody of child-bearing years, that is. Sally narrowly escaped. I ran into him once when I was visiting a publisher on Lake Muskoka. I gather that he enjoyed upsetting some of the old Muskoka traditions: taste, decorum, manners, things like that." Vanessa had taken my hand in hers. There was no suggestion of intimacy or romance. No, it was just a curious object that was handy, and she thought she wanted a closer look. It didn't hold her interest long after I pressed her for more information.

"I do remember hearing that Dermot threw Devlin out one time. I forget what it was about, but he was banned from Dermot's cottage, forbidden the use of his boats. You know, cut off at the ankles. And Dermot wasn't hard to get along with."

"Well, that's something. Who would be your source on that?"

"Probably Philip Rankin. He'd be good on Dermot too, of course."

"It's *your* bacon I'm trying to keep from frying, Vanessa. It's too late for Dermot. Although, from what I've heard, I would like to have met him."

"If you like walking tightropes. He was quirky, Benny. For instance, he couldn't abide sharp objects: sharp pencils, knitting needles, knives. He'd go crazy if he saw a blade of any kind. You can imagine what it was like trying to edit audio tape around him in the old days. It was all done with razor blades. He would never allow anything sharp in that place of his on Clarence Square. Blades were just one thing. There were lots of them. You could never tell when you were crossing him until he was so peeved at you, you were done for."

"Was he peeved with Renata?"

"Renata Sartori? No! Of course not. He was in love with her. She was with him when he was drowned. She was in the boat, helping Foley manage the rafts and equipment."

"Does the name Bowmaker ring any bells with you?"

"That's what he used to call Renata: his little bowmaker. I never understood why."

"It doesn't have to mean anything. It's enough to know that it means Renata. Who saw him up in Muskoka last year?"

"From around here?" I nodded. "Ken Trebitsch, I guess. Ken is addicted to power and money. Dermot had both. I don't think Dermot liked him much, but he was fascinated by Ken's hunger for making it. Ken's a simple sort, really. Deadly, but uncomplicated. I think Dermot wondered how someone like that could climb so high. He didn't come around often enough to see that there are hundreds just like him."

"Did you go to the service for Alma Orchard?"

"Alma? How do you know about . . . Oh! From Ed Patel. You do get around, don't you, Benny? Yes, I was there. The place was thronged. When I'm depressed, I think they were morbidly curious, but usually I remember that she had lots of friends. I hope I have that many when it's my turn to go. Do you think of dying, Benny?"

"Only when I'm a passenger. I don't think about the things I don't think about." We finished up our drinks, had another round and went out into the un-air-conditioned world below. Vanessa was hungry, so we took a taxi to the Montreal Bistro where she had another Scotch and some roasted eggplant. I didn't choose very well. I had a salad with goat cheese on top. It looked like an albino hockey puck.

The bistro was located in an old building on Sherbourne Street. The brick walls inside were supported by huge foot-thick wooden beams. Music was supplied by a quartet of jazzmen from Cuba. The piano player, Hilario Duran, was great; a blend, as Vanessa whispered to me, of Art Tatum and Rachmaninov. As soon as we were seated, the waiter reminded us that while the musicians were playing, there was a no-talking policy in place. Even whispering was frowned upon. No wonder Vanessa chose this place. If sitting with Vanessa hadn't so many other redeeming features, I could have become peeved with this woman.

TWENTY-ONE

● Wednesday

I was up not long after the sun, also after a night of diving a sunken wreck in cold waters, to a day that looked like it was going to be a burner. This spring was turning into midsummer without a murmur from the weatherman or the man on the street. Most of my stay in Toronto had been in air-conditioned comfort. I'd been spoiled. My few excursions outside had been brief exposures to the frying elements. I try to keep track of my blessings when I remember.

After showering and getting dressed, I looked fairly presentable in the mirror over the bathroom sink, while I did my duty by my whiskers and teeth. My trousers had won back an echo of a crease under my mattress overnight. The shirt I was wearing represented the last of the clean clothes I'd brought from Grantham. If this case lingered on much longer, I was going to have to do some shopping, my least favourite activity. In returning my wallet, pen and handkerchief to my pockets, I came across the name and phone number of Vanessa's sister out west. I called the number and left a message on her machine about where to find me.

Outside the front door, the heat I'd guessed at through my window made good on its threats. I found Chuck Pepper at a table at the back of the Open Kitchen just a few doors north of my hotel. He was dressed for the heat in a short-sleeved shirt and a tan hat with a wide brim. It sat at the edge of the table on top of a newspaper.

"Good morning!" he said, shaking hands rather formally. I could see he had already finished at least one cup of coffee. Soon we both had cups in front of us. It was fresh and only slightly bitter when I tasted it.

"What luck did you have with the lock?" Chuck grinned and shook his head.

"I wasn't able to fool Jack and Jim," he said. "They knew what I was on about."

"So you took a ribbing on my behalf. I'll owe you for that. But did you get the numbers?"

"In the end Jim gave them to me." Here he reached into his breast pocket and brought out a slip of pink paper.

"Just a minute!" I said, reaching into my own back pocket and retrieving from my wallet my own slip of paper. "I don't know how to organize this, but let me try." I flagged down a waiter, who came to the table at once. I told him that I wanted him to watch and listen to what happened next. He looked puzzled, but folded his arms and nodded to show that the entertainment could begin. "Chuck, give your paper to the waiter." Pepper did so. I handed Chuck the paper I'd taken from my wallet. Chuck's eyebrows shot up. "Read the numbers on your paper," I said to the waiter. He did so, while Chuck's eyes followed an invisible bouncing ball on the paper he held.

"Right 2 turns to 25, left 1 turn to 11, right to 39."

"It's the same combination!" Chuck said. The waiter leaned in to see the paper Chuck was holding. He nodded agreement. Later, I got the waiter's name, in case any of this should end up in a courtroom.

"Okay, Benny, what does all this mean? You used to feed rabbits for Blackstone the Magician when you were little, right? What's going on?"

"Your paper has the number from Vanessa Moss's locker, right?"

"That's what he told me."

"Fine. This is the number I wrote down in the shed behind Bob Foley's place. You know, the one with the motorcycles inside?"

"Yeah. So Foley . . . ?"

"Foley put his *own* lock on Vanessa Moss's locker. It makes it more than a little probable that Foley picked up the shells at the scene of the Renata Sartori murder and took them to the NTC building where he put them in the locker. First, he had to cut off Vanessa's own lock."

"Does that mean that he killed Renata Sartori?"

"It makes him a damned good suspect. It also makes sense: he was a professional electronics technician. He had access to tools, including bolt cutters, and keys to offices."

"But what's the point? Why would he do it?"

"Foley and Vanessa go back a long way together. He attempted to rape her years ago at the CBC, and at the time, Vanessa tried to get him fired. She was trying again three weeks ago. He hated her guts."

"That's interesting, but what does it explain about the murder? Was Foley out to kill Moss but killed Sartori by mistake? Or does it mean that Sartori was the intended victim all along and that Moss engineered it all?"

"Who's Moss?" asked the waiter.

"Could you find us some cinnamon toast?" Chuck asked through his teeth. The waiter, hurt, moved back to the kitchen.

"It means that Foley's lock was on Vanessa's locker. That's all we have that we know for sure."

"Okay. But on that premise, what may we build?"

"Let's see. It means that if Foley wasn't at Moss's house for the shooting, he arrived later and took the spent shells. It means that he saw the body and that he probably took it to be Vanessa's unless he knew for sure that Vanessa was still up north."

"So, you think that Foley may not have been the principal bad guy here?"

"Could be."

"There's stuff missing. You know something you haven't said. What is it?"

"I know—and I don't want to say how I know right now—that Sartori's murderer left the scene with the spent shells lying next to the body. I have a witness who will come forward, if we need him."

"So that makes Foley the clean-up man for the real killer."

"Fits him, doesn't it? He was the gofer for Dermot Keogh. He was the boat wrangler, the buyer of arrowroot biscuits for the cello player."

"Huh? Arrowroot biscuits?"

"What are you having to eat?" The waiter was hovering near again. If it wasn't for more games, it could be that he was waiting to get on with his job. He placed some cinnamon toast between Chuck and me. I told him I now wanted some dry brown toast, a fried egg, orange juice and more coffee. With the addition of some back bacon, Chuck Pepper ordered the same. We didn't talk again until the breakfast was partly demolished. And, even then, it didn't prove very interesting.

When I arrived at the twentieth floor, twenty minutes later, Sally was at her desk, wearing a broad pink hair band. "Benny! There are two *men* in Vanessa's office waiting for you!" She paused and added in a whisper: "I think they're policemen." I don't know whether the last bit was to give me a chance to make a run for it or what. I squared my shoulders, gave Sally my best "damn the torpedoes" look and vanished into Vanessa's sanctum. The cops were Jack Sykes and Jim Boyd, as I'd expected. Both were wearing the same clothes I'd seen them in last time. They looked the same, anyway. Maybe they had whole closets full of these mass-market outfits, designed to show off every overweight ounce they were carrying. Boyd was wearing that silly straw summer hat in his lap, like it was the only thing handy to protect his otherwise naked body.

I gave each of them a friendly grin and the opening for some wisecracks. They were not in the mood. "Benny," Sykes said, "I gotta know when your boss is coming down here. I can't get anything from the girl out there."

"'Girl' usually means pigtails and freckles, Jack. You know: sugar and spice, skipping ropes and hopscotch, barrettes and—"

"I didn't come here for a lecture on political correctness, Cooperman. You know goddamned well who I mean: the receptionist, secretary thingy, whatever she is. I know Moss is back from Los Angeles."

"Back from the coast, you mean? That's how we say it around here."

"Save it, Ben," Boyd said, showing that he was in a sober mood. He crossed his long legs, hiding most of the hat.

"She got back yesterday."

"We know that. We know what plane she was on and where she went from the airport. We know what she did last night and who she was with until two-thirty this morning. What we don't know is when she's going to walk in that door." I blinked at the efficiency of the local cops. I didn't give them enough credit. I had been planning to skip the end of Tuesday, since it didn't seem to advance the story any. But, perhaps I owe a word or two to the unsatisfied. From the Montreal Bistro we went back to Vanessa's temporary residence. I would like to flatter myself that it was my company that recommended me to my employer, but I have to be honest. Any company would have done as well. We went through the motions, without the handgun this time, and I let myself out into the quiet street at the time noted by the stake-out guys, wherever they were hiding. On the way back to the hotel, I thought of Anna and groused inwardly about what a low-life I can be on occasions. The thought of Tuscany and the Californian mushroom king salved only twenty percent of my conscience. I spent the remainder of the night sweating out the rest.

Sykes cleared his throat theatrically.

"There's a big PR reception and press conference this afternoon," I said. "She'll be there. She won't miss that. Why all the interest?"

"You can guess the answer to that. The shells that killed Renata Sartori that we found in Ms Moss's locker were fired from the shotgun you left with us on Monday night. That makes her our leading suspect as of right now."

"That was fast work. Good on the boys in Ballistics. Must be a new record: this is only Wednesday."

"Whatever. Anyway, we know now what we only suspected before. She's moved up a rung on the ladder of suspicion."

"What are you *talking* about? That shotgun didn't belong to my client! You don't know where I found it. *I'm* the one you want to question. Vanessa can wait. Hell, you let her skip off to California for the weekend. If she was going to do a bunk, do you think she'd be here now?" I'm glad Vanessa missed this welcoming committee. A jet-lagged suspect, even one who has just outfoxed the network brass and saved her skin, is hardly better than no suspect at all.

Jack Sykes ran his fingers through his hair. Besides some red fuzz, there wasn't much of it. He moved his hands to a fallback position with his fingers intertwined at the back of his head. "Our bet is that she had access to the shotgun, and *she* had the spent shells. Benny, Jim and I are thinking of driving north to check out that cottage of hers."

"Wait a minute and think before you waste the taxpayers' money on trips to Muskoka. Why would she bring the shells back here? I found the shotgun on Lake Muskoka. If she drove back with the gun, why didn't she get rid of the used shells along the road, toss them into a lake or a ditch? Why did she plant these deadly mementoes in her own locker? It doesn't make sense."

"Benny—!"

"If she wanted to take credit for the murder, why didn't she call the chief of police, or send a note to Whatshername, Barbara Turnbull at the *Star*? Why not give an exclusive interview to *The Toronto Sun*?"

"Benny—"

"And while she was at it, how did she pop back into town and head back up the highway to Muskoka without anyone noticing? Have you checked her gas receipts? Maybe she flew? Maybe she knows a road that hasn't been discovered yet by people trying to beat the traffic on a Victoria Day weekend."

"Benny, shut up for a second! We don't like it any better than you do, but it's the best we've got."

"That's not enough to run her in."

"Who said anything about running her in? We want her to assist us in our inquiries. What's the matter with that?" He looked into Jim Boyd's blue eyes: the final arbiter of what was reasonable.

"You already talked both her ears off. Now you're after blood."

"We are just looking for things that we might have missed the first time around. We've got her statement, sure. We just want her to amplify it, that's all."

"That's a load of garbage and you know it, Jack!" I wasn't going to fall into the trap of thinking they weren't already building a case against my client.

"What can you tell us that will make our trip north—when we make it—as short as possible? And I don't mean tips on where we can buy worms and fishing licences."

"It's a clear conflict of interests, Jack. I'm working for Vanessa Moss. When she cuts me loose, I'll tell you what I saw up there. In the meantime— Hell! I brought you the gun in the first place! What more do you want from me?"

"Okay, okay. Don't rupture yourself. I hear you."

"Jack, I had breakfast with Chuck Pepper this morning. Talk to him about the tie-in with Bob Foley. I think it's important."

"To you everything's important except the answers to my questions."

On their way out, I introduced Jack and Jim to Sally, who looked worried they were going to take me downtown with them. She disguised it by appearing decorative enough to make them run for the elevator in disorder. She was still wearing that expression when I came back from seeing them off.

"A call came for you while you were in there with those men. I didn't think I should interrupt you." She handed me a blue slip of paper, and I went over to my desk and dialled the ten-digit number. The phone was answered by a bright-sounding youngster named Hugh. He was Vanessa's nephew. The things I learn in this business! He told me that he was home from school because he'd injured his knee long-jumping at the school field day.

I asked to speak with his mother, Franny, Vanessa's sister. When she came on the line, she said, "I'll be happy to talk to you. But call my sister 'Stella.' That's her name. I don't know where she picked up 'Vanessa,' probably from her arty friends in Toronto."

We went on from there to have a pleasant chat. In the course of it I discovered that Franny's ten-year-old son, Hugh, had been notoriously neglected by his auntie Stella for all ten of his years. Hugh and his mother were in Calgary on the day that Renata was killed. I thought that with the kid along, it would have been harder to concoct an alibi than it was for Barry Bosco. I dropped that line of inquiry. Franny, it turned out, was the head psychiatric nurse in a Calgary hospital. She had not been in Toronto for three years and didn't expect a Christmas invitation to visit her sister this year or the next. I got off the line as soon as I could, feeling vaguely guilty. I neglect people too. I thought of a few of them as I wandered into the outer office where Sally sat nibbling on the corner of a sandwich.

"I hope you aren't in some kind of trouble, Benny."

"Naw. It's just that the cops want me to do all their work for them, that's all."

CHAPTER TWENTY-TWO

The big event of the day to all the regulars of NTC was the press conference and reception at the Royal York Hotel that introduced the joint creation of Dermot Keogh Hall by the network and the Keogh estate. The hall was to be located deep in downtown Toronto, on a site between Jarvis and Church Streets, north of Carlton.

Instead of describing what was said, I should just attach some of the many PR releases that were available all over the Library Room on the mezzanine floor, but maybe you'll take my word for it. In a few words, the Dermot Keogh Hall would change the centre of gravity of the music scene in the Ontario capital. It would, according to the speeches, surpass in acoustics, comfort and intimacy all the older halls in the country. Ted Thornhill made a fine speech, so did Raymond Devlin. One called it "the event of the decade," the other "the first great architectural marvel of the century." They introduced the architect, whose firm had been engaged to carry out the plans designed by I. M. Pei and to do all the work involved. They answered questions from the press before everybody was released from being on their best behaviour and allowed to resume their eating and drinking at the bar and buffet provided. Vanessa was there, but she kept her public comments to a minimum. Ken Trebitsch was there, pressing flesh for a news angle. His rival, Philip Rankin, spoke briefly, but only to introduce Raymond Devlin to the hundred and fifty journalists and guests crowded into the attractive room.

I stayed close to Vanessa through most of this. Press cameras reminded me of assassinations in old Hitchcock movies. One reporter tried to quiz my boss about the ongoing murder investigation but didn't make many yards with her. She was magnificently turned out for the occasion in a suit by Donna Karan. I had read the label when the jacket was hanging in her office earlier. She didn't have much to say to anyone and, when asked a question, gave short answers or forwarded the question to either Thornhill or Devlin. The overhead light shining on Rankin's head did nothing for the illusion his hairpiece was attempting to create. He was talking to a tall Japanese reporter. His expression was stuck in a pout, which was supposed to look like rapt attention, I guess. "Why, yes," I heard him say, "NTC can only become more and more involved in developing its own label of high-quality recordings. I needn't remind you," he went on—and I guessed at what he was going to say—"NTC has a duty to bring out and make available the works that Dermot Keogh himself had recorded before his untimely death last year."

As the crowd began to thin out, I grabbed some smoked salmon on a dry biscuit. There was quiche for quiche aficionados and, to the evident delight of Ray Devlin and Ted Thornhill, no trays of orange and yellow cheddar lumps on toothpicks. The booze included wine, rye, gin, vodka and Scotch. There was even a bottle of Campari. The Perrier ran like water.

"Well, Mr C., how do you think that went?" It was Barry Bosco.

"I'm no judge, you know. I'm off my turf. But if appearances are anything to go by—"

"Mr C., in television appearances are *everything* to go by."

"Mr Cooperman! Good to see you!" It was Ray Devlin. "Still guarding Vanessa's lovely backside, are you? Think we have assassins among us?"

"You never can tell, Mr Devlin. You looked mighty fine up there," I said, inclining my head in the direction of the microphone-bedecked podium.

"I'll have to get used to doing this sort of thing, won't I, Barry? Not much like talking to a jury, I can tell you."

"Will you be personally supervising the building of the hall, Mr Devlin?"

"Please call me Raymond. I'd like that. And you're . . ." Here Barry helped out with a full reintroduction. This time Devlin took it all in. "So, it's Ben, is that right?" I nodded. "And as to the building of the hall, I intend to keep my distance from the builder's people—give them a free hand once we are all agreed on the direction of the project. You know the local architect's a direct descendant of one of the architects of the Houses of Parliament in Westminster. I didn't know that until today. No, I will keep my distance this summer. I can be reached on my boat in Toronto harbour or up on Lake Muskoka if I'm needed. And heaven help anybody who bothers me unnecessarily."

"You're quite a sailor, I hear."

"Oh, I like to knock about in boats, you know. Are you a sailor at all, Ben?"

"Only in a small way." I quickly reviewed my knowledge of canoes and rowboats at Camp Northern Pine. And wasn't the phrase "mess about in boats"? I was losing confidence in Devlin's abilities as a sailor before I'd even seen him in his commodore's cap.

"Well, you must come out with us one day, when your duties here will allow it."

"I'd like that," I said, grinning broadly, I suspect.

"Do you know Muskoka?"

"I was there over the weekend. I went to pay a visit to an old colleague of yours in hospital in Bracebridge."

"Oh?"

"Yes. You might have run into Ed Patel on the lake. Unfortunately, he's in a bad way just now. He loves talking about Lawrence of Arabia and about Dermot Keogh. We had a very interesting chat. Even now he's a mine of information."

"Bit of a bore on Lawrence."

"Maybe, but illuminating on Keogh. He seems to think that Mr Keogh left his motorcycles to a British collector. But

I could find no reference to that in Keogh's will. Funny, isn't it?"

"Ed must be far gone at this stage. I wouldn't credit too much of what he says from now on."

"He also spoke of a palliative care unit that Keogh was going to have set up. Did you ever hear about that?"

"You didn't know Dermot, did you, Ben? Well, Dermot had a new scheme every ten minutes. He had a wonderfully fertile mind. He took a lot of time from the people closest to him. He was a great one for delegating jobs. Right and left. Tote that barge. Lift that bale! That was Dermot."

"I see, you think Ed Patel's reference to a palliative care unit was just one of those flights of fancy?"

"Wonderful idea, great scheme, but he just didn't have time enough to bring it off. We often talked about it."

"You were a great friend of his right to the last?"

"May I be bold enough to say that I felt like a brother towards the man? He often asked my advice in areas well beyond my capacity as his legal counsel."

"Ed Patel was his lawyer too, wasn't he? I'm not at all clear about that."

"Ed was a small-town country lawyer. He did small local favours for Dermot. Things where a local knowledge is an advantage. For instance, there was an easement for a road crossing Dermot's property on the lake. Ran right through the house! Ed took care of it. No man better. I'd have tried to make a federal case of it and made a mess, I'm sure. Ed's well liked up there, Ben."

Vanessa hove into view. I could see her taking in the conversation between me and Devlin. She weighed it and fixed it somewhere in her memory for later use. It was part of her system. I was beginning to understand her more and more.

Meanwhile the conversations of other NTC people and reporters raged around us:

". . . He can get Leo any time he wants. Day or night . . ."

". . . I'm going on his boat this weekend. Then it's off to Thailand . . ."

". . . Power goes to my head like fast food. It's not good for me . . ."

". . . Everybody in town's playing up this murder thing. Our News isn't on top of it. Trebitsch is sitting on his hands. It's like that Palango thing last year."

"Yes, that was an unnecessary scandal. Less said about it the better."

"Save us from necessary ones too, old boy."

"Say, isn't that Hy Newman over there?"

"You've got to be kidding. Where? *My God!* Yes, it is. *Hy Newman!*"

I followed the direction of their gaze and recognized Hy Newman, the burned-out producer that Vanessa had banned from the building. He'd got in somehow and was cleaning up one side of the buffet with efficient ease. Next to him stood a little man with fuzzy salt-and-pepper hair exploding out of an impressive dome. He looked as though he was wearing a pair of party glasses, the kind that come with large plastic noses attached. On closer inspection, I could see that the nose was his. He was working hard on the smoked salmon.

I was nearly derailed on my way to the buffet by a tall woman in a black suit making her way to another woman. I skipped out of the way.

"Trish Jackson, how are you?"

"How are you, Bev? Tell me, how did the date go?" Trish looked like a lawyer. She was beautifully turned out in a cool grey suit in which she could reargue Magna Carta and have it come out any way she wanted.

"I told you I was taking a chance dating somebody who said 'very unique.' It compromised my standards. He knew that if he said 'between you and I,' he'd never get laid."

"You came down equally hard on 'good' and 'well,' I remember."

"That's right, but he split all his infinitives, which is very with it at the moment."

"How does he stand on 'hopefully'?"

"Trish, I led him down that path, but he wouldn't bite. He confuses 'loan' and 'lend' and 'lay' and 'lie' too, but that's cute and he's putting it on. But I think he's on to me. He's starting to sound like Henry James. I'd better watch my step."

Devlin allowed his eyes to farm the crowd. In the end, I was left to my own devices as Devlin and Bosco began talking about a case I'd never heard of. Bosco saw my distress at being excluded, but did nothing about it. He wasn't much better than his colleague Cavanaugh, the one who gave him his alibi for the night of the murder. They both knew where the money was coming from.

Vanessa was over by the buffet, three reporters away from Newman. I joined her. "Benny, are you carrying any aspirin?" I had a secure vial in my pocket and handed it over. She swallowed two with the aid of some white wine. "What do you think of all this?"

"It reminds me of the part of *Alice in Wonderland* where Alice shouts 'You're nothing but a pack of cards!' Remember that?"

"No. Beatrix Potter was never my thing." I decided not to correct her. She *was*, after all, still paying the bills. What works for Bosco and Cavanaugh rubs off on me. But does it stop me criticizing? Not a bit. Corruption, thy name is pay-day.

"You know, Vanessa, the cops want to talk to you again."

"Benny, now that *this* is over, I don't give a damn. Today was a special sort of hell, but I weathered it. And look! Everybody's still *talking!* Who'd have guessed?"

A tap between my shoulder blades proved not to be the tip of a silenced Walther, but the knuckles of Ken Trebitsch's right hand. I turned and saw what he was wearing as his public face for the occasion. "Look, Cooperman—"

"I got your message. I don't need it repeated."

"I deserved that. Look, is there a way for us to try this again? If I admit to being a horse's ass for a start? I've called off the hounds, by the way. You may move about the city as you please without my knowing all your moves."

"Why the change of strategy?"

"Practical reasons. The other wasn't working. When you leave here, can I tempt you to a glass of beer somewhere? You name the place, just to put off my execution squads."

"What do you want to tell me? Why not tell me now?"

"You can't have a conversation at a press reception: too many interruptions. Besides, what I have to tell you is for your ears only." Trebitsch frowned meaningfully. What a flim-flam artist he was!

"You know that I'm on Her Majesty's Secret Service. She has first call on my time," I said, cocking my head in Vanessa's direction.

"I suspect that you can get around that. Give me twenty, twenty-five minutes. Choose the place." I tried to think.

"There's an Irish pub up on Bloor Street, near Walmer Road, called the James Joyce."

"I know it well."

"Say in an hour? And come alone. Acolytes and disciples make me nervous." He paused a moment, as though decoding a message, then nodded assent.

"That's a promise." Having said that, he shook my hand, which I didn't remember holding out, looked at his watch and vanished into another conversation it was impossible to have at a crowded press reception. I went back to the refreshments to rescue some salmon. The little man with the fuzzy hair was still there.

"What do you do in television?" he asked, licking the length of a finger.

"Nothing," I said. "What about you?"

"I write detective stories. I'm Sheldon Zatz."

"I've always admired the authenticity of your police work," I said. "You must do a lot of research."

"I'm tireless when it comes to the details," he said, taking the last piece of smoked salmon in the room.

Philip Rankin swam towards me through the smiles and metallic chatter, already well supplied with a fistful of salmon. With his fish-like features, he and the salmon looked like an illustration of the food chain. "Ah, dear boy, still with us, I see. Ken hasn't mewed you up in one of his oubliettes?"

"Sorry, I don't recognize the word."

"Dungeon. It's rumoured that he has places where he hides things and people."

"He's just offered to buy me a beer. Shouldn't I trust him?"

"Far be it from me to inform on a colleague, but you might ask him about the files on a certain Tory backbencher. They just disappeared. Quite amazing."

"But just the files?"

"Yes. Of course. As far as we know. I think news people are still essentially children, don't you? They take no responsibility."

"I haven't given it much thought," I said as another thought crossed my mind. "Mr Rankin, while I have you on the phone, so to speak, may I ask you one last question?"

"Granted. You see what hard liquor does to me in the early afternoon? What is it, dear boy?"

"Dermot called Renata—I'm almost sure it was Renata—bowmaker, his little bowmaker. Did you ever hear him say that?"

"Oh, goodness me, yes. It was his nickname for her."

"Could you explain it?"

"Mr Cooperman, I wouldn't expect you to know this—hardly anyone does—but Renata bore the last name of one of the very great bowmakers in Italy. Just as great cellos are remembered by the men who made them, so are fine bows. Sartori was one of the finest bowmakers the world has ever seen. Dermot used the word enchantingly to, and of, Renata. It made her blush in company. That's why he did it, of course. He had the devil's own mischief about him. Any more questions?"

"No, but thanks for the answer to that one. I'm sorry, I don't know whether it's important or not. Maybe I'll know later on."

"You seem to have developed an insatiable appetite for information about my friend Dermot Keogh. Any special reason?" I'm not sure, but Rankin's brow looked moist from this angle. Was he beginning to feel the pressure?

"No. It's just that I've been told that you're the authority. Being in charge of all of his unreleased recordings is a grave responsibility."

"Ha! How I wish I could hear those words from my boss, Ted Thornhill! You're a man of fine sensibilities, Mr Cooperman. I wonder, would you like to see where Dermot's tapes are prepared and mastered before their release to the public?"

"You mean at Sony's studios in New York?"

"Oh no, no, no. Much closer than that. In fact not very far from where we're standing. Dermot's studio is at 18 Clarence Square, just below King Street at Spadina."

"I heard that he had a glory hole somewhere in the city."

"*Glory hole* indeed! Yes, I spent many spellbinding hours with him as he worked with his editor, looking for just the right take on a particular piece of music. Dermot never thought in terms of union rates. He scarcely knew what 'overtime' or 'time and a half' meant. But it was all worth it. If you'd ever care to have a guided tour of the studio, I'd be glad to show you around."

"That would be a treat."

"As a matter of fact, I have to go over there later this afternoon, say around 4:30. If you happen to be in the neighbourhood, just bang on the door. I'll hear you. Now that I think of it, there's something most particular I'd like to discuss with you in the privacy of that place. Nobody can talk at cocktail parties, can they?"

"I might be free about then. I'll bang on the door, as you say."

"Excellent! I must confess that I never tire of giving a tour of Dermot's inner sanctum. It's a hobby horse of mine, I fear. Shall we say around 4:30, then?"

The press reception had been going on for a good hour. The place was beginning to look like the lettuce on the edge of most of the trays on the buffet: a little wilted. I began scouting to see whether Vanessa was getting ready to leave. She wasn't. Not quite, anyway. She was standing forehead to forehead with Ted Thornhill and arguing the future of Entertainment, with an increased budget, I'm sure. Hy Newman was passing behind her when she grabbed him by the arm and brought him into the charmed circle. Thornhill turned quite red in the face when he saw him. Vanessa clapped him on the back and everybody shook hands as if they'd never held a dagger in them.

"Ben!" It was Devlin. I turned and wondered what was on his mind so soon after our recent conversation. "Ben, a few of us are going over to ROYC tomorrow for a sail at six. That's my yacht club over on the Island, you know? We'll just take a run around the Island, nothing fancy. If you'd like to come, I've got all the gear you'll need stowed on board. It's just a thought. Chance to get to know you better."

"How soon do you need to know? I've got some things to do tomorrow, but I should be clear by six."

"Great! If you can swing it, we'll be catching the six o'clock ROYC ferry at the foot of Spadina. I want you to meet some of my friends. They're as crazy about boats as I am."

I nodded assent. I thought it might prove an interesting trip. Besides, I'd never been to a proper Upper Canadian yacht club before. I thought it might be instructive to put myself among people who had the right clothes for every situation.

Ten minutes later one of the limos hired for the occasion dropped us in front of the network building on University Avenue. George Brenner was standing in front with his hair trimmed and wearing a shirt and tie. It was a new George, or at least a new side of him. He and Vanessa exchanged looks that I wasn't supposed to see. He even spared me a grin as Vanessa preceded me through the revolving doors.

I could tell from Sally's face that there was a reception committee just inside the closed doors of Vanessa's office. Vanessa caught the look on Sally's face too and coolly asked her to hold all her calls until further notice.

Inside her large office, the three cops I had been talking to were sitting together on a couch. Rub-a-dub-dub. On our entry, they shot to attention, looking like schoolboys caught smoking behind the gym.

Sykes was the first to speak: "Ms Moss, I told you that we might have to have another talk with you. Well, the time has come." He thanked her for her frank and open co-operation so far and hoped that in this same spirit of helpfulness they would be able to continue their inquiries. Then he introduced Detective Sergeant C. R. Pepper. Vanessa made for the door to beg coffee of Sally. Boyd had half risen as she moved, then tried to regain his seating surreptitiously when she returned to sit down in front of her desk.

"I want to get to the bottom of Renata's death as much as you do, Sergeant Sykes. Tell me what you want, and I'll do my best to respond. But, just for the record, am I under arrest?"

"No! Certainly not. We just have a few questions."

"I see. Then, fire away. Oh, do you mind if Mr Cooperman stays? He's as close to an attorney as I have handy. Besides, as you know, he has been giving this case a good deal of attention. He might help us all."

"Yes, we know *all* about Benny. And I have no objection to his staying. What about you, Chuck?"

Pepper shrugged. "No objection from me. I reckon Benny's been more of a help than a hindrance since he got here." With that settled, we stalled around until the coffee arrived. Sally caught my eye, and I tried to reassure her with a look that we weren't all about to be taken downtown in handcuffs.

"Well, then, let's get started. We don't want to waste any more of your time than necessary. First of all, Ms Moss, why was Renata Sartori staying in your house on the night of the murder?"

"You may remember that I told you that. It's in my statement, the one I made when I came back to town from Muskoka."

"I have a copy here. You said that she had been using your house while you were up north. She had an apartment of her own, I believe?" said Sykes.

"Please don't patronize me, Sergeant! You *know* she had an apartment; you've probably searched every inch of it. I know the address too. I've been there twice. The first time, when my husband and I began having difficulties, Renata offered me her spare room. The second time I stayed with her was when my house was being decorated. When Renata's apartment was being redone, she came to my place. I was simply returning the favour. Oh, I should say that she'd stayed with me once before. It was just after Dermot Keogh drowned. She was in bad shape and somebody had to take her in. She was with me over a week, until we started getting on each other's nerves. A good sign that she was on the mend."

"It was just redecorating? She wasn't having trouble with the current boyfriend?"

"She *may* have been. And I've heard that story. Perhaps both are true. I know we never had time to discuss it. I was off to Muskoka when she arrived. I had a bag full of pilot scripts, and I had to get out of Toronto."

"Did you visit anyone while you were up north?"

"I saw the man at the marina where I keep my boat. Is that what you mean? I didn't have any appointments. I was alone the whole time, except when I was foraging for food, visiting the bookstore in Port Carling or stopping in Bracebridge just to look around. I took my canoe out at least once a day."

"So you didn't see anyone connected to NTC?"

"Isn't that what I just said?"

"I'm only trying to get things clear."

"May I ask a question?" I said to Sykes. He nodded sharply. I guessed it allowed me one short question. "Besides yourself and Evans at the marina, who else has keys to Ed Patel's cottage?"

"Who?" Boyd glanced at Sykes, as though he'd slept through act two of a three-act play.

"Local lawyer, not far from the marina."

"I don't know of any other keys. Maybe Alma. Alma had keys to everything."

"Benny, what's going on here? We've never heard of either of these people."

"Patel's in the Bracebridge hospital, dying, I think. Alma Orchard was his secretary until she died about four weeks ago in an accident."

"Accident?"

"She took a radio into the bathtub with her."

"That'll do it all right. How is she mixed up in all this?"

"She had been watching over Ed Patel's affairs since he went into hospital."

"And? Come on, Benny, don't ration it!"

"There's not much more to tell. Patel knows Vanessa, and knew both Renata and Dermot Keogh. He also knows those NTC executives who have places on Lake Muskoka. There are more of them than you might expect, because a bunch of properties came up for sale or rental a few years ago. Called the Bradings Trust. People like Philip Rankin and Ken Trebitsch. Now don't go asking me whether that's important or not. I don't know."

Jack Sykes looked at me a full ten seconds and then moved his eyes to Vanessa. "Are you planning to leave the city during the next week, Ms Moss?"

"I have no plans to do anything but ride this desk. I've been away and there's catching up to do."

"Good. Are you moving back into your house?"

"No. I'll stay where I am, and when I decide to go home, I'll let you know."

"That's the answer I was expecting." Sykes got to his feet, and with a moment's delay, Boyd and Pepper followed suit. "Thank you for your co-operation, Ms Moss. I hope that we will get to the bottom of this quickly and that you'll be able to return to your normal life without the fears of the last couple of weeks."

"Thank you for that wish. I hope you're right." The police officers and I left the office and headed for the elevator. Vanessa followed us as far as Sally's desk, where she found that she had a stack of telephone messages to answer. I caught her miming a monosyllable under her breath as she winnowed them into two piles. I was about to return to my own desk, when Jack called out to me.

"Benny, can I borrow you for ten minutes?"

"I'm on the job, Jack. I'm trying to see to it that Ms Moss is alive at the end of the day."

"Well, lock her in her office for fifteen minutes. I won't keep you."

Vanessa, who had heard this, came to my aid. "Gentlemen, take him by all means, but please return him so that he may be blamed for any more attempts to marginalize me with malice aforethought." She said it as a joke, but just touched with a bite of gallows humour. The cops made way for me and we disappeared into the elevator.

"Benny, I—"

"We don't talk in elevators, Jack. Unless you want to send Commander Dunkery a greeting from 52 Division. His eyes and ears are everywhere." Pepper looked at me, up at the ceiling of the car and then at Sykes and Boyd. He shrugged as we made our way down twenty floors to a still largely unbugged Mother Earth.

TWENTY-THREE

We were back in the Second Cup across from the police station on Dundas Street. We had coffee and biscotti in front of us and nobody was talking. The café was nearly full of people coming from or going to a show at the art gallery across the street. They looked bright and motivated, which was more than I was feeling. Jack, Jim and Chuck sat looking at me to see if I dared chew a biscotti under their gaze without talking first. I chanced it and they all pounced at once.

"Benny, you've got to—"

"Cooperman, we know what you're up to—"

"Damn it, Benny, what the hell are you messing about in?"

I shrugged to show my complete ignorance of what they were talking about and picked up my coffee. "Wherever I go in this town, somebody's always leaning on me. What's the matter with you guys? I've just agreed to do three things that may get me killed and all you want is for me to spill my guts out."

"Who's going to kill you? Outside this room, I mean?"

"Ken Trebitsch, head of News at NTC, one swell suspect, has just invited me to have a friendly beer with him. Philip Rankin wants to show me around Dermot Keogh's old studio down on Clarence Square. He says he has something 'most particular' he wants to discuss with me. And to top it off, Ray Devlin, the legal whiz, has just invited me for a sail aboard his yacht tomorrow."

"How are these invitations dangerous?" Boyd wanted to know.

"All of these invitations are out of character; that makes them highly suspicious. Devlin doesn't go sailing with sharpies from Grantham, not when they fail to make one hundred and sixty thousand a year. I'm not in his social group. Rankin has no reason to be nice to me. And Trebitsch even admits that the meeting is just another way to get from me what he's wanted all along."

"What's that?"

"The sight of my tail lights heading for the nearest road out of here. He'll settle for that. Maybe he'd like to see a little blood. I don't know him well enough to guess."

"Where are you meeting him and when?"

"In about fifteen minutes," I said, with a glance at my watch. "At the James Joyce Irish Pub on Bloor Street."

"I'll go along," said Chuck Pepper. "Trebitsch doesn't know me. And he knows you guys too well. Remember the trial involving Whatshername? That nurse? NTC News was all over that one." Both Sykes and Boyd looked at one another. That case was not one of their scrapbook cases.

"When are you meeting Devlin?"

"The ROYC ferry dock at the foot of Spadina at six tomorrow night."

"He say there would be others coming?"

"Yeah, but I won't be surprised to find myself alone on his slow boat to China."

"I'd like to wire you before you talk to these guys. You ever worn a wire, Benny?"

"There's no time. I have to meet Trebitsch right now."

"Okay, Jim and I'll head down to Clarence Square now and try to set something up. What's the number?"

"Eighteen."

"You won't see us, Benny, but we'll be there. Someplace."

"This is too much like the movies. The ones where the point man gets hit."

"It could be the breaking of this case. Rankin, Trebitsch or Devlin. You could take all of them, Benny. If there's a fight, I mean. They're in worse shape than you are."

"Good. At least I'm not meeting them together." Our gang was adjourned after that, with Chuck heading out the door before the rest of us.

I took a taxi to Bloor and Spadina and walked west. A young woman was interviewing a panhandler sitting on a milk crate in a doorway. He looked like he'd been interviewed before; his answers to her questions were well expressed. I tried to look through the clear sections of the frosted glass that covered the windows of the James Joyce Irish Pub. I walked in. To my right stood amps and microphone stands and stools on a rudimentary stage in a window alcove. It was a set-up for some music group who were nowhere in sight. Clearly visible in a seat at the far end of the bar sat Chuck Pepper, with his jacket removed and the sleeves of his shirt rolled up above the elbow. I'm not sure whether the tattoo visible on his left forearm was from the police academy or not. The blond head of a Guinness in front of him had everything under control. Chuck's upper lip looked like a milk ad. I looked around for Trebitsch or one of his boys, but I couldn't find them. I ordered a draft of Smithwicks, which sounded suitably Irish, and carried it to a table near a window. To pass the time, I started watching the people passing outside. I divided them into men and women, getting five men to every four women. Then I tried checking men with hats against men without them. Most men didn't wear them. By the time I was checking skirts and dresses against pants and shorts, I saw Ken Trebitsch step out of a navy blue BMW driven by someone who drove off, while Trebitsch came into the gloom of the pub. He didn't take long to find me. Then he didn't waste words.

"Why are the city police letting you meddle around in their investigation?"

"How can they stop me? I'm not corrupting their crime scenes. I'm not strong-arming their suspects. Even when the chief of police gets word of me, and he warns his men about me, I still manage to find things out and put your back up."

"You think that was me?"

"You'd be my first guess." Trebitsch didn't like to feel so transparent. He looked around for a waitress, and found her hard to get, reminding me of Marlowe. I enjoyed watching him flounder; it annoyed him and his image of himself surrounded by yes-men. At last attention was finally paid to this man and he ordered a Coors Lite. "Why do I put your back up? You're not the only suspect in this murder who works for NTC. How is it that you imagine yourself their best bet?"

"I knew Renata. We go back a long way. I knew she was staying at Vanessa's house while she was away. I also talked to her on the day she died."

"Okay, I revise my opinion. Frankly, I didn't know that. So, you see, I haven't dug a deep trench into you yet. If you knew that Renata was in the house, not Vanessa, then you're unlikely to be accused of trying to kill Vanessa. We all know she had enemies, and you were one of them, but you wouldn't shoot the wrong woman."

"*I* didn't shoot anybody. Yes, I want Vanessa out of Entertainment. I want a bigger share of the time she controls. She won't compromise because she can generate sweetheart deals for every second of that time. Her successor, who is already waiting in the wings, will cut me more slack. Look, even Vanessa knows her time here is finished. Why is she fighting it?"

"Why do you take it so personally?"

"Because it's my fucking *life*. I'm ambitious. That's not a crime in television."

"What did you talk to Renata about?"

"She started in about some huge conspiracy. Couldn't make head nor tail of it. Something to do with Dermot Keogh. I was taking another call and being briefed by one of my people while I was on the phone. Frankly, I never listened to Renata with both ears. She was great, don't get me wrong, but she was more fun to be with than to listen to. There was a physical dimension. Ask anybody. But that day she *was* upset. I got that part of the message. Now, tell me when you'll be returning to Grantham. I'm looking forward to that event. You know that."

"Why do you want that so bad?"

"The longer you stick around NTC, Mr Cooperman, the longer Vanessa will keep her job. You bring a whole ambience of unsettled mayhem with you wherever you go. Ted Thornhill's terrified of you. I know this. Once you're gone, things will return to normal and Vanessa Moss will leave."

"I was hired to protect Vanessa. She'll turn me loose as soon as she's convinced she's in no further danger. I think that might be sometime before the weekend."

"Can you be more precise?"

"I'd like to be out of here by Friday."

"This is Wednesday."

"Yes, it usually follows Tuesday. But why are you so worried? There's something more, Mr Trebitsch; something you've left out. How have I been stamping on your corns?" Trebitsch stared into his beer for a moment, then looked up.

"The first thing I ever sold to this network was an interview with a gravedigger who'd grown disenchanted with his profession. It proved to be a great hit. The guy was really funny. People remembered me as the producer."

"Well?"

"The interview was a fake. The gravedigger was a struggling filmmaker who'd never held a shovel or dug a grave. That didn't matter. The item *made* me. But it continues to haunt me and could *un*make me. I've never faked anything since, but that four-minute item—we allowed longer items in those days—gives me nightmares. Vanessa knows the truth about that piece. She watched me edit it. She could expose me at any moment."

"You underestimate her. If she wanted your scalp, she wouldn't dig up your past. In News, you're your own worst enemy. 'The Trebitsch Look' gets in the way of the stories. Back off on the personal signature, and your stock will go up. Not only here but in California."

"Who have you been talking to?"

"Never mind, but hear this: Winkler of Warner Brothers is watching you and you keep spoiling the picture. Were you on Lake Muskoka when Dermot Keogh drowned?"

"No. I have a place up there, but Phil Rankin warned me that Dermot had suddenly taken a dislike to all NTC types,

Renata Sartori excepted, of course. So, I stayed clear of him. So did Phil, Ray and others. It was too early in the season: April."

"Why was Raymond Devlin lumped in with you NTC types?"

"He was chief NTC counsel in the CRTC hearings that year."

"What's that?"

"Canadian Radio-Television Commission. They supervise and grant licences to broadcasters. They could theoretically pull the plug on all or any of us. But they don't, no matter how badly we misbehave. That's the way so-called 'arm's length' politically appointed bodies operate in this country."

"So Dermot spent that last summer well away from all you broadcasters?"

"The lake held other attractions. Hamp Fisher and his wife, the movie star Peggy O'Toole, had started coming up there. And there were other points of interest." He smiled at the memory, whatever it was. I tried to imagine his sort of "interest." Then I examined my watch.

"I've got to go. I hope I've told you what you wanted to hear."

"Hey! You haven't told me about Winkler at Warners!"

"More news, less personality. That's the ticket." I could almost see his lips repeating my invented comment. I could see that I might have a future in this business.

"Goodbye, Cooperman. Remember, what I told you was said in confidence."

"Look, Trebitsch, if I didn't respect confidences, I wouldn't stay in business a week. It's a habit. But I have to find things out in order to find things out. So long." I got up, and left it to Ken Trebitsch to pay for my beer.

There was a taxi hovering near Ye Olde Brunswick House across the street. I grabbed it, and the driver whisked me down to King and Spadina. It was a neighbourhood of ancient sock factories and seed warehouses. The old garment district was just north of King. Here, traffic caught its breath for the ramps of the Gardiner Expressway at the last-chance gas station. In the middle of all this, I found a lush, green patch: old trees with wooden seats running around the trunks and park benches. On the north side stood a solid wall of townhouses going back to the 1870s, the remnant of a square that once boxed in the park. Number eighteen was the easternmost of the houses. It looked as though it had once had a bigger building to lean against, but that had been bulldozed away, leaving the exposed, windowless flank to the elements.

The house had a Georgian feel to it: fanlight over the door, fluted brass doorknob. The entrance looked like one on a poster I once saw of front doors of Dublin. I banged on the black woodwork. When nothing happened, I tried the huge knob. It turned. I stepped into a hall that was big enough to accommodate the walking sticks of all the elected members of the 1890 House of Commons. White stairs led up to a second floor that looked dark and uninviting. The hall leading into the back of the ground floor looked more promising.

It was a huge room, originally the kitchen of the house. An old-fashioned sink and drip board in heavy porcelain dominated the side of the room with a window. But stuffed chairs, overstuffed couches, recording machines, loudspeakers the size of boxcars, racks and racks of recording tape, and cans of film formed the focus of the studio. A double door, such as you find in a radio studio, cut off the room from the rest of the house. A wall of sound-absorbing tiles had been built against the back wall, killing noises from King Street, which backed on the property. The studio was also littered with paper: paper on desks, paper on chairs and couches. A stack of magazines overflowed against a table leg upon which half a dozen film scripts, no two lying parallel, had been scattered. They say that there is such a thing as the genius of a particular room: the room where Bach composed or where Robert Louis Stevenson wrote carries something of the essence of its owner through time. Although Dermot Keogh had been gone a year, his personality and quirks were etched on everything in the room, from the battered upright piano, a bench so broken and dangerous that it might have belonged to Glenn Gould, to the open cello case carelessly left open on a couch. The cello itself rested against a heavy music stand, the base of which was buried in music manuscripts.

"Mr Rankin?" I called out over deadly silence. My voice sounded as crisp as a rifle shot. But there was no answer. I looked at my watch. I was on time. "Mr Rankin!" I shouted again. Again, no answer.

Quickly I made the rounds of the rest of the place. It was plain to see that the house was not now lived in, nor had it been inhabited for a good long time. In one room, long regimental photographs on ancient wallpaper showed that the room had not been used since shortly after the First World War. The front room, which looked out on the park, had been more recently used. The walls had been painted over embossed wallpaper. Bookshelves had been rigged on the right and left of a marble fireplace. A lone peacock feather sat in a corner with a portrait of the solemn, bearded founder of the Salvation Army. (He was identified in small print at the bottom.)

The third floor was full of rooms, all of them empty, except for a pile of warped cardboard backings that photographs had once been pasted to. Now the photographs were curled into shapes like giant pasta shells. I tried to straighten one of them out, and it broke with my effort. It was a picture of a curly-headed bus driver leaning from the window of his rustic bus, holding a rose in his smiling teeth.

I returned to the studio and made a better search. To one side of the piano, under an old drafting table, I found Philip Rankin. His stillness suited the quiet of the studio. When I turned him over, I could see a bloodstain on the front of his shirt. I thought it was odd that the smell of a gunshot wasn't still hanging about in this airless room. But there was no hint of powder in the air. I poured myself a glass of cloudy water. The pipes groaned at the intrusion.

Rankin had been alive half an hour ago, according to his face. His fingers were still flexible and lividity had only just started, as I could see through his shirt. The little blood that surrounded the wound was hardly sticky yet. Stepping back, and holding on to the piano for support, I could see where he'd been dragged. He must have been standing or sitting in one of the few chairs that weren't burdened with papers. I lifted the cushion. There was blood on the other side, and more under it on the chair.

No murder weapon was in sight. If it hadn't been a gun, and the lack of the right smell convinced me that it hadn't, then Rankin had been stabbed. But then I remembered what I'd heard about Dermot Keogh: he hated sharp objects. A quick look in the drawers under the shelves near the sink showed nothing sharper than a pencil or a cake of rosin.

"Well, well, what have we here?" It was Jack Sykes, with Jim a step or two behind him. "Your pal Rankin stand you up?"

"Not exactly," I said. I hadn't heard them come in. Neither had the murder victim heard the murderer, I thought. A possibility.

"What's the matter, Benny? You look like you need to sit down."

"Yeah, you're as white as the walls," added Jim. "Sit down."

"Can't," I said. "Can't foul the murder scene." Their surprise was noted and I pointed to the body under the drafting table. Jim quickly got busy on his cellphone, while Jack examined the body. I tried to stay out of the way. I had to excuse myself and run up the stairs to the bathroom when Jack lifted the body again to look at the mortal wound. Rankin's toupée had slipped to one side, adding a dimension something like the unkindest cut of all. By the time I came downstairs, cops of all sizes, shapes and ranks had appeared. I gave my statement to two different officers before I was allowed to leave.

When I got back to the New Beijing Inn, I reached for soap, a washcloth and the shower. Shortly after that, I was in a deep sleep, more like oblivion than a real snooze. And that's the way I stayed for the next hour and a half.

CHAPTER TWENTY-FOUR

● Thursday

I attended to my chores all the next day. Ted Thornhill stopped me in the hall and asked me some probing questions about what I was doing there. He was leaning over me a little like an unhappy bank manager, and talking a little louder than necessary, when I decided that I had no reason to live in fear of the CEO of NTC. I put him to bed by dropping Hamp Fisher's name. Somehow, I brought up the fact that I'd rather be back on Lake Muskoka on the deck of *Wanda III* and hearing stories about my old friend, the director Jim Sayre, from the matchless lips of Peggy O'Toole. That did it. That ended any idea of starting a range war with the kid from Grantham.

Sally brought me lunch. She knew how Vanessa moved from meeting to meeting without taking nourishment. She told me that Crystal's ex-husband had spent last evening talking to Gordon, *her* soon-to-be ex. After a bottle of Chivas Regal, Gordon was seeing the whole matter of his fractured life in a new and more law-abiding light. He promised not to harass her from now on.

In the course of the day I made three trips to the drugstore for Vanessa, and working with Sally and George Brenner, helped create a CV for that parking attendant and man of all work.

At about 5:30 in the afternoon, I caught a cab and let the driver take me south on Spadina, past the collection of police cruisers still parked along Clarence Square to the placid, cooler lakeshore. There were four men and a couple of women sheltering from the late-afternoon sun in the ROYC shelter at the foot of Spadina Avenue. Ray Devlin wasn't any of them. I watched the ferry grow bigger as it approached the dock, wondering what I would do if Devlin failed to appear. This was turned into an idle speculation by Devlin's sudden arrival in an orange-and-black taxicab. "Sorry I'm a little late," he said, shaking hands with me. "Do you mind if I continue reading this brief? My girl just handed it to me as I went out the door."

"Sure, I don't mind. Wish I'd brought along something myself." Devlin sat down inside the shelter for three or four minutes while the ferry arrived and made itself fast to the bollards. Then he got up, had a card punched and went aboard. I followed, giving up real money to the purser, if that's what he's called, and found a seat below decks. Ray continued to study the brief he was holding, but it didn't make him safe from interruptions. A woman said she'd seen him on the news that afternoon. A man asked if he had had much luck with a certain anti-fouling paint. Ray gave him a short, crisp answer, which discouraged further commerce.

The trip across to the Island took about fifteen minutes and ended when we reached the dock in front of the impressive, white-and-blue-shuttered ROYC clubhouse. Here, for the first time, I saw that the initials stood for Royal Ontario Yacht Club. There was a plaque. Inside the door were photographs of commodores of the past wearing their yachting caps, paintings of yachts and their crews, a few cabinets dedicated to silver cups in annual competition and time-oranged oars hung up on the walls as decorations in commemoration of something or other. The people I saw were older than the people passing the window of the James Joyce pub. They were wearing English sweaters or club blazers. The dress code probably frowned on sandals and T-shirts, but the moment that notion crossed my mind, I saw three teenagers in sandals and T-shirts. I recognized the fact that I had to overcome a certain bias against people who could afford to own and operate boats out of this place.

I looked around for Devlin for a few minutes without any luck. He was probably making contact with his crew. They may have taken the ferry before ours. I also couldn't find any sign of Boyd or Sykes. If they were prepared to protect me from Devlin, as Chuck Pepper had protected me from Ken Trebitsch, they were well disguised. I walked out on the well-rolled lawn, examining closely the members and their guests with their drinks and snacks. A suspicious-looking gull was watching the marina, where boat crews were busy getting a large assortment of boats ready for sailing, or battening them down after bringing them back up the cut to the club. There was a stiff breeze blowing. Anyone venturing out that afternoon wasn't going to have to use auxiliary motors. As far as I could see wind-filled sails dotted the bright blue water. Spinnakers were deployed on some boats, giving the crews a good run for their membership fees. As backdrop to all this, the city's silhouette loomed with its office and communications towers. The SkyDome's open roof turned that stadium into an oyster on the half-shell.

A hand on my arm made me turn suddenly. "I'm sorry, Benny, but none of my regulars is here this afternoon. Philip Rankin told me he'd be here for sure. Nick Trench is always here looking to crew for somebody. Bill Keiller's often agreeable. But I don't see any of them. Say, I don't suppose that we could manage with just the two of us?" Devlin had shed his city clothes and was now wearing an ROYC-approved sailing outfit: white shorts and light yellow nylon slicker.

"Raymond, I don't know your yacht, but most of the boats I've been on can be handled by two. Where is your boat?"

"She's in the last slip at the north end of the dock, the *Sir Ed Cook*, spelled 'Coke.' I'll have another look around in case I can find somebody wanting to crew. Tell you what," he said, "you start off, begin taking the wrappings off, while I get my flask refilled. There's a stiff wind out there this afternoon, and I know there's not much to drink on board. Here's the key to the hatch. Once that's open, you can find yourself some clothes and shoes that will make you more comfortable. All that gear is stowed forward. Okay?"

"Aye, aye, sir." Devlin laughed and retreated back to the clubhouse. I tried to catch the sharp eye of a gull that had followed me from the clubhouse lawn. It gave no sign that it was working undercover. Very professional.

I walked down to the end of the dock, which was connected to smaller wooden docks, which in turn created the slips where about fifty or sixty small craft of all kinds were tethered. The yacht seemingly at the end was bigger than any I had ever been aboard, barring one owned by an east-coast brewer. But on that one I'd had to line up, and velvet ropes prevented unimpeded exploration below decks.

Next to this, but masked by the larger boat, was moored a much more reasonably sized vessel. Across the stern of the white hull, the words SIR EDWARD COKE TORONTO were painted in bold golden capitals. I struggled aboard, feeling, as I always did, heavy and awkward. I tried the key that Devlin had given me, and the hatch opened easily on well-lubricated tracks. I opened it fully, and went backwards down the inside ladder, turned and headed towards the front. Here, as instructed, I found an assortment of boating wear. Most important, I found a pair of soft running shoes that almost fit.

Back on deck, having brought some of the running tackle with me, I began unbuttoning the boom cover. When I'd removed it and stowed it below, and was wondering what to do next, Ray Devlin appeared with drinks and snacks. "Ahoy!" he shouted, slipping into the mock nautical banter that I had initiated a few minutes earlier. "The wind's getting stronger. We're going to have us a real sail, Ben." Coming aboard, he saw what I'd started and lent a hand to complete things. He opened a hatch forward to let in some light, and began running the sheet lines through the left- and right-hand cleats and then hitching them up to the boom. Meanwhile, I took the sails out of their plastic bags and began slipping the toggles into the slot running up the mast. Devlin clipped a line to the top of the sail and made it ready for hoisting aloft. We managed the foresail in similar fashion, not talking, not getting in each other's way.

On a boat I become subservient. It comes naturally to me. I've tried at various times to sail by myself, but it is always awkward, like trying to climb stairs in roller blades. I am a natural first mate, never the skipper. It's as though I hold the craft of seamanship sacred. While I might manage well as altar boy, I wouldn't attempt to serve the mass myself. I don't know where I got that comparison. It's as foreign to my experience as sailing a yacht. The plain fact is that the wind is an abstraction that is beyond my frail brain.

Finally, we cast off and were on our way out of the slip. Despite my earlier guess, it was necessary to use the auxiliary motor to back away from the dock, turn and make our way out into the channel. While Devlin manned the tiller and the motor, I kept out of the way and sat on one side prepared to be useful. I watched other boats returning to the club, their crews and skippers red in the face from the growing blow moving across the north end of the Island.

"This is going to be exciting!" Devlin said, nodding in the direction of the nearest returning boat. It looked wet and so did its crew. When we reached the middle of the channel, Devlin raised the mainsail and the one in front, cut the motor and settled down for a good sail. "You know, there are some people, a good part of the active membership, who only come out for races. Now, I like to race too, but I also like to sail without having to round marker buoys. Know what I mean?" I knew and nodded. He had to raise his voice to be heard. "Last year, we sailed across for the Shaw Festival. It was rough going to Niagara, but it was even harder changing into black tie for the opening-night show below decks."

The trees along both sides of the channel were getting smaller. Soon they were well behind us. In front, off the port bow, as Conrad might say, the end of the runway of the Island Airport kept us company for a few thousand metres, then dropped away. After that, Oakville and Hamilton beyond lay hidden in the summer-like haze that sat on the lake. We were running with the wind, making good speed. When Devlin told me he was going to come about, we were a good mile west of the Island. The clouds above looked bruised. There were few boats near us and not a gull in sight.

The sail luffed briefly, then caught the full blast of the wind. The boom slammed across the boat with stunning force, narrowly missing my head. Devlin and I changed sides, as I brought the foresail around and adjusted the sheets. We were launched on a southeasterly tack, which would take us well out into the lake, before coming about again and heading around the east end of the Island.

"Did you do any sailing last weekend, Ben? On Lake Muskoka?"

"No, I was out in a canoe and aboard *Wanda III.*"

"Took the tour ride, did you?"

"It amounted to the same thing, but I ran into an old friend who had rented *Wanda* for a few weeks."

"What took you north just at that time?" he asked, looking up at the fluttering streamer that showed the wind direction. Then he made a small adjustment in the sheet he was holding.

"My boss was out of the country, so I thought I'd check out her cottage. I hadn't had a holiday since—"

"You can speak more frankly than that. I know what you do, Ben. Do you take me for a fool?"

"Well, I may have done some snooping. I did some canoeing, a little hiking, some—"

"That's a little unusual, isn't it? Checking up on your boss?"

"Maybe, but I didn't like the idea of working for someone I didn't entirely trust. The trip made that better."

"In what way?"

"The condition of the cottage seemed compatible with what she said she'd been doing at the time of the murder."

"You actually thought that *she* might have done it?"

"I didn't rule it out. Not until I'd been there."

With his arm steadying the tiller, Devlin found two stainless-steel cups and poured a healthy dram into each of them. He handed me one. I took it just as the boat heeled over with a sudden blast of wind, and we toasted each other with spray flying about us. I didn't try my drink until I saw Devlin finish off his in one gulp. Maybe I've seen too many movies for my own good.

There was a good swell now, and the water was thumping the hull under my bum steadily. I handed my cup back to Devlin, who stored both of them in a safe place. The last thing you need on a sailboat is a lot of tin cups rolling around underfoot. With the flask also tidied away, Devlin hunched over the tiller, like a gargoyle sitting on the gallery of a big French church. He wasn't looking up ahead: he was looking at me.

"You think you've got it all figured out, Ben?"

"Me? Figured out what?"

"Let's have a minimum of pretending, Ben. I know more than you think." Devlin was staring straight into the weather now, with his eyes narrowed to slits. I decided that being frank was part of what I'd set myself up for.

"There are still things I don't get yet. Like Foley's role." Devlin was silent for a few seconds, and then he smiled.

"Foley was in it to begin with. He was closest to Keogh. Without him, it wouldn't have happened."

"But he was the least reliable. You didn't trust him, nor he you."

"Yes, I could handle Philip. Philip Rankin. As long as I buttered up his ego regularly, he was a happy camper. Until I overheard him saying that he wanted to talk to you. At the reception yesterday. I couldn't let that happen. And Foley was happy enough, too, most of the time, as long as his hands were busy. But thinking upset him, made him nervous, made him a poor colleague."

"Tell me about the breach with Dermot. That had to be the start of it."

"Ever since Foley had introduced me to Dermot, I was in the charmed circle. I was a made man. I was soon doing all of his important legal work. Oh, there were crumbs left for old Ed Patel, but I was doing all of his deals with Sony and the other New York connections. I did the contracts with NTC too.

Rankin got me that and much more. The very nature of my practice changed. The firm got bigger. Had to, to keep up."

"And you were close with Dermot personally as well?"

"Sure. He depended on me to listen to his stories late into the night, when Renata or some other girlfriend wasn't around. I tried to please him. Gave him stock tips, gave him presents, flattered him. He needed that. Where I went wrong was trying to prepare some biographical material on him. Just for the record, you know. I wasn't going to publish it. It was just so that it would be there."

"You interviewed Dermot's father."

"Yes. That was a big mistake. Nearly finished me. I didn't know he was all that sick. I didn't know that I'd broken the unwritten law with Dermot. 'If you want to know about *me*,' he said, 'ask *me*! Leave my father and my family out of it!' I'd never seen him so angry."

"That wrecked it?"

"That's right. First he became morose, then formal. Soon I couldn't get near him. He wouldn't take my calls. I was *exiled, banished!*"

"That must have hurt."

"Of course, personally it was a great blow. It was like being thrust back into black-and-white after a summer of Technicolor. In business, it was more than a great blow. More like a catastrophe. I'd rebuilt my law firm on the expectation of a continuing relationship with Dermot. He tried to ruin me. I was haemorrhaging. I was overextended. You saw our offices. That sort of thing costs money."

"Where did the actual plan come from?"

"Dermot suggested it himself. Before he dropped me, I mean. He'd told me of his plan to dive the wreck of *Waome* with Hampton Fisher. That was the perfect time, and Bob Foley would be there. He hadn't been shut out. All I had to do was stay away."

"I see."

"But you wouldn't stay away, would you, Ben? All Vanessa wanted was a bodyguard. That wasn't good enough. You had to nose around, compete with the authorities, stir things up."

"It's my nature, Raymond. I can't help it."

"I suppose not. Makes things rather awkward, though."

"I think I see what you mean."

"You see the position you put me in?"

"Oh, I've seen that right along."

"But you came along anyway?"

"I wanted to hear it all from you. I wanted to understand whether it was just about the money."

"Of course, the money was a big part of it. But not all. He shouldn't have treated me like that. I was his friend. He was peeved with me. That's his word, not mine. And he cut me off as casually as though he were deadheading roses. I couldn't stand that. I wouldn't put up with it."

"But the scheme wasn't foolproof. From the beginning there were flaws. Other people knew and had to be hit."

"You make me sound like a common gangster!"

"Oh, there's nothing common about you, Raymond. You're memorable. You're a keeper. You won't slip into obscurity again. I can promise you that."

"So many loose ends that had to be taken care of. The ones I foresaw and the ones I didn't. Foley, now. I always knew that he wouldn't go the distance, but I couldn't tell exactly where along the line I'd have to deal with him. He followed me to Vanessa's that night. Thought he'd spoil things for me and implicate Vanessa. It was muddled thinking, you see. He didn't have the head for it. Neither did Rankin. He only wanted the glory of the association with the great man. He'd always let me look after the practical things."

"And you did very well. The police up north never suspected; the ones down here are still confused. Killing Renata at Vanessa's was a master-stroke. It muddied so many waters at once."

"A lot of that was luck. And timing. I didn't know about Renata's going to Vanessa's until the day before I had to act."

"But you had the rest planned?"

"Not really. As soon as Vanessa's house came into it, I remembered Ed Patel's gun over his fireplace. It was a lucky stroke. Like the wonderful things that come to you when you're summing up a case and staring into the faces of a jury. Only the one last detail to put in place now."

"Me, you mean?"

"Naturally. As they say in the movies, 'You know too much.'"

"So you planned this little trip in the *Sir Edward Coke*." Devlin was sitting upright now. He looked like an insect about to strike, except that he was carrying too much weight to be any insect I could think of.

"I'm sorry about this, Mr Cooperman. But you see the necessity." By his moving from "Ben" to "Mr Cooperman," I could feel that he was getting ready to make his move. It's easier to kill someone with whom you are on rather formal terms.

"You may have forgotten a thing or two, Raymond."

"Such as?"

"I'm not a complete fool. Do you think I'd have accepted your kind invitation without taking out insurance?" I could hear the wind whistling around the mast as Devlin weighed what I'd said.

"You can't bluff your way out of this. All the cards are face up. There are no more surprises on the table." He was sneering slightly. "You'll have to do better than that."

"What if Ed Patel comes home from the hospital? That would be another complication."

"Ed Patel isn't getting out of there except to go to the funeral home across the street. Even *he* knows that." The boat was heeling over again, the sails were bellied out. The sheets were squeaking in their cleats.

"Are you sure he hasn't contacted anyone? Friends, visitors?"

"Who'll believe him? He's wandering in his mind. When he's not going on about Lawrence of Arabia, he's telling you who owned which cottage on the lake at the turn of the last century. He's a colossal bore. He can't spoil things. Only *you* can."

"The police know I'm here."

"More bluff. But not good enough to save you." Here, Devlin swung the tiller hard over, ducking his head down as he went. I ducked as well, just as the boom slammed over hard, parting my hair as it went. But Devlin had a second part to his plan. He was up on his feet now, and I could see that there was a gun in his right hand. It looked like a toy. It was the circumstances that told me it was real. He made a start for me, silhouetted against the light, as I cowered in the cockpit. He added the support of his left hand to his right as he took aim. I closed my eyes just as the boom crashed back to where it had been. The boat had refused to come about. Devlin was struck full in the chest and knocked off balance. He went over the side without my being able to either see him properly or get to him. The gun went off as he fell, and I heard the zing of the bullet as it hit the aluminum mast. By the time I got to his side of the boat, there wasn't even a ripple showing where he'd gone down. Then, I saw his head come up and saw his yellow slicker as he thrashed around.

I was surprised how quickly the yacht was moving away from him. He was becoming smaller, vanishing under the swell. I looked for a life preserver and tossed it overboard. I tried to turn the boat to get back to the place where he'd disappeared. But, as I said, I'm no skipper. I've felt helpless before, but this was a new issue, nothing like any earlier experience. I attempted to come about, but by the time I managed it, I was half a mile from where I'd last seen Devlin. I tried again, got closer, but could see nothing.

Then I remembered the motor. I turned the key and pushed the button; it caught the first time. I tried the throttle, moving it back and then forward to get the hang of it, and then sped back where he'd last been seen. I passed the empty life preserver, made another turn and came around again. I wanted to criss-cross my path as well as I could, but the sails had their own plans. At last I had to admit that we were totally out of control. The boom had come loose and was under water on the side away from the wind. I tried to straighten it, but by the time I'd got the sheet firmly caught in the cleat, I couldn't tell where I was. I'd lost sight of the life preserver and, with it, all chance of finding Devlin. That's when I gave up the search. By now I was sailing a piece of the lake that had not witnessed any of this. Innocent water. That's when I turned my mind to getting *Sir Edward* back to the Island.

CHAPTER **TWENTY-FIVE**

I arrived back at the ROYC *main dock,* towed by a police launch that had been alerted by the duty commodore of the club. My erratic thrashing around, my many attempts to sail directly against the wind, finally attracted attention. If ever a fine boat hung its head, *Sir Edward* did. The police corporal at the controls of the launch that towed me back to the club had never heard of Sykes or Boyd. Later, Jack Sykes told me that they had had a helicopter circling above the *Sir Edward Coke* all the time. I never heard it. It's one of those stories you'd like to believe.

They never found Devlin's body. He was gone. Maybe he got to the life preserver and made it to the American side of the lake. Maybe he is now searching titles in a Rochester registry office. In a pig's eye. He was gone in another way: gone not meaning simply not here. And I couldn't make myself feel good about it.

Someone rescued my street clothes from the cabin of the yacht. I remember glimpses of ROYC members fussing over me as though I were Robinson Crusoe thrown up on Centre Island. A woman with blue hair gave me half a sandwich. A shot of rye was administered; I never found out who paid for it. I recall trying to explain that I was unharmed, that it was the other guy who could use some help. But by now it was dark and far too late to launch a search-and-rescue operation. So all of this unsolicited energy for good deeds centred on me. I fell asleep on the ferry, and the taxi left me at the New Beijing Inn without my being fully aware of the fact. The rest of the night was divided equally between unruffled sleep and nightmares of a nautical nature that I don't want to go into right now.

 Friday

When I awoke, the sun was stealing the colours from my bed-clothes, and the bed was not quite fixed firmly to the floor. The phone was ringing. I don't know when the ringing started. It was Vanessa. "Benny, Sergeant Sykes just called me and told me all about it. What a narrow escape!"

"Thanks. What time is it?"

"Time you started looking for another job, Benny. I don't need protecting any more. You're fired!" I thought that there would be more, but she'd left the line. I was fired, and she'd hung up.

I pulled myself from the bed and into the shower. My body felt tender all over. A few bruises had appeared where I don't remember hitting myself. My face in the steamy mirror looked wraith-like. I tidied it as well as I could and took the elevator down to the ground to find something to eat.

Sykes and Boyd were waiting for me in the Open Kitchen. Pepper was late, by the look of it. He arrived after I'd got down my first swallow of morning coffee. We sat staring at one another. I crunched dry white toast. Orange juice helped. So did a second cup of coffee.

"Are you going to tell us about this or what, Benny?" Sykes asked. "We tried to discourage you from getting involved with this thing, but you didn't listen. Now it's time to pay the consequences. Spill your guts, or we will spill them for you."

"Jack, I wouldn't hold out on you. Just let me wake up a little, okay?"

"Sure, take all the time you need, just so long as you're talking in ten seconds."

"Where do you want me to start? I'm not sure where the beginning is. Where a guy like Devlin steps off the curb into a set-up like this is more a matter for a shrink. He had a screw loose, that's certain."

"Save the theorizing. We'll settle for a few gory details."

"Okay, okay. The basic scam was this: Devlin and his pals tried to suppress the last will and testament of Dermot Keogh, late of this parish."

"What? What are you talking about? All through this case we keep bumping into Keogh's will. That's what set up the Dermot Keogh Hall. That's what Devlin was administering."

"That was Keogh's *second*-last will, and as such, it doesn't count. The will that set up the concert hall, that put Devlin and Foley and Rankin in the business of managing Keogh's estate, was superseded by a later will, which they tried to bury."

"Take your time, Benny. We're listening. When did all this take place?"

"Dermot made the first will—well, it may not have actually been his *first*, but it is the first one that involves us—while he was pals with Devlin, Foley and Rankin. It set them up in good style forever. Only trouble was, Raymond spoiled things. He got Dermot peeved at him trying to research Dermot's past: visited his sick father, asked him to paint for him a portrait of the artist as a young man. Guess who became angry at him and went off and made a *new* will? Ed Patel was the lawyer who drew it up. He's in hospital in Bracebridge and unaware that the earlier will is the one probated. Renata Sartori was a witness to this will. So was Alma Orchard, Patel's long-time secretary. Both of these women were murdered to keep them quiet. Dermot was killed too, so that he couldn't make more trouble and to get the estate established. Only a few people knew about the new will."

"Three murders! Is that what you're saying?" Chuck Pepper looked stunned.

"More than three. Bob Foley was killed too, because he was getting out of hand. He planted the spent shotgun shells in Vanessa's locker. He thought it would confuse things. That undermined Devlin's plan. Foley was turning into a liability. Loose cannon rolling across the gun deck. His petty crimes, such as keeping Keogh's Jaguar and motorcycle collection, threatened to expose the bigger deception."

"Correct me if I was hearing things, but did you just say that Dermot Keogh was murdered?"

"I said that."

"Who killed Keogh?"

"Foley, under orders from Devlin. He monkeyed with the regulator of Keogh's aqualung after they picked up the equipment at McCordick Brothers' Marina. Renata was there, as well as Hampton Fisher and some strangers. Nobody'd suspect Foley because he was always tuning up the gear. That was the only killing last year. For a few months it looked like Renata was going to be a team player. She kept quiet about the suppression of the new will for nearly a year. But the conspirators could see that she wasn't going to stay bought. At any time she could go public with her story. She had a new boyfriend; she could easily tell him. Ray killed Renata and Alma Orchard the same day. He drove up north, collected the shotgun from Patel's place, where he'd seen it many times hanging over the fireplace. He took shells from there too. He dropped in on Alma, Patel's legal secretary, surprising her on her way to a church bake sale and thumped her on the back of her head. He removed her clean clothes, put her in the tub and added the radio to the bathwater."

"Nasty touch," said Boyd. Sykes just made a face.

"Then he went through Patel's office using her keys. That's when he destroyed copies of the new will. He returned the keys and drove home to Toronto.

"That same night, Monday, the fifteenth, he shot Renata. She was about to spill her guts to Barry Bosco, her boyfriend. While he headed north again, to return the gun, Foley came in and took the spent shells. For him, it was easy to get into Vanessa's office. He used a bolt cutter to remove Vanessa's lock on her locker. When he'd put the evidence inside, he snapped on his *own* lock, thinking that nobody would check the combination of a cut-off lock."

"Still harping on that damned lock!"

"Things remained calm for a while. First, everybody was convinced that it was Vanessa who'd been murdered. That suited Devlin fine. Later, the idea that Renata had been an accidental victim suited him just as well. Everything was coming up roses, until Foley walked off the Vic Vernon show. He was showing an independence above his station. That worried Devlin. It drew attention to Foley's powers under Dermot's will. When you test the fingerprint you found on the rubber glove in Foley's kitchen with one of Devlin's, I think you'll get a match."

"What did Trebitsch have to do in all this?"

"Not much. He didn't kill anybody. He's basically a busybody; has to know what's going on. Insecure, you know?"

"What about Philip Rankin? How deeply involved was he?"

"He kept his mouth shut about suppressing the later will. He made the most of his Keogh connections at the network. But I don't think he had the guts to kill anybody. But he knew that the killing was part of the plan. He was guilty of keeping his mouth shut, of conspiracy, of fraud and of being an accessory to one, two, three, four murders. Take your pick. He may not have known the details, but he collected all the benefits, including a cello named Hector."

"Rankin was stabbed all right. We established that much before you left. But, Benny, there wasn't a knife found at the scene. Not a knife, blade, shiv, nothing that could have made that single, deep, deadly wound in Rankin's chest. I'm not talking about a tiny weapon: this one had to be at least a *foot* long."

"Yeah," said Jim Boyd. "And our searches haven't turned it up. We've been into every sewer and gutter in the neighbourhood. We've been behind billboards and in empty warehouses: no murder weapon. Nothing like what we're looking for at Devlin's home or office."

"That's right. It wasn't at the scene and it wasn't in the vicinity. Nor did we get reports of somebody running down the street with a bloody knife in his hand."

"I'd heard that Keogh was very strict about having sharp objects in his studio," I said. "But I went over it in a dream last night. In my sleep I went through the room with a fine-toothed comb."

"It's your time. What did you come up with?"

"The murder weapon."

"Don't kid, Benny. Nobody likes a kidder."

"That's right," said Chuck Pepper.

"Tell us about this dream."

"Who's buying breakfast?"

"I am," all the others said together.

When we had all had our coffee cups refilled and finished off what was left of toast, bacon or egg on our plates, I took another deep breath and got back into the story. "You remember that studio room on the ground floor. It was crowded with stuff. Well, last night in this dream, I let my closed eyes wander over the whole room. You know, the way a camera scans a room in the movies when there's some point to be made by a slow pan across the set?"

"Sure, I know the movies," Jack said. "Get on with it."

"Well, from one end to the other, there was nothing that could have killed Rankin, unless you pushed the piano over on him. And that's what unlocked it: the idea that a musical instrument could be used in such a sinister way. Then, in my sleep, I saw Hector—"

"Hector who, damn it?"

"Hector was the name Dermot Keogh gave to his Strad. You know, his cello."

"What about Hector, then?"

"Cellos don't sit on the floor, Jack. They are supported by a peg or pin at the bottom. Some early instruments don't have them. Keogh's Strad did."

"When are you going to finish? Next Tuesday?"

"I remembered that Keogh's Strad was supposed to have gone to the University of Toronto's Hart House Collection of old stringed instruments. Under Keogh's will, the one that Devlin and the others were using as their magic carpet. If it was supposed to go to the university, why was it still in Dermot's studio a year later? Then I could see, Rankin was as greedy about Strads as Foley was about motorcycles. Devlin couldn't handle that. And when he overheard that Rankin wanted to meet me at Dermot's studio to tell me something, Devlin got homicidally angry again."

"Are you saying that Rankin was stabbed with a Stradivarius, Benny?"

"That's what I said. You can check for blood on the retracted pin. But don't let your forensic people cut it open or carve it up. Then there won't be anything for the university or whoever its new owner is."

"Christ, Cooperman, you're breaking my heart!"

"Where did you get this from, Benny?" Jim asked.

"I remembered Bob Foley's shed, back of his house. He had been doing some metalwork not long before he was killed. On the bench was a rubber ring, a ferrule, the sort of thing you put on the cello's pin, the strut-thingy, the leg it stands on so it won't slip. Foley had sharpened the end to a sharp point, then covered it with the usual rubber tip."

"Why?"

"Maybe he didn't want to be alone in Keogh's weaponless studio with people like Devlin around. How Devlin found out about it, we'll never know."

"Maybe Foley and Devlin had been planning to get rid of Rankin for quite a spell," said Chuck, who had been quiet for some time.

"How do you know for a fact that Devlin didn't remove the spent shells from the scene of Renata's murder by himself? Why bring Foley into it?" Jack was looking just a little like a well-fed cat just then.

"We know that Foley hid the shells where they would be found so that blame would fall on Vanessa. That had nothing to do with Devlin's plan of killing Renata and letting you think that she was killed in error. So, if Foley was involved in disposing of the shells, it's a safe bet that he removed them from the scene."

"You once said you had a witness to this."

"That's right. I have, but we don't need him. We've got a case without him."

"What have you left out?" Jim Boyd wanted to know.

"Lots of things, but from what I've said, you can see all the big pieces."

"Does that wrap things up, Benny?" Sykes wanted to know.

"Probably not. But it's as close as I can get to it right now. Detecting's a hit-and-miss operation the way I work it. I don't have the staff to be methodical. Maybe there will be a clearer picture up ahead somewhere."

"If you guys are finished with your breakfast," Chuck Pepper observed, "I reckon it's nearly time to start thinking about lunch. Anybody second that?"

TWENTY-SIX

After lunch, I dropped around to the NTC building on University Avenue. I got no flack from Security when I went past the desk. Later, I found out that Vic Vernon, the egomaniacal talk-show host, had been questioned by a security guard the night before, and instead of calling upstairs for help, he went home to bed and let everybody else in the studio tear their hair out. I hope that it's the beginning of a new era: enlightened security.

Sally was there and gave me a big hug when I came up to her desk. She showed me the write-up of the Island adventure in the morning paper. There wasn't a word about first wills or even second ones. Devlin was still described as "missing, and believed drowned." Poetic justice for the architect of Dermot Keogh's death. Sally had a million questions, which I dodged or answered on a random basis.

"Cooperman! Get in here!" It was Vanessa, of course, looking like a spread in *Vogue*. She settled me on the couch and came over where she could watch me, and where, incidentally, I could watch her. "Okay, give me the dirt. You owe me that much."

I gave her a short rundown of who did what to whom and saved the thunderbolt until the end. "Of course, Vanessa, now there will be no Dermot Keogh Hall. At least, there won't be one that was foreseen in Dermot's last will and testament. Maybe there are some legacies you can snag from the will when they get a copy from the hard drive in Ed Patel's law office in Bracebridge. But I would be surprised if Keogh didn't give the works to charity. Maybe he endowed a palliative care unit at a hospital or a puppy farm to look after stray, unwanted dogs. You never know with that guy."

"Benny, you owe me a better explanation than this! Are you telling me that my life has *never* been in danger? Were you leading me on all this time just to bleed more money from me? My lawyer's not going to like this."

"Never mind your lawyer, Stella. I don't think *you're* going to like this. The plain fact is, dear heart, the plain fact is that this case wasn't about *you* at all. You were a smoke-screen, a red herring."

"You won't get me to believe that in a thousand years."

"Nevertheless." Vanessa tried to hide the kick to her vanity by taking it out on me. An offensive is always a good play when you've been taken off guard.

"You're in league with the rest of them."

"Your pills are in your top drawer." She started to open it, then slammed it shut again.

"Vanessa, I was always as up front with you as you were with me. Remember the first day in my office, when you told me you never owned a gun?"

"You're a cheat and a liar, Benny. You should be disbarred."

"Stella, how can you accuse me like that? Me, a friend from Grantham Collegiate Institute and Vocational School."

"Stop calling me that! I ought to fire you right now."

"But I'm not even on the payroll any more. You fired me already. I'm sure that Staff Sergeant Sykes—"

"You're still on salary until *Saturday*. I changed my mind. But I'm moving you out of here. Hy Newman needs your space. Did I tell you about that?" I raised a surprised eyebrow while she told me about what I'd seen at the press reception. "I think that bringing Hy back was a stroke of genius, don't you? He'll save me hours a week. Some days I know I earn my pay. I may never have to go into a studio again. What bliss!"

"Great."

"Now what are you going to do?"

"I think I'm due for a holiday."

"Taking off to Dittrick Lake or back to Muskoka?"

"I would like to go back to Muskoka some day. Maybe you'll rent me your cottage. But right now I think I'm heading for Paris. Paris will be a rest cure after looking out for you, Vanessa." I didn't think it would be polite to mention that I had hopes of seeing my own Anna Abraham in Paris. I really can keep some things to myself.

"I'll bet you're glad to be leaving here. Leave the cleaning up to others."

"They were doing it before I came to Toronto, Stella."

"Stop *calling* me that!"

"You have my Grantham address, right?"

"Sally has it. Was it all work, Benny? We did have some fun, didn't we?" I looked over at Vanessa Moss in her big corner office, sitting with her lovely legs crossed. I thought of the last ten days at out-of-town rates. I thought of Dermot Keogh, Rankin, Devlin. I thought of Renata Sartori, whose death had brought me to Toronto.

"Didn't we have some fun?" Vanessa repeated. I didn't know how to answer that one.

Anna's face moved through my head, reminding me of all I wanted to forget. Like I said in the beginning, I should have seen the writing on the wall.

"It was more than fun, Stella. It was an education."